A Collection of Lies

Also available by Connie Berry

Kate Hamilton Mysteries

The Shadow of Memory

The Art of Betrayal

A Legacy of Murder

A Dream of Death

A Collection of Lies

A Kate Hamilton Mystery

CONNIE BERRY

CROOKED LANE

NEW YORK

Published in the United States by Crooked Lane Books, an imprint of The Quick Brown Fox & Company LLC.

Crooked Lane Books and its logo are trademarks of The Quick Brown Fox & Company LLC.

Library of Congress Catalog-in-Publication data available upon request.

ISBN (hardcover): 978-1-63910-666-0
ISBN (ebook): 978-1-63910-667-7

Cover design by Alan Ayers

Printed in the United States.

www.crookedlanebooks.com

Crooked Lane Books
34 West 27th St., 10th Floor
New York, NY 10001

First Edition: June 2024

10 9 8 7 6 5 4 3 2 1

This book is dedicated, with my thanks,
to the Romany and Traveller Family
History Society in the UK.

"A harmful truth is better than a useful lie."

Thomas Mann, "The Magic Mountain"
Translated by John E. Woods

Chapter One

Thursday, January 2
The Old Bell Inn, Devon, England

"Murderers can be perfectly ordinary people." Tom was stretched out atop the duvet, bare chested and wearing his navy sweatpants. He looked at me over his reading glasses. "I'm serious, Kate. They're often people you'd never suspect. Small irritations build up, and then one day they just snap. I once arrested a pensioner for stabbing her neighbor to death with a garden trowel because she was sure some of the weed killer he was spraying had drifted onto her prize roses."

I started to laugh, and my coffee went down the wrong way.

"That's not funny." He looked slightly hurt.

I thumped my chest, trying to breathe. "I'm sorry, but do you think all newlyweds chat about murder on their honeymoon?"

To be fair, the topic was hardly surprising. Tom was a detective inspector in the Suffolk Constabulary. But I was an antiques dealer and appraiser. Not a particularly treacherous profession.

"I was leading up to something." Tom reached over and placed his mug of coffee on the bedside table. He picked up a blue folder. "We'll be on Dartmoor tomorrow. It's time to think about our investigation. Listen to this: 'Of all the crimes in Devon's history, the most mysterious may be the case of Nancy Thorne, a thirty-year-old lacemaker from the lost Dartmoor village of Widdecombe Throop.'"

"Wait a minute," I interrupted him. "What do you mean by 'lost village'? How can an entire village be lost?"

"Lots of reasons. Climate change, for one. Settlements that thrived during the Medieval Warm Period were abandoned as the climate cooled. And during World War II, there were villages that—"

I gave him a playful shove. "In other words, you don't know. Keep reading."

Tom grinned at me. "'At one AM on the night of seventh September 1885, Nancy returned to the cottage she shared with her sister, a seamstress, in a state of incoherence. Her hair was disheveled. Her dress was torn and soaked with what appeared to be blood. For reasons never explained, neither the village doctor nor the local constable was called.'"

"This happened in 1885?" I propped myself on one elbow. "When was the piece written?"

"Nineteen forty-two. It's the script of a radio documentary on crimes in Devon."

"Hardly an eyewitness account, then. Go on." I kissed his shoulder.

"'Witnesses testified that Nancy arrived as usual for the six o'clock service at the village church but left soon afterwards. The vicar, Edward Quick, assumed she had been taken ill. Later, concerned for Nancy's well-being, he called at the cottage, where her sister, Sally, told him Nancy had not returned home. She wasn't concerned, however, as Nancy often stopped after evening service to visit a friend, a local widow who'd been housebound. The widow, when questioned later, said she had indeed been home but had not seen Nancy Thorne in several days. When Nancy finally did appear, she claimed to have no memory of the events of that night and could offer no explanation for the blood on her frock. The police launched an investigation, but as no person in the surrounding area had gone missing and no body, human or animal, was ever discovered, the case was closed. Nancy died at the age of forty-six without ever speaking of the events that occurred that night.'" Tom closed the folder. "Well, that's the case."

"Please don't tell me we're expected to solve a hundred-and-forty-year-old murder."

"No."

"Well, then, what does Grahame Nash expect us to do?"

Nash, Tom's friend from his early days in the Suffolk Constabulary, ran an international private investigations firm based in Toronto. He'd been trying for at least a year to convince Tom to take early retirement from the police force and join his firm—an idea that appealed to me no end. When I weighed the dangers of discreet private investigations against drugs, domestic violence, organized crime, and terrorism, there was no contest. I had a new husband, and I didn't want to lose him.

Tom laid the folder on his chest. "If we take the case, our task will be—" He broke off. "No, best to hear it directly from the horse's mouth." He opened the folder again and pulled out a sheet of letterhead bearing the logo of Nash & Holmes, Private Investigations. "I received this from Grahame a few weeks before our wedding," he said, and proceeded to read the letter in its entirety.

November 29

Dear Tom,

My hearty congratulations on your forthcoming marriage. If Kate has captured your heart, she must be a very special lady indeed. I look forward to meeting her. Sadly, I will not be able to attend the wedding ceremony. On that particular day I will be traveling in one of the countries currently in the crosshairs of the former Soviet Union.

There's no need to tell you I'm delighted you have decided to give the case in Devon some thought. As you know, this is not a criminal matter. Here's a quick overview:

The Museum of Devon Life, a small but highly regarded institution led by Dr. Hugo Hawksworthy, formerly of the Mary Rose Museum in Portsmouth, has received a sizeable grant for a new exhibit to be called 'Famous Crimes in Devon's History.' You can imagine the sort of thing—reconstructions, photos where possible, perhaps a skull or two thrown in to attract the kiddies. Construction of a new wing is currently underway, with a grand opening scheduled for spring. The proposed centerpiece for the new exhibit is a dress said to have belonged to a Victorian lacemaker from a village in Dartmoor. I trust you've read the enclosed file. The dress, along with a collection of items found with it, has been donated to the museum by a colorful gentleman named Gideon Littlejohn. Perhaps you've heard of him. If not, Hawksworthy can fill you in. At any rate, your assignment will be to establish, if possible, the provenance of the dress. Did it really belong to the lacemaker in question? Are the stains on the dress human blood? Can we identify the blood type or retrieve any DNA material?

I know you've made no long-term commitments, but I believe this case will be of interest to Kate as well. With her experience in the antiques trade, she may be able to provide valuable help. I'm more than happy to put her on the payroll. As I told you earlier, while our monthly stipend is nothing to write home about, we do pay all expenses—generously, if I say so myself. The real money comes from commissions on investigations resolved to the client's satisfaction. And that, my dear chap, is what you do best. If you have questions, get in touch. If I'm out of the country, Ellie, my PA, will know how to reach me.

I remain, as always, your friend,

Grahame Nash

Tom looked at me over his glasses. "What do you think?"

"Interesting," I said in an offhand way, trying to hide a smile. I was fascinated, and Tom knew it. "Sounds a lot safer than policing."

"Hmm, yes." He lay back and put an arm under his head. "Leaving the force is a major decision. Our lives would change."

"We've already made one life-changing decision—spending the rest of our lives together. That's turned out pretty well so far."

"*So far?*" He gave me a cheeky smile. "Jury still out, then?"

"The real test will be when we get home. Figuring out who cooks and who does the dishes, seeing who squeezes the toothpaste tube from the middle—that sort of thing." I glanced around our suite. "This isn't exactly real life."

"The Old Bell?" Tom frowned. "If I remember correctly, you called it 'nothing in the middle of nowhere.'"

"I meant it as a compliment."

"I know you did." He reached over and touched my cheek.

The Old Bell, a former coaching inn near Okehampton, was perched on a rise overlooking a wild, rushing stream. No fancy spa. No gourmet restaurant with tiny portions artistically presented. No signature cocktails. Just comfortable beds, excellent cooking, gorgeous surroundings . . . and privacy. Every night we'd fallen asleep to the hoot of an owl. Every morning we'd awakened to the clear winter sun gilding the thick stone walls of our suite. Frankly, I was getting a bit restless.

I needed a challenge, and a bloodstained Victorian dress sounded right up my alley.

A discreet knock on the door sent me scrambling for my cashmere robe—a wedding gift from my friend Lady Barbara Finchley-fforde.

"Coming." I pulled the soft fabric around my body and tied the sash.

"Breakfast, madam," came a voice from the hallway. "I'll leave it outside, shall I?"

"No, no." I opened the door. "Come in."

A middle-aged woman in a black skirt and white apron entered, balancing a large tray. "We don't like to disturb our honeymoon couples."

"It's no problem."

"I can see that." She raised an eyebrow, probably assuming our matching black eyes and the gash on Tom's forehead—souvenirs from an encounter with a drugs dealer just before our wedding—were the result of a domestic dispute. Placing the tray on a table, she started to leave, then turned back. "Always best to talk things out, my luvs."

We waited until the sound of her footsteps died away, then collapsed into laughter.

An hour later, the coffee cold and our plates nearly empty, we were still in bed.

I was studying the ancient oak beams holding up the ceiling.

"Thinking about Nancy Thorne's dress?" Tom asked.

"Actually, I was thinking about historical mysteries in general. Uncovering the past. Everyone involved is long gone. No crime, no danger."

I never learn.

Tom tossed the blue folder on the bedside table. "This is our last day at the Old Bell. How shall we spend it?"

We'd been married exactly eight days. Due to an administrative delay—something to do with retirement dates and pensions—Tom's boss, DCI Dennis Eccles, wouldn't be taking up his new post at the Suffolk Constabulary headquarters until February 1. Which meant Tom wouldn't become the new detective chief inspector at Bury St. Edmunds until then either, and since he'd accumulated more than a month of vacation time, we'd planned to spend the first three weeks of our honeymoon in Devon and the rest of January settling into our new home in Long Barston.

"The weather's supposed to be lovely," I said. "Sunny. Not too cold. Why don't we do that guided-trek thing on the moor today? It may be our last chance."

"We should think about making a move."

"I suppose so." I looked over at Tom's profile, the straight nose, the angles of his cheekbones, the slight scar near his ear. Life, miraculously, had given me a second chance at love. A whole new life with this charming, gifted, gorgeous, irresistible—

"Come on, then." He started to get up.

I pulled him back down. "Oh, not yet."

Chapter Two

Friday, January 3
Coombe Mallet, Devon

Late the next morning, Tom and I checked out of the Old Bell, stowed our gear in the rear of our Range Rover Discovery, and headed south toward the Museum of Devon Life, fifteen miles or so from the southeastern edge of Dartmoor.

The day had dawned cold and clear with a bright winter's sun. I felt a pleasant sense of anticipation. We had a one o'clock meeting with the museum director, Hugo Hawksworthy, and his newly hired textile conservator, Julia Kelly. I'd dealt with antique textiles before—mostly fine tapestries, exquisitely embroidered Chinese panels, and a sampling of girlhood embroidery—but nothing involved in a murder. Now we were about to see a dress that might have belonged to a murderous Victorian lacemaker. To say I was intrigued would be an understatement.

As we entered Dartmoor National Park, our car climbed through old oak forests and hidden valleys to windswept moors punctuated by weathered granite cairns, spiky evergreen gorse, and fernlike bracken in its winter colors of amber and treacle. Scattered sheep grazed near the craggy outcroppings. A few sturdy Dartmoor ponies with their long-flowing manes and tails eyed us with mild interest.

We'd spent the previous afternoon walking on the moor, led by one of the Dartmoor Rangers who offered guided treks to supplement his income. Having grown up on one of the farms dotting the national park, he knew every rock and tuft of bracken by heart.

As we walked, our guide had kept up a running commentary. The bleak, nearly treeless moor had once been a vast forest, first cleared by humans in the Bronze Age. Many of the old stone fences dated from early medieval times, some even earlier. "The moor is a rare and irreplaceable ecosystem," he'd told us. "Abundant rainfall creates mires and wetlands. The soil is covered by a layer of peat that soaks up the rain, spreading and deepening with the decomposition of the vegetation."

"You mean bogs," Tom said, clearly interested. "Tell us about them."

"Two main types. Blanket bogs are found on the high moor, where the moss-covered peat forms what some describe as a giant sponge, absorbing and capturing the rainfall. Basin mires form in the valley bottoms. They're called 'featherbeds' or 'quakers,' because when you walk over them, they feel like a huge, wobbling jelly."

"Can they really pull you under?" I shuddered, picturing Arthur Conan Doyle's Grimpen Mire.

"Fiction—mostly." The guide squinted against the sun. "Just don't go wandering off on your own."

No worries there.

A fine rain spattered the windscreen, blurring our view. Tom flipped on the wipers.

Our route to the market town of Coombe Mallet joined a ribbon of paved road bisecting Dartmoor from Tavistock in the west to Ashburton in the east. In the distance, we could just make out Dartmoor Prison, the stark, mist-shrouded Victorian structure where, in the past, the most notorious of England's criminals had been incarcerated. Very likely, some of the criminals to be featured in the museum's new exhibit had languished within the prison's lichen-covered walls.

"Do you think we'll see the bloodstained dress today?" I asked.

"I hope so. We'll get the mini-tour this afternoon. Tonight they're holding a gala fundraiser at the museum. We're invited." I must have rolled my eyes, because he added, "I know—not my favorite thing either. But we might learn more about the new exhibit."

"Like who's funding it?"

"Oh, I know who's funding the exhibit." Tom downshifted on the steep decline. "Uncle Nigel."

"You're kidding. To tempt you into leaving the police?"

"Nothing to do with me. Nigel supports lots of local endeavors—the lace museum in Honiton, the Devon Wildlife Trust, Salvation Army, Age Concern, several children's charities."

We rounded a sharp turn and entered the village of Coombe Mallet. A sign pointed us to the museum with its pay-and-display car park.

"What are we hoping to learn at the gala?"

"A bit more about the man who donated the items, I hope—the one Grahame Nash described as 'colorful.' He's our starting point."

"Colorful how?"

"Good question. I spoke with Grahame just before our wedding. He described Littlejohn as eccentric, but when I asked *how*, he just laughed and said, 'You'll see.'"

Now I really was intrigued.

* * *

The museum occupied a four-story former woolen mill, constructed of gray stone rubble with redbrick dressings and a half-hipped slate roof. The mill had been—we learned later—one of the last in Devon, built in the early nineteenth century near Dartmeet, where the east and west branches of the River Dart converge. After the mill closure, the building was used as a storehouse. In the 1990s, the site was purchased by the museum.

A sign pointed us to the entrance. Construction of the new wing, a wooden structure, appeared to be well underway. A set of large, plate-glass doors led into the reception area with its information desk and ticket counter.

The director, Hugo Hawksworthy, was waiting for us. "Mr. and Mrs. Mallory—welcome to Coombe Mallet."

"Call me Tom, please. And my wife uses her professional name—Kate Hamilton."

"My apologies." Dr. Hawksworthy was an attractive man, somewhere in his late forties or early fifties—athletically built, clean shaven with a thick brush of brown hair, lightly tanned skin, and unusual light hazel eyes. His clothes were expensive and meant to be noticed—tweed jacket over a cashmere quarter-zip and immaculate wool trousers. "You're here to authenticate the Nancy Thorne dress. Shall we make a start? Ms. Kelly is working on the garment now."

Tom gave me a surreptitious thumbs-up.

We followed Hawksworthy from the reception area, through a central atrium that served as the museum shop, to a forged-iron staircase with a balustrade in a neo-Gothic design. On the first floor—what Americans would call the second story—a series of rooms were arranged in a circular pattern around the atrium, which was open to a high glass dome on the roof. Metal railings in the same neo-Gothic design circled all three upper floors.

Hawksworthy noticed my interest. "It was an innovative design for its time. Open-air skylights have been used since Roman times, but it wasn't until the Industrial Revolution that glazing became affordable to anyone but royalty. Since gas lighting didn't reach this part of Devon until the end of the nineteenth century, the architect created a source of natural light and ventilation in the center of the building. The design also gave the mill foreman a bird's-eye view of all the floors at the same time."

We walked past several rooms, each showcasing a particular aspect of Devon life. A free-standing sign reading *Gypsies, Romanies & Travellers* pointed us toward a large, open space. That surprised me. Wasn't the term *Gypsy* and its implications of illegality and irregularity considered offensive? I made a note to ask Dr. Hawksworthy privately. Further on, I caught a glimpse of another room featuring the lacemaking industry in Devon. That might prove helpful. Nancy Thorne had been a lacemaker.

Hawksworthy opened a set of double doors, and we entered a large workroom dominated by a table covered with sheeting. A dress printed in a small tobacco-and-white-sprig pattern lay spread out and covered with fine netting. From what I could see, the dress had a high neckline with a white collar, long sleeves cut short on the forearm, and a full-length gathered skirt.

A young woman was bent over the table. She straightened, brushing back a fringe of dark-auburn hair. "Hello, welcome. You must be the Mallorys."

Tom started to correct her, but I touched his arm. Professionally, I was still Kate Hamilton, but Mallory was a name I was more than happy to claim.

"Tom, Kate—may I call you that? This is Julia Kelly, our textile conservator." Dr. Hawksworthy smiled expansively. "She's been with us just over a month. In addition to the crimes exhibit, part of the new wing will be dedicated to a collection of historic costumes. If we get the funding, of course."

Julia Kelly was an attractive woman in her early thirties with a shaggy pixie-cut hairstyle and a slim, almost boyish figure. "Have you always been interested in antique textiles?" I asked her.

"At uni, I started out in theater costuming." She smoothed a hand over the fine netting. "We were doing *As You Like It* with a medieval theme, so I spent a month studying design in Copenhagen. The National Museum there has a wonderful collection of fifteenth-century garments." She shrugged. "I was hooked. After getting my degree, I was an intern with the Historic Royal Palaces—an amazing experience—but when Hugo offered me a position here, I couldn't turn it down. It's a wonderful opportunity to be in on a project from the ground up. Under Hugo's leadership, the museum is getting lots of positive press coverage."

Hawksworthy made a small, dismissive gesture, but I could tell he was pleased. "We've all worked very hard. To follow the Devon crimes exhibit with a collection of historical costumes and textiles should boost our standing nationally."

Tom leaned over the table to peer at the dress. "Can you explain what you're doing?"

"Certainly." Julia beamed. "Each garment I work with is unique, fragile, and irreplaceable. The initial step is an overall assessment of condition, followed by the gentle removal of surface impurities—dust, lint, that sort of thing. I'm using a regular canister vacuum on the lowest setting. Not all conservators agree, but I like to protect fragile textiles with netting. Then I gently vacuum the garment in sections. The next step will be to make decisions about any stains, tears, insect infestation, mildew. Damage is usually stabilized rather than repaired. Stain removal depends upon several factors. Those decisions come later."

"Based on what?" I asked.

"Conservation of textiles is always subjective. The significance of folds, stains, tears, and soil is evaluated in light of what we refer to as the textile's 'true nature,' meaning its history and context. Stain removal is an irreversible process. If this dress belonged to Nancy Thorne, the stains and areas of repair will be historically important."

"Yes, I see that," I said. "Part of the story." *And a sensational draw.* A bloodstained dress owned by a possible murderess? Grisly but irresistible. I looked more closely at the fabric under the netting. "Is it cotton?"

"Calico. A plain-woven textile, coarser than muslin, made from unbleached cotton—often not fully processed. See here?" She pulled back a section of the netting and pointed out small irregularities in the weave. "These are actually parts of the husk. This particular fabric was machine printed in an overall sprig pattern. Typical of the period. Unremarkable—except for the stains, of course."

Julia rolled back another section of netting, exposing most of the skirt.

My breath caught. The front of the skirt was discolored by large swaths of what looked very much like old bloodstains. A rip in the fabric near the hem had been almost invisibly repaired by someone. I moved closer to examine the damage.

"The repair was done sometime in the past," Julia said. "Makes you wonder, doesn't it? Why would such a dress have been preserved?"

"Yes, and by whom?"

Leaning farther over the table, Julia uncovered the narrow bodice. More bloodstains.

She turned back the front button placket so I could view the construction. "The dress was made entirely by hand, a very fine hand. I'm told Nancy Thorne's sister was a seamstress."

"I believe so," I mumbled, unable to tear my eyes away from the bloodstains. *So much blood.*

Julia ran her finger over an impossibly fine seam. "I've seen this level of workmanship in French couture garments created around the turn of the twentieth century. Unusual, I should think, in a remote village."

"Very unusual." My pulse quickened. My fingertips tingled. I bent closer.

What had appeared under the net to be an ordinary white collar was actually made of intricately patterned lace, a dense botanical design of flowers and leaves, woven of threads as fine as spider webs. Without thinking, I reached out to touch the lace, my fingers lightly brushing the intricate motifs. "I'm sorry," I said, realizing I should have asked permission. "I'm not wearing gloves. I just—"

"It's all right," Julia said, smiling.

As my fingers hovered over the old fabric, I felt a pulsing of heat or energy. Was it coming from the blood?

"I, ah . . ." I stopped to swallow as I pulled my hand away, tucking it under the opposite arm. "It's just I've never seen lace like this. It's exquisite." My brain was thrumming. My cheeks had gone hot, and my mouth was dry. Yes—my normal reaction to objects of great age and beauty. But this was an ordinary dress—finely made, yes, but not even that old by British standards. Why was I reacting this way?

I watched, horrified, as the dark stains seemed to spread and quiver before my eyes. I caught the metallic scent of . . . blood? But surely that was impossible.

"The dress was washed," Julia said. "Someone tried to save it." She pulled the netting back over the bodice.

An image flashed in my brain. A woman, on her knees. Sobbing inconsolably.

Blood. So much blood.

I took in a breath, louder than I'd intended. The image fled.

"Kate?" Tom was looking at me, concerned.

"It's nothing. I'm just feeling a little . . . strange."

"Glass of water?" Hawksworthy asked.

"Yes, please. I'm a bit light-headed." The wave of heat, the pounding of my heart, was beginning to subside.

"We have bottles of water in our staff kitchen. Be right back." Hawksworthy rushed off. He probably assumed I was overly squeamish. Or pregnant.

That struck me as funny, which helped.

I smiled at Julia, feeling embarrassed. "Tell me about the lace."

"Each part of England produced its own particular patterns and styles," she said. "The lace made in this area, Honiton lace, is a bobbin lace created with small, individual motifs, such as a single leaf or flower. The elements are then joined using plaits. The overall designs can be extremely complex—so complex it would have taken a worker from eight to ten hours to make just one square inch. Can you imagine?"

I shook my head. "It must have been unusual for a dress like this one—an everyday dress, I mean—to have such an elaborate lace collar. If the dress was Nancy Thorne's, would she have made the lace herself?"

"Another mystery. I can't imagine she'd have had time to make something for personal use. One lacemaker near Honiton wrote in her journal that she'd stayed up all night finishing a job so her children could have breakfast."

Dr. Hawksworthy returned with a bottle of water. I thanked him, screwed off the top, and took a drink.

"I understand it was a local man named Gideon Littlejohn who found the dress," Tom said. "What can you tell us about him?"

"An interesting character, to say the least," Hawksworthy said. "Unfortunately, my assistant just informed me that a potential donor is expecting a return call. We don't like to keep them waiting." He grinned. "Let's table the question of Mr. Littlejohn until after you've met him."

"Of course." Tom shot me a look.

First Grahame Nash. Now Hugo Hawksworthy. What was the mystery surrounding Gideon Littlejohn, and why was everyone so reluctant to tell us about him?

We thanked Julia and followed Hawksworthy back through the displays toward the stairs.

"I hate to cut this short," Hawksworthy said, "but you'll have plenty of time to examine the dress later—and a collection of items found with the dress. They may help you trace the origins. If authentic, the dress will be displayed, bloodstains and all, on a mannequin as visitors enter the exhibit."

"Very dramatic," Tom said.

"We hope so," Hawksworthy said. "Ironic, really, because with an exhibit called Famous Crimes in Devon's History, you'd think the area was a hotbed of villainy. The truth is, out here in the villages, we haven't had a serious crime in years."

Chapter Three

After leaving the museum, Tom and I checked into the Crown, a stunning fifteenth-century thatched inn in the center of the small market town of Coombe Mallet. We'd booked in for a week, courtesy of Nash & Holmes. After that, assuming we completed our investigation, we hoped to spend a week at Fouroaks, the country estate that had been in Tom's family for generations. As Tom's uncle Nigel was currently aboard the Eurostar, speeding his way toward his villa in the south of France, we'd have Fouroaks to ourselves. I was sorry not to have more time with Nigel. He was an old charmer, in the nicest possible way. But I *was* looking forward to exploring Fouroaks with Tom. He'd spent his summers there as a boy. The house, the grounds, and the nearby villages held so many fond memories for him. I wanted to share them.

After settling into our large and old-fashioned but comfortable room at the Crown, we spent an hour or so exploring Coombe Mallet. The small town, built on land rising from the River Dart, had a lovely old church, the remains of a motte-and-bailey castle, a winding High Street lined with shops, and a sixteenth-century guild hall built on the remains of a medieval priory.

As we walked, Tom said, "I wonder if either of the Thorne sisters married and had children. The dress may have been passed down from mother to daughter to granddaughter."

"Oh, that would be way too easy." I took his arm.

"All right, let's hear your questions. I know you have some."

"Okay, here's one—why didn't Nancy's sister go to church that night?" I raised an eyebrow. "Here's another—was Nancy ever examined by a doctor? The blood could have been her own."

"Excellent questions. Which we'll do our best to answer."

"This case is going to take a lot of research."

"Which begins tonight when we meet Gideon Littlejohn at the museum gala."

At six, we dressed in the best we had—Tom in wool trousers and a sports jacket and me in the little black dress and heels I'd packed for the New Year's Eve celebration at the Old Bell, a low-key event attended almost exclusively by locals.

An hour later we arrived at the museum, where it took us all of two seconds to realize we were decidedly underdressed. Dr. Hawksworthy had neglected to tell us the evening was black tie. Not that we could have done anything about it.

Inside the museum, the atrium shop had disappeared. A raised platform and a number of high-top tables had taken its place. A bar had been set up on the opposite side of the room. Long tables tucked into the alcoves were laid with fancy finger food. Servers in black trousers and white tuxedo shirts moved through the glittering crowd.

We spotted Hawksworthy at the bar with a group of older couples.

Seeing us, he excused himself and strode over. "Welcome back to the museum."

"You've attracted quite a crowd," Tom said.

"A testament to how much the new exhibit means to our community. The bloodstained dress is exactly what we need. Something 'sexy'"—he put the word in air quotes—"as a draw."

"If it's genuine."

"Of course—if it's genuine." A forced heartiness in Hawksworthy's tone told me he was counting on the dress being genuine and us proving it. "When I was hired as director here, I promised to take the museum to the top of its field. With the help of the good people of Devon, that dream is about to become reality."

I'd opened my mouth to offer my congratulations when a tall, dark-haired woman in a shimmery gold cocktail dress joined us. Handsome, middle-aged, full-bodied but fighting it. She'd obviously been listening to our conversation. She threaded her hand through Hawksworthy's arm. *His wife?* "Did he tell you the Museum of Devon Life has been short-listed for Art Fund Museum of the Year?"

"Quite an honor," Tom said.

"It takes a team." Hawksworthy shot us a small, self-deprecating smile. "Tom, Kate, meet our assistant director, Isla Ferris. We couldn't have done it without her."

She flushed with pleasure. "Hugo's being too modest, as usual. With his impressive credentials, Devon is very lucky to have him." She looked at him adoringly. "First the prestigious museum studies program at the University of Glasgow, then a full scholarship for a doctoral program in heritage studies at Georgetown University in the States."

"Isla," Hawksworthy protested, "I don't think the Mallorys are interested in my academic career." He was obviously enjoying this immensely.

"But you returned to the UK," Tom said.

"I was interning at the Smithsonian when I was offered the job with the Mary Rose. Hard to turn something like that down."

"You have quite a record," Tom said.

"Driven by a love for preserving our heritage."

"Which is what he's doing here." Isla beamed. "Preserving our heritage. The gala tonight is important—not only the celebration of what we've accomplished, the new wing, but also a fundraiser for the proposed historic textiles exhibit."

"We met Julia Kelly this afternoon," I told Isla. "I was impressed by her expertise."

"Yes." Isla's lips twitched slightly. "Nice girl." She brushed an invisible piece of lint off the front of Hawksworthy's jacket, a proprietary gesture.

Not his wife, but clearly more than a colleague. And she doesn't mind us knowing it.

"The textiles project will require the support of individual donors—lots of them," Hawksworthy said, "but we're rather counting on a grant from ACED—Arts and Culture, East Devon. Our speaker tonight is our new MP. His support will be key."

A silver-haired couple drew Hawksworthy aside. He excused himself, and we found ourselves alone with Isla Ferris.

"Has Gideon Littlejohn arrived?" Tom asked. "We'd like to meet him."

"There he is now," she said. "The man in the tailcoat and breeches."

Gideon Littlejohn was tall, perhaps in his midforties, and well built, with a neat mustache and long muttonchop sideburns. He was dressed in a snug-fitting tailcoat over a patterned waistcoat, dark trousers, a white shirt with a standing collar, and a wide black silk cravat. He leaned on a silver-headed cane.

"Is he supposed to be Prince Albert or something?" I asked, meaning the prince consort, Queen Victoria's husband.

Isla laughed. "This isn't fancy dress, Kate. Gideon dresses like that all the time. He calls himself a historical re-creator."

"What does he do for a living?" Tom asked.

"That's the irony. He's a freelance cybersecurity expert. One foot in the past, the other very much in the present. Come. I'll introduce you."

Seeing us, Gideon Littlejohn gave a little bow, making me feel as if I'd wandered into a television costume drama.

Isla lifted a glass of champagne from a tray. "Gideon, may I present the Mallorys—Tom and Kate."

"A great pleasure to make your acquaintance." Littlejohn bowed again. "Hugo told me you've come to authenticate the dress. Have you had a chance to see it yet?"

"We had a look this afternoon," I said. "It's certainly old, and the dark stains do look like blood. Whether the dress belonged to Nancy Thorne is another question—one we hoped you could help us answer."

"At your service, madam."

I didn't know how to respond. Was he putting us on?

"How did you come to be in possession of the dress?" Tom asked.

"Purely by accident. I purchased an entire household—furniture, old kitchen and bath fittings, tools, books, all sorts—mid to late Victorian mostly, the property of an elderly man, never married, never threw anything away, lucky for me. I own a historic house in the village, the Old Merchant's House. I'm slowly taking it back to its original condition—or as close as I can come. It's not easy to find antique fixtures in restorable condition. I purchased the household mainly for the cast-iron woodburning range and the original Victorian bath and water closet. Everything else came along for the ride."

"And the dress?" Tom asked.

"I found that in a trunk, neatly folded with a note saying it had once belonged to the murderess Nancy Thorne. Naturally, I was curious, so I did a little research. Then I contacted the museum."

"Did you keep the note?"

"I gave it to Hugo along with the dress. I assume it will be part of the exhibit."

A note? Hawksworthy hadn't mentioned a note. "Did you find any personal papers, estate inventories, photo albums?"

Provenance, the history of an item—its chain of ownership—is most reliably determined by written documentation. When that isn't possible, old photographs can help. Gideon Littlejohn had purchased a houseful of objects from a single source. If we could prove a connection between the owner of those items and Nancy Thorne, we might be able to document the history of the dress. Or come close enough to justify attribution. Someone had saved the dress, folded it carefully away. Who and why?

"There may be papers and photographs," Littlejohn said. "I haven't had time to sort through everything. You're welcome to look."

"We'd like to see the trunk," Tom said.

"Of course." Littlejohn tapped his cane on the floor. "My work keeps me pretty busy, but I do work from home and set my own schedule. You're welcome to visit anytime you'd like."

"The sooner the better," Tom said.

"Well, then, how about tomorrow around eleven? I should be free." Littlejohn removed his wire-rimmed glasses and began polishing the round lenses with a white linen handkerchief. "Number ten Park Terrace—just off the High Street."

Chapter Four

It was a quarter to nine when Dr. Hawksworthy stepped onto the stage and tapped the microphone. "Welcome, everyone. What an amazing night. I trust you've all received the packet of information about our plans for the museum—and, of course, the all-important donation envelopes." He held one up, his eyes twinkling. "Which you may drop in the box as you leave or mail in at your convenience. Right now, it is my distinct pleasure to introduce one of our most enthusiastic supporters. Everyone, please welcome our newly elected member of Parliament, Theodore Pearce."

Applause was enthusiastic.

A well-muscled man of medium height, possibly in his late forties, leapt onto the stage. With his shaggy hair, flat lopsided nose, and distinct underbite, he had the look of an amiable bulldog. He clapped along with the audience. "Not bad for an ex-juvie, eh?" He pointed a thick forefinger at Hawksworthy. "And no *Theodore*, got it? It's Teddy."

Hawksworthy steepled his hands and bowed in mock apology.

"Nah, you're all right, mate." Pearce grinned. "I'm told we're here tonight to cough up some serious cash, eh? And what better reason to do it than for the Museum of Devon Life. Our museum. Our way of life. And just to be clear, I will *not* be part of the famous criminal's exhibit."

Laughter.

Pearce's expression became serious. "But I could have been. Some of you know my history. Grew up on the streets. No point lying. Dad was a worthless drunk. Mum scrubbed floors. By the age of nine, I was on me own. Never got an education." He held up his hands. "My own fault. Thought I was the dog's bollocks, I did. Headed for hard time until social services stepped in. Literally saved my life. That's why I stood for Parliament. To change the lives of other kids—kids like me who didn't have the best start in life. Make a difference, you know? But tonight we're here to talk about the Museum of Devon Life. Our museum—yours and mine."

I watched Pearce, fascinated, as he responded to the audience, inserting humor, adjusting his tone and body language until he had them in the palm of his hand. I couldn't help liking him. Pearce might lack a formal education, but he had boatloads of charisma. And he knew how to give a speech.

Gideon Littlejohn stood beside me, his hand gripping the silver head of his cane.

Pearce adopted a confidential tone. "I don't need to tell you lot—Devon has suffered a decline in our core industries. Fishing, mining, farming. You know what I mean—the rise in crime, the drugs epidemic, the loss of good jobs, especially for our young people. We rely on tourism, and this museum is slated to become a major attraction. If we want it to be. If we're willing to back it up with cash. And that's just the beginning. Hotels, restaurants, shops, service industries, all sorts, will grow up around the museum. Bringing prosperity. Bringing hope. And hope isn't something we take for granted in this part of Devon."

Applause. Murmurs of agreement.

"That's why I stood for Parliament, folks. Didn't do it for myself. I did it for you and you and you." He pointed at several faces in the crowd. "Think about it. A lad from the streets in Parliament? My old mum would never have believed it. And job one is rooting out and putting an end to corruption. You know what I'm talking about—eighty percent increase in raw sewage dumps. Thousands of Council homes with expired electrical safety certificates. Long waiting lists for essential surgeries. The elderly and most vulnerable having to choose between the cost of care or remaining alone in their homes. How did it happen? Short story, ugly but true: Corruption. Local politicians, bureaucrats, even the police."

"Mind what you say, lad," came a voice from behind me.

I turned my head. The voice belonged to the tall, silver-haired man I'd seen speaking with Hawksworthy when we arrived. His wife was silver haired, too, and almost matched him in height.

"You know what they say." Pearce flashed a smile. "If you don't make someone mad, you're not doing your job." The audience laughed. He shrugged. "We're talking real crime here, and trust me, folks, it takes one to know one. But I can't fight decades of corruption alone." He was serious now. "I think that's why you elected me. You care about preserving our way of life. You want our young people to have the hope of a living wage, the chance to have a family, hold their heads up. And you know what we're up against, don't you? Powerful people. People with money and influence who are profiting from crime. They fly off to their holiday homes in Spain and turn a blind eye to the suffering of the little people. The ones with no power. They're determined to stop me. I'm their worst nightmare." He laughed. "Hell—I've been someone's worst nightmare me whole life." More laughter from the crowd. "But seriously, folks. I've been threatened. Phone calls in the middle of the night. My house vandalized. Rocks tossed through the windows." He stopped and bowed his head. "They can't intimidate me, because this is important. If we're going to make a change, we have to stand together. That's why we're here tonight. To stand together. Together we can accomplish anything. End corruption. Fund this museum. Bring pride and prosperity back to our community. We're here to celebrate our heritage, our history, our way of life. So get out those checkbooks, eh? Be generous, because we're ordinary people who know what's important in life. Some of us had to learn the hard way, but it's going to take all of us working together to finish the new wing—to bring hope back to East Devon. And while you're at it, I wouldn't say no to a wee check for my campaign." Pearce saluted the crowd. "That's enough of me blathering on, eh? Enjoy the evening, folks."

He jumped off the platform to thunderous applause. A woman joined him. His wife? She was younger than Pearce and slightly taller, platinum blond and incredibly beautiful yet almost too thin. She was dressed in a long Wedgwood-blue velvet gown that bared her pale, wand-like arms. A crystal-studded clutch in the form of a winking cat hung from a silver cross-body chain. Pearce put his arm around her, and they moved toward the bar, Pearce shaking hands all the way.

This man was extraordinarily gifted. I could see why he'd won in the general election—plain-spoken, humble, likable. "An ordinary bloke like us," I heard someone say.

Hugo Hawksworthy was back at the podium. "If that doesn't get your blood pumping, I don't know what will. Thanks, Teddy. Folks, you can slip those checks in the envelopes provided. Mail them in, drop them off in person, send a herald on horseback. We'll take them any way you like. But now, enjoy the food and the drinks. Take time to wander through the museum. We have guides stationed in every room to answer your questions. Unfortunately, the new wing isn't ready for visitors, but you can have a look through the reveal on the top floor. I think you'll be impressed. And for those interested in the mechanical clock, I'll meet you at ten on the first floor for a demonstration." He clapped at the crowd. "Thanks, folks, for coming out tonight. It means so much. And thank you in advance for your generous support."

The hum of conversation rose as small clusters of guests moved off in all directions. I looked for Gideon Littlejohn but didn't find him.

"Wonderful speech," Isla Ferris said. I'd forgotten she was still with us. "Teddy's support will make a big difference. Would you like to meet him?"

"Yes, of course," Tom said. "Interesting fellow."

Teddy Pearce stood near the bar, a drink in one hand and the other around the waist of the woman in blue.

"That's Teddy's wife—Quinn," Isla said. "Her father's one of the largest landowners on Dartmoor. Gorgeous, isn't she? And fabulously wealthy. She was studying business at Exeter when she announced she was dropping out to marry Pearce. As you can imagine, Mum and Dad weren't best pleased. They have twin daughters now." She took Tom's arm. "Come on. I'll introduce you."

In heels, Quinn Pearce was several inches taller than her husband, with porcelain skin and amethyst-blue eyes. Her white-blond hair was pulled into an intricate knot at her neck. A silver chain set with a curved bar of diamonds rested between her collarbones. She smiled as we approached, revealing perfect white teeth. She was older than I'd first thought—late thirties?

"Mr. and Mrs. Pearce—I'd like you to meet Detective Inspector Tom Mallory and his wife, Kate Hamilton. They're from Suffolk, here to investigate the provenance of the Victorian dress."

"Quinn and Teddy, please. Welcome to Devon." Quinn's handshake was stronger than I had expected. "Hugo told us you were coming."

Teddy Pearce stuck out his hand to shake Tom's. "We've got our fingers crossed about the dress."

"You've seen it?" I asked.

"Of course. Hugo had us over when it first came in."

"You know Gideon Littlejohn, then," Tom said.

"Hard to miss, I'd say." Pearce glanced at his wife. "I wouldn't say we actually know each other."

I noticed Dr. Hawksworthy signaling Isla from the other side of the room.

"Sorry—I'm needed." She excused herself.

The tall silver-haired couple approached. Without acknowledging our presence, the man took Pearce's arm. "A word, if you don't mind."

Pearce looked embarrassed. "Great to meet you, Tom and . . . Kate, is it? We should get together while you're here. Share a meal. How about it, Quinn?"

"Yes, of course." She turned away from the older woman. "We'll have you over. Sometime next week?"

"That would be lovely," I said.

Teddy and Quinn headed off with the older couple.

* * *

Tom was thumbing through the museum brochure. "The Rise of Transport exhibit on the ground floor has a 1962 Ford Anglia Deluxe. The Harry Potter car. Care to have a look?"

"Very tempting," I said with a generous hint of sarcasm, "but I think I'd rather check out the lace exhibit."

Isla appeared again. I was beginning to wonder if she'd been ordered to follow us. "You mentioned the lace exhibit. It's one of my favorites. Why don't I show you around?"

"You don't mind, do you, Tom? We can meet up in forty minutes or so in the atrium."

"I'll be there."

Isla and I made our way toward the staircase. A sign told us the first-floor exhibits included lacemaking in Devon, the West Country's Romanies and Travellers, village schools, and the mechanical clock.

"The lacemaking exhibit is one of our first and best," she said. "It's really about people, you know, the way they lived their lives. Mostly women, of course, although there were men who made lace—ex-fishermen, mostly."

The exhibit was fascinating. The term *Honiton lace*, I learned, was taken from the town of Honiton in East Devon—the center of Devon's lacemaking industry from the end of the sixteenth century. Even then, the cost of handmade lace was affordable by only a few wealthy locals. Most of the lace was sent to London and the continent—which made me wonder again why that exquisite lace collar had been sewn onto a plain calico dress.

The display featured gorgeous examples of lace—collars and cuffs, edgings, flouncings, veils—but the heart of the exhibit was the stories of the lacemakers themselves, told in photographs and in their own words. I wandered through, reading the captions. Isla followed.

"Very young girls were sent to lace schools," she said, "in existence in Devon until around 1870. They were taught songs, or 'tells'—slow, chant-like rhythms to help them memorize the patterns and work more quickly. Many of the tells spoke of hardship and domestic violence by fathers or husbands."

I thought about Nancy Thorne and the bloodstained dress. Had she been mistreated? I pictured that breathtaking lace collar. A reminder of the life she'd never have? A badge of courage? Or a symbol of something darker, like Hester Prynne's embroidered *A*?

Isla looked at her watch. "I'm afraid I'll have to cut things short. The mechanical clock demonstration in the atrium area begins in ten minutes. I'm expected to have everything ready when Hugo arrives. I hope you'll stay to see it, Kate. It's quite remarkable."

"I'd love to see it. Tom won't mind waiting." As we moved toward the atrium, I saw that a large number of guests had already gathered around a long-case mahogany clock with a brass face and a platform upon which the hidden mechanical figures would revolve. I'd seen similar clocks in other museums.

Isla, wearing cotton gloves, opened both the clock's upper and lower doors, exposing a complicated mechanism of weights, gears, and pendulums.

More guests were joining the crowd, among them Quinn Pearce. She was with the tall, silver-haired couple—the man who'd warned Teddy Pearce to tone down his accusations and his equally tall wife.

I leaned over the railing, gazing down at the ground floor to see if Tom had returned yet. He hadn't, but I noticed Dr. Hawksworthy in what looked like a tense conversation with Gideon Littlejohn. Hawksworthy stabbed his finger into Littlejohn's chest. As Littlejohn turned away, Hawksworthy grabbed his arm. Littlejohn wrenched free. Hawksworthy shook his head and strode off toward the stairs. He was needed for the clock demonstration.

I was still watching Littlejohn, puzzled by what I'd seen, when Teddy Pearce appeared. He gestured sharply, causing Littlejohn to step backward. Pearce threw up his arms.

What was that all about? Were there undercurrents swirling around the museum that Tom and I hadn't detected? Apparently so.

"Excuse me, folks—coming through." The crowd gathered around the clock hushed as Dr. Hawksworthy made his way to the front. "The Museum of Devon Life is truly fortunate to have this early-nineteenth-century automaton, thought to have been made in Gloucester." Hawksworthy was slightly out of breath, perhaps from his dash up the stairs. "Throughout the day, on the hour, a series of figures from ordinary life appear—a butcher, dairymaid, parson, doctor, banker, country gentleman, blacksmith, and so on. I think you'll recognize them. We don't wind the clock on a regular basis—too much wear on the mechanisms. But you'll see all the figures tonight because Ms. Ferris has set the clock for twelve. At that time, twice a day, all the figures appear, turning one by one to face the observer as they make their way across the stage, followed by the ominous figure of Death carrying a scythe. When that figure reaches center stage, you'll see him swing the great curved blade, signifying the brevity of life and the certainty of death."

Hawksworthy reached for a bank of switches on the wall, dimming the overhead lights and adjusting a spotlight that shone on the clock. Then, donning his own pair of cotton gloves, he signaled Isla, who stepped aside so he could set the automaton in motion. A bell sounded, and as the first of the mechanical figures appeared, Dr. Hawksworthy and Isla Ferris retreated into the crowd. Near me, at the back, stood the tall, silver-haired couple with Quinn Pearce. On their right, a woman with bright-red hair held a small boy. Opposite her was a tall man with a red face and a short man bouncing on his toes in an attempt to see over the crowd.

I watched, fascinated, as the mechanical figures began their slow, jerky procession. One by one, the wooden figures made their way across the stage of life, bowing before disappearing through the door on the opposite side. I thought of Jacques's melancholy soliloquy in *As You Like It*: *All the world's a stage, and all the men and women merely players. They have their exits and their entrances . . .*

All eyes were fixed on the clock as Death made his entrance—a pale, gaunt figure, carrying a scythe nearly as tall as he was. I felt a chill, thinking about the lives of those who had witnessed this marvel for the first time. Death had been a constant and tangible presence in their lives. Their forebears were the lucky ones who'd survived the Black Death. Their descendants would experience the horrors of the First World War and the Spanish flu pandemic that killed one-third of the world's population.

The clock struck slowly—twice, three times, four. Death had reached the center of the stage. You could have heard a pin drop. Was it my imagination, or did he appear to grin? I felt a sudden frisson of fear. I'd had enough. I wanted Tom and his solid warmth.

Backing away, I took a final look at the tableau vivant—Isla's gold dress, shimmering in the light; the tall, silver-haired couple, leaning forward; the outline of Quinn's spine as she bent her pale neck; the redheaded woman and her son; the tall man with the red face; the short man craning his neck to see.

I flew down the stairs, the bells still tolling. Scanning the crowd, I found Tom with Gideon Littlejohn near the drinks trolley.

"There you are," Tom said. "I was about to—"

I heard a pop.

A tray of drink glasses shattered. People screamed. Then, bizarrely, there was a moment of shocked silence, broken only by the tolling of the clock's twelfth and final chime.

"*Get down, everyone*," Tom shouted. "Take cover. Active shooter."

People around me scrabbled on their hands and knees. I crawled behind the drinks trolley. "Tom," I called. "Are you all right?"

"Littlejohn's been grazed." Then, in a louder voice, "I'm a police officer. Where did the shot come from?"

"Upper floor," someone called back. "First, I think."

"Hawksworthy. Where are you?"

"On one. Everyone's safe up here."

"Same on two," came a woman's voice from high above.

"Stay where you are," Tom said. "Don't anyone move. I'm calling 999."

"Already on the way, mate." The voice was close, and I knew it. Teddy Pearce. I hadn't seen him in the atrium, but he'd apparently taken cover close to the spot where Tom and Littlejohn were crouched.

Pearce stood. "It's over, folks. They won't try again."

"You don't know that, Pearce," Tom shouted. "Get down. Stay where you are until the police arrive."

"Sorry, mate. If they think they can intimidate me, they've got it wrong."

"What do you mean?" Tom asked.

"It's obvious, isn't it? I was the target."

Chapter Five

The police arrived in about fifteen minutes. Tom and I followed Dr. Hawksworthy to the main entrance, where he unlocked the double glass entry doors.

A tall, dark-skinned man in a wool overcoat and black fedora stepped across the threshold. He held up his police warrant card. "Detective Chief Inspector Elijah Okoje. Major Crimes Unit, Newton Abbot." Okoje looked to be about Tom's age, with a neatly trimmed stubble beard and mustache. He removed his hat, revealing a shaved head. From a distance, he might have been mistaken for Idris Elba.

Three men entered behind him, one in plain clothes, the other two in police uniform.

"This is Detective Sergeant Veejay Varma," Okoje said. The man in plain clothes was young, of South Asian descent.

Varma held up his warrant card. He wore a leather jacket and expensive-looking shoes with pointed toes. "You probably know your local constables, Doaks and O'Brien."

The constables, both quite young, stood behind their officers, stony-faced and, I thought, a bit awestruck.

Tom brought out his own warrant card. "DI Tom Mallory, Suffolk Constabulary. I'm here unofficially. This is Dr. Hugo Hawksworthy, museum director, and my wife, Kate Hamilton."

"Ma'am." Okoje nodded once. "Anyone hurt?"

"Single shot. One person grazed. Close, though. Another inch or two and we'd be looking at a fatality."

"Singled out or just unlucky?"

"Unclear. The local MP, Teddy Pearce, seems to believe he was the target."

"Ah, yes. I understand the lad's ruffled a few feathers."

I wondered if I should mention the silver-haired man who'd objected to Pearce's speech but decided they'd find out, one way or another.

Inspector Okoje turned to Hawksworthy. "How many ways in and out of the museum?"

"In and out?" Hawksworthy shook his head as if to clear it. "Ah, besides the main doors, there are three exits, one at each side and another at the rear. All locked and bolted."

"Holding them prisoner, eh?"

Hawksworthy looked at him blankly.

"Just my little joke, sir." Okoje cast an eye around the room. "How can you be certain the doors were locked?"

"I did it myself, just before Pearce's speech."

"Who else has keys?"

"My assistant, Isla Ferris, and our textile conservator, Julia Kelly. She isn't here tonight."

Odd, I thought. With the bloodstained dress and the potential new historical costumes exhibit, I'd have thought Dr. Hawksworthy would have insisted she come—and be introduced to the donors.

Hawksworthy was still explaining the keys. "There is a cleaning company. They have keys, but they aren't due for another week."

"Sergeant Varma will take the details. Anyone see the shooter?"

"Not as far as we know," Tom said. "I told everyone to stay where they were until you arrived."

"Lucky you were here, Mallory." Okoje turned to the two young constables. "Doaks, O'Brien, begin a search, top floor down. We're looking for a weapon. As soon as you've finished, have the guests come down in ones and twos. Varma, take the victim's statement first. Then check everyone as they leave for GSR."

"GSR?" Hawksworthy looked confused.

"Gunshot residue. Simple process."

"You can't detain these people all night," Hawksworthy said. "Some are elderly."

"Won't take long if everyone cooperates." Inspector Okoje rubbed an eyebrow. "You say all doors were locked? No one in or out?"

"I don't see how."

Okoje's dark eyes took on a steely glint. "Well, now. That means the shooter's still in the building, doesn't it? And so is the weapon. Sorry. No one leaves without being searched and checked for gunshot residue. We'll do our best to clear the most elderly first." He looked at the two constables. "Got it?"

"Yes, guv." The constables left.

Hawksworthy's face had drained of color.

"If the shooter was smart, he or she wore gloves," Tom said. "No residue. No fingerprints."

"What are those, sir, if I might ask?" Okoje indicated a pair of white cotton gloves hanging out of Hawksworthy's pocket.

Hawksworthy stared at the gloves as if seeing them for the first time. "It's, ah, the mechanical clock. We . . . we always wear gloves to operate the mechanism. The oils on human hands can, over time . . ." He trailed off.

"We'll need those, I'm afraid."

DS Varma stepped forward with an evidence bag.

"Anyone else wearing gloves tonight?" Okoje asked.

"My assistant, Miss Ferris," Hawksworthy said. "And the servers."

"Shooter would have ditched the gloves, but you never know. We might get lucky. I'd like to interview Pearce tonight, Hawksworthy. Is there an office I can use?"

"Staff lunchroom is free. Will that do?"

"Fine. Mallory, would you care to sit in? I could use another set of ears."

They left, and I wandered back toward the atrium. DS Varma was speaking with Gideon Littlejohn, who held a white handkerchief stained with blood. The bullet had cut a two-inch swath across his right cheek. Isla Ferris dabbed at the wound with a tissue. Varma must have suggested a trip to the hospital, because Littlejohn shook his head. "I don't need medical attention. Yes, I'm sure."

Tom was right. Another inch or two and he might be dead.

I noticed Quinn Pearce sitting on the edge of the band platform. She looked ill. "May I join you?"

"Yes, of course." She was trembling, her already pale face drained of color. "Thanks for checking on me." She put her hand on mine. It was cold as ice.

"You need a cup of tea," I said. "I'm sure I can find one somewhere."

"I'll be fine." Quinn pressed a knuckle to her upper lip. "It's just been so hard lately. The attacks on our family—now this."

"Who's staying with your children?"

"My mother. I phoned her. She's prepared to stay the night."

"Do you have any idea who did this?"

"None at all." Quinn shook her head. "I'm not involved in politics; that's Teddy's interest. He tries to shield me and the children."

"Do you mean it could be a political opponent?"

She looked at me, her blue eyes swimming with tears. "Most of the local politicians are lovely, caring people who just want to make Devon a better place. We might not always agree on the way to do that, but we have a common goal. But there are some who are out for themselves, who profit from the status quo—*the swamp*, as you Americans call it. It doesn't want to be drained."

"You were on the first floor when the shot was fired. I saw you with an older couple."

"The Jamiesons, yes. They're old friends. Teddy and I had been visiting the school exhibit. Education is one of his interests. They have a classroom set up as it would have been during the Second World War. One of the guides was explaining how the educational system in Devon has changed. Teddy was getting a bit bored, so he excused himself. I stayed to be polite. Then someone said, 'The clock's about to go off,' so we all moved into the atrium. The demonstration was nearly over when we heard the gunshot."

"The police think the shot came from that floor. Did you see anything?"

"No. There was such a crowd. When the shot went off, we all sort of fell to the floor. I panicked. All I could think was 'They've finally done it—they've shot him.' Your husband told us to stay where we were. Then I heard Teddy's voice." She began to tremble again. "I was so relieved."

I put my arm around her thin shoulders. "I can imagine how frightened you were." It was true. I remembered the previous spring when I'd thought I'd lost Tom in the collapse of a house. I never *ever* wanted to experience anything like that again.

The arguments I'd witnessed from the first-floor railing kept running through my mind. "How well does your husband know Gideon Littlejohn?"

"Gideon?" She looked surprised. "Teddy told you, Kate. They're not friends. I mean, they've met because of the museum. Why do you ask?"

"It's not important."

The museum patrons were beginning to file down from the upper floors. No one was complaining. They were probably still in shock.

Isla Ferris appeared with two paper cups of tea. "I added milk and sugar. I hope that's all right."

We thanked her and assured her the tea was perfect. Just what we needed to settle our jangled nerves.

Shortly after that, we saw Tom, Teddy Pearce, and Inspector Okoje emerge from the staff lunchroom.

"May I take my wife home now, Inspector?" Teddy asked.

"Yes, of course, sir. Let me know when you've completed the list we talked about; I'll send someone around to collect it."

The Pearces headed for the cloakroom.

Tom took my arm. "Let's go." He must have seen the look on my face, because he said, "Tell you when we get to the Crown."

* * *

It was close to midnight when Tom and I got back to the Crown. We were both exhausted, but we knew we'd never sleep until we'd talked things through.

Fortunately, the snug bar was still open, although the fire had burnt down to a few glowing embers. We ordered small glasses of brandy and sat by the stone hearth on a battered leather sofa.

"What was that list Inspector Okoje mentioned?" I asked.

"They've asked Pearce to make a list of his political enemies."

"I had a talk with Quinn. She said they've been the target of threats, vandalism. When she heard the pop, her first thought was that someone had shot her husband."

"He's convinced he was the target, and he may be right. They've reported the attacks to the police, but so far no one has been arrested."

"Pearce didn't seem intimidated."

"Buckets of self-confidence, that man." Tom put his arm around me. "Comfortable in the role of disrupter. Six years ago he was elected to his local council and stirred things up. Made some enemies. He admitted as much. Last year he stood for Parliament. He's popular with the people, not with the bureaucrats and those who've been in charge for years. Pearce's election was an upset."

"What do you know about that older man who called him out, the one with the silver hair? Quinn said his name was Jamieson."

"Richard Jamieson. He's an architectural consultant by trade, specializing in the structural remediation of heritage buildings—and a member of the East Devon District Council. Claims he sympathizes with Pearce. Says his words were meant as a warning."

"Do you believe it?"

"The better question is, does Pearce believe it? I think he does. Jamieson is Labour, like Pearce, so they're technically on the same team. Besides, he couldn't have fired the shot. He and his wife were on the first floor, but they were standing next to Quinn Pearce."

"Yes, I saw them, just before I came down. The police are certain the shot came from the first floor?"

"That's what it looks like. They found the bullet. A ballistics expert has been called in. They'll work out the trajectory."

"No one thinks Gideon Littlejohn was the target?"

"Not even Littlejohn, apparently."

"But what if he's wrong? Isla Ferris said he's in cybersecurity. That involves computer hackers, right?"

"Littlejohn works behind the scenes—preventing data breaches, setting up firewalls, encryption. Stuff like that."

"While dressed in a Victorian frock coat?"

"Now that's a picture."

"Tom—" I hesitated, working things out in my head as I spoke. "What if the shooter wasn't one of the guests?"

"Go on."

"Someone could have entered the building earlier and hidden, out of sight, until the time was right."

"An interesting theory." His brow furrowed in thought. "You mean they stayed hidden until the appropriate moment, emerged to fire the shot, and then exited quickly while people were still scrambling for cover. Probably lots of places to hide on the first floor. One problem—how could an intruder escape when all the doors were locked? Unless they had a key."

"Julia Kelly has a key. Dr. Hawksworthy said so. But why would she want to kill Teddy Pearce?"

"It might have been a random shooting. Someone wanting to disrupt the gala or discredit the museum." Tom yawned. "Or maybe Littlejohn was the target after all. He's almost a celebrity around here. He produces a video podcast. Several thousand followers, he says, not all in the UK."

"What does he talk about?"

"Living like a Victorian gentleman. Dressing like one. Giving up modern conveniences for a simpler, less complicated lifestyle."

"Living without modern conveniences doesn't sound less complicated to me. How would you like to heat water for your bath on a coal-fired stove—or cook on one, for that matter?"

"A more authentic lifestyle, then. Back to one's roots."

I made a face. "You know I love history, Tom, but I have no desire to live there. I wonder why he does?"

"Do you think Littlejohn was the target?"

"Not really. He seems pretty harmless. But I did notice some hostility this evening." I told him about the arguments I'd witnessed, first between Littlejohn and Hugo Hawksworthy, then between Littlejohn and Teddy Pearce. "I couldn't hear what they were saying, obviously, but neither conversation looked cordial."

"Interesting." Tom nodded slowly. "Littlejohn and Pearce were standing near each other when the gun went off."

And near you as well, I thought with a shudder.

"I'll tell Okoje what you witnessed." Tom stood and yawned again. "Come on. Let's go to bed. The Devon & Cornwall Police can handle the shooting. Our concern is a mysterious bloodstained dress."

I didn't quite believe him. I'd seen the spark in his eyes when Okoje asked him to sit in on the interview with Pearce.

Chapter Six

Saturday, January 4
Coombe Mallet

We woke earlier than planned. Still keyed up from the shooting, we showered and dressed and headed down for an early breakfast. After shamelessly indulging at the Old Bell, I'd promised myself I'd have something light, maybe fruit and an English muffin. But when Tom ordered the full English—scrambled eggs with locally made sausages and all the trimmings—I weakened. And enjoyed every bite.

With our stomachs full, we headed back up to our room. The crime scene team was still processing the museum, and since our appointment at the Old Merchant's House wasn't until eleven, we had time to read and answer emails. Tom fell asleep almost immediately. I woke him at ten fifteen. "Time to go soon."

The day was cold and gray. Since rain was drizzling down, we layered waterproofs over our warm jackets and took the Rover. We arrived at Gideon Littlejohn's house a few minutes early and parked on the street.

The Old Merchant's House was a four-story, flat-fronted brick structure built directly on the pavement. The entrance was framed by glossy white columns. We stood on the doorstep, huddled under our umbrella. Tom used the door knocker, and in moments a small, neat woman opened the door. She was dressed in a long, dove-gray dress with a high buttoned collar and a starched white bib-top apron.

Her gray hair was pulled into a bun and topped with a lace-trimmed mobcap. She stepped aside, allowing us entry into a paneled hall with an unlit fireplace and a steep, U-shaped staircase. "Good morning, sir, madam. May I help you?"

I stared at her, speechless.

Tom, unruffled as always, jumped in. "I'm Tom Mallory. This is my wife, Kate Hamilton. We have an appointment at eleven with Mr. Littlejohn."

"Very good, sir. If you'll wait here, I'll see if Mr. Littlejohn is at home." She must have seen the question on my face, because her mouth curved up in a smile. "The answer is he pays well." She scurried off.

I looked at Tom. He shrugged.

I noticed a small keypad on the wall near the entrance. Interesting. A Victorian gentleman with a security system.

The housekeeper reappeared, completely back in character. "This way, if you please. Mr. Littlejohn will receive you in the morning room."

We followed her along a corridor to an octagonal-shaped room with banks of windows overlooking the back garden.

Littlejohn stood to greet us. He was dressed in a dark frock coat, buff-colored trousers, and a plaid waistcoat. In spite of the bandage on his cheek, he appeared to be in high spirits. "Ah, the Mallorys." He consulted his gold pocket watch. "Right on time. Welcome to the Old Merchant's House. Mrs. Grey, will you kindly bring tea?"

"Of course, sir." She bobbed a curtsey.

"Must be nice, having a housekeeper," I said when she was out of earshot.

"Housekeeper and cook. Beryl has been with me for nearly a year now. I've begun to advertise for a live-in cook and butler. If you're going to do something, why do it by halves?"

Why indeed, if you have the money. Cybersecurity must pay well.

"How's your injury?" I asked.

"It's nothing," he said, nonchalant for someone who'd been inches from death mere hours ago. "Come, let's sit by the fire."

Tom and I chose a small, patterned sofa. Littlejohn sat across from us in one of two matching scroll-arm chairs. I wanted to ask him about his conversations—arguments?—with Hugo Hawksworthy and Teddy Pearce the night before but couldn't think how to broach the subject without sounding intrusive. It was, after all, none of my business.

"I feel as if we've stepped into a museum," Tom said.

"Oh, it's very much a home. I mentioned last night that I'm taking the house back to its original condition—or as close as I can come. There are a number of health-and-safety regulations I can't get around. And a few practicalities."

I smiled. "Like a security system?"

He looked almost embarrassed. "Yes. The work I do requires a high level of security."

"When was the house built?" Tom asked.

"It was completed in 1838. The original owner was a draper—a seller of fine wool, linen, and silk. The ground floor was his shop, which is why there's no front garden. In the early 1880s, he retired and sold the house to a lawyer with a wife and three children. They did extensive updating, including adding this room at the rear of the structure. The real architectural damage was done around the time of the First World War when the house was divided into flats. Later it was a boarding house."

"And you've rescued it."

"Yes, I suppose I have."

I thought of Teddy Pearce. Sometimes people needed rescuing too.

Beryl Grey appeared with a tea tray. She bumped the door closed with her hip and set the tray on a drum table near the windows. Besides tea, she'd brought several kinds of biscuits.

"When did you become interested in the Victorian era?" Tom asked.

Littlejohn smiled. "What you really mean is why do I live like a Victorian?"

"That too," Tom admitted. "You've chosen a unique hobby."

"Oh, it's not a hobby," Littlejohn said. "It's a way of life, and the answer's simple. I choose to live this way because it makes me happy."

"A very good reason, then," I said.

"I'm part of a group—an unofficial club, you might call it. We all choose to re-create the past, although we're each at a different stage.

Some simply dress occasionally in Victorian clothing. Others, like myself, extend our interest into our daily lives. I publish a bimonthly video podcast on YouTube. It's become quite popular."

"How do you take your tea?" Beryl Grey hovered over me with the teapot.

"Milk and two sugars." She poured milk, added the tea and two sugar cubes, and handed me the porcelain cup.

After pouring out for Tom and Littlejohn, she bobbed another curtsy and left the room.

As we drank our tea, Littlejohn told us more about his fascination with all things Victorian. "It started when I was a child. One day I met an old man in the park, feeding the ducks. He was terribly deformed—something wrong with his spine. Looking back, I think he must have been in great pain, but he never complained. He lived in a terraced house not far away. I started going there, occasionally at first, later almost every day. He was lonely. So was I. We became friends. Everything in his house was ancient, or so it seemed to me then. He told me stories about the old days. Showed me old books—histories, old maps and engravings. I was fascinated. His house was a kind of sanctuary for me. I was a little chap then. Didn't get my growth spurt until later, so I was bullied. The old man was too. It was a bond between us. He was the one who instilled in me an interest in history."

"Was it his household you purchased?" I asked.

"Oh, no. I wish I'd had the chance."

"What happened to him?"

"He died in a house fire." Littlejohn placed his teacup carefully in the saucer and looked away. A door had been shut and barred.

He'd told us more than he intended.

A sudden smile transformed his face. "But you're not here to learn about my past. You're here about the bloodstained dress."

"Which you purchased at auction," Tom said.

"As I told you last night, the entire household was sold as a lot. Seems the family of the man who'd passed away wanted a quick sale."

"When was this?" I asked.

"Last summer. I found the dress in a trunk with a collection of other objects—sort of a time capsule. I don't think anyone had looked inside for years."

Time capsule? That sounded promising.

"I gave the smaller items to the museum along with the dress. One thing I saved for myself." He got up and went to a side window, where he pulled back a heavy drape. Within the alcove formed by a wide bay sat a small domed-lid trunk, the kind used for travel.

Littlejohn carried the trunk to the hearth and opened the lid. The interior was lined with a fine-print fabric in pale yellow. Folded inside was a patchwork quilt, cunningly patterned from various scraps of fabric in a riot of colors. "I thought about using the quilt on one of the beds, but some of the fabrics are quite fragile. Even so, I'm reluctant to let it go."

Littlejohn placed the quilt on my lap. The design was the kind the Victorians had loved—irregular shapes of fabric, mostly silk-satins and velvets, sewn onto a foundation and outlined with a variety of elaborate embroidery stitches. The beauty was in the design and the colors, skillfully chosen and placed for maximum effect. I peered closer, feeling a sort of warm glow or something akin to the buzz you get after a couple of glasses of wine—my usual reaction to beautiful objects and fine workmanship. The stitching was incredibly delicate and precise. I thought of Julia Kelly's comment about the bloodstained dress—workmanship rivaling that of the French couturiers. Had Nancy Thorne's sister, Sally, made both the dress and the quilt? If so, I could see her using scraps of fabric from the dresses she'd created for wealthy village women. Once before, in Scotland, a quilt had been a clue to a mysterious death. "It's gorgeous. A real treasure."

Tom placed his teacup on a side table. "What can you tell us about the man who owned these things?"

"Almost nothing except that he died. His niece, his only surviving relative, didn't want the hassle of going through everything, so her lawyer organized an auction."

"Was he someone you knew?"

"Never heard of him. I was looking through the listings and saw the Victorian fixtures."

"You realize we're looking for a connection between this man and the Thorne sisters," I said. "Have you found one?"

"Just the note I told you about last night. As I said, I haven't had a chance to look through the other items in the lot. I plan to do that when my work settles down."

"Would you mind if we took the trunk and the quilt with us?" I asked. "I'd like Julia Kelly to see them."

Littlejohn looked up sharply. "No—that's not possible." His tone was almost harsh, which he seemed to realize. "But you're welcome to return and study the quilt anytime. Or look through the other items in the lot if you wish. I'll tell Mrs. Grey. She can prepare a room for you to work in. The dining room still has electrical outlets, and the Wi-Fi signal is strong there."

"I understand," I said, although I didn't—not completely. Did he imagine we'd steal something? "Is tomorrow too soon? As Tom mentioned earlier, our time here is limited."

"Tomorrow afternoon should work. Mrs. Grey will be free by twelve forty-five. I always take my midday meal at twelve thirty. Would you care to join me?"

"Very kind," Tom said, "but we'll get straight to work, if that's all right."

I felt slightly disappointed. It would have been interesting to see what a Victorian gentleman had for lunch.

Tom stood and extended his hand. "Thank you for your time."

"My pleasure. I hope to see you tomorrow."

On the way out, we made arrangements with Beryl Grey to return at twelve forty-five the following day. She showed us to the door, and, donning our rain gear again, we emerged into the twenty-first century.

Back in the Rover, I pulled off my hood and shook out my hair. Storm clouds were gathering. At least we'd been warned. In the winter, Devon and Cornwall are the wettest counties in England.

"It'll be interesting to see the other items found in the trunk," I said. "The ones at the museum. They might offer a clue."

I tried to picture the trunk as Littlejohn had found it. The lovely quilt. A calico dress, washed but stained with blood. And pinned to it, a note saying it belonged to the murderess Nancy Thorne. Who'd written the note—and why hadn't Hawksworthy shown it to us?

Chapter Seven

Sunday, January 5
Coombe Mallet

A drenching rain had come, all right, and kept up most of the night, drumming on the thatch and sluicing down the windows of our room at the Crown. But by morning, the skies had cleared, the sun was shining, and the temperature had settled at a relatively mild twelve degrees Celsius—about fifty degrees Fahrenheit.

"We're not expected at the Old Merchant's House for another four hours," I said, pouring Tom a cup of coffee. "Do you think the museum will be open today? After the shooting, I mean."

"Not to the public." Tom slipped his mobile into the pocket of his fleece jacket. "Okoje texted while you were in the shower. The crime scene team didn't finish up until three AM last night. The museum staff will be there today, cleaning up. Lots to do before they can open their doors again. They'll probably let us in. What do you have in mind?"

"We need a place with reliable Wi-Fi. I'd like to search for any contemporary newspaper accounts of Nancy Thorne and the mystery surrounding the bloodstained dress. That means logging on to the British Newspaper Archive and finding out which newspapers were published in mid-nineteenth-century Devon. If I can find an account of the incident online, it will save us time and effort. Patience isn't one of my virtues."

"You can't have them all." He placed a coffee pod in the room's Keurig.

After a second cup of coffee, we threw on our jackets and headed out into the crisp morning.

We arrived at the museum at nine fifteen. Two men were wiping down the glass entrance doors, which had been dusted for fingerprints. Inside, a man in a dark jumpsuit was running a floor-polishing machine, and several young women in floral smocks were setting up the gift shop.

"It's the Mallorys. Good morning." Isla Ferris stood in the reception area, a dustcloth in one hand and a bottle of glass cleaner in the other. "You're up bright and early." She seemed especially cheerful, which puzzled me.

"Dr. Hawksworthy said he'd make a room available," I said. "Would we be in the way?"

"Not at all. Hugo told me you might be coming."

"We'll need access to your Wi-Fi," Tom said. "Kate brought her laptop."

"Of course." Isla beamed. "Such a lovely morning. Too bad they're predicting snow later." She ushered us into what appeared to be an employee break room. A long table and chairs shared space with several vending machines and tea-making facilities. "I'm afraid there's only one really comfortable chair, but the cleaners are here. Shall I ask them to move one of the chairs from Hugo's office?"

"Don't bother," Tom said. "I promised to stop by the police enquiry office this morning."

"The shooting, of course. Such a shock. Unbelievable." Isla's somber face lasted only a few seconds. She smiled and spread her arms. "Make yourself at home, Kate. There's tea, coffee, cappuccino. I'll stop by later to see how you're doing."

Isla's demeanor was almost—well, celebratory. I gave Tom a side glance. *What's with her this morning?*

"You're in a good mood today, Ms. Ferris," he said, echoing my thoughts. "Have you had some welcome news?"

"I won't deny it." She positively twinkled. "Not for public knowledge quite yet."

"We can't wait to hear," I said, smiling with her. Had the museum received the grant they were hoping for? Had one of the donors coughed up a large check?

Tom bent to give me a kiss. "Text me if you find anything interesting."

I plugged in, logged on to the British Newspaper Archive, and immediately found at least a dozen local Devon newspapers published in the mid-nineteenth century. I began with the *Cornish & Devon Post*, which appeared to be an old standard.

It was just before ten when Isla popped her head around the corner. "Making progress?" She was wearing a long fawn-colored coat.

"Still looking." Truthfully, I was getting restless. "Would it be possible to see the other objects donated to the museum by Mr. Littlejohn?"

"I'll have to ask Hugo. He's meeting with one of his donors this morning. I'm leaving as well, I'm afraid. Stay as long as you like. Someone will be here all day."

That was disappointing—and a bit curious. The night of the gala, Hawksworthy had introduced Isla Ferris as assistant director of the museum. Why did she have to get his permission to show me the collection of items found with the dress? Was Hawksworthy a control freak?

It was ten thirty when Tom returned to find me frustrated and fuming.

"How's it going?" He kissed the top of my head.

"A whole hour wasted—that's how it's going. I found a bunch of newspapers published in Devon in the mid-nineteenth century, but would you believe not one of them so far mentions Nancy Thorne?" I held up my hand. "Sorry for the rant. Ignore me. What did Okoje have to say?"

"Quite a bit, actually. The ballistics expert confirmed the bullet came from the first floor. Given the trajectory, the shooter had to be standing close to the railing. Which is odd, because it's a fairly open space, and yet no one admits seeing him—or her."

"Incredibly dangerous, shooting into a crowd like that. Anyone could have been hit. *You* could have been hit."

"Yes—and that's odd too." Tom pulled off his jacket and draped it over the back of one of the folding chairs. "Why take the chance of killing the wrong person?"

"Maybe the shooter was desperate. Or overconfident. Or, as you said, just wanted to create havoc."

"Anyway, the good news is they recovered the weapon—a semiautomatic pistol, small but deadly. Easy to conceal." He pushed a couple of coins into the vending machine slot. "Fancy a cappuccino?"

"No, thanks. Just had one." I held up my empty paper cup, still feeling slightly sick from the excessive sugar and artificial cream. "Where would someone buy a gun like that in the UK?"

"Plenty of guns floating around." Steaming liquid filled Tom's cup. He took a tentative sip. "Guns can be bought or rented on the black market. Criminals use antique guns as well. It's actually a trend. Not long ago, a North London gang member used an eighteenth-century blunderbuss to ward off a rival gang." Tom took another sip, made a face, and put his cup down. "Way too sweet."

"Where did the police find the gun?"

"In a bin near the staircase on the first floor. Wrapped in a plastic bag." He sat down next to me at the table. "No fingerprints, which means the shooter wore gloves—probably the same latex gloves worn by the catering staff. Easy to slip off and discard in one of the many rubbish bins. Hundreds of gloves were discarded that night. Finding the exact pair worn by the shooter would be like finding a needle in a . . . well, in a stack of needles." Tom got up, poured the rest of his cappuccino down a small service sink, and tossed the paper cup in the rubbish bin. "About the newspapers, maybe Hugo can point you in the right direction."

"I never thought of that."

"You have a sarcastic streak."

"I'm sorry. Hitting dead ends all morning has put me in a bad mood. Hugo isn't here at the moment. Neither is Isla. She got me settled and then left soon afterwards."

"How's Julia Kelly coming with the dress?"

I checked my watch. "If she's here, we can ask. I think I've done all I can online for now."

We found Julia in the workroom, on her knees, draping a length of flesh-colored fabric over a molded white mannequin. The dress hung nearby on a padded hanger.

"Oh, hello." Julia inserted a long T-pin to hold the fabric in place. She stood, brushing back her fringe of hair. "I can't believe what happened at the gala. Lucky no one was seriously hurt. Poor Gideon. What are the police saying?"

"Still gathering information," Tom said. "They've scheduled a press conference for this afternoon."

I noticed Julia had called Littlejohn by his first name. "You were lucky not to be there." I watched for her reaction.

"I wanted to go, but Hugo—Dr. Hawksworthy—would have insisted on making a big deal of the restoration work on the dress. I'm not good with publicity. Just give me something to work on and leave me alone. Besides, I'm trying to keep a low profile. In case you haven't noticed, I'm not Isla's favorite person."

"Oh? Why is that?" I had noticed but decided to let Julia tell me about it.

"She keeps our esteemed museum director on a tight leash. I think she sees me as a rival, although it's ridiculous. He's way too old for me. Not my type anyway."

"Isla's jealous?" Tom asked.

"It goes deeper than that. Hugo's been giving me lots of kudos lately. He's excited about the new exhibits, and he knows how to build team loyalty. Part of the reason he's so good at his job, I suppose. A museum is a collaborative effort. Lots of people with lots of different skills pulling together. I think Isla resents the fact that Hugo values me. She doesn't like that."

"Are Hugo and Isla a couple?" I pictured her brushing invisible lint off his jacket at the gala.

"In her mind, maybe." Julia rested one hip on the felt-covered table and tucked a strand of hair behind her ear. "Isla's good at her job. She's been with him for years—since the Mary Rose. His success is important to her, and I suppose she rises with him. Hugo has big plans—the new wing, the proposed textiles exhibit. With Isla's help, he seems to be pulling it off."

"I hope the shooting doesn't discourage the donors," Tom said. He was examining the dress, which, on the hanger, looked impossibly small.

"Oh, it hasn't. Donations are already well above target, and more are bound to come in."

Another dress lay on the worktable, the rich garnet-red silk covered with netting. "Will this dress be part of the new exhibit?" I asked.

"The historic textiles exhibit, yes—not the crimes exhibit." Julia pulled back the netting. "It's gorgeous, isn't it? Donated by a local family. The fabric is warp-printed silk taffeta, probably woven in France. See the shimmer? People often think Victorian clothing was dark and drab. It's not true. Victorian women loved color, especially after 1856, when aniline dyes were invented, producing richer, more vivid colors—like this."

Tom had wandered over to the mannequin. "So that's Nancy Thorne. Or the owner of the dress, whoever she was."

"Where did you find a suitable form?" I asked. "Body sizes and shapes were so different in the past."

"You're right, Kate. We ordered her from a costume institute in Japan. They make four female body types from four different historical eras. Nancy—that's what we're calling her—is a nineteenth-century mannequin, slightly sloping shoulders, high bust, fuller rear. I ordered it without a middle section—the waist—so I can create the exact dimensions we need. We fit the form to the garment rather than adjusting the garment to fit the mannequin."

"Museumgoers will see Nancy Thorne exactly as she was in 1885," Tom said. "If the dress was hers."

"I believe it was hers." Julia blushed. "Just a feeling, of course."

"That's what we hope to find out." Tom took my arm. "Come on, Kate. If we want lunch, we should leave now. Beryl Grey is expecting us in less than an hour."

"Give me a minute," I told Tom. "I'll meet you in the car park."

When he'd left, I said, "How well does Dr. Hawksworthy know Gideon Littlejohn?"

"You mean personally?" Julia frowned. "I don't think he does. I went out with Gideon a few times last year. He never mentioned knowing Hugo."

"What is he like—Littlejohn, I mean?"

"Serious about history. Obsessed, I'd say. And rather sad. He doesn't like to talk about his past, but I have the feeling there's something there, a shadow."

On the way to the car, it struck me that so far we hadn't come up with a single irrefutable fact linking the dress to Nancy Thorne—or to anyone else, for that matter. All we had was an anonymous note, a note Hugo Hawksworthy hadn't mentioned. And yet the museum was putting considerable time and resources into the exhibit. Were they overconfident, or did they know something we didn't?

* * *

The street outside the Old Merchant's House was quiet. The sky had clouded over and a few hopeful flakes of wet snow floated down, melting as soon as they hit the pavement. Tom claimed the same parking spot we'd found the day before. We climbed the steps leading to the shiny black door. Tom used the knocker. When there was no response, he knocked again.

From inside came a blood-curdling scream. Tom tried the door. It was unlocked. Rushing in, we vaulted up the stairs toward the horrible sound.

The housekeeper, Beryl Grey, stood with her back to us in the upstairs hallway.

"Mrs. Grey, what's happened?" Tom took a step toward her.

She turned. Her hands were covered with blood. She stared at them in horror. More blood soaked the front of her white apron. "It's Mr. Littlejohn. He's in there." She indicated an open door. "He's *dead*."

Instantly, Tom went into policeman mode. "Kate, call 999. Stay with her until they arrive. I'm going to check on Littlejohn."

As Tom disappeared, I called emergency services. Then I put my arm around Beryl Grey's shoulders and led her to a chair in an alcove off the upper hallway. She wasn't screaming anymore, but I had no doubt she was in deep shock. "Take some breaths. That's right. In and out, nice and slow. I'll get you some water." I stopped. "Where's the bathroom?"

"On the left, s-second door." Her face was ashen. I felt for her pulse. Fast but regular.

Satisfied she wasn't in immediate danger, I rushed to the bathroom and found a glass resting upside down on a clean towel. Rinsing it out, I filled it with cool water from the brass tap and hurried back.

"Here, drink this."

She took a small sip.

Tom appeared in the doorway. He caught my eye and shook his head.

"Police will be here any moment." I put my hand on Beryl Grey's arm. She flinched. "We'll stay with you until they arrive."

Tom crouched beside the housekeeper. "What happened? Can you tell us?"

"He told me not to come till twelve noon today, as he had a meeting in the morning and wanted privacy." She covered her face with her hands—not a smart move, as her face was now smeared with blood. "I couldn't find him, so I went upstairs." She stared down at the horrible red stains on her crisp white apron.

An image of the bloodstained Victorian dress flashed in my mind.

Car doors slammed. We heard voices.

"Upstairs," Tom shouted.

Inspector Okoje came bounding up the stairs, followed by DS Varma and several EMTs in dark uniforms with high-vis yellow vests.

"In there." Tom pointed toward the open door.

The EMTs had fitted paper booties over their shoes. They pulled on latex gloves.

Inspector Okoje did the same and handed a set to Tom. "You went into the room?"

"Briefly," he admitted. "Had to find out if he was still alive."

"Yes, I see."

DS Varma knelt beside Beryl Grey. "There, there." His tone was unexpectedly gentle, like a father comforting a frightened child. "Tell us what happened."

She began to sob.

While DS Varma questioned the housekeeper, I slipped down the hallway and peered into the room. Gideon Littlejohn lay on the floor in a pool of dark-red blood. I swallowed hard and forced myself to concentrate on the details. The long, curved desk. Multiple displays, keyboards, and computer towers. A tangle of cables and power cords.

The EMTs crouched over the body. That's when I noticed Littlejohn's clothing. Instead of his Victorian getup, he wore jeans, a hooded sweatshirt, and a pair of black Nike trainers.

His escape into the past wasn't complete after all. Someone, very much in the present, had brought an end to his fantasy.

Chapter Eight

With Gideon Littlejohn's body on its way to the morgue in Plymouth, Tom and I followed Inspector Okoje, DS Varma, and the housekeeper, Beryl Grey, into the parlor. After taking samples of the blood on Beryl's skin, the police had let the poor woman wash her face and hands. They'd also confiscated her shoes and the bloodstained apron. Fortunately, she kept a pair of old shoes in the scullery.

I made a pot of tea, adding a fair amount of sugar. After downing a cup of the hot, sweet liquid, Beryl Grey regained some of her composure. "Thank you, dear."

"We'll ask the three of you to provide formal statements later, at the police station," Okoje said. "Right now I'd like to get an overview. You all arrived at the same time?"

DS Varma pulled out a small notebook and tested his pen.

"Kate and I got here a little before twelve forty-five," Tom said. "We heard a scream. The front door wasn't locked, so we rushed inside to see if we could help. You know the rest."

"What about you, Mrs. Grey?" Okoje leaned forward in his chair, his dark eyes focused on her.

"But I told the sergeant—" She broke off and started again. "Mr. Littlejohn said I should begin work at twelve noon today. I arrived five minutes early—he was a stickler about time. I came in through the servants' entrance as usual, hung up my coat, and put the kettle on."

"Where exactly is the servants' entrance?"

"Around the back."

"Did you see anyone coming or going?"

"No one—not until they arrived." She tilted her head in our direction. "Mr. Littlejohn likes to take his lunch precisely at twelve thirty. I'd made the sandwiches the night before. The soup just needed heating, and—"

"I get the picture." Inspector Okoje nodded encouragingly. "What made you go looking for your employer?"

"Because he wasn't in the dining room, of course." Beryl Grey fiddled with her high collar. "Mr. Littlejohn is *always* in the dining room at twelve thirty, already seated in his chair at the head of the table and waiting for me to serve his meal."

"Do you work every day, Mrs. Grey?" DS Varma asked. He was taking notes.

"I have Wednesday and Saturday afternoons off. On those days, I make his evening meal ahead and leave it for him in the fridge. He's been threatening to get one of those old iceboxes. I told him fine—if you want to die of food poisoning."

"Go on."

"I carried the tureen through, and—" She took in a sharp breath.

"He wasn't there," said Inspector Okoje.

"That's right, and I thought, where can he be? Did he forget to wind his pocket watch? But then it occurred to me he might have taken ill."

"Why would you think that?"

"Mr. Littlejohn is *always* where he says he'll be. Very punctual, he is. Reliable."

"You didn't think, perhaps, that you'd mistaken his instructions?"

"Certainly not." She shook her head firmly. "I was to come at twelve noon. He would have his lunch at twelve thirty as usual. When the Mallorys arrived, I was to show them the old housekeeper's room belowstairs."

"He told you to come at twelve today," Okoje said. "When do you usually arrive?"

"Eight o'clock. Only Mr. Littlejohn had a meeting this morning."

I could almost see Okoje's ears perk up. "Did he say where this meeting was to be held?"

"Well, here, of course."

"You're sure about that, are you? Did he actually say it was here?"

Beryl Grey thought for a moment. "Yes, he did. He said, 'I'm expecting a visitor tomorrow morning, Mrs. Grey, so you may take the morning off. I'll be in the study, and I don't wish to be disturbed. Come at noon. I'll take my lunch as usual.'"

"Did he tell you who he was expecting?"

"He did not."

"Did he mention the time of the meeting?"

"No, and I didn't ask. It wasn't my business."

"Do you happen to know if this anonymous visitor showed up?"

"He must have, because I found two teacups and a plate in the sink. I'd left a plate of biscuits. Mr. Littlejohn could make tea himself when he wanted to."

DS Varma scribbled something in his notebook.

"Are the dishes still there?" Okoje's voice was hopeful.

"I washed them and put them away as soon as I arrived."

If Okoje was disappointed, he didn't show it. "Did Mr. Littlejohn keep an appointment book, by any chance?"

"He must have. He was a busy man. But I never saw it."

"He probably kept his appointments on his computer," Tom said.

"Yes, that's it." Beryl Grey brightened. "I expect you'll find everything you want to know on that computer of his."

"The techs are on the way. Now," Okoje said, "if you'll just walk us through your movements again, Mrs. Grey."

For the first time since having her tea, she looked shaky. "Must I? I've told the story several times."

"I'm afraid so. Take it step by step."

Beryl Grey's hands trembled. She clasped them in her lap. "Like I said, I got everything ready for his lunch and went through to the dining room with the tureen of soup." Her brow wrinkled. "I set the tureen on the sideboard. Then I went into the hall and called, 'Mr. Littlejohn, your lunch is ready,' as usual. When he didn't answer, it occurred to me there might be something wrong. So I climbed the stairs and knocked on his bedroom door. I didn't dare go in, of course, so I called out again, through the door, like, 'Mr. Littlejohn, are you in there? Is everything all right?' but there was still no reply."

"Did you try the door?" Okoje asked.

"Certainly not. I'm never to disturb him if a door is closed."

"What did you do next?"

"Well, I didn't know what to do, did I? I stood there for a moment. Then I noticed the door to the bathroom was open, so I looked in. All his shaving things were there, and his nightshirt was hanging on the hook. Then I saw the door to his computer room standing partly open, which it never is. He'd made it clear from the start I wasn't to tidy in that room. But I had to look, didn't I?" She gulped down a sob.

"Take your time, Mrs. Grey. What did you do?"

"I saw him, the blood, and I . . . I had to find out if he needed help, so I went over, to feel for a pulse." She stared at her hands as if expecting to see blood. "I couldn't find a pulse, and there was . . . I mean, his . . ." She buried her face in her hands. "I suppose I must have screamed."

Her shoulders began to shake.

"It's all right now." Inspector Okoje patted her arm stiffly. "You did the right thing, Mrs. Grey."

Beryl Grey sniffed. I handed her a tissue, which seemed to make things worse. The tears started flowing again.

"We have just a few more questions, Mrs. Grey. Are you able to continue?" Inspector Okoje looked at me. *Do something.*

"Best to get it over with," I said. "You're doing well. This is all very helpful."

She nodded and wiped her eyes.

"What sort of man was Mr. Littlejohn?" Okoje asked. "Was he a good employer?"

"Oh, yes. Private, he was. Very private. Respectful. Good at his work, I believe."

"When did you start your employment here?"

"Last February. Eleven months now."

"Did he pay well?"

"Very well. On account of"—she looked down at her lap—"his requirements."

"His requirements?"

"That I dress like this, for one. I know it's silly, but it was important to him. At our first interview, he said, 'Outside this house it is the present day, Mrs. Grey. But inside it is 1855. Do you understand?' I said, 'Oh, yes.' I was that eager for the job. The pay was excellent. He didn't require any *heavy* work. He was always pleasant—as long as I followed the rules. The worst part was the laundry. No modern conveniences. I had to use one of those old flatirons like people had in the old days—heated on the stove. Hard not to burn things, you know. But my husband is disabled, and I needed the money, so I decided we were in a sort of play. It was fun, because I used to be in a community theater company—years ago, before I met my husband. I was pretty good too, if I say so myself."

"What exactly did Mr. Littlejohn expect you to do?"

"As I said, the laundry. That was a pain, and not just because of the heavy old iron. I had to wash everything by hand in a copper pot in the cellar. The shirt collars and cuffs had to be starched. He insisted I use one of those old mechanical wringer things. Then there was the dusting, hoovering, washing up. Answering the door, of course. Cooking was the main thing. And baking. Mr. Littlejohn liked his biscuits and cakes. I'd prepare his evening meal, and he'd let me take something home for my husband's tea."

"You say he was pleasant as long as you followed the rules. Was he ever unpleasant?"

Beryl Grey massaged the bridge of her nose. "Not unpleasant as such, no. Strict-like. He caught me on my mobile once. I was checking on my husband. From then on, he told me I had to leave my mobile at home. I didn't, though. Kept it in my purse." She shot us a guilty glance. "Funny when you think of it. It was supposed to be 1855—with all that computer equipment he kept in that room upstairs. Anyway, I had to walk from the bus stop, even in the rain. Originally he wanted me to live in, but I put my foot down there. I couldn't do it, could I, because of my husband. So he agreed on condition that I arrive and leave on foot."

"And you've been perfectly happy with the conditions of your employment?"

Mrs. Grey glanced at me, then back at Varma. "To be honest, I've been worried about that wood-fired range he was so in love with. How was I meant to cook and bake on that thing? Lucky for me, it needed extensive restoration, and he was having a hard time finding anyone to do the work. I decided to face that problem when I came to it. As my old gran used to say, 'Don't get your knickers in a twist until the elastic goes.'"

Varma started to laugh, quickly turning it into a cough.

"Is there anything else, Mrs. Grey? Do you know anyone who would wish your employer harm?"

"No. But then, I didn't really know him—as a person, I mean. He never talked about anything personal—his work or his friends. Like I said, we were in a sort of play. We weren't ourselves, neither of us."

"How about his family?"

"He had a sister, Donna Nixon. I know that because she and her husband, Clive, came to the house last week. Mr. Littlejohn asked me to bake a Victoria sponge. Had to look up the recipe, didn't I? But it turned out well enough."

"Do the Nixons live in the village?"

"Exeter, I believe."

"A social call?"

"Something to do with a legal matter."

"Mr. Littlejohn told you that, did he?"

"Just what I picked up serving tea. I believe one of them mentioned a solicitor."

"The name?"

"Well, let me think now." She screwed up her face and chewed her bottom lip. "Something like Rutledge, I think. I wasn't *listening*, you understand."

The expression on her face told me she had indeed been listening but wasn't about to admit it to anyone, much less a police officer. I made a mental note of the name. Littlejohn had told us the lot he'd bought had been handled by a solicitor. If Rutledge was that solicitor, he'd be a solid lead.

"How did Mr. Littlejohn get on with his sister?"

"Fine, for all I know. It was the husband he didn't care for. I could tell. Unpleasant sort of man." She made a moue of distaste. "*Words* were spoken, if you take my meaning. I don't know what was said, but I heard raised voices." She must have realized how the remark sounded, because she added, "I'm not saying he would have *shot* Mr. Littlejohn, mind. Heavens, no."

"Were there any other visitors to the house in the last few weeks?"

"A woman came about a week ago. Thursday—no, it was Friday. Day after Boxing Day. She didn't stay long."

"A friend?"

"More than a friend would be my guess. They seemed . . . well, familiar."

"In a romantic way?"

"No, not that. Just familiar. Someone he knew."

"Did he tell you anything about her. A name? Why she came?"

"He did not."

"Can you describe her?"

"Only saw her for a minute. She was all bundled up in a hat and coat. She was tall. That was all I could see. Cold as a cat's nose that day and rain pelting down in great lumps."

"Young? Old?" Okoje asked.

"She wasn't a girl, if you know what I mean. I thought Mr. Littlejohn would want tea brought, but he didn't. He made it clear he didn't want me to bother them."

I immediately thought of Clare Jamieson. She was tall.

"Had you noticed a change in Mr. Littlejohn recently—anything at all, Mrs. Grey—however insignificant it might seem?"

"Not a change, no. He was a very private man. Reserved. Secretive, some might say." Beryl Grey furrowed her brow in thought. "I got the impression he was keeping a secret."

Inspector Okoje looked up. "Do you have an idea what that secret might have been?"

"None at all. I'm sorry."

Chapter Nine

The police enquiry office in Coombe Mallet occupied a brick building on a side street near the market square. Small as it was, DCI Okoje had set up his local headquarters there, although Okoje and Varma weren't staying in the village. Newton Abbot, their home base, was only a twenty-minute drive away. At three that afternoon, after Tom and I had been fingerprinted and had given our written statements, we found ourselves with Okoje and DS Varma in one of the small offices.

"A nasty business, murder," Okoje said. "I'll come straight to the point, Mallory. We could use your help. The Devon & Cornwall Police may not be the largest force in the UK, but we have the largest area to cover—eight thousand miles of roads, nearly a thousand miles of coastline. We don't often deal with murder in the rural villages. The fact that you were present for both crimes is fortuitous."

"Not suspicious?" Tom asked. I think he meant it as a joke, but Okoje took him seriously.

"You and your wife were having breakfast at the Crown when Littlejohn was killed. You couldn't have committed the crime, even if you'd had a motive."

They'd checked up on us—not surprising, I supposed. We were outsiders.

"I've spoken with your DCI—Eccles," Okoje said. "He's given you permission to help with our enquiries. If you're willing, of course. He also told us you're here"—Okoje cleared his throat—"on your honeymoon."

"That's right," Tom agreed. "We were married on Christmas Eve."

"Congratulations to you both. Yet, if I'm not mistaken, you have some sort of project at the museum." He spread his large hands. "May I ask why you chose Devon for your honeymoon? A lovely spot, to be sure. But in January I would think you'd have chosen somewhere a bit warmer."

Tom might have explained we weren't beach people and didn't care for the kind of all-inclusive resorts where you make new best friends you'll never see again. Instead he said, "I spent summers in Devon as a child." He glanced at me. "But you're right. Kate and I are here partly to look into a potential case for a friend, a private investigator—ex-police." He proceeded to tell them about Nash & Holmes and the Victorian dress. "I'd rather you kept that to yourselves, if you don't mind. My superintendent doesn't know I'm considering retirement, and we haven't made our decision yet."

"No reason to mention it." Okoje turned to me. "Eccles told us about *your* involvement in several previous cases, Mrs. Mallory . . . erm, Hamilton."

"I'm part owner of an antiquities business in Long Barston. I was hired last spring as a consultant on a case involving a collection of fine art. In October, my colleague and I were asked to authenticate a medieval painting, which turned out to be related to a cold case on the Suffolk coast."

"Eccles also mentioned something quite recent—a drugs operation?"

"That was purely accidental. I was helping a friend who owned a valuable gold coin."

Okoje scooted his chair closer. "Perhaps you would consider helping us here in Devon, Mrs. Hamilton. Not with the murder, you understand, but with Mr. Littlejohn's connection to the museum—and his unusual lifestyle. The most obvious motive for his murder is his work in cybersecurity, but I intend to keep my mind open. It's possible the motive lies in his rather unusual personal choices."

"What exactly are you asking us to do?" Tom glanced at me sideways, gauging my reaction.

DCI Okoje planted one huge hand on the table "Here's the proposal. We handle the official investigation. Mallory, you'll help us with the routine work—taking statements, for example. In the meantime, the two of you do what you came here to do—investigate the origins of the Victorian dress. Talk to people who might know something. Ask questions. You have free reign as long as you remain in the role of investigators working for the museum. Just keep your eyes and ears open. Did Littlejohn own something of value, for example—antique furniture, paintings, jewelry?"

"Was there evidence of a burglary?" Tom asked.

"Hard to tell. The crime scene team is at the house now, but to be frank, our lads wouldn't know a valuable Wedgwood bowl from a secondhand chamber pot."

I braced myself, praying he wasn't going to ask me to make an inventory of Gideon Littlejohn's possessions. I'd done inventories for the police twice before and knew how tedious and time-consuming it would be. Besides, two of our three weeks in Devon were almost gone, and I didn't want to spend our final week cataloguing Victorian antiques. I don't even particularly like them. "As far as I know, Mr. Littlejohn wasn't interested in collecting antiques, and I didn't see anything in the house of great value. I'm not sure how I can help."

Okoje's response wasn't what I expected. "I think you may have got the wrong end of the stick, Mrs. . . . er, Hamilton. We're not asking you to consult. If we have a question, we'll certainly ask. But you're here to do research—so do it. While you're at it, you might learn something important. Just keep us informed. That's all we're asking. My team will proceed with the criminal case while you look at things from the historical angle."

"When your team is finished, we'd like to get into the house," Tom said. "We're looking for something that will shed light on the origin of the dress."

"I'll let you know when that's possible." Okoje sat forward, his dark eyes gleaming. "So, what's the verdict? Will you help?"

"If you don't mind," Tom said, "we'd like time to consider your proposal. We can't stay in Devon indefinitely."

"I understand. But remember, you're already involved. First the shooting. Then the murder. You're witnesses."

It was time to voice my suspicion. "You said the most obvious motive for the murder was Mr. Littlejohn's work in cybersecurity. Could he have been the intended target at the museum after all? If he wasn't, the two shootings would be quite a coincidence."

"They do happen, coincidences." DS Varma spoke for the first time.

"I don't believe in coincidences." Okoje's eyes shifted, and I got the impression he was deciding how much to reveal. "I'll tell you this, but you're going to have to keep it to yourselves. It may not be related. Three months ago someone broke into Littlejohn's house. He wasn't home at the time. Once inside, they forced the door to his computer room, which was always kept locked. Just then, Littlejohn returned, and they fled through the rear of the house. Littlejohn didn't get a description, and he said nothing was missing. No fingerprints. We found traces of DNA but no matches on our database. The point is, whoever it was may have returned."

* * *

Tom and I were lucky to get a table for dinner at the Crown that night. The whole village, it seemed, had turned out to celebrate the first weekend of the New Year. Or maybe, based on the snatches of conversation we overheard, it was the shooting at the gala and the murder of Gideon Littlejohn that had gotten the residents of Coombe Mallet out on the town. Just about everyone had a theory about Littlejohn's death. Most centered on his mysterious computer work. What did a cybersecurity expert do exactly? No one seemed to know.

A harried but jovial waitress escorted us to a tiny table in a side room. The inn had been constructed, we learned, in the fourteenth century as a place for stonemasons to live while building the village church. The restaurant occupied the original core—low ceilinged, with ancient timber beams, ridiculously thick stone walls, and open, warming fires. We'd read through the menu while we waited for our table, so we knew what we wanted—the house specialty, a minted lamb casserole with crusty bread and a side salad. I ordered a glass of Pinot Noir, and Tom opted for one of the West Country pale ales.

"I can see your mind working," Tom said. "What are you thinking?"

"I'm thinking about that break-in. The one Okoje mentioned. It happened three months ago, and yet Mrs. Grey didn't mention it. Do you think that's odd?"

"Seeing his body may have driven everything else out of her mind. Or maybe she didn't know."

"Maybe—but that's another thing. Why does this always happen to us?" I tasted the wine. "We come to see a dress and end up with a dead body."

"Fate." Tom scooted his chair in as another couple squeezed past us on the way to their table, which was so close to ours we might have been a party of four. The man nodded and said something we didn't catch in a thick West Country accent.

"Seriously," I said, trying to keep my voice down, "we came to solve a nice historical puzzle. Suddenly we're in the middle of a murder investigation."

"We can always tell them no—both of them, Okoje and Hawksworthy—and spend the rest of our time at Fouroaks."

"You mean Grahame Nash would send someone else to authenticate the dress?"

"He'd probably decline the case. They have too much work as it is. A shame, really." He tapped the rim of his glass. "The mystery of Nancy Thorne's dress would probably never be solved." The corner of his lip curled up, not quite a smile.

"That's unfair." I had to smile too. "You know it would kill me not to find out if that dress is the real thing."

"I know." Tom leaned over the table and kissed me.

The couple at the next table frowned. *We came for dinner, not a show.*

"We're on our honeymoon," Tom told them, making things worse. Then in a low voice, he said, "I was teasing, Kate, but truly—we can tell Okoje we're not available. Is that what you want?"

"What I want is you out of harm's way."

"Harm's way? We're talking routine stuff here. There were a hundred and twenty-three people at the museum Friday night, not counting the caterers and waitstaff. Okoje asked me to take statements. Look into their backgrounds. See if there's any connection with Gideon Littlejohn."

"That's it?"

"Maybe speak with Littlejohn's sister and her husband. Actually, you could help with that. They may know something about the Victorian dress. More importantly, they may know the identity of the woman who visited him recently." I started to protest, but he went on. "If you agree to help with the investigation, Kate, you'll have a perfect reason to ask questions. You said it—there might be a connection between the owner of the household he purchased and the dress. If you find the connection, you might solve a hundred-and-forty-year-old mystery. At the same time, you'd be on the lookout for anything unusual or suspicious in Littlejohn's death. Right up your alley, I'd say."

"You know me too well, Tom Mallory." I *tsk*ed. "We've been married less than two weeks, and already the glamour and mystery are gone."

"You, my darling, are the epitome of glamour and mystery." His face softened. "Speaking of mystery, there's something I'd like to know."

"What?"

"Your face, the first time you saw that bloodstained dress. I've seen that look before."

"Oh, that." I attempted a laugh. "My overactive imagination. Runs away with me sometimes."

I could see Tom wasn't convinced, but at that moment, the waitress squeezed past us to take orders at the next table. "What will it be?" she asked the older couple.

"Give us a few more minutes, luv," the man said.

Tom's mobile must have vibrated, because he pulled it out of his pocket. "Sorry—it's Okoje. I should take this."

As he left, I felt a twinge of guilt. Tom was my husband. I owed him the truth. But what could I say—*I get emotional around fine antiques*?

Fortunately, these experiences didn't happen often—or they hadn't until recently. I was beginning to think there was something about England that brought them on. Perhaps it was the sense of the past and the present existing simultaneously. But then I'd had these episodes since childhood. They always began with physical symptoms, then the impression—real or imagined—of the emotional atmosphere in which an object had once existed. My father had called me a *divvy*, possessing the instinctive ability to discover the single treasure in a roomful of junk. That wasn't strictly true, although I usually do know a treasure when I see one. But I was beginning to realize it wasn't the monetary value of an object that triggered these experiences—or even its age and beauty. What I sensed were emotions. Strong emotions. And sometimes those emotions manifested themselves in a word, a phrase, a feeling.

This time, with the Victorian dress, I'd gotten a rather frightening image. A woman, sobbing. *Blood. So much blood.*

Had I really been given a glimpse into the past? Or had I, as I'd always tried to convince myself, simply allowed my imagination to run away with itself?

I shook my head. This wasn't helping. How could I explain it to Tom? How could I put into words something I'd never understood myself? And what would telling him accomplish except to make it more real—and more disturbing? Still, I would have to tell him sometime.

I'll wait for the right moment, I told myself.

Coward, chided my snarky inner critic.

Tom returned. His face told me something was wrong. "There's been another attack on Teddy Pearce's house. Brick through the front window this time, and a threatening note: *Back off or your family is next.*"

"Poor Quinn." I stared at him in horror. "When I spoke with her at the gala, she was already terrified. You really want to help with this investigation, don't you?"

"I won't deny it. But if you say no, that's it. We're a team, Kate. We don't make independent decisions now. Especially when they involve us both."

I sat there for a moment, suspended in time, hearing my mother's voice. *What will you do, darling? Wrap him in cotton wool? Refuse to let him out of the house?* I wasn't giving up on the job opportunity with Nash & Holmes—not at all. I really wanted Tom to take it. But I couldn't allow fear to dictate our decision. I'd married Tom for better, for worse, for richer, for poorer. I'd married him for love. I had no desire to change the man he was.

"I want to help too," I said truthfully. "Tell Okoje we'll do it."

"You're sure?"

I nodded.

"I'll call him tomorrow." Tom took my hand across the table. "Tonight let's celebrate. We are still on our honeymoon, after all." He leaned over and kissed me again.

The couple at the next table raised their menus.

Chapter Ten

Monday, January 6

Early Monday morning, Tom and I had breakfast at the Crown and went our separate ways. He walked to the police enquiry office, where he anticipated a tedious day poring over statements from the gala. I took the Rover. We planned to meet for an early dinner at the Pig & Whistle, the second pub in town—no rooms, according to Constable Doaks, just bags of history and excellent food.

Fortunately, the Museum of Devon Life was closed to visitors on Mondays, which meant an extra day for cleanup. It also meant Hugo Hawksworthy and Isla Ferris would be available for questions. At least I hoped so. I phoned ahead, and Isla let me in. Her ebullient mood was gone. Not surprising, given the news of Gideon Littlejohn's death. "You must be in shock," I said. "A murder in a quiet village like Coombe Mallet seems unbelievable."

"Have the police formed any theories yet? About the killer?"

"Early days." I repeated the meaningless phrase I'd heard DCI Okoje voice in the brief television interview he'd given the evening before. "I'm sure they'll find out who did it."

"Yes. I expect so."

I asked to speak with Dr. Hawksworthy, and Isla escorted me to his office. She knocked softly before opening the door. "Hugo, Kate Hamilton is here."

He looked up from his elegant elmwood desk. He'd been working on a slim silver computer. "Thank you, Isla."

She left the room, closing the door softly behind her.

He rose to greet me. "Mrs. Hamilton—welcome back to the museum." He grimaced. "I do apologize. *Welcome* sounds callous, doesn't it, given the circumstances?"

"I'm not sure what would be appropriate in the circumstances."

"Nor I." He slid the gold fountain pen he'd been holding into the pocket of his jacket.

On the wall behind his desk hung an impressive collection of degrees, diplomas, and commendations. In one, he stood beside Princess Anne, receiving some sort of award. In another, he was shaking hands with Boris Johnson. Hawksworthy certainly wasn't shy about displaying his credentials. On the wall to my right hung two large maps—one a contemporary map of Devon and the other a reproduction of an early map of Dartmoor.

"Shall we sit? Coffee? Tea?"

"No, thanks." I took one of the white leather chairs grouped around a low live-edge oak table. A Turkish carpet of crimson and terra-cotta softened the painted concrete floor.

"How awful for you—finding Littlejohn's body," he said. "I can't believe he's gone. Just a week ago I was chatting to him about a possible bequest. Apparently he hadn't put anything in writing. Terrible news, isn't it?"

"Terrible," I agreed, wondering if he meant the loss of the man or the money. "Was that what you and Littlejohn were discussing at the gala—a bequest? I noticed you speaking with him just before the gunshot."

Hawksworthy blinked. "Ah, yes." He sat forward and fussed with a stack of brochures on the table. "He was considering putting the museum in his will. He doesn't have children, as you know. The night of the gala, we were actually talking about the quilt and the trunk. I wanted to display them along with the dress. Littlejohn refused. I don't know why."

Why this should have caused the heated argument I witnessed, I couldn't imagine, but I remembered being surprised myself by Littlejohn's refusal to let the trunk out of his sight.

"How well did you know Littlejohn?" Julia Kelly had said they weren't close, but I wanted to hear his own version.

"Not personally. He was a very private man."

Everyone agreed about that. Was reticence part of Littlejohn's personality, or did he have something to hide? Increasingly, it was looking like the latter.

"At the risk of sounding callous," Hawksworthy said, "will you and your husband continue your investigation into the origins of the dress? I must ask. A lot of people are counting on the success of the new exhibit."

"Actually, yes," I said, thinking Hawksworthy himself would be at the top of that list. "We've decided to continue our research—if you still want us, of course."

"We do. Very much so. Recent events have been upsetting for our patrons. First the shooting at the gala. Then the murder. Scandal tends to dry up the sources of funding." He straightened his shoulders. "At any rate, the crimes exhibit will go forward, and so, I'm glad to hear, will the investigation of the dress. That's what Gideon would have wanted. How can I help?"

"Some background information, to start. The Thorne sisters lived in a village called Widdecombe Throop. I understand it vanished sometime in the early twentieth century. Is it on that old map, by any chance?"

"It is." Hawksworthy got to his feet. "This map of Dartmoor was made in the early eighteen hundreds. It's marvelously detailed. "Widdecombe Throop is just here." He put his finger on the map. "In a valley about twenty miles northeast of Coombe Mallet, near Evelscombe, the deepest mire on Dartmoor." He tapped what looked like a small brown pool surrounded by an uneven rim.

The village itself appeared to be little more than a widening at the intersection of two lanes. "When did the village disappear? Is anything still standing?"

"If any structures remain, they're under thirty feet of water. Widdecombe Throop was one of two small villages and several surrounding farms that were submerged in 1906 when the land was flooded to create a reservoir. Tenants were served with eviction notices, landowners were compensated, and that was that."

"Along with Evelscombe?"

"No, the famous mire still exists—part of a protected wetland, spring fed, covered most of the year by a domed layer of sphagnum moss growing over twelve meters of liquid peat. Every year, a few sheep wander into the mire. Farmers pull them out when they can, dead or alive."

I was trying to get the dates straight in my mind. According to the information in the radio documentary, Nancy Thorne was thirty in 1885 and died at forty-six. That meant she died in 1901. By the time the reservoir was created, she'd been gone five years. Her sister, Sally, was probably still alive in 1906, though. She would have been forced to move to another village.

"Do you know where the villagers were relocated?" If I could discover the name of that village, I might find some of Sally's relatives still living there.

"I don't. I'm sorry. It was a long time ago."

"You'd think people would remember a lost village."

"Oh, they do. For years people have claimed that on stormy nights, they can still hear the church bells ringing out of the depths."

"Ghostly bells. Makes a good story." We returned to the white leather chairs. "Speaking of the church, did they preserve the parish records? The vicar in 1885 was a man named Edward Quick."

Hawksworthy crossed one leg over the other, revealing a pair of expensive-looking leather shoes and an inch or so of fine wool sock in a jaunty stripe pattern. "The parish records disappeared along with the village. Believe me, I checked that straightaway—although they could be lurking, unnoticed, in someone's library. That kind of thing happened a lot around here. People weren't as careful with records as they should have been. You know the sort of thing—*The past is dead. Look to the future.*"

I did know and had often regretted the willful or careless destruction of documents. I still hadn't forgiven Jane Austen's sister, Cassandra, for burning all those letters. "Are there any Thornes still living in the area?"

"No Thornes that I know of—not anymore."

"I checked the British Newspaper Archive for the name Nancy Thorne, but I didn't find a single article. Were there any small, local newspapers in the mid-1880s that might have reported the incident?"

"Local papers popped up from time to time all over Dartmoor. I know someone who might be able to help. Maggie Hughes. She's an archivist at the public library in town. I'll email her and copy you. That way you two can chat." He raised his eyebrows. "Anything else I can do?"

"I'd like to see the collection of items Mr. Littlejohn donated along with the dress. They might be helpful."

"Of course. Isla told me. They're ready for you now." He moved to his desk and picked up the telephone. "Isla, I'm sending Ms. Hamilton up." He walked me to the door. "I'll be interested in your thoughts. Bit of a puzzle there."

Chapter Eleven

The museum's storage facility was on the second floor, directly above Julia Kelly's workroom. It was a large, well-lit space with floor-to-ceiling metal shelving that held, I imagined, items not currently on display. I remembered the local history museum on the Isle of Glenroth, the small Hebridean island where Tom and I met. There, musty treasures had been mashed tooth-to-jowl with thrift-shop rejects and the detritus of home-clearance auctions. At the Museum of Devon Life, everything was in perfect order—a testimony to Hawksworthy's high standards or Isla's administrative skills? Maybe both.

"I've laid everything out for you," Isla said.

A number of objects, fewer than a dozen, rested on a long, laminate-top table. Among them were several small pieces of jewelry and other trinkets, a colorful teapot, a lovely carved wooden box, and an unframed photograph.

My eyes went first to the photograph. It was small, about two and a half by four inches—one of the so-called cartes de visite, the inexpensive mass-produced photo cards that dominated Victorian photography. The image showed a group of young girls, perhaps seven or eight years old, sitting outside a vine-covered building. Each held a large cushion from which hung a number of bobbins. The photograph was titled *A Group of Young Devonshire Lace Workers.* I turned it over. No names or location. If Nancy Thorne was among them, we'd probably never know.

"We intend to use the photo in our lace exhibit," Isla said, "especially if we can identify the particular lace school pictured. Many

Devon villages had lace schools in the nineteenth century. The building may be gone, but someone may remember."

"Too bad someone didn't write the girls' names on the back." The lace-school photograph, found with the bloodstained dress, suggested the first real connection with Nancy Thorne. Psychologists call it synchronicity, the theory that seemingly unrelated but simultaneously occurring events are connected. My mother had a simpler explanation: *When you see things together, there's always a reason.* Truthfully, it wasn't much of a lead. Of course, there were always the census records. They'd provide basic information about Nancy Thorne—her age, place of birth, the names of her parents and siblings, her occupation.

"I don't know much about lacemaking," I said, "except what you told me at the gala. What were the cushions used for?"

"Honiton lace is really a type of weaving," Isla said. "Only hobbyists attempt it today. It's far too complicated and time-consuming to be commercially profitable. Individual motifs were created on pins inserted through a pattern into the cushions you see in the photo, which were typically stuffed with barley straw and covered with white calico. The bobbins were either bone or turned wood. The number of bobbins reflected the complexity of the pattern. The motifs, usually objects from nature—flowers, leaves, fruit, birds—would then be joined together with tiny plaits or bars into larger patterns and sewn onto fine silk netting."

I looked at the photo in more detail. The girls wore white smocks over short, printed dresses. Some had bows in their long hair. Behind them stood two adult women in dark dresses, tight under the arms and fitted high at the neck. "The girls look well cared for."

"Photographs can be deceiving." Isla's left eyebrow arched. "Children, usually girls, were sent to lace schools as young as five or six. It was thought that if they didn't begin early, their fingers would never develop the dexterity to produce the kind of high-quality lace that would earn them a decent income later. The youngest would have worked four or five hours a day, the oldest girls up to sixteen hours a day—can you imagine? The little ones must have been terribly homesick, and the conditions were appalling. In summer the girls could work outdoors, but for most of the year, they worked indoors. No electricity, of course, or even gas lamps. Candles were fixed to metal poles. Water-filled glass flasks called 'flashes' reflected the light onto the girls' cushions. Open fires weren't allowed, as the soot could blacken the lace, so the young lacemakers sat with a pot of hot ashes at their feet. Ventilation was nonexistent. Breathing difficulties were common, The lace mistresses were strict, often harsh."

"You're very knowledgeable. Did you design the exhibit?"

"I helped. The original exhibit was created long before Dr. Hawksworthy took over, but he's added significantly to the display. He's really a genius." Isla's face glowed. "I lead group tours—mostly for schoolchildren and sometimes for local pensioners' outings. Lacemaking is an interest of mine."

I picked up the earthenware teapot, admiring the designs in brilliant shades of cobalt blue, copper lustre, yellow, burnt orange, and green.

Hawksworthy appeared in the doorway. "Ah, the teapot. What's the verdict?"

"It's certainly colorful." I turned the pot over in my hand, making sure to hold the lid in place. "It's called Swansea Cottage in the UK—Gaudy Welsh in the States. Popular in the nineteenth century, inexpensive, highly decorative, and very collectible."

"We have a similar teapot on display in our Romani exhibit," Hawksworthy said. "The ware was popular among the Romanichal people."

"Romanichal? I'm not familiar with the term."

"I'm sure you know the Romani people have their roots in the Indian subcontinent. Most scholars agree they began migrating west in the eleventh century. The Romanichals, sometimes called English Gypsies, probably came through France around the end of the fifteenth century and mixed with local Travellers. They speak English and Angloromani, a language that blends English syntax with Romani vocabulary. Some have settled in the larger cities, but most still move from place to place, valuing their ancient traditions and way of life, which we've tried to display in a culturally appropriate manner. On

Thursday we're hosting two of the West County Gypsy leaders. I hope you'll attend. Isla, do you have one of our programs handy?"

Hawksworthy's use of the word *Gypsy* was making me uncomfortable. "I thought the term *Gypsy* was considered a racial slur."

"I understand it is in the States. Things are rather more complicated here. If you come on Thursday evening, I'm sure you'll hear all about it."

Isla handed me a brochure listing the museum's monthly community programs. I leafed through, seeing topics ranging from flourless baking in the Second World War to the ninth-century Viking invasions to a video presentation about A la Ronde, England's only sixteen-sided house. January's program was titled *England's GRTs and the Crime of Travelling.* "What are GRTs?" I asked.

"It's an acronym, an umbrella term meaning *Gypsy, Roma, and Traveller.*"

"I'll talk to Tom, but I'm sure he'll be delighted. We both will."

Hawksworthy picked up the carved wooden box and removed the lid, showing me a number of gold coins inside. "Eight gold sovereigns with the head of Queen Victoria. Issue dates ranging from 1874 to 1882. Another possible connection with the Romanichals. They valued visible signs of wealth and often used gold and silver coins as jewelry—a status symbol, and when times were hard, easily pawned."

"My colleague and I recently appraised a similar coin from 1838. These aren't as rare, but they're certainly valuable."

"I consulted a coin collector I know in Exeter," Hawksworthy said. "A sovereign represented more than a month's wages for a nineteenth-century laborer. A substantial sum."

He handed me the wooden box, which was carved in a design of oak leaves and ivy. "This box is another possible Romanichal connection. Some of the men were skilled woodworkers. Most of what they made was functional—bowls, platters, pegs, and so forth—but they made decorative items as well."

"It's beautiful. Like a small treasure chest." I frowned, trying to understand the overall context. *There's always a reason.* Had the box held the pieces of jewelry laid out on the table? I saw a string of glass beads in a pretty coral color and a silver ring in a design sometimes referred to as "movable hands"—three narrow bands that, when stacked, bring two hands together in a clasp of friendship. Both pretty and collectible but not especially valuable. More interesting to me was an elaborate jet-bead choker necklace, the shiny black beads actually faceted spheres of fossilized wood, strung in an elaborate three-inch-wide pattern. Jet-bead jewelry was wildly popular in the nineteenth century. This choker was in poor condition. One of the strings had broken. Some of the beads were missing.

"We found this in the box as well." Hawksworthy handed me a gold ring, slightly domed and set with a deep-blue sapphire framed by two mine-cut diamonds. I held the small gold circle up to the overhead lamp, checking for hallmarks and watching the gems capture the light.

The pounding of my heart took me completely by surprise. The ring was interesting but certainly no treasure. Much of the gold had worn away. The gems were not fine quality. Yet there was something there. I could feel it—an intensity of emotion or some kind of weird physical reaction. I felt my face flush.

"It's lovely," I said, taming my breath into something resembling mere academic interest. "It's seen lots of wear. The marks are nearly worn away, and the shank is thin—there, where the finger would bend." I reached into my handbag, pulled out my lighted magnifier, and trained it on the band. "I can just make out the sovereign's crown. That means the ring was cast of British-made gold. Oh—and there's the number *18*, meaning eighteen carat."

"The setting is unusual," Isla said. "The stones are actually embedded into the gold."

"It's called a hammer setting," I said, feeling my heart returning to its normal rhythm. "Most rings use prongs to prop up the gem, allowing light to refract. In hammer settings, the gems are hammered into the band itself. Clean, minimalistic. It's an attractive design, almost contemporary in feeling."

I looked at the objects laid out side by side on the table. A photograph of young lacemakers. A woman's jewelry. Eight gold sovereigns in a carved oak box. A Gaudy Welsh teapot. An unusual gold ring.

What did they have in common with the bloodstained dress and the quilt?

"Littlejohn told us he'd found a handwritten note pinned to the dress," I said. "I've been wondering why you haven't shown it to me."

"Oh, that." Dr. Hawksworthy looked embarrassed. "I haven't shown it to you because it's worthless—a forgery. Intended to look like old handwriting, but it's actually quite recent."

"How do you know?"

"The usual way—too perfect. Forgers try too hard to get it right."

A forgery? That didn't make sense. Who would do that—and why? "Do you still have the note?"

"I didn't keep it. It was an obvious fake."

"Do you remember what it said?"

"It said, 'Dress belonging to Nancy Thorne, a murderess.'"

The mystery surrounding the bloodstained dress was murkier now than ever.

Chapter Twelve

It was four o'clock by the time I got back to the Crown. I found a comfortable chair near one of the open fires and decided to make a few phone calls before meeting Tom for dinner at the Pig & Whistle. Eager to learn more about the items stored with the bloodstained dress, I called Ivor, my colleague at the Cabinet of Curiosities, the antiques and antiquities shop where I worked in Long Barston. As far as I was concerned, Ivor knew everything.

"Well, I didn't expect to hear from you for a while," he said. "Everything all right?"

"Everything's fine, but there's been a murder." I heard a small choking sound. "I'll tell you about it when we get home. We were first on the scene—well, almost first. Tom's helping the Devon police. I'm trying to authenticate a late-Victorian dress supposedly belonging to a lacemaker and possible murderess. Look," I said quickly, before he could get a word in, "I know how this sounds, but I think you might be able to help."

Ivor was silent for a beat longer than necessary. "Isn't this meant to be your honeymoon?"

"It's complicated." I gave him the CliffsNotes version, but even that took time. "Today I saw the items Gideon Littlejohn donated to the museum along with the dress. He said he found everything in a trunk—part of a household he bought at auction. Among them was a very beautiful but well-worn hammer-set ring. Is there something I should know?"

"They were called Gypsy-set rings in Queen Victoria's time."

"Gypsy-set?" Was this another Romani connection? "Why?"

"Because the design seems to have originated in the Romani culture. Many Romani men were skilled metalworkers. The design was sturdy and easy to make with the tools they possessed. By the late Victorian era, Gypsy-set rings were all the rage, so it might have belonged to anyone."

"We've found several possible links between the bloodstained dress and the Romanichals in Devon. It's puzzling."

"And you love a puzzle. How's the honeymoon going—other than investigating murder? Black eyes fading? Tom's gash healing?"

I had to laugh. "We're having a wonderful time. The black eyes are more yellowish green now. You can hardly notice them. How's everyone in Long Barston?"

"Fine and dandy. Vivian misses having you to fuss over. She's looking for a new lodger—someone to take your place. Lady Barbara's over the moon in her private apartment in the west wing. You know the National Trust is scheduled to open Finchley Hall to the public in April. They've begun hiring locally. A good thing for the village."

Lady Barbara Finchley-fforde, daughter of the late marquess and last of that titled family, had gifted her family estate, Finchley Hall, to the National Trust the previous November when it became clear she could no longer afford to maintain the crumbling Elizabethan manor house. Vivian Bunn, the bossy but lovable woman with whom I'd boarded before the wedding, lived in a cottage on the Finchley estate with her elderly pug, Fergus. To be truthful, I missed them too. Especially Ivor.

"How are things at the shop?"

"Quiet. Almost no walk-ins this time of year. Internet sales are ticking along. Back to the Victorian dress. What are you doing to authenticate?"

"Trying to find the name of the family that sold it to Gideon Littlejohn, for starters. The problem is, I don't know exactly when he bought the household—or where. Sometime last summer, he said. I wish I'd asked him for details."

"I could check the past-auction listings."

"Would you, Ivor?" This man was a wonder. "The solicitor handling the estate *might* have been named Rutledge." It was a leap, I knew, but since leads were thin on the ground, worth checking.

"That will help. I'll let you know if I find anything."

"Marvelous. In the meantime, say hello to everyone."

We hung up, and I was about to phone my mother in Wisconsin when I saw an incoming phone call from a number I didn't recognize.

"Hi, Kate. It's Julia Kelly. I just noticed something about the dress. It's rather unusual, and I thought you'd want to know. The dress has been altered at the waistline—significantly. I think it was made for a pregnant woman, then cut down after she gave birth."

"A pregnant woman? How do you know that?"

"I don't know for certain, but at one time, the dress was considerably larger in the waistline. Tiny breaks in the seam finishing tell me that. The dress fabric is calico, but the seamstress bound the seams with a fine cotton lawn, probably left over from another project—nothing wasted, you know. The fabric binding on the seams around the waistline is also lawn, but not from the same bolt. The color is off, for one thing, and the thread count slightly different. I think it was done later."

"Was it unusual to repurpose a maternity dress?"

"Not for poor women. But the unusual part isn't that the dress was altered. It's the bloodstains. You saw them on the bodice and the skirt. The stains at the waist continue into the seam allowances. Best if I show you. Come tomorrow if you can. I'll be here."

"Why would someone go to the trouble of resizing a dress stained with blood? Who would wear it?"

"I can't answer that," Julia said. "But the dress was definitely worn after alteration—and for some time. The new seams show signs of wear."

None of this was making sense. "But Nancy Thorne was never married."

"Doesn't mean she didn't have a child."

* * *

I arrived at the Pig & Whistle ahead of Tom and chose a table near the open hearth. I've always loved log fires. There's something comforting about a fire, the smell of burning wood, the crackling of the flames. In most parts of the UK, log fires burn almost year-round. The Georgian house Tom and I would live in when we got home had several fireplaces, and I intended to make sure they were all in safe, working condition.

Because I had a few more minutes to wait, I took out my notebook and began jotting down the facts I'd learned about the bloodstained dress. Everything about it—the style, the printed fabric, the workmanship—placed it as mid to late nineteenth century. The bloodstains on the skirt and the bodice were massive, suggesting that someone, or possibly an animal, I had to admit, had been terribly injured, perhaps fatally. The woman wearing the dress had either tried to help the victim or was herself the killer. If Julia Kelly was right, the dress had been made for a pregnant woman, then altered after she gave birth. This didn't mean the dress couldn't have been passed down from someone else, of course, but most puzzling of all, the dress had been worn with the visible stains. I knew poor people at that time couldn't just go out and buy something new, but still.

The dress had been found by Gideon Littlejohn in an old trunk, part of a lot auctioned off after the death of an elderly man. I'd seen the trunk briefly when Littlejohn showed me the quilt, but I hadn't had a chance to examine it. I'd do that as soon as the police gave me clearance to enter the Old Merchant's House. Some of the items in the trunk suggested a Romani connection. Strangest of all, according to Hugo Hawksworthy, the note found pinned to the dress, calling Nancy Thorne a murderess, had been a forgery, written much later. But to what end? I couldn't imagine.

My cell phone pinged—an email had arrived from Maggie Hughes at the Coombe Mallet Public Library:

> *Hello, Kate. I'd love to help if I can. Tomorrow I have a meeting in Exeter, but I'm free Wednesday afternoon. Say one o'clock? Dr. Hawksworthy explained what you're doing. I'll try to have some information ready. Let me know.*

I replied, thanking her and telling her I'd be at the library at one on Wednesday.

Tom arrived, unwinding his scarf and hanging his jacket on a hook near the table. The yellowish-green shadow around his eye had nearly faded, but the gash on his forehead was still red. He'd probably have a scar. "Hullo, darling." He bent and kissed me lightly. "How was your day?"

"Frustrating." I told him what I'd learned about the bloodstained dress. "Three things bother me—no, actually four. First, why was the dress kept in a trunk with items suggesting a Romani connection? I don't get it. Second, the blood. Whose blood was it—Nancy Thorne's or someone else's?" I explained Julia Kelly's theory that the dress had originally been made for a pregnant woman. "Third question—why would a woman continue wearing a dress like that after it was so badly stained? And fourth, the note pinned to the dress naming Nancy Thorne as a murderess. Dr. Hawksworthy says it was a forgery. Who would write such a thing, and why?"

"Maybe the writer of the note knew about the transcript from the documentary—the one naming Nancy Thorne as the suspect in an unsolved crime—and wanted to capitalize on it."

"Well, yes—I suppose that's possible." Tom was right. I knew from long experience in the antiques trade that people love to connect their families with well-known people and events in history. I couldn't count the number of times customers had sworn on their grandmother's grave, for example, that the old bowling pins they'd found in their attic had come from the first White House bowling alley or that their signed photograph of Abraham Lincoln (an obvious fake) had been gifted by the Great Emancipator himself to their great-great-grandfather after the Battle of Vicksburg.

Tom got up to kick an errant ember back into the fire. "There's something else. The trunk. Why did Littlejohn refuse to part with it?"

"You're making it worse," I said. A waiter in black jeans and a white apron handed us menus.

Tom stowed his menu on his lap. "So we're no farther ahead at all?"

"We do have leads. Ivor's checking the auction listings. Our best chance of authenticating the dress is to learn the name of the family who put the items up for auction. I told him to look for a solicitor named Rutledge."

"That's good, but if the note was a fake, why not the dress as well?" He rubbed the back of his neck, a sure sign he was frustrated.

"Bad day?"

He huffed. "This is the part of an investigation I like least—the beginning, when it's all questions and no answers."

"Haven't the police learned anything?"

"About the shooting at the gala or the murder of Gideon Littlejohn?"

"Start with Littlejohn."

"The police found traces of DNA on the front door and in Littlejohn's study. More than one individual, ours included. The problem is finding matches—impossible unless we're dealing with known criminals. We can't ask everyone in the village to take a DNA test."

"Did they try matching the DNA possibly left by the intruder three months earlier?"

"No match." He scanned his menu briefly, then closed it. "The Hi-Tech Crime Unit from Exeter has taken away all the computer equipment, including a large number of USB flash drives. Going through that lot will take time. They have learned one interesting fact, though. Gideon Littlejohn wasn't his real name. He was born Gordon Little. Changed his name sometime in 2014."

"Really? I wonder why."

"I imagine his sister, Donna, would know. She and her husband, Clive Nixon, have been informed of his death."

"Where do they live?"

"West side of Exeter. They told the police they know nothing about his murder, and they didn't mention the name change, although, to be fair, they weren't asked. When they were asked about their recent visit to the Old Merchant's House—the visit Beryl Grey mentioned—they said it was purely a social call. They denied it had anything to do with legal matters and insist they've never heard of a solicitor named Rutledge."

"Is there a solicitor in the area with that name?"

"No, but then Beryl Grey might have got the name wrong—or perhaps he's not from around here." The waiter delivered our drinks. Tom tipped his ale down the side of a tall glass. "DCI Okoje would like us to speak with the Nixons."

"Us? Why?"

"The idea is, if we go there asking about the dress, they might tell us something they wouldn't tell the police. Like why Littlejohn changed his name."

"They're under no obligation to tell us anything, Tom."

"That's the point. Most people don't like talking to the police. There's an instinctive reluctance, a mistrust. It feels like interrogation—especially when you've had prior experience with the legal system. Clive Nixon has form. Nothing violent, but still. Private investigators are in a different category, especially those doing research into the distant past. Nice and safe."

I thought of my friend Sheila Parker, whose deceased husband Lenny, a minor criminal, always said, "Never get involved with the rozzers." In his case, with good reason.

"What do you think?" Tom asked.

"Let's do it. Why not?"

"How about tomorrow, then? We can drive into Exeter, see the Nixons, be back in time to debrief Okoje, and still have an early dinner at the Crown, just the two of us."

"Sounds lovely." I reached out and took his hand. "Technically, we're still on our honeymoon, right?"

"Absolutely. Is there such a thing as a working honeymoon?"

"There is now." I still hadn't looked at the menu. "Have the police learned anything more about the shooting at the museum gala?"

"We've spoken with everyone present that night, including the caterers and their staff. No one admits to bringing a gun, of course, and no one saw the shooter. We've been mapping out all four levels, placing people where they say they were at the time of the shooting and then trying to find corroboration."

"And?"

"A number of people could have done it—those on the first level—but of course they all deny it. And so far we haven't come up with a motive."

"The Jamiesons were on the first level. So was Quinn Pearce. I saw them during the clock demonstration."

"True, but Quinn Pearce wouldn't risk harming her own husband, and Richard Jamieson and his wife, Clare, insist they're big Pearce supporters."

"Jamieson was the one who called Pearce out during his speech."

"He says he was warning Pearce not to say too much too soon. There's an ongoing investigation into the possible corruption of three local bureaucrats. There may be others involved. Jamieson was warning him not to jeopardize the investigation. I got the impression he's had to rein Pearce in on more than one occasion."

"Were any of those local bureaucrats at the gala?"

"No."

"Have the police traced the gun?"

"No prints, no serial numbers."

As I tucked that thought away, our waiter appeared. "Have we decided?"

"What do you recommend?" Tom asked.

"I'm partial to the sole and the venison myself—both local."

We ordered one of each, planning to share, and drinks—wine for me and another of the local ales for Tom.

The waiter had just left with our orders when we heard a loud crash coming from the bar area. Tom, always the policeman, sprinted toward the commotion. I followed him.

One of the barstools lay on its side. Two men stood facing each other, fists raised, faces flushed. One was heavyset, with the unhealthy complexion of a drinker. The other was Teddy Pearce. Blood ran from his nose. He wiped it away with the back of his hand. "You're dead wrong, *eegit*. It's not like that."

"Inn'it?" The other man growled, his accent pure West Country. "You blather on 'bout ending corruption, but yer up t'your bloody neck in it."

Pearce dabbed at his nose. "That's a damn lie, and you know it."

"Oh, aye?" The other man turned to the crowd. "It's yer wife's bloody father who's behind everything."

The bartender in his white apron had come around the bar. He stood with his hands up. "Come on, both of youse. I won't have it."

The older man moved toward Pearce. One of his fists was bleeding. "How much is he payin' you to keep 'is name out of it?"

Pearce sprang at the man.

Tom grabbed him from behind. "Pearce—that's enough. This isn't helping."

Pearce whirled around and threw a punch, catching Tom on the right cheek before recognizing him. His face went slack. "Oh, geez. I'm sorry, man. I just—" He subsided onto a stool, shaking the pain out of his fist.

The bartender handed the other man his coat and led him to the exit. "Banned for a month, Charlie. Won't tolerate fightin'. You know better than that."

"What about 'im?"

"You started it."

Charlie, whoever he was, didn't argue. He slammed out the door.

Someone handed Pearce a napkin. He wiped his face. "Tom—sorry, man. I just . . . what he said, I—" He broke off, took a long breath, and blew it out. "I'm sorry."

A bruise was coming up on Tom's cheek. He touched it gingerly. Turning to the waiter, he said, "Can you bring him some water?"

The bartender brought a glass of water. Pearce downed half of it.

"Where's your car?" Tom asked. "Can you drive?"

"Yeah. Had barely half a pint before the man attacked me."

"Want to press charges?"

"Nah. Not worth it." Pearce stood. "Sorry. Thanks. I'm leaving."

He grabbed his jacket from a hook on the wall and left the bar.

"Oh, Tom," I said. "Your face." His left cheek was already turning an ominous shade of purple. At least he wouldn't have another black eye.

Our waiter approached us. "Er, sorry. Your dinners are ready."

Chapter Thirteen

Tuesday, January 7
Exeter

The Nixons lived in a flat above a barbershop on Cowick Street in Exeter St. Thomas, an urban area on the west side of the River Exe. At nine AM, the street was already bustling. Shopkeepers were arranging their front windows, pensioners pushed personal shopping trolleys, and adults with newspapers under their arms waited for the next bus.

Tom rang the buzzer.

"What d'you want?" I could hear the surliness through the crackly intercom. "Don't need insurance, luv. Not interested in joining your church, and we're not gonna sign no petitions."

"We're here about your brother, Gordon Little," Tom said, using Gideon's birth name. "My name's Tom Mallory. My wife, Kate, and I have been asked to look into the origins of a dress he recently donated to the Museum of Devon Life. We're sorry to intrude. We know you've just heard about your brother's death, but we won't be in the area long and we'd like to ask you a few questions, if it's all right."

There was no answer, but the buzzer sounded. Tom pushed open the door, and we climbed a set of narrow steps to the first floor.

The woman who opened the door wore so much makeup it was nearly impossible to tell what she actually looked like. Her eyes, set in half-moons of sparkly purple and heavily fringed with fake lashes, were small and suspicious. Only her wrinkled neck and freckled hands revealed her age. She wore shiny black leggings and a cheap nylon blouse in a riotous pattern of purple, hot pink, and lime green. She stared at Tom's bruised face. "What happened to you?"

Tom touched his right cheek. "Ran into a door."

Her lips pleated in a skeptical moue, but she stepped back, allowing us to enter.

The parlor was neat—sparsely furnished with a three-piece suite in tattered mauve upholstery. A man sat in one of the chairs, holding a can of beer. He was thin, almost unhealthily so, his knees jutting in a pair of gray track pants. His hair was sparse, and his fingernails were bitten to the quick. They looked sore.

"I'm Donna Nixon." She wasn't pleased to see us. "That's my husband, Clive. You said you're here about my brother. How did you know him?"

Tom and I sat side by side on the sofa. "We met him briefly at the museum fundraiser in Coombe Mallet," I explained. "He invited us to the Old Merchant's House the next day."

"So you went to his house, did you?"

"Your brother was an interesting man," Tom said.

"You mean eccentric."

"They mean weird." Clive's lips thinned in a sneer.

"We really are very sorry for your loss," I said. "This must be a difficult time for you."

"Of course. I'm absolutely gutted." She didn't look gutted. "What did you say your interest was? Something about a dress?" Donna sank into the other chair—literally. The springs had gone.

"We're private investigators," Tom said. "The Museum of Devon Life has hired us to authenticate a Victorian dress your brother recently donated."

"Nothing to do with us."

"Did your brother tell you about the items he purchased at—well, it must have been an estate sale?" I asked.

"Gordon and I had little contact. I'm eight years older. Left home when he was ten."

"But you knew about his hobby—living like a Victorian gentleman."

"We knew." Clive Nixon cackled. "Whatever floats yer boat."

"Did he ever mention a bloodstained dress?" I asked.

Donna wrinkled her nose. "Why would we be interested in something like that?"

"Did he show you an old trunk with a quilt inside?"

"No."

"But he told you about the household he bought?"

"He told us he'd bought this lot at auction," she admitted. "There was some old furniture he didn't want. Thought we might take it."

"Did you?" Tom asked.

"We don't need castoffs, thank you very much," Clive said. "Weren't our style anyway, all that fancy carving."

"Not that it wasn't kind of him, you understand," Donna added.

"Oh, he was kindness itself, your brother." Clive bared his teeth. "Couldn't do enough for us—right, Donna?"

Something was being communicated between them, but I had no idea what it was. "Did he happen to mention anything about the family of the man who died?"

"Why would he tell us?"

We weren't getting very far. "Did your brother have a solicitor—a will?" Tom asked.

"The police asked that when they came to tell us he was dead," Donna said. "We couldn't help them. We didn't see my brother all that often."

"You're sure he never mentioned a solicitor?" I asked.

"Not that I remember."

"His housekeeper mentioned someone named Rutledge."

"Police mentioned the name. Never heard of the chap," Clive snapped. "Shouldn't believe everything that so-called housekeeper tells you anyway."

"Why is that?" I asked, wondering why Beryl Grey would be *so-called.*

"Tell 'em, Donna."

Her false eyelashes flicked. She was deciding what—and how much—to tell us.

"She was taking advantage of him." Donna held up one spotted hand. "I know—poor woman with a disabled husband, right? Played on people's sympathies. But my brother caught her stealing. He told us. Buying more food than necessary and taking some of it home. Skimming off the household budget. Then he caught her red-handed, pocketing a silver box—some old thing with gulloon edging."

She meant *gadroon* edging, a decorative motif popular on Victorian silver. "Did Mrs. Grey admit it?"

"Course not. She said she was taking the box home to polish. He didn't believe her. In fact, he was going to give her notice. Soon as he could find a replacement."

I looked at Tom. He gave a brief shake of his head. No, Beryl Grey had not mentioned any of this to the police.

"What was your brother like as a boy?" I asked, hoping to lower her defenses.

"Sensitive. Bookish. Private. He wouldn't allow anyone in his bedroom. And he wasn't home a lot—I remember that. There was an old man on the estate. Gordon spent a lot of time with him, according to our mother."

"Was this in Exeter?"

"Burnthouse Lane. Council estate. The old man died in a house fire. Tragic, it was. Hit Gordon pretty hard. Mum said he hardly spoke for weeks. But that was after I left home."

"How old was Gordon when the old man died?"

"I don't remember. Twelve or thirteen, maybe."

"We understand your brother changed his name," I said.

"Oh, that."

"Poncey git," Clive muttered.

"Plain Gordon Little wasn't good enough for him when he started making money," Donna said. "Like he were ashamed of us."

"We know your brother was a cybersecurity expert."

"Hacker, more like," said Clive. "He liked uncovering people's dirty little secrets."

Donna gave Clive a sharp look. "Gordon was good at computers, that's all. He had clients—people hired him to make sure no one could hack into their systems. He protected them from criminals."

"Takes one to know one," Clive muttered.

"Gordon was *very clever*," Donna said, settling the matter.

"When was the last time you saw him?" I asked.

"Months and months," Clive said quickly. Unfortunately for him, Donna had said "Last week" at the same time.

They looked at each other, momentarily confused.

"You forget, Clive. We went to look at that furniture, remember? We told the police."

"Thought she meant a proper visit," Clive muttered. "Didn't stay long."

"Your brother told us he was part of a club—historical re-creators," I said. "One of them might know something about the dress. Are you able to give us any names?"

"I don't think it was an official club—like with dues and stuff." Donna crossed her legs and folded her hands primly. "I don't know any names. They were just people who shared Gordon's interests. He always was a different sort of person. Thoughtful, like."

"Peculiar." Clive crumpled his beer can.

"Is there anyone else who might be able to help us trace the dress?" Tom asked.

Donna screwed up her mouth in thought. "His wife, maybe?"

"Your brother was married?"

"Divorced in 2014. Her name's Freya—Freya Little."

"Do you know where she lives?"

"Torquay, last we heard." She rubbed her forehead. "Oh, and there was another woman a bit later. A girlfriend. Mercy something. I think her surname began with an A."

Back in the car, I pulled up UKPhonebook.com on my phone and typed in *Freya Little, Torquay*. "No listing. Either Littlejohn's ex-wife isn't living in Torquay anymore or she doesn't have a landline."

"Maybe she remarried." Tom turned the car around and headed back toward Coombe Mallet. "The name Mercy A-something won't get us very far."

"Okoje was right," I said. "We did learn a few things he'll want to know."

"Good timing as well." Tom downshifted as we pulled onto the A30. "We're meeting him at Queenie's at three."

Chapter Fourteen

Queenie's Cream Teas occupied a half-timbered building on Paddock Close, just off the High Street in Coombe Mallet. The medieval structure had settled so much over the centuries that the adjoining building appeared to be holding it up—and maybe it was. We entered through the crooked red door and hung our jackets on the pegs lining the entrance hall. Tom stowed our umbrella in an iron rack.

DCI Okoje and DS Varma had already arrived. They stood to greet us. "What happened to you, man?" asked Okoje, wincing. "Looks painful."

Tom fingered the bruise on his cheek. "Stepped into a fist."

At least Tom's black eye had almost faded to normal. Mine was taking a bit longer, but I'd bought a color corrector makeup kit, which did a pretty good job of concealing any lingering olive shadows.

"Any news on Littlejohn?" Tom asked as we took our seats. "Neighbors see anything?"

"We're still conducting door-to-door interviews." Okoje signaled the waitress. "We've had a piece of luck. The CCTV at a corner shop near the Old Merchant's House was recording that morning. PC Doaks is getting the footage."

"The coroner's report?"

"Bullet through the heart. Thirty-eight caliber. Death would have been almost instantaneous. Whoever shot him was lucky or knew exactly where to aim."

"Would neighbors have heard the shot?" I asked.

"Sure, but the sound could easily have been mistaken for a car backfiring or a door slamming. Most people don't think of gunshots first." He looked at me. "Not in the UK, anyway."

"Time of death?"

"They've narrowed the window slightly. Between nine and twelve Sunday morning." Okoje pushed a plate toward us. There was one scone left. "Help yourselves."

"Thanks, but we'll order something in a minute."

Varma, who looked relieved, reached for the last scone.

Tom took out his notebook. "We need to find out who Littlejohn had the appointment with that morning. The report of his death has been in all the papers. If that person wasn't the killer, he or she should have contacted you by now."

"Especially if he arrived and no one answered the door." Varma was carefully spreading a layer of strawberry jam on his scone.

A young woman in a frilly apron brought two menus, handwritten on parchment. "Here you are."

I glanced at the menu. "How do you feel about a pot of Earl Grey and a couple of those Devonshire apple scones?" I asked Tom.

"Fine by me."

"Anything else, luv?" the waitress asked.

"No, thanks." I handed her the menus and turned back to Okoje. "Have you learned anything about the attack on Teddy Pearce's house?"

"Not yet. Fortunately, Pearce was the only one home. We've posted a guard until he can get cameras installed. Should have had security a long time ago, if you ask me."

It was a good point. As Pearce was a member of Parliament, I would have thought security would be mandatory. "What about the shooting at the museum?"

"Nothing new. The shot came from the first-floor balcony, but we've known that. We've interviewed everyone present at the time. No one saw anything. No one was alone. No one had a motive." Okoje shook his head. "I need some good news. Actually, I need any news. Tell us about the Nixons. How was your visit?"

"They weren't thrilled to see us." Tom shot me a smile. "Donna claimed she and her brother weren't close. Clive made no secret of the fact that he didn't like Littlejohn. They were vague about the last time they saw him but agreed it was about a week ago. He'd offered them some furniture, which they didn't take."

"You believed them?" Varma's tone implied that he, for one, didn't believe anything anyone said, ever, simply on principle. "Nixon drives an old dark-blue Vauxhall. If the car shows up on the CCTV footage, we've got enough to bring them in. After all, he's got—"

"Early days," Okoje said, cutting across him. "Keeping an open mind."

I got the impression they were keeping something from us. If they had evidence against the Nixons, why didn't they say so? Maybe because I was there.

"Let your open mind dwell on this," Tom said. "According to the Nixons, Littlejohn recently caught his housekeeper, Beryl Grey, pocketing a valuable silver box. She claimed she was taking it home to polish, but he didn't believe her. He suspected her of stealing some of the household money as well. The Nixons said he'd decided to replace her."

Okoje raised his eyebrows. "She neglected to mention that."

"Imagine that." Varma grinned.

"We'll follow up." Okoje lifted his teacup by the delicate handle—not a simple task when you have hands like baseball mitts. He took a sip. "In the meantime, Ms. Hamilton, I think you should pay her a visit. Woman to woman. Tell her you've been worried about her. She may confide in you."

"Sure. I can do that." The words came out before I had a chance to run them through my brain.

"Learn anything else?" Okoje asked Tom.

"Donna told us her brother, when he was Gordon Little, was married to a woman named Freya who used to live in Torquay."

"Is that so? Bad blood there?"

"No idea."

DS Varma made a note. "Were they in touch?"

"Donna didn't know, and we couldn't find the ex-wife in the telephone directory." Tom checked his notebook. "I'm interested in the woman Beryl Grey mentioned—the one who recently visited Littlejohn. Mrs. Grey got the impression they knew each other well. It might have been Freya Little."

"I'll work on it," Varma said. "If she's still in England, we'll find her."

"Back to the Nixons," Okoje said.

"Clive implied that Littlejohn used his computer skills to dig up secrets on people," Tom said.

"Blackmail?" Okoje folded his arms across his chest. "It's a motive."

The waitress arrived with our order, a pot of tea and a pair of scones on a lovely Blue Willow–patterned plate. They looked amazing. Tom poured tea into the delicate teacups.

"What about the sister?" Okoje addressed his question to me.

"She defended her brother," I said, "but I'm pretty sure she resented his success—and his money. She implied he changed his name to disassociate himself from the family." I added milk and two sugar cubes to my tea and stirred slowly. "What I don't understand is how they would benefit from her brother's death."

Varma was smiling like the Cheshire cat.

"You've asked the right question," Okoje said. "Littlejohn's solicitor in Coombe Mallet—and before you ask, her name is Anna Tran, not Rutledge or whatever—said the Nixons recently asked Littlejohn for a loan. Ten thousand pounds for some business proposition her husband had going. He'd loaned them money before. This time he refused."

"No wonder Clive wasn't best pleased," Tom said.

"Tran also told us Donna Nixon is the sole beneficiary of her brother's will." Okoje's lips parted in a rare smile, revealing a gold tooth. "She inherits the lot."

"Does she indeed?" Tom said. "How much are we talking?"

"Just over a million."

"The day Littlejohn died," said Varma, "was their lucky day."

I thought of the cheap mauve furniture and Donna Nixon's flashy nylon blouse. She'd wanted to give the impression she had style and money. Now she had it—money, anyway.

"I wonder if Donna knew she was the beneficiary," I said. "She claimed to know nothing about his finances."

"We're wondering the same thing." Okoje stood. "Let's go, Varma. The case won't solve itself."

Tom and I stayed to finish our tea.

"I forgot to ask for Beryl Grey's contact information," I said. "If they want me to see her, I should telephone first."

"I'll get it for you. But remember, as far as anyone knows, our purpose here is the dress. Who else should we contact?"

"Littlejohn's ex-wife, if we can find her. They divorced in 2014, but she'd probably be in the best position to tell us about him—and the members of that club he belonged to. He would have told the club members about the dress. That's what they were all about—re-creating the past. Maybe the club has a website. I'll check online." I took a last drink of my tea. "Have you heard anything more about that dinner at the Pearce's?"

"Maybe they've forgotten. You know how people are. 'We simply must get together,' and then you never hear from them again."

"Just as well. After the incident at the bar last night, it might be awkward."

Tom's mobile rang. He glanced at the screen, then at me. "It's Pearce. He must be telepathic." He put the phone to his ear. "Mallory." He listened for a moment. "Why not the police?" He nodded. "Hmm, yes, I see. All right, if you're sure."

"What was that all about?" I asked when he'd rung off. "Did they cancel?"

"No, Kate. Seems there's something they want to tell us about Littlejohn's death—privately. Tonight. He said to arrive at seven."

I sighed inwardly. There went our romantic dinner for two.

Chapter Fifteen

Quinn and Teddy Pearce lived in a contemporary house perched on the edge of a ravine about ten miles from Coombe Mallet. Seen from the road, the unassuming timber-and-granite walls gave the impression of solid utility.

Teddy must have seen our headlights, because the door opened as soon as we'd climbed out of the car. "Welcome to Chez Pearce." He stood under the porch light, wearing faded jeans and a finely knit black crew-neck sweater.

We dashed from the car, eager to get out of the icy drizzle.

When Teddy saw the bruise on Tom's face, he flushed with embarrassment. "Sorry again, man. Thanks for stepping in. My temper can get me into trouble."

"No worries." Tom glanced around. "Where's the constable? I thought the police sent security."

"They did. Poor guy was freezing his . . . toes off. Told him to go home and put the kettle on. Don't fancy livin' in a fortress."

A policeman assigned to security duty, I knew from Tom, would never abandon his post. But then again, when a member of Parliament orders you to leave, do you have a choice? I hoped one of the constables we'd met, Doaks or O'Brien, wasn't going to get into trouble.

Pearce led us through the central corridor to an enormous open-plan kitchen and living area with a vaulted ceiling and a long wall of glass that looked out on a spacious courtyard garden and the ravine beyond. I couldn't identify all the plants in their winter forms, but I did recognize yew hedging, what looked like drifts of pruned lavender, and a water feature.

"Your house is stunning," I said. "When was it built?"

"Two years ago. Quinn's money, of course. She has a trust fund from her grandfather." He must have remembered the accusation made against him at the bar, because he added, "I've done lots of things in my life—in the past, I mean. Taking bribes isn't one of them."

If Teddy was uncomfortable living in a house built with his wife's money, he didn't show it. On the contrary, he seemed proud of the house and eager to tell us about it.

"The chief materials are weathered larch and concrete. The roof is zinc—low maintenance, self-healing, eco-friendly. The weight is borne by a massive steel girder, which means in summer the sliding glass panels can be fully opened to incorporate the courtyard—or the garden room, as Quinn likes to call it." He laughed. "Listen to me. I sound like a bleedin' architect. Before I met Quinn, the poshest houses I knew were semidetached."

"Don't you have to live in London now you're in Parliament?" I asked.

"Most MPs don't these days. Not since the expenses scandal in 2009. Now we spend as much time in our constituencies as we can. I'm home every weekend. People know me. They know I have their interests in mind. I keep a serviced studio flat in Churchill Gardens. Hardly room to swing a cat, but it suits me fine. Furnished. Fitness center. Twenty-minute walk to Parliament House. Train to Exeter takes less than three hours. Keep a car there."

"When does Parliament reconvene after the holidays?" Tom asked.

"They reconvened yesterday, but nothing much happens until next week. I'll go up on the early train the morning of the thirteenth. Be there in plenty of time for voting."

"Where's Quinn?" I asked.

"Getting the girls ready for bed. She'll bring them down to say good-night."

He led us into the living area, which featured a long, U-shaped sectional in pale-grey tweed. The reception rooms were expensively furnished in a subdued palette of white, gray, and black—pared down, minimalistic. Not my style but stunning. The tile floors gleamed. No artwork interrupted the expanse of museum-white walls. The side tables held no objects of any kind, and yet the effect wasn't sterile or bleak, just impossibly chic.

I sat facing the kitchen with its pristine white cabinets and an island topped with black granite. The only spark of color was a red-glass-tiled backsplash behind the sink counter. I could picture the kitchen in *Architectural Digest.*

"Make yourselves at home," Teddy said. "What would you like—red wine or mineral water?"

We both chose mineral water.

Twin girls in pink-striped flannel pajamas scampered into the room.

"I'm Ivy, she's Lily," said one of the twins. They looked around seven to me—beautiful children with their mother's white-blond hair and amethyst-blue eyes. "Mummy said we could stay up to meet you."

"We're glad you did." Tom shook hands with them. "I'm Tom. This is Kate."

"Daddy said you just got married." Lily took my hand. "Did you look like a fairy princess?"

"Exactly like a fairy princess." Tom gave me a wink. *With a black eye.*

"We're going to be princesses when we get married," Ivy said. "If we *do* get married."

"We haven't decided yet," Lily explained. "We might be ballet dancers."

"Or astronauts." Ivy jumped up and down.

"You still have plenty of time," I said. "I'm sure you'll make the right decision."

Quinn entered the room. Tonight she wore a black bias-cut silk midi skirt and a chambray blouse wrapped tightly around her torso. The open neckline exposed sharp collarbones. She looked even thinner, if possible, than she had at the gala.

The girls ran to her. "Mummy, Mummy, come and meet Tom and Kate."

"Nice to see you again," Quinn said, peeling them off her silk skirt. "Time for you girls to climb into bed. Say good-night to Tom and Kate."

We all got hugs, and Quinn herded the girls toward the far end of the room. "Uma," she called. "Will you put the girls to bed, please?"

"Uma is our nanny," Teddy explained. "Lovely girl. Bilingual—French and English."

"I'll just see them off," Quinn said.

"They're adorable children," I told Teddy. "As bright as they are beautiful."

"Won't argue with you." Teddy beamed. "Sometimes I can hardly believe they're mine. We didn't have them right away, you know. We were married in 2006. Quinn was twenty-three. Never been on her own. Wasn't sure she wanted children. Once I talked her into it, things didn't happen right away. She was thirty-five when the twins were born. I was forty-five."

They were both older than they looked. "Well, you have them now, and they're absolutely gorgeous."

His expression became serious. "Things could have ended very differently for me. Even now there are folks who wouldn't be exactly gutted to see me fail."

"DCI Okoje told us about the attack on your house," Tom said. "What happened?"

"Drive-by. Brick thrown through the window by the door. Good thing the girls weren't home. Uma had them at the pool. Quinn was shopping. Luckily, we were able to have the glass replaced the same day."

"The note was wrapped around the brick?" *Do people actually do that?*

"Sounds like a penny dreadful, doesn't it?" Teddy attempted a smile.

"You said there was something you wanted to tell us."

"We do." The voice was Quinn's. "But let's get dinner on the table first. So much easier to talk over food and wine, don't you think?" She slipped on a pair of oven mitts and pulled an enameled baking dish from the commercial-style range. "Lasagna. Hope you like it."

A three-photo frame stood on the counter. In the first photo, a much younger Quinn, fourteen or fifteen, perhaps, knelt beside a black-and-white dog. In the second, she stood in front of a gray stone house, wearing jeans and a wax Barbour and holding a rifle. In the third, she sat astride a beautiful chestnut horse, dressed in traditional hunting livery, fawn jodhpurs and a fitted black coat.

"What a gorgeous horse. Where were these taken?" I asked.

"My family's hunting lodge on the moor. That's Hector. He was a Welsh gelding. Loved to jump. The dog was Bella. She wasn't ours, but she might have been. She spent most of her time on our land, trying to herd our sheep. I spent a lot of time at the lodge growing up. Summers, most school holidays."

"The house looks old."

"It is. The oldest part dates from the 1550s."

"Is it far from here?" I asked.

"About forty minutes. Daddy owns land north of the Dart. I don't go there much anymore. I miss it." She handed me a pair of wineglasses. "Would you put these on the table? Two more in the cupboard over there."

Along with the lasagna, Quinn had prepared a lovely green salad and a loaf of homemade garlic bread. Teddy poured glasses of a dark-red Brunello di Montalcino.

We were nearly finished with the main course when the mood changed. Quinn was eyeing Teddy, who was drumming the table with his thumb. "We didn't plan this, you know. Tonight was meant to be a social gathering. But after the incident at the bar, we realized we'd have to tell someone."

"Why us?" Tom asked.

"Because the police will jump to conclusions." Quinn downed the rest of her wine. "We thought if we told you first, you might be able to explain things to them."

"I can't conceal information," Tom said.

"We're not asking that," Quinn said. "It's just awkward. We could use your advice."

"About the incident at the bar?" Tom asked.

"That, yes. And Littlejohn's murder."

Tom lifted his eyebrows. "You'd better start at the beginning."

"More wine?" Teddy held up the bottle, but we declined. "You know my background." He poured another glass for Quinn and corked the bottle. "What I didn't mention at the gala was the fact that I'd been married before. Gemma and I were just eighteen. It should never have happened. She got pregnant. We married, she lost the baby—all within the first five months. After that, we realized we'd made a mistake, but it was expensive to get a divorce, so we let things slide. Years later I met Quinn. I'd gone to the university in Exeter to speak about responsible government. She was the student organizer. Love at first sight, at least for me." He grinned. "Took you a bit longer, didn't it, luv? By then I had a good job and could afford a divorce. Gemma didn't mind. In fact, she was all for it—as long as I paid."

Quinn reached out and took his hand. "The problem was my parents—Daddy, mostly. He took against Teddy straightaway. He was ten years older, barely divorced. Neither of them agreed with my decision to pull out of university. Then there was Teddy's past. Daddy actually had him investigated. I'll never forgive him for that. In the end, he didn't find anything Teddy hadn't already told me."

Teddy huffed. "Don't be too hard on him, luv. Imagine what I'll do when it's Ivy's and Lily's turn." He laughed, but there wasn't much humor in it. "You have to understand." Pearce turned to us, his bulldog face earnest. "Quinn's father is Karl Benables. That may not mean anything to you, but he's a big deal around here. Owns land, property, a number of local businesses. On several environmental boards. Well thought of in the community and the nation. Twice he's won the . . ." He looked at Quinn. "What is it?"

"The Queen's Award for Enterprise."

"That's it—outstanding achievement in the areas of innovation and sustainable trade. He was appointed OBE in the 2020 New Year's Honours list for services to the environment and the rural community." A drop of red wine had spilled on the glass table. Teddy wiped it away with his finger. "I'm telling you this so you can understand how

Quinn's parents felt when she turned up with me. Not exactly their dream son-in-law."

"They forbid me to see him." Quinn's nostrils flared. "It had the opposite effect."

"I can't blame them for that either," Teddy said, "but Quinn and I were in love, and that was that."

"Daddy threatened to disinherit me," Quinn said. "I told him to go ahead. I have money of my own."

Quinn's trust fund from her grandfather must have been substantial.

"Did he follow through?" Tom asked.

She huffed. "He always does what he says."

"There's been no reconciliation?" I asked. "Even with Teddy's election to Parliament?"

"That made it worse," Quinn said. "Daddy's on the opposite side of things politically. He actually backed Teddy's opponent."

"What about the twins? They must have made a difference."

Quinn shook her head. "It's been hardest on my mother. She has to go behind his back to see the girls. He refuses to have anything to do with them—or me."

"That must be difficult," I said.

Quinn was twisting her gray linen napkin. "Difficult and bloody unfair. He had no right to tell me what I could and couldn't do. I didn't ask for his money. I was an adult. I had my own life. Teddy was the one who opened my eyes to the privilege I'd taken for granted—not that he intended to turn me against my father."

He reached out for her hand. "*Luv.*"

"I'm fine. My father and I have never gotten along anyway." She was grasping the napkin so desperately her fingertips had turned white. "He was never home, for one thing. When he was home, he thought he had the right to control me—what classes I should take, who my friends were, how I spent my free time, what my future would be. I was never good enough or smart enough in his eyes. He was always waiting for me to fail, and when I did, he'd tell me it served me right for not following his advice. Now he's biding his time, waiting for our marriage to fail, which *isn't* going to happen." She raised her chin. "The result is he's lost his grandchildren. Rather a high price to prove yourself right, don't you think?"

I was thinking exactly that, picturing the sweet faces of the twins.

"Forgive me," Tom said, "but what does this have to do with Littlejohn's death?"

"This," Teddy said. "Quinn and I eloped. I'd just been elected to the East Devon District Council. Full of myself, I was—I admit it. Decided to do something about corruption. Raw sewage dumps. Expired electrical safety certificates. I mentioned all that at the gala. We began an investigation, and Quinn's father got caught in the net."

"Your father's one of the men under investigation?" Tom stared at Quinn.

"Not yet." She sneered. "But he's in it up to his neck."

"We don't know that, luv," Teddy said. "That's what the guy at the bar was talking about. He thinks I'm protecting Quinn's father. Not bringing charges because he's family. He's wrong. I have no power to protect Benables now, even if I wanted to. It's out of my hands."

"Oh, he's guilty," Quinn said. "No one gets where he is without cutting a few corners."

Teddy put up a hand. "You know that's not fair. Your father may not have known what his people were up to. There's no evidence he did." To us he said, "You can imagine how it went down—lawsuits, adverse publicity. He blames me, thinks I'm out for revenge."

"Daddy's the one bent on revenge—as usual." Quinn's upper lip twisted. "When he feels threatened, there's no telling what he'll do." Quinn's eyes glittered. She might be physically frail, but I wouldn't want to cross her.

"I wasn't out to get him." Teddy crossed his heart. "But there he was, and when it went public, I couldn't stop it."

"I still don't understand what this has to do with Littlejohn," Tom said.

"Sorry—didn't I say?" Teddy lifted his wineglass. "Littlejohn was the one who found the evidence against Quinn's father and the others. The council hired him to investigate."

"And now Littlejohn is dead."

"You can see how it looks," Quinn said. "I resent my father, and if he's guilty, he's guilty. But I don't want him falsely accused. Physical violence isn't his style. Besides, he wasn't home when Gideon was killed. He's been in Germany on business since the second of January."

Tom glanced at me. It wasn't hard to read his mind. People like Quinn's father don't do their own dirty work. Maybe Karl Benables had hired someone to break into Littlejohn's computer lab. And then kill him.

"I'm sorry to ask," I said, addressing Pearce, "but is that what you and Littlejohn were arguing about at the gala? I happened to notice your conversation from the first-floor gallery."

Pearce's face went slack. Then he shrugged and put both hands up in surrender. "No point denying it. I know the committee can't conceal evidence—I wouldn't ask that. But I wanted Littlejohn to consider the possibility that Quinn's father may not have been personally involved." He shot a glance at his wife. "He is the twins' grandfather. I thought Littlejohn might be able to prove that somehow."

"He refused?" Tom asked.

"He said facts were facts. His job was to uncover them. What others did with the evidence had nothing to do with him."

I looked at Tom. "What about the three men named in the local corruption? They might harbor a grudge against Littlejohn."

"I'm pretty sure they do. Pretty stupid if they followed through on it, though," Pearce said. "The police already have the evidence Littlejohn found."

"Do you know anyone else who might have wanted Littlejohn dead?" Tom asked.

Pearce fiddled with a gold watch on his left wrist, twisting it. "No, but if Littlejohn dug up dirt on three of Karl Benables' colleagues, he might have done the same to someone else."

Clive Nixon had said the same thing. Littlejohn liked knowing secrets. "You're still certain the gunshot at the gala was meant for you?" I asked.

Pearce pushed his chair back from the table. "Decide for yourself." He went to a small desk tucked into a corner of the living room and pulled out a creased sheet of paper, which he handed to Tom. He read it and passed it to me.

Next time I won't miss.

The carefully formed letters had been carefully anonymized. In fact, it looked to me as if someone had used their nondominant hand.

Tom handed the note back. "The police need to see that."

"No, mate." Pearce crumpled up the paper. "Intimidation—that's all it is."

* * *

We said good-night, thanked the Pearces again for dinner, and promised to break the news about Quinn's father to DCI Okoje—for all the good it would do. Okoje wasn't one to jump to conclusions, Tom said, and he wasn't in the habit of listening to gossip.

The temperature had dropped, turning the walk between the house and our car into a skating rink. I held on to Tom's arm, wishing I hadn't worn heels. Tom scraped a layer of ice off the windscreen. Once inside, he turned on the defroster. As we waited for the wiper blades to clear fan-shaped windows of visibility, Tom asked, "What did you think of their story?"

"About Quinn's father?"

"Exactly. Why would they bring it up? Was it really to soften the blow, or was it just the opposite—to plant suspicion about Karl Benables in our minds?"

"Quinn clearly resents him." I clicked my seat belt. "But is she angry enough to drop her own father in the middle of a murder investigation?"

"I wondered that as well."

"I'm wondering about the break-in, the one at the Old Merchant's House three months ago. Did Benables hire someone to find and destroy evidence of his guilt?"

"Maybe," Tom said. The windows were clearing. He put the car in gear and began backing out of the driveway. "Think about Teddy, though. He seemed eager to cut his father-in-law considerable slack."

"Yes, and I wonder why, when Benables did everything he could to prevent the marriage?"

"Pearce knows how bitter Quinn is. I think he also knows it's not healthy."

"Two things bother me," I said. "First, the handwriting. The only reason to disguise your handwriting is because someone will recognize it."

"You mean Pearce knows who wrote the note?"

"Or has his suspicions. Why else would he refuse to show it to the police?"

"And the second thing?"

"Nothing to do with the Pearces, but I'm still thinking about the death of that old man years ago. The one who befriended Littlejohn and died in a fire. I think we need to find out more."

Chapter Sixteen

Wednesday, January 8
Coombe Mallet

The sound of Tom's mobile startled me. I peered around the darkened room, experiencing a momentary sense of panic. No one calls in the middle of the night with good news.

Tom grabbed his mobile and raised himself up on one elbow. "Mallory. I see. Sure. I'll be there in"—he squinted at his watch on the bedside table—"half an hour." He clicked off his phone.

"Who was it? What's going on?" I was still trying to focus.

"Okoje. CCTV footage the night before Littlejohn was murdered shows a dark Vauxhall saloon turning onto Park Terrace just after midnight. Single driver. Clearly visible number plate, registered to Clive Nixon. The police are bringing him in for questioning."

"What time is it?"

"Almost seven." He headed for the shower. "Sorry to leave you on your own."

"No problem." I yawned. "I'm meeting Maggie Hughes at the library at one o'clock. I might look in at the museum this morning if Julia Kelly's available."

"What about Beryl Grey? You promised Okoje you'd speak with her."

"I'll call her and set something up." I yawned again.

Ten minutes later Tom emerged, fully dressed. He bent down to kiss me.

"You're going to miss breakfast, Tom. The kitchen doesn't open until seven thirty."

"No worries." He grabbed his jacket and headed for the door. "No such thing as a police station without food. Text you later."

After Tom left, I showered, dressed, and made my way down to the breakfast room. I chose a table against the stone wall and slid onto the long bench. A young waitress brought coffee and took my order for scrambled eggs and sausages with brown-bread toast. It was becoming a habit.

The coffee was strong and hot, just the way I like it. I cradled the cup in my hands and thought about Clive Nixon. Was he under arrest? Would he confess?

Nixon had a motive for killing his brother-in-law—the inheritance. That is, if he'd known his wife would inherit her brother's considerable estate. And then there was the fact that Littlejohn had refused his request for a loan. Nixon might have been the person Littlejohn was expecting Sunday morning. Except the CCTV footage had captured him turning into Littlejohn's street around midnight the night before. Why?

I hate unanswered questions. One thing was clear—the Nixons had lied to the police.

The waitress delivered my breakfast.

"I really shouldn't have sausages every morning," I told her. "I can't resist."

"We get them locally—butcher's shop on the High Street."

I pushed my plate to one side to make room for the small notebook and pen I always carry. Putting my thoughts on paper helps me make sense of things.

I took a few bites of egg and buttered a piece of toast. Chewing thoughtfully, I began to write:

1. *Who besides the Nixons profits from Gideon Littlejohn's death?*
2. *What was Clive doing in Coombe Mallet the night before Littlejohn's murder?*

3. *Was Littlejohn the target at the museum gala after all? Shot fired from first floor of the museum. Ask Tom to show me the site map they produced.*
4. *Had Littlejohn uncovered dirt on someone other than Quinn's father and his colleagues? Is the break-in three months ago related to his murder?*
5. *Death of the old man in Exeter—obviously important to Littlejohn. How did he die? Accident or murder?*

I finished one of the sausages and started on the second. I'd forgotten about the bloodstained dress. That was a separate issue. Or was it? I began to write again:

6. *Why did Littlejohn refuse to give trunk to museum? Who forged the note pinned to the dress and why?*
7. *Was Nancy Thorne a murderess? Whose blood was it on her dress, and what could it possibly have to do with the murder of Littlejohn? (probably nothing)*
8. *Connection between the dress and the items found with it? (Romani?)*
9. *Where is Littlejohn's ex-wife, Freya Little?*
10. *Who are the other historical re-creators? What can they tell us about Littlejohn or the dress?*

I massaged the back of my neck. So many questions. So few answers.

"More coffee, luv?" The voice came from behind my shoulder. I was pretty sure the waitress had been reading my notes.

"Thank you, yes." I closed my notebook. "Is there a place to set up my computer? The Wi-Fi in our room isn't very strong."

"Oh, I know. We get complaints all the time. It's the thick stone walls. Try the library. Through that door and past reception. Toward the back of the inn."

I thanked her and, taking my coffee with me, returned to our room to collect my computer.

The library was a small, cozy space that doubled as a bar. I commandeered a table near a window that looked out on an outdoor beer garden, closed for the winter. When I turned on my computer, I was delighted to find a robust Wi-Fi signal.

My computer search began with Freya Little. DS Varma had promised to track her down, but who knew when he'd have time? Questioning Clive Nixon was his first priority at the moment, so it was up to me. And unless Donna Nixon had been wrong about Torquay, Freya Little's name should show up somewhere there, even if she'd moved on.

I was right. It took me nearly an hour, but the effort paid off when I found not only the name Freya Little mentioned in one of the local Torquay newspapers but also the name Mercy Abbott. The girlfriend Donna Nixon mentioned? Maybe. They'd both attended a dinner in 2015, part of the annual Agatha Christie festival. The article included a photograph of about fifty people, all dressed in the clothing of the 1930s. As no names were listed beneath the photo and as the faces of the participants were miniscule, I could only guess which, if any, were Freya and Mercy. Nevertheless, it was a starting point. I looked for contact information, a phone number or email. Finding nothing, I emailed the festival committee's generic info@ account.

Hello, I typed, and then decided I needed a plausible reason for asking for personal information. *I'm working with the Museum of Devon Life in Coombe Mallet, tracing a Victorian dress donated by a man who is now deceased. I'm trying to locate his former wife, Freya Little, and a woman named Mercy Abbott. I believe they are pictured somewhere in this photo. If you have any information, please contact me.*

I attached a copy of the photo and pushed send. Hopefully someone would respond.

My next priority was learning more about death of the old man in Exeter. I honestly didn't see how it could have anything to do with the murder of Gideon Littlejohn, but I couldn't help feeling there was more to the story than I'd been told. Was the old man's death really a tragic accident? Probably, but it wouldn't hurt to find out. My mother, whose curiosity could easily exhaust the extra lives of several cats, always said, *Keep asking questions until you run out of them.*

I was a long way from running out of questions, not only about the bloodstained dress but also about the old man who'd instilled a passion for history in the heart and mind of a rather lonely young boy.

Chances were that a death in a house fire would have been mentioned in the newspapers. Donna had said it happened after she'd left home, when Gideon was twelve or thirteen. If she was right, that meant the fire occurred in the early 1990s. Maybe the village library had some sort of newspaper index. Waiting patiently for information has never been my gift, but I wasn't in the mood to waste time with a blind search. I needed a few facts first.

I was shutting down my computer when a woman I recognized as the pub's owner entered the library and began dusting the liquor bottles at the bar. Somewhere in her sixties, she was on the heavy side—sturdy might be more accurate—with a pleasant face and thick salt-and-pepper hair. She wore a smock and low-heeled shoes.

"Am I disturbing you? I can come back later." She smiled, revealing a slight overbite. "I'm Yvie. Pronounced *E-V* but with a Y. Short for Yvonne. Yvie Innes. My husband and I own the inn.

"You're not disturbing me at all. I'm Kate Hamilton. My husband and I checked in last Thursday."

"Yes—we understand you're on your honeymoon. Thank you for spending part of it with us. Your husband just reserved your room for another seven nights, just in case."

He did? I just smiled.

Yvie polished a bottle of clear spirits—probably gin—and gave me a sidelong glance. "I understand you're also here in a . . . well, professional capacity." She anticipated my question. "Before you ask, dear, nothing stays hidden for long in a village. We're just sorry you've got mixed up in this terrible business. Coombe Mallet is normally a peaceful place—dull even, one might say."

"Did you know Mr. Littlejohn?"

"Everyone knows everyone in Coombe Mallet. Gideon's club used to hold their quarterly meetings at the pub. They called themselves the Society of Victorians. We would get anywhere from five or six to maybe twelve. Some from as far away as Plymouth. I believe the club meets on

Zoom these days, but I can't imagine what will happen to them now, with Gideon gone."

"When was this?"

"Well, let me see. It must have been around 2014 or 2015 when they started."

"Did you know Mr. Littlejohn's wife, Freya?"

Yvie Innes stared at me. "He was married? No, luv."

"Do you remember any names? Anyone Mr. Littlejohn was especially close to?"

Yvie pursed her lips and consulted the ceiling. "Well, let's see. There was one young woman—Mercy Abbott, I think her name was. She was lovely. Chinese, I think. She used to come regular, and I got the impression she and Gideon were close. I haven't seen her for a several years at least. There was a young man as well. Daniel something. Never knew his surname."

So I'd been right about the name in the Torquay newspaper. "What were the meetings like?"

"Food and drink, of course. Lots of drink. Some stayed overnight. There was always a presentation on some aspect of Victorian life. The last one I remember concerned the Romani culture in Devon and the trope of the Gypsy in Victorian literature. Gideon gave the presentation himself."

"When was this?"

"Probably 2019. Like I said, they began meeting on Zoom."

So Gideon Littlejohn had an interest in Romani culture. I didn't know whether to be excited or disappointed. It meant the items he'd donated to the museum—the carved wooden box, the gold sovereigns, the Gaudy teapot, and the Gypsy-set ring—might not be connected to the dress after all but simply part of his collection. That begged another question. Had Littlejohn actually *said* the objects were found in the trunk with the dress? I was pretty sure he had, but then he might not have been telling the truth.

"Tell me more." I smiled at Yvie, encouraging her to continue. "Do you know anything about Romani camps near Coombe Mallet?"

"If you mean today, they've banned wild camping on Dartmoor. Shame if you ask me. Back in the day, a large Romanichal family arrived every spring and set up camp near the River Dart. People looked forward to their arrival. They provided useful services—mending, lambing, shearing, helping with the harvest. They sold horses—good stock too. Part of our local history."

"The museum has an entire room dedicated to the Romani culture in Devon."

"Mind if I take a load off?" Yvie eyed the chair across from me. "Been on my feet since five."

"Please—join me."

Yvie tucked her dustcloth into a pocket and lowered herself into the chair. "I've lived in this village my whole life. My parents and grandparents before me. There's not much about the history of this area I don't know." She paused, grimacing as she kicked off her shoes and wiggled her toes. "The Romanies were an important part of life in my grandparents' day. We heard stories. Some of the women told fortunes, but I think it was mostly because people expected it. The men did odd jobs, mending pots, iron gates, repairing stone fences—they could put their hands to just about anything that needed doing. Everyone over the age of fifty remembers the old tales. Take the tea shop—Queenie's. Named for the matriarch, Queenie Squires. My old gran told me about her. Ran the camp like a true queen. Honest, they were, and hardworking. Queenie insisted on it. She was quite a character by all accounts. Died at the age of eighty-something, fit as a fiddle till the very end. Her funeral was held on the moor. Everything done in the old, traditional way. They packed all her personal belongings in her vardo—that's what they called their caravans—and set it on fire. Folks could see the blaze for miles around."

"Do you remember hearing about a village just north of here called Widdecombe Throop?"

"The one that got flooded."

"Yes. Did your gran ever mention a lacemaker from there, Nancy Thorne—actually anyone named Thorne?"

Yvie screwed up her face in thought. "I don't think so. No Thornes around here now, anyway." She slipped her feet back into her shoes. "Best get back. Work doesn't do itself."

My cell phone buzzed—it was a British number, one I didn't recognize.

"This is Kate."

"Oh, Kate. It's me—Donna Nixon. The police have taken Clive away." I heard a sob. "They think he killed Gordon. What am I going to do?"

What could I say? "If Clive is innocent, the police won't charge him," was all I could come up with. Why had she called me? Didn't she know Tom was a policeman—or was that the reason she'd called me?

"The thing is . . ." She took in a ragged breath. "We lied to the police, and I don't know what to do. Can you meet me? I can be in Coombe Mallet in thirty minutes."

"All right, but I'm not sure what I can do either. I'm at the Crown."

"No, not there. Meet me at St. Petroc's."

Chapter Seventeen

St. Petroc's, the parish church in the center of Coombe Mallet, had been built around the same time as St. Æthelric's, Long Barston's fifteenth-century jewel, but was smaller and plainer. The exterior was limestone with a Norman tower and shingled slate roof. With the cold wind whipping my hair, I ducked inside.

Morning prayers were over. The sanctuary was empty, so I took one of the free informational flyers and slipped into a square-ended pew near one of the ancient radiators chugging out warmth along the perimeter. I'd started to read the flyer when Donna Nixon arrived, red-faced and out of breath.

"I've been in a flap all morning." Donna wiggled out of her puffy jacket. "At least we have some heat. It's usually like the grave in here." She was in distress, but she hadn't neglected her makeup. Sparkly green eyeshadow matched her sparkly green top. "I don't know what to do about Clive. The police came to the house, read him his rights, and took him away."

"What did they tell you?"

"They know he went to see my brother the night before he was murdered. They have him on camera."

"You said you were together the night before the murder."

"I know." She groaned. "Had to say that, didn't I? Clive'll kill me when he hears I contacted you." Her eyes opened in horror. "I don't mean he'd actually *kill* me. He'd never harm anyone. Might shout a bit, wave his arms about."

"I heard about the CCTV footage, Donna. Why did Clive drive all the way from Exeter to Coombe Mallet on Saturday night?"

"I told him Gordon wouldn't let him in, but would he listen to me?" She pulled a tissue out of her cleavage and wiped her eyes. "He was desperate."

"Why? What was he hoping to do?"

"Talk my brother into loaning us money, of course. Beg him if necessary. We'd asked Gordon, but he'd refused point-blank. He said it had to stop—the foolish get-rich-quick schemes. It's not that Clive's dim, exactly, but he's always looking for that pot of gold."

And now he's found it. I watched her for signs she'd known about the inheritance, seeing none.

Donna wiped her eyes, smearing the green eyeshadow. "He's fallen for every scam in the book—gambling on the horses, Bitcoin, work-from-home gigs that required cash up front, investment scams, pyramid selling—he called it 'multilevel marketing.' If he'd put as much energy into a regular job as he has into those worthless swindles, we'd be sitting pretty by now."

"Your brother loaned you money in the past?"

"Twice. Once when Clive signed a contract to open a mobile chippy—only to find out he'd committed to a large cash outlay up front with no way to buy the equipment he needed. The second time, Gordon paid off a debt Clive incurred when the value of Bitcoin tumbled. I don't blame my brother for refusing to fund his latest scheme. This time it was some new technology, replacing gasoline with a synthetic made from sweet potato peelings or something. He said it was a sure thing. He borrowed fifteen thousand pounds from a loan shark. He has to pay it back, or—" She made a throat-slashing motion with her hand.

"So he drove all the way to Coombe Mallet and didn't get there until after midnight? Did he suppose your brother would be awake at that time of night?"

"Thinking ahead has never been Clive's gift. I pleaded with him not to go, but he was up and out of the house before I could talk sense into him. He just had to have another go."

"What happened? Did he see your brother?"

"Never got the chance. When he arrived, the house was dark, and it finally dawned on the fool that Gordon'd be even less likely to agree to the loan in the middle of the night. So he decided to wait until morning. Stayed there all night—in his car. Near froze to death."

"Wait a minute—are you saying he saw your brother in the morning?" She was making things even worse for Clive.

"No. He was about to open the car door when someone else showed up."

I felt the skin on the back of my neck tingle. "Who was it?"

"Who knows? All he saw was the back of someone climbing the stairs. Naturally, he ducked out of sight, and when he dared look again, no one was there."

"You're saying this person was admitted to the house?"

"Probably."

"Man or woman?"

"He's not sure."

"When was this exactly?"

"He doesn't know. Never wears a watch. But it must have been midmorning, because the sun was glinting off the hood of his car. Maybe around ten?"

Apparently *froze to death* was a relative term. "When did he leave?"

"Soon after that."

"Did he see anyone else?"

"No."

"Has he told the police?"

"No, and he won't."

"Why not, Donna? This information could exonerate Clive and lead the police to your brother's killer."

She looked up at me through her lashes. "Because this time, Clive's in real trouble. He'd have to explain why he went there. He owes money, lots of it, and the people who loaned him the cash won't be best pleased if he tells the police who they are. They aren't nice people, Kate. I know Clive. When he's threatened, he'll deny everything and clam up."

"But if he doesn't tell them, he may be charged with murder." A chubby-cheeked cherub smiled sympathetically down from the altarpiece. Donna was going to need more than sympathy. "If Clive won't tell the police, *you* have to."

"I don't know." Donna bit the side of her lip. "Doesn't seem right."

"You've already told me. Let me tell Tom. He'll know what to do."

Donna took a deep breath. "Clive's going to kill me."

* * *

By the time I got to the library for my meeting with Maggie Hughes, Donna Nixon was already being interviewed by the police. Tom had texted me. Once she'd agreed to talk, they couldn't shut her up. What Okoje would do with her information, I had no idea. Some of Clive's schemes over the past few years hadn't sounded precisely legal, but it was clear, at least to me, that his actions in this case had less to do with criminal intent and more to do with his entirely unwarranted belief that riches were waiting for him around the next corner. I still had questions—most importantly about Littlejohn's mysterious visitor the morning he was killed. Had he or she been captured on the CCTV footage from the corner shop? Only the police could answer that question, so I put the matter aside and turned my thoughts to the bloodstained dress.

The Coombe Mallet Public Library occupied a wing of the Village Hall on Church Street. I arrived exactly at one and found Maggie Hughes waiting for me. She was a pleasant-looking woman, middle-aged, dressed in a dark woolen dress. Her blunt-cut silver hair fell just below her ears, and she wore a pair of oversized horn-rimmed glasses.

"Welcome, Kate." Her smile was as warm as the glint in her eyes. "I think you'll be interested in what I've found. It's not a lot, I'm afraid, but it might point you in the right direction."

I followed her through the stacks to a small, glass-walled room. On a boat-shaped conference table sat a computer, a monitor, and a pile of papers.

"Come, sit here. I've printed everything off for you, but I thought you'd like to see what I found on the monitor first."

We sat side by side in front of the screen. Maggie clicked a few keys. An image of an old newspaper appeared. "This is the only account of the Nancy Thorne mystery I could find—and I looked through no fewer than thirty newspapers printed in Devon at that time." She zoomed in so I could read. A small article had appeared in the *South Devon Post* on the second of October 1885:

> *An event of the strangest and most puzzling nature has come to us from Dartmoor. At one a.m. on the night of 7th September 1885, Nancy Thorne, a thirty-year-old lacemaker from the village of Widdecombe Throop, returned to the cottage she shared with her sister, a seamstress, in a state of incoherence. Her hair was disheveled. Her frock was torn and soaked with what appeared to be blood.*

I stopped reading. The account had been copied, almost word for word, and dropped into the radio documentary from 1942. "Maggie, you're a genius. Unfortunately, the article doesn't tell me anything I don't already know—except that it actually happened, or at least people believed it happened."

"Don't give up yet." Maggie tapped a few more keys. "I was intrigued, so I decided to dig deeper. The UK census has been taken every ten years since 1801. After 1841, personal information was included—names, occupations, stuff like that. Unfortunately, the census of 1921 is the last one available online. The hundred-year rule. Privacy, you know, for those still alive."

"What did you find?" I was almost salivating.

"This." Maggie pulled up a file on her computer—a spreadsheet she'd created with census dates on the left and columns headed *Name of House, Name and Surname, Relation to Head of Family, Condition, Age, Rank*, and *Profession or Occupation*.

"Nancy Thorne first appears on the 1861 census for the parish of Widdecombe Throop." She directed my attention to the first line. "If you read across, you'll see she was living at number four Brook Lane. She was six years old, the daughter of Henry and Sarah Thorne. Her father is listed as a laborer. She's listed as 'Scholar at Home.'"

"And Sally?"

"Second line—just there. Sally was eight. Listed as 'Apprentice Dressmaker.'"

"Sewing dresses at *eight*—my goodness."

"Yes. Now look at the next line. That's the 1871 census. There's been a major change in the family. Henry is gone, and Sarah is described as a 'Laundress, widow of the parish.' Sally is eighteen now, and her occupation is listed as 'Dressmaker.' Nancy is absent, which tells me she wasn't living at home on the second of April when the census was taken. She would have been sixteen. Maybe she was a boarder at one of the lace schools in the area."

I'd already gone on to the next line. "In 1881 Sally and Nancy are living together at number four Brook Lane. Their mother, Sarah, is gone, and—" I stopped, surprised. "Sally is married." I read, "'Sally Tucker, age twenty-eight, dressmaker. Nancy Thorne, twenty-six, lace-maker.' Her relationship to the head of household is listed as 'Sister.'" I looked up. "Where was Sally's husband?"

Maggie shrugged. "It doesn't say Sally was a widow, so separated? In the army? I think England was fighting the First Boer War at that time. Or he could have been in the workhouse—or even jail." She looked back at the screen and scrolled down. "The next census in Devon was taken on Sunday, the fifth of April, 1891, five and a half years after the incident with the bloodstained dress. Take a look."

Another surprise. "Yes, I see. Sally and Nancy are still in residence, but now there's a child. 'William Tucker, age five.' And Sally is described as a widow." This was interesting. Sally had given birth to a child. Had the bloodstained dress been hers, then?

"Census records can tell us a lot," Maggie said, "but there's so much more we'd like to know. They're a snapshot in time, but a lot happened during those ten intervening years. People grew old. They died. Children were born. Life circumstances altered, and all without explanation." She removed her glasses and polished them with a small square of cloth. "The missing information can often be found in church records, but as Hugo told you, the parish records for Widdecombe Throop have been lost."

"Is there any way to find out when Sally's husband died? It's probably irrelevant, but I'm curious."

"I can check the military records. If he was a soldier, I should be able to find him. Burial records are trickier. Depends on where he died. Some are available, others not."

"Do you know if the graves from the churchyard in Widdecombe Throop were relocated?"

"I don't, but I would think the living residents would have insisted on it. I'll see what I can find."

Several lines on the spreadsheet remained, but they didn't contain any useful information. In the 1901 census, Nancy was no longer listed as living at number four Brook Lane with her sister and nephew. According to the radio documentary, she'd died in 1901 at the age of forty-six—evidently before the census was taken. By the time of the 1911 census, the village of Widdecombe Throop no longer existed.

"Is there any way to tell where Sally and her son, William, moved when the village was flooded?"

"I thought you might ask, so I did a preliminary search for Sally and William Tucker in the 1911 census. Unfortunately, there were thousands of people by that name—more than four hundred Sallys and over seven hundred Williams—and that was Devon alone. They could have moved anywhere. I didn't have time to go further. But I will. And I'll try to find information about Sally's husband and the graves."

"There is one other thing. The death of an old man living on or near the Burnthouse Lane estate in Exeter in the early 1990s. I've been told he died in a fire, but I don't know his name or age except that he was elderly."

"A tall order, Kate, but I love research. I'll see what I can find. In the meantime, I've printed everything out for you." She handed me a folder.

"Maggie, I can't thank you enough." I gave her my business card. "If you learn anything else, call me—especially if you can trace William Tucker. He might be the one who preserved the bloodstained dress."

"Will do, Kate."

For the first time since arriving, I felt optimistic. We might be able to trace the dress after all, and if it went through the Tucker family, originally of Widdecombe Throop, they might be able to tell us whether the dress belonged to Nancy Thorne or her sister, Sally. They might even know what really happened that night.

I pulled on my jacket. "There's one other area I'm interested in—the history of the Romani Travellers in Devon. Yvie Innes at the Crown said a Romanichal family camped near the River Dart in her grandparents' day. Was there much interaction between them and the villagers?"

Maggie took what might have seemed a strange request in stride. "It might take me a day or two. Check back tomorrow. Or Friday. I'll be here both days."

I thanked Maggie again, picked up the printouts, and headed for the Museum of Devon Life.

Chapter Eighteen

I arrived at Julia Kelly's workroom around two. The museum was quiet. A few visitors, mostly senior citizens, strolled leisurely through the exhibits. Everything, as far as I could tell, was back in perfect order.

Julia was arranging the garnet-red dress, the one I'd seen earlier, on another of the mannequins. Now, displayed on a human form, I realized just how truly spectacular it was. The ball gown had a wide, open neckline, a tightly boned bodice, and yards and yards of the self-patterned silk fabric gathered into pleats, drapes, and ruffles. But the eye-popping feature was an enormous bustle that stood out from the back of the dress at a ninety-degree angle.

"Hey, Kate." Julia looked up from her work. "Can you imagine wearing this? The bustles were so heavily padded people claimed they could support an entire tea service."

"How did the wearer sit?"

"Perched on the edge of the chair, I imagine—if they sat at all. The weight of these gowns was so great, an infrastructure had to be created with flexible wire, cane, and whalebone."

"When would a dress like this have been worn—the period, I mean?"

"We can place it almost exactly to the years between 1885 and 1888. Before that, bustles had been mostly replaced by draped or pleated trains. Suddenly they reappeared—with a vengeance. Then, after 1888, with the increasing popularity of what was called 'the Rational Dress Movement,' dresses returned to slimmer, more natural silhouettes."

"Women came to their senses."

Julia laughed. "Fashion has never been a matter of sense. Remember the huge shoulder pads, head-to-toe sequins, and neon spandex of the eighties?"

"I could show you photos." I made a face. "You said the dress was donated by a local family. Do you know the name of the woman who wore it?"

"I don't. You could ask Hugo or Isla." Julia drew my attention to the waistline. "You can see an hourglass shape was attempted—she would have worn a corset—but this woman had some weight on her. She might have been pregnant."

Like the wearer of the bloodstained dress. "What else does the dress tell you?"

"This isn't the kind of frock one would have worn to a country ball. The woman who owned it probably spent the social season in London. That and the silk fabric, almost certainly imported from France, tells me she was wealthy—landed gentry, maybe even titled."

"The color is spectacular—and it hasn't faded."

"Thanks to those newly invented aniline dyes." Julia peeled off the white gloves she'd been wearing. "There's one other thing, Kate—the most important thing. I'm convinced the seamstress who made this dress also made the calico dress with the bloodstains."

"Really?" Nancy Thorne's sister, Sally Tucker, had been a dressmaker.

"Every seamstress had her own unique way of working—almost a signature."

"Wouldn't the family who donated the dress know her name?"

"That's Hugo's job. My interest is the garment itself."

"I met with a librarian today. She's helping me trace Nancy Thorne's family through the census information."

"You mean Maggie Hughes. She's been incredibly helpful with local history." Julia leaned in as if someone might be listening. "Actually, Maggie saved Hugo from some embarrassment last year. He'd purchased what he thought was an English copy of Bede's *Commentary on the Gospel of St. Luke* from the scriptorium of a ruined Benedictine monastery near Bovey Tracey. It was very exciting. We had several pages on display in the room dedicated to Devon's religious history—until Maggie Hughes pointed out, privately, that two words in the commentary—*unearthly* and *auspicious*—weren't coined until a half century after the monastery was dissolved. That prompted a scientific analysis of the so-called sheepskin parchment. It turned out to be old shoe leather, aged with a coating of animal-skin glue. Can you imagine? If Hugo's mistake had become public, his reputation would have been damaged. I can't think how the forgery slipped past him. He should have suspected something. Isla still hasn't forgiven Maggie."

"Forgiven Maggie? For what—pointing it out?"

"Completely unfair, of course." Julia was arranging a series of pleats along the side of the red dress. "Hugo is nothing if not ambitious. I'm sure he *wanted* the commentary to be authentic. Like he wants the dress to be authentic."

"Dr. Hawksworthy is the one who gave me Maggie's name."

"He owes her." Julia inserted a pin to hold up a sagging flounce. "Maggie could have written an article about the forgery. It would have enhanced her academic reputation. And yet Isla acts as if Maggie was a traitor or something by pointing out the error."

"Isla's very loyal."

"I think Hugo takes advantage of her. She's been with him for years. I'm sure she's in love with him."

I'd thought that as well. It was fairly obvious. "Is he in love with her?"

"I don't know. Hugo's single. Divorced." She straightened. "But you're not here for museum gossip. Let's have a look at the calico dress. I'll show you what I found."

The dress, covered with protective sheeting, was spread out on the worktable. Julia removed the sheeting, opened the bodice, and folded it back to reveal the interior structure.

The room felt hot. I swallowed against the dryness in my throat.

"This humble dress was constructed with as much skill as the red silk. The calico fabric was meticulously underlined with undyed muslin and the seams bound with fine cotton lawn. Can you see the subtle shade difference—right there? I'm sure the binding between the bust and the waist was applied later, after the dress had been worn for a while. I've removed a section of lining so you can see the stains." She pointed at one of the curved seams along the front. "Analyzing stains is partly science, partly intuition; but if the bodice of the dress came into contact with blood—lots of it—the stains would have been less pronounced on the interior seams, which were partially protected by the bodice lining and the seam finishing. That's not true in this case. Look for yourself."

I did, noticing that the blood had soaked fully into the cut edges of the fabric. *Blood. So much blood.* An image swam in my brain. The same image I'd seen before. A woman on her knees, sobbing. I stepped back, distancing myself from the blood.

"There—see what I mean?" Julia looked up. Could she hear the pounding of my heart? "You can see blood on the finished edges. That tells me there was more fabric there at one time."

I took a deep breath. "You mean when the blood came into contact with the dress, the garment was larger around the waist."

"Yes. When Victorian women became pregnant, they wore the same style of clothing but altered to accommodate their increased girth. Most, even poor women, wore maternity corsets. The lacings on the sides could be loosened as the baby grew, but many women continued to tight-lace—working women especially in the first five months or so. Pregnancy often meant a loss of employment. In other words, they hid their pregnancies as long as they could."

I focused on Julia's explanation, forcing myself to breathe normally. "And when they couldn't hide it?"

"They simply withdrew from public exposure." She looked at me curiously. "Do you need to sit down, Kate?"

"I'm fine. Just hot." I peeled off my jacket to prove it. "The 1891 census records for Widdecombe Throop show that the Thorne household included a child born around 1885 or 1886. His name was William Tucker, the son of Sally Tucker, Nancy's older sister."

"As I said, my job is to observe and analyze the garments and to gather data. I leave the interpretation of that information up to others."

Once again, the deep lace collar drew my eyes, with its exuberant motifs taken from the natural world. I noticed tiny, perfect acorns incorporated into the design, and an unusual slipper-like blossom. "Is that a real flower?" I asked Julia, determined to focus on details and information.

"Bird's-foot trefoil. You'll see it everywhere around here in summer. The local people call it 'eggs and bacon' because of the egg-yolk-yellow flowers and reddish buds."

"Why bird's foot?"

"Because of the clawlike seed pods." She re-covered the dress with sheeting. "Have the police made any progress on the murder—or aren't you able to tell me? Gideon was a friend."

I didn't want to lie, but I couldn't tell her about the Nixons. "The police are moving ahead with their investigation. I'm sure we'll know more soon."

I couldn't wait to get out of there.

* * *

Back at the Crown, I found Tom waiting for me. "Hello there, beautiful. I was about to phone you." He pulled me in for a kiss. "What d'you say we take a walk before dinner? We still have a good hour of light, and the weather isn't bad."

"I'd love that. Let me change my shoes. Be down in a minute."

Ten minutes later we donned our parkas and gloves and left the pub by the rear entrance. Tom waved a brochure. "The front desk gave me a map of the footpaths. Oh, and speaking of maps—DCI Okoje would like you to look at the floor plan of the museum we put together. You were on the ground floor when the shot was actually fired, but you'd just come from the mechanical clock demonstration on the first floor. That's where the shooter was located. Okoje would like to know if you see anything on the plan that sends up red flags."

"Of course, but I was focused on the clock like everyone else."

"I know. The shooter chose the perfect moment."

The hotel parking area led to a series of footpaths crisscrossing the landscape around Coombe Mallet, skirting open fields and winding through impressive woodlands. We chose the Dartmeet Walk along the river, which reminded me of the walks we loved to take along the Stour near Long Barston. I loved the sound of water rushing over the stones and the possibility of spying the creatures that made their homes on the riverbank. It always reminded me of *The Wind in the Willows*, one of my favorite childhood books.

"What will happen to the Nixons?" I asked.

"I don't know." Tom pushed a low-hanging branch out of the way. "Clive isn't one of nature's geniuses. He's got himself into real trouble this time with loan sharks."

"That's what Donna said. Can the police help him?"

"The important thing right now is prising whatever information he might have about Littlejohn's early-morning visitor out of his thick head."

"Donna said he didn't see anything, not even if the person on Littlejohn's doorstep was male or female."

"Turns out he did see something—or rather heard it. When Gideon answered the door, Clive heard him say, 'Oh fine. Let's get this over once and for all.'"

"Is that important?"

"It could be. It means Littlejohn wasn't happy this person turned up."

"And it narrows the time of death even further. Donna said the visitor showed up midmorning, around ten AM."

"You think like a detective."

"It's rubbing off on me."

We'd reach a stile. Tom went first and then helped me over. "The police are pinning their hopes on the computer files, but Littlejohn knew what he was doing. He used something called a two-hundred-fifty-six-bit AES key. Don't ask me to explain it. It's a high level of security. The digital forensics team in London needs a password. They've asked the software publisher to provide the digital key. The problem is they might not agree to give it to the police."

"Did you tell the police about the three men Littlejohn was hired to investigate?"

"Another dead end. When Littlejohn was shot, all three of them were in a meeting with their legal team. Lots of witnesses."

"What if they hired a hit man?"

"Hit men don't usually make appointments in advance, Kate, and the victim usually doesn't know them. It looks like whoever killed Littlejohn was known to him."

The path led us to a narrow section of the River Dart where a series of flat granite slabs formed a bridge. Tom consulted the route details. "The map says it's a medieval clapper bridge." He held out his hand. "Can you make it?"

"I can if you can."

The bridge forded the river at a narrows. We hopped from slab to slab. Once across, we entered a wooded area with the remains of an old, ruined cottage.

"Did you tell DCI Okoje about Karl Benables?"

"Turns out they've had their eye on him."

"For the alleged corruption or for the attacks on his daughter and son-in-law?"

"Both."

"I can't imagine he staged the attacks." I shook my head. "As much as he might resent his son-in-law, I don't believe he would risk harming his own daughter and grandchildren."

"For the record, they haven't found a shred of evidence against him. Either he's innocent or knows how to maintain deniability."

"There's got to be more to the story."

"I agree." The path took a sharp rise. Several large tree roots snaked across the footpath. "How was your day? How was Maggie Hughes?"

"Helpful." I told him about the census records. "Now all we have to do is find a family named Tucker that traces their descent back to Widdecombe Throop."

"And *that* won't be a problem." I saw the corner of his mouth go up. "Seeing that Tucker is one of the most common surnames in Devon."

"At least English people didn't change their surname every generation like the Scandinavians. My father and grandfather were both Larsens—literally 'the son of Lars.' But my great-grandfather was Lars Jensen—'the son of Jens,' and his father was Jens Pedersen, 'the son of Peder.'"

"I'm getting a headache."

"I know. Makes genealogy challenging. Seriously, though, it would help if we could locate the solicitor who handled the sale of that household. I'm counting on Ivor."

"Speaking of solicitors, Anna Tran contacted the Nixons about the will. She told Okoje they were shocked. Or seemed to be."

"If they didn't know about the inheritance, it pretty much eliminates their motive."

Tom didn't answer. The footpath had opened up into a field. Although the light was fading, we could see the path where feet had trodden. "We should head back," he said, looking at his watch. "We'll be able to see where we're going until at least five, but crossing that clapper bridge in the dark wouldn't be a smart idea."

My cell phone pinged, and I pulled it out of my jacket pocket. "It's an email from someone named Max Newlin."

"Max who?"

"Newlin. Wait—this could be interesting. He's responding to my query about Littlejohn's wife and Mercy Abbott." I clicked on the message and read it aloud:

> *Hello Kate. You asked about Freya Little. I'm sorry to tell you that she died in 2015. Single-car crash on the Barton Road. I'm afraid that's all the information I have. Mercy Abbott's still around. She was quite active on the festival committee for a time, but she left the area. I'm not at liberty to share her contact information, but if you give me your mobile number, I'll pass along a message. She may be willing to contact you. Max Newlin, International Agatha Christie Festival.*

"The ex-wife's a dead end, then," Tom said.

"Literally. But Mercy Abbott's out there somewhere." I typed in my cell number and pushed send.

* * *

That evening as Tom and I were finishing an early dinner at the Crown, we heard raised voices, not coming from the bar this time but from the entrance to the dining room.

Quinn and Teddy Pearce were standing at the hostess desk with the older, silver-haired couple we'd seen at the gala.

Quinn was complaining to a very young hostess, "I *specifically* asked for the round table near the fire." She indicated a table on the far side of the room where two couples sat, just beginning their meals.

"It wasn't noted on the booking, madam." The hostess looked close to tears.

"Well, it should have been. I made a point of it on the phone."

"I'm terribly sorry, madam."

Teddy took her arm. "It's all right, luv."

"No, it's not all right." Quinn turned back to the frightened girl. "My husband is your newly elected MP. We eat here frequently. We have guests tonight."

"I *am* sorry, madam," the girl repeated. "Someone must have mixed up the bookings."

"It's not a problem, luv—really," Teddy said. "Plenty of other tables."

"But I asked for the *round* table." Quinn's face was flushed. "And I made the booking a week ago. You'll just have to do something."

"I don't know what can be done at this point, madam. We can hardly ask—"

Her words were cut short by the arrival of Yvie Innes, who smiled pleasantly. "Now, what's this all about?"

Quinn had started to tell her story again when the older woman, Mrs. Jamieson, put her arm around Quinn's shoulders. "It's not important, dear."

"It's the principle."

"There's really no problem," agreed Mr. Jamieson. "We're happy to sit anywhere."

"You see, Quinn?" said Teddy. "Everything will be fine." He turned to Yvie Innes. "Sorry for the disturbance. We'll take that nice table by the window."

Yvie grabbed menus. "Sorted, then? All hearts still beating?"

As they made their way to the new table, Teddy spotted us. "Hullo, Tom, Kate. Sorry for the . . . mix-up." He shrugged.

Quinn managed a tiny smile.

"Anyway," Teddy said, "I'd like you to meet our good friends, Richard and Clare Jamieson."

We both stood, and Tom held out his hand. "We met briefly at the gala."

"Yes, I remember," said Richard Jamieson. "The policeman from Suffolk."

"And your very charming wife," said Clare Jamieson, smiling. "What beautiful blue eyes you have, dear." She reached out and touched my hair. "Has anyone ever said you look like Charlize Theron? When her hair was dark, of course." She went on before I could answer. "This whole thing has been a terrible shock. I always liked Gideon Littlejohn."

"I'm sure we all did," agreed her husband.

Yvie Innes stood, waiting, with the menus in her hand.

"Don't let us delay your dinner," Tom said. "Lovely to see you all."

Yvie led them to a table on the far side of the restaurant.

"Now that's interesting," Tom said when we were alone.

"What's interesting?"

"Quinn Pearce accused her father of throwing his weight around, but she doesn't mind throwing her own around, does she? All seven and a half stone of her."

Chapter Nineteen

Thursday, January 9

I was still thinking about Quinn Pearce the next morning at breakfast. "I don't really get her at all," I told Tom. He'd finished his breakfast and was checking his phone for messages. "When you first meet her, she seems sort of passive, almost fragile. Like a sharp breeze would knock her over. Maybe it's because she's so thin. But when you go deeper, you realize she's got a core of steel. I think she's the one who runs that household."

"I know what you mean. I get the impression Teddy would do just about anything to please her—including backing down when they disagree." He looked at his phone screen. "It's Okoje. I've been waiting for this." Tom scanned the message. "He'd like us to stop at the police enquiry office this morning. I'm going to be there most of the day, but he'd really like you to have a look at that museum floor plan. Any reason why you can't?"

"None at all. I'd planned to stop by the museum sometime today to visit the Romani exhibit. And I'm hoping to speak with Maggie Hughes again. She's been doing some research into the Squires clan. But I don't have any fixed appointments."

Tom tapped in a message. "All set. I told him we'd be there in about twenty minutes."

When we arrived at the policy enquiry office, one of the community support officers showed us into the conference room, where DCI

Okoje and DS Varma were studying three large pieces of paper, each representing one of the upper floors of the museum. Small squares of paper had been tacked onto the floor plans. On each was written a name.

"This is the floor we're most interested in." DCI Okoje stabbed his forefinger on the first-floor area where the mechanical clock was on display. "We know the shot was fired from here. According to forensics, the shooter would have been standing near the railing overlooking the ground floor."

I mentally shuddered, realizing that I'd stood in that exact spot just minutes before the mechanical clock demonstration. Had I seen anyone? Heard anything? I leaned closer to the floor plan and saw a small paper square with my name on it.

"Is that about where you were standing when the demonstration began?" Okoje asked.

"Yes, I think so. Quinn Pearce and the Jamiesons were in front of me, on the right. A woman with a child stood next to them. Oh, and two men—one short, the other tall with a red face."

"Sounds like Eddie Smith," said DS Varma. "I interviewed him myself. He runs Fire Flies, the outdoor gear and sporting-goods shop in town. He was there with his store manager. Neither of them saw a thing."

I was still studying the floor plan. "You've placed Dr. Hawksworthy and Isla Ferris on either side of the clock." I straightened.

"That's where they said they were just before the shot was fired," Varma said.

"But that's not right. I mean, they *were* there, but when the mechanical figures actually began their progression, they moved away into the crowd."

Okoje handed me a pencil. "Mark an X on the plan where you think they were."

"I don't know exactly. Everyone was watching the clock. But I know Dr. Hawksworthy moved this way and Isla that way." I drew two small arrows from the original squares of paper toward the edges of the crowd on the left and right respectively.

I looked at the layout again. Something else wasn't right, but I couldn't think what it was. Were the squares of paper too close together, or was it something else? "I'm sorry," I told Okoje. "I wish I could be more helpful."

"You've done fine," Okoje said. "But if you think of anything—"

I smiled at him. "I'll let you know."

* * *

The Museum of Devon Life was literally jumping. A group of what looked like twelve- or thirteen-year-olds were on a field trip—the girls looking years older in the latest gear and makeup; the boys struggling to control their long limbs and clownishly oversized feet. Having raised two teenagers, I remembered those days—the moodiness, the concern about body image, the peer pressure.

A group of boys lurched past me, nearly knocking me off balance.

"Sorry, miss," said one of the boys, then to the culprit, "Mind where yer goin', tosser."

They careened off.

Isla Ferris appeared. "Sorry, Kate. We've got the lower sixth formers from St. Andrew's in Totnes today. They're headed out soon, thank goodness."

"Tom and I do plan to attend the program tonight. I thought I'd prepare by having a look at the Romani and Travellers exhibit. You're a wonderful guide, but if you're busy, I can wander through on my own."

"Today's perfect." She looked delighted. "I'm glad you're coming tonight. Our speakers are two of the most prominent Romani leaders in the West Country. You'll have a chance to ask questions."

"We're looking forward to it."

I followed her up the staircase to the first floor, where a large space was labeled *Gypsies, Romanies & Travellers: Devon's Oldest Cultural Minorities.* The centerpiece of the exhibit was a colorful wooden caravan, perhaps sixteen feet long, painted red with lavish detailing and gold trim. "It's beautiful," I said. "Yvie Innes at the Crown told me they're called vardos."

"The best of the surviving examples date from the late-nineteenth and early-twentieth centuries—what the Romanichals affectionately call 'the wagon time.'" Isla directed my attention to a poster showing the various configurations. "Ours is a Reading vardo, which refers to the shape, like a miniature train car, and the maker, Dunton & Sons of Reading. The interior is quite spacious. Take a look. I think you'll be impressed."

What impressed me was Isla's knowledge. I climbed the access stairs and peered inside the vardo. At the rear was a built-in box bed, lavishly made with lace-trimmed sheets and a colorful quilt. Windows were hung with rich red velvet panels trimmed with gold fringe. Along the right side were benches with built-in storage, several wall-hung cupboards, and an armoire of carved wood, the designs accented with more gold paint. The left side of the wagon had been fitted with a vented stove, above which, on wooden shelving, stood a collection of colorful Gaudy Welsh pottery. "That must be the teapot Dr. Hawksworthy mentioned," I said, indicating a particularly attractive example. "He's right. It's very like the one Gideon Littlejohn found with the dress."

"Every aspect of the vardo was intended to showcase the wealth of the owner, and thus his status. The gilding you see, inside and outside, was applied simply for the sake of opulence and beauty."

"You must feel privileged to own such a fine example."

Isla nodded her agreement. "Most surviving vardos, the authentic ones, reside in museums or private collections. We're fortunate to have this one at all, because traditionally, when the owner died, the vardo and all the deceased's personal possessions, even valuable objects like china and jewelry, were burned."

"Interesting, then, that the collection of objects Littlejohn found in the trunk seems to have a Romani connection. And I'm still trying to figure out what they had to do with a lacemaker."

"I agree. It doesn't make sense. The Dartmoor clans didn't mix with the settled population—at least not socially. I wish I could help."

"I hope to speak with the research librarian at the library later today. She's been collecting information for me about the Romani camps on Dartmoor."

"Maggie Hughes." Isla rolled her eyes. "Don't believe everything she says."

The comment was so unexpected, I spoke before my brain kicked in. "But didn't she help you last year? Julia Kelly said something about a medieval document that proved to be a fake?"

"*Helped?*" Twin red blotches bloomed on Isla's cheeks. "She was *lucky*. All right, there were discrepancies, but Hugo would have found them. Maggie has no idea how busy he is, how many projects he juggles every day—keeping the board happy, managing the funds, creating publicity"—she rolled her hand—"overseeing the displays, applying for grants, conducting research. No one can do everything at once." She took a breath.

"Of course not," I said, before she could continue. "I didn't mean to imply—"

"No." She held up both hands. "My fault. It's just that woman gets right up my nose. Implying that Hugo was *lacking* in some way. How dare she, a village librarian, criticize someone with an academic record like Hugo's?"

I couldn't think of a single thing to say.

"I'm sorry," Isla said. "I must get back to my office. Feel free to wander around."

I watched her march off. Isla definitely had a trigger, and I'd just pulled it.

* * *

"I was hoping you'd stop by today." Maggie Hughes placed the stack of books she'd been carrying on a rolling cart. "I'm sorry, Kate. I couldn't find any information about the graves at Widdecombe Throop. I'm still looking. And I wasn't able to learn anything at all about William Tucker in the census records. There were lots of Tuckers in England, but none with a birth year of 1885 or 1886 *and* a mother named Sally. That doesn't mean he isn't there. Lots of people lied about their pasts for lots of reasons. Some simply didn't want to be counted."

"I know what you mean. Every time the census taker came round, my great-grandmother shaved a couple of years off her age."

Maggie laughed. "Good for her. I did find something you'll be interested in, though. Come. I'll show you."

I followed her through the stacks to the same conference room we'd used earlier. She strode ahead, excited by what she'd found.

"I should apologize," I said as Maggie booted up her computer. "Julia Kelly at the museum told me you spotted anachronisms in a forged medieval commentary. I'm afraid I mentioned it to Isla Hughes."

"Yes, I see." Maggie gray eyes looked amused. "Then you'll know I'm not her favorite person. Not that I mind. She's completely obsessed with the museum—or should I say with the museum director?" She gave me a wry smile. "What was I meant to do when the Bede commentary was an obvious forgery? Let it go for the sake of appearances? I couldn't do that."

"Of course you couldn't." I was interested to hear Maggie's version of the incident. "Why hadn't Hugo caught the anachronisms himself?"

"Why indeed? It wasn't even a sophisticated forgery. All I saw were the two pages on exhibit, and there they were—words invented by Shakespeare nine hundred years after Bede's death. I spotted them because I'd done my thesis on the words Shakespeare coined and their likely etymology."

"To be fair, Hugo isn't a Shakespearean scholar."

"No." Her mouth compressed in a disapproving line. "Neither am I. The point is, Kate, he didn't check. He didn't call in experts on medieval paleography, which he should have done. He *wanted* the manuscript to be real, so that's how he presented it to the museum board. They went along with it because Hugo's supposed to know these things."

"How did Hugo take it?"

"Embarrassed—chagrined. That's the kind of miscalculation that could have marred his professional reputation. Nobody wanted that, least of all me, so we kept it private. We're still keeping it private." Maggie tapped a few keys on the computer. "I will say Hugo owned his mistake right away. Isla's the problem. She thinks I'm waiting for an opportunity to damage Hugo's reputation. I assure you, I'm not."

"But the forgery still troubles you."

"Of course." Her computer screen lit up. "Anyone can make a mistake, but I think Hugo's eagerness to make a name for himself clouded his judgment. I just hope he's learned his lesson." She tapped a few more keys and pulled up an old photograph in black and white—a group of dark-haired men rounding up ponies. The men wore what looked like woolen trousers and jackets. Most wore flat caps. Some had scarves tied around their necks. The ponies had compact, sturdy bodies with broad chests and small, neat heads.

"Are the men Romanies?" I asked.

"That's right. I found the photograph in a news article on an upcoming horse auction near Totnes in September of 1881. Finding reliable sources on Romani culture in Devon isn't easy. They avoided scrutiny, a tendency shaped by centuries of racism and persecution. They left few written records. What has been written by outsiders is often filled with exaggeration, stereotypes, romanticism, and prejudice. Photographs are often the best source of history—moments in time, captured forever." Maggie touched my arm. "Don't look now. We're being observed."

A small boy peered at us through the glass, made a face, and ducked below the half-wall.

"Ignore him, little monkey." She pulled up another photograph. "Most of the camps in Devon were near Teignmouth or Plymouth, but in the 1880s there were several private landowners on Dartmoor who allowed Romanichals to camp on their land in spring in exchange for help with the livestock and the Dartmoor pony herds—surveying the population and checking the ponies for injuries or diseases they might have picked up over the winter."

"So they arrived in spring and stayed until when?"

"Autumn. After the Drift, they were gone."

"The Drift?"

"For generations, the Dartmoor ponies have been rounded up in an annual autumn event known as the Drift. New foals are claimed by their owners. Some are branded and returned to the moor. Others are auctioned off. The Drift has always been a social event as much as a commercial one, but animal-rights organizations have long argued that the experience is traumatic for the wild ponies, some of whom are young and have been forcibly separated from their mothers. It probably is. They've also worried that buyers aren't properly vetted, and they've been concerned about overbreeding. Now the yearly auction is carefully monitored, with a focus on the well-being of the animals. My point is the Romani men would help with the Drift and then move on until the following spring."

Maggie clicked again, and the photo on the computer screen changed to what looked like a family portrait taken outside a vardo similar to the one I'd seen in the museum. A group of individuals, perhaps twelve in all—men, women, and children—surrounded an imposing-looking elderly woman sitting on the wagon's footboard, her booted feet on the shafts. She was wearing a dark mutton-sleeve dress and what looked like a man's porkpie hat. Bracelets, probably gold, encircled her wrists. And she had on some sort of necklace. It was hard to see the details.

"This is the prize, Kate—an actual photograph of the Squires family. Their camp was on land near Hexworthy, along the banks of the Dart. That's Queenie, the matriarch, in the middle—a colorful character by all accounts. You probably know the village tearoom was named after her. I'm pretty excited to have found the photo, which is rare. It took some digging in the archives."

Words printed in white ink along the bottom of the photo read *August 1884*. "Yvie Innes at the Crown told me a little about Queenie Squires," I said. The photo was grainy, but it would have been hard to miss the expression on the old lady's face—stern, proud of her clan, secure in her place in the family. "Was her husband gone by this time?"

"Long gone. He died in a farm accident in the 1820s, and Queenie took over as leader of the clan. Unusual for a woman, but I suppose it speaks to the force of her personality. Before her husband died, she'd produced a daughter and a son. By the time this photograph was taken, Queenie had seven grandchildren and four great-grandchildren. Seems only a part of the family was present that day. The names are on the reverse side." She zoomed in a little. "That's Queenie in the middle, the old woman. The man on her right is her son Leverin and his wife Daisy. Their son, Tawno, is in front with his wife, Cleopatra, and their three children."

Tawno Squires was a muscular man, perhaps thirty-something, with the thick neck and huge arms of someone used to physical labor. A small boy stood next to him, clasping his leg. His wife held an infant wrapped in a shawl. Next to her was a girl of perhaps ten or eleven.

"On the left are Queenie's daughter, Naomi, and her husband, Elias Heron," Maggie said. "The good-looking young man sitting on the wagon tongue is their son, Luke."

Young Luke Heron stared directly into the camera, his regular features, thick black hair, and piercing light eyes visible even in the poor-quality image.

"The eyes grab you, don't they?" Maggie said. "Light eyes were an unusual feature among the Romanichals but not unknown."

"Where was the rest of the family?"

"I don't know. A few of the grandsons may have been out working. It's interesting that Naomi and her husband are there. Romani women typically joined their husband's family, so maybe they were visiting. Or maybe Naomi stayed with her mother because of her advanced age." Maggie pushed her glasses farther up on her nose. "Are you and your husband planning to attend the program at the museum tonight? I've heard the speakers before. Powerful."

"Wouldn't miss it." I looked up from the monitor. "Do you know where the Squires family camped?"

"Sure. I'll pull up the online Ordnance Survey." While she was doing that, she continued speaking. "As I said, Queenie Squires was a fascinating character—something of a legend in Devon. She lived well into her eighties and ruled her clan with an iron fist. She had high standards and expected her sons and grandsons and their wives to maintain those standards—honesty, order, cleanliness, respect for the past, respect for the land and the animals."

Outside the conference room, the little boy was making faces again, crossing his eyes as he pulled at the corners of his mouth and stuck out his tongue.

"That's Jack Hedge." Maggie stuck her own tongue out at the boy. "Too much energy for one little body. A bright boy. His mum's a doctoral student, so they come here a couple of afternoons a week so she can do research." She tapped the online map with a fingernail. "There—see that large open area just west of the Dart tributary? That's approximately where the Squires family camped every year."

"Could you zoom out a little?" I asked. "Interesting. The camp isn't far from the old village of Widdecombe Throop."

"Yes. Submerged now in that reservoir—the blue shaded area there. The owner of the land thereabouts was Sir Henry Merivale, one of the wealthiest Dartmoor landowners at the time—excepting the Crown, of course. He had a large estate near Widdecombe Throop—Merivale House."

I thought of the gorgeous red silk dress I'd just seen. If Nancy Thorne's sister, Sally, made dresses for wealthy local women, she might very well have sewn for the Merivales. They would have been thrilled with a dressmaker trained in the finest French techniques. "Merivale House is underwater too, I suppose."

"No, actually, it's not. Run-down a bit now—well, quite a bit if I'm honest. Lady Helen Merivale still lives there. Heaven knows what will happen to the house when she dies. She offers tours these days to bring in a little extra income."

"Oh? When are the tours?" I didn't want to get my hopes up, but if Lady Helen Merivale was anything like my friend, Lady Barbara Finchley-fforde, she might have a keen interest in her family's history. And she might remember hearing about a dressmaker named Sally Tucker. She might even have been the woman who donated the red silk dress.

"There's a Merivale House brochure in the lobby. Ask the librarian on duty."

Outside the conference room, Jack Hedge was bouncing up and down like a jack-in-the-box. A young woman, his mother, I presumed, finally noticed. She rushed over, grabbed him by the arm, and led him away.

Good luck, Mom.
On my way out, I picked up a brochure for Merivale House.
In the car, I phoned Tom's mobile and left a message:

Remember, tonight's the program at the museum, 7pm. Free for a road trip tomorrow? I may finally have a lead on the dress.

Chapter Twenty

The crowd that had gathered for the museum's January program was impressive for a small village—fifty or so people, including a few older children. We met in the Romani exhibit room, where several freestanding displays had been moved to make room for folding chairs. Hawksworthy and Isla Ferris were there, of course. So were Julia Kelly and Maggie Hughes from the library.

"Kate." Maggie waved at us. She'd saved two seats, which was a good thing, because most had already been taken.

"Thanks, Maggie. This is my husband, Tom."

They shook hands. "We really appreciate your help with research," he said. "And thanks for saving us seats. We should have started out earlier."

It was a few minutes before seven. The speakers, a man and a woman, sat on high stools at the front. The man, perhaps sixty, looked like a university lecturer—tall and slightly stooped with thinning gray hair and a pair of wire-rimmed spectacles. He was dressed conservatively in tailored trousers and a blue V-neck sweater over a white shirt. The woman was probably a little younger. Fifties, maybe—short and compact with iron-gray hair pulled back into a thick ponytail that fell to her waist. Her high coloring, sparkling eyes, and a wide, white-toothed smile gave the impression of robust health and a good nature. She was dressed in a dark-purple cardigan over a printed jersey dress that reached almost to the floor.

Hugo Hawksworthy took the microphone. "Welcome, everyone, to January's program on Romani culture in Southwest England. I'm

Dr. Hugo Hawksworthy, director of the Museum of Devon Life. We are privileged tonight to welcome back two of our West Country Romanichal leaders. Dr. Bob Smith is an author and retired professor of Romani studies at Christ's College, Cambridge. He's an active member of Friends, Families and Travellers, a national charity; the Gypsy Lore Society; and RTFHS, the Romany & Traveller Family History Society. Dr. Smith is joined by Lula Boswell-Cooper, an internationally known advocate for human rights and a tireless worker for improving educational opportunities for Gypsies, Roma, and Travellers across the British Isles. Ms. Boswell-Cooper works closely with the National Federation of Gypsy Liaison Groups as well as the Dorset-based charity and advocacy group Kushti Bok. Our speakers tonight are going to talk about the most important issues currently facing the Romani and Traveller communities. After that, they'll take questions. Please make them welcome."

The audience clapped enthusiastically.

Dr. Smith stood and took the microphone. "Evening, folks. Lula and I are glad to be with you again. At our last visit in October, we focused on the history of the Romani peoples and the persecutions in medieval Europe and, later, under the Nazi regime. Tonight, as Dr. Hawksworthy told you—"

I watched as the two Rominchal leaders took turns speaking. The presentations were interesting, informative, and disturbingly clear. Lula Boswell-Cooper spoke about a recent report by the UK's Equality and Human Rights Commission, documenting the failure of the educational system in the UK to meet the needs of children in the Gypsy, Roma, and Traveller communities. She struck me as a deeply competent person, sure of her facts and brave enough to tell it like it is. Even though she followed the bleak report with a summary of efforts underway on both local and national levels to bend the curve, I asked myself if those efforts would be enough. The problems were so massive. And yet her passion was undiminished. She was doing what she could, confident that others would pick up the banner in the future.

Dr. Smith was soft-spoken, with a charming air of self-deprecation. I noticed the *OBE* after his name on the museum brochure, but he hadn't mentioned it. His presentation concerned the passage of new laws restricting the rights of Gypsies and Travellers to follow their traditional way of life. "Our culture has been criminalized," he said, "and our crime is our itinerant way of life. Most of our families travel for work in trailers, chalets, or wagons. We are a mobile workforce, and yet public lands are now off-limits, and legal sites are becoming fewer each year." Dr. Smith went on to identify the needs of the GRT community—access to health care and education, stabling for their horses, improved utilities, and green spaces for their children to play in. "What we're asking for is the right to exist, to honor our culture, and to raise our families."

When they opened the floor to questions, my hand was the first to go up.

"In the US," I said, "the term *Gypsy* is considered a racial slur. Can you explain why that isn't so in the UK?"

Dr. Smith smiled. "Well, now, the question isn't an easy one to answer, but I'll try to keep it simple. The umbrella term GRT—Gypsies, Roma, and Travellers—includes many individual communities with distinct ethnicities. And we don't agree on everything. English Gypsies—the Romanichals—are people of Romani origin who have been present in England since the end of the fifteenth century. We bear the name Gypsy as a badge of honor. After all, our ancestors were persecuted and murdered for the name. We're proud to own it.

"The Roma are a distinct ethnic group. They migrated to England and America from Eastern and Central Europe during the large waves of immigration beginning around 1880. They're offended by the term *Gypsy*. They see it as a racial slur, and they also resent being called *Travellers*, because they typically don't travel.

"The Travellers, now, were traditionally people of Irish origins, although several groups today claim that name—including Showmen and even some hippies."

When another hand didn't immediately go up, I said, "Could you explain a little about Romani funerals—why the deceased's possessions were burned?"

"I can speak to that." Ms. Boswell-Cooper took the microphone. "Traditionally, there was no such thing as inheritance among the

Romanichals. Anything still owned at death would be burnt—however valuable. To keep anything was considered *bokky*—cursed. Any intergenerational transfer of wealth or goods had to occur during life. More recently, during the last sixty years or so, land ownership has complicated the matter. Some families have found a solution by setting up family trusts."

I had more questions—lots of them—but decided to see if others would step in. They did, asking all sorts of questions about the past and the present, but none had a direct bearing on our research. By eight thirty, just about everyone had drifted away.

Tom and I introduced ourselves to the speakers. "Thank you both," Tom said. "Your talk was eye-opening."

"That's why we do events like this." Ms. Boswell-Cooper's face lit up in a smile. "We feel it's our responsibility."

"We understand from Dr. Hawksworthy," Dr. Smith said, "that you're conducting research into the origins of a Victorian dress—a dress that may have connections with the Squires family."

"That's right," I said. "Do you know anything about the Squires and the Heron families on Dartmoor?"

"Everyone knows about Queenie Squires," Ms. Boswell-Cooper said. "A legend in her own day. I've heard the surname Heron, but it's less common. Probably Welsh. Can you add anything, Bob?"

Dr. Smith appeared to be deep in thought. "Heron, did you say?" He looked up. "I have heard that name—and fairly recently. At the Romany & Traveller Family History Society, we help people trace their roots. It must have been about a year ago that someone contacted us, asking about a Luke Heron in the 1891 Devon census."

Luke Heron—the man in the photograph, the one with the mesmerizing eyes. I hadn't even told Tom about him yet. "Who was asking?"

"I don't remember. It was an online contact. A man—I'm sure of that. We got the impression he wasn't a Romani himself."

"What did you tell him?"

"We couldn't tell him anything. There is no Luke Heron in the 1891 Devon census. Perhaps he died."

The thought came unexpectedly. *Or was murdered.*

Chapter Twenty-One

Friday, January 10
Dartmoor National Park

Tom and I awoke to a cold, crisp, and unexpectedly sunny day. The night before, as we lay in bed, discussing what we'd learned about the Romanichals in Devon, I'd explained about the photograph of the Squires and Heron families Maggie Hughes had found in the archives.

Tom was still thinking about it when, after a late breakfast at the Crown, we set off for Merivale House. "The Luke Heron in that photograph has to be the same Luke Heron someone was hoping to trace through the Romany & Traveller Family History Society—Queenie Squire's grandson. Ms. Boswell-Cooper said Heron wasn't a common Romani name in Devon." Tom turned onto the road toward Hexworthy.

"And I think the person who contacted the RTFHS must have been Gideon Littlejohn."

"I agree." Tom pulled to the right, overtaking a slow-moving caravan. "He was probably trying to figure out himself why the bloodstained dress was packed up with items suggesting a Romani connection. He must have made the same link we did, between Widdecombe Throop and the Squires family who camped on Merivale land. Funny he didn't mention it."

"That reminds me. There's something *I* haven't mentioned—something Julia Kelly told me. I meant to tell you right away, but that fuss Quinn Pearce made at the Crown that night put it out of my mind. It's about Dr. Hawksworthy. I don't think it's related, but it is odd." I told Tom the story of the medieval commentary that turned out to be a fake. "Maggie Hughes from the library was the one who caught the discrepancies, and she's no medieval scholar. So why did Hugo, with all his training, miss them? We know he's eager to make a name for himself. Julia said he wanted the commentary to be legitimate, so he didn't follow normal procedures and brushed aside any suspicions he may have had."

"You mean like he wants the bloodstained dress to belong to a murderous Victorian lacemaker."

"Exactly, and that means we need to follow every lead, even if it means *not* completing the assignment to the client's satisfaction."

"That's the problem with private investigation." Tom pulled down his visor. "Police are successful when they establish the truth. Nash & Holmes is successful—at least financially—when they complete the job to the client's satisfaction."

"And if the dress isn't authentic, Hugo won't be satisfied."

We drove in silence for a few minutes.

"Tell me about Merivale House," Tom said, changing the subject. "What are we to expect?"

I read the description on the brochure aloud:

> *Merivale House, a historic five-bedroom Grade II-listed residence dating back to 1109, has changed hands only twice in the last 500 years. Set in fifty-three acres of woods and pastureland, the stone house and traditional buildings are arranged around a central quadrangle. Lady Helen Merivale, the current owner, welcomes visitors on Wednesdays and Fridays from one to three p.m. Tours begin on the hour and cover three reception rooms, the great hall, the kitchen, and three bedrooms on the ground floor, plus several outbuildings, a small chapel, and an interesting stone-and-timber barn. Admission: £20 adults; £12 children under 12 when accompanied by an adult. No appointment necessary.*

Twice before in the UK I'd encountered once-grand houses that had fallen into decrepitude. And I'd watched a documentary the previous autumn about a so-called "urban explorer" who'd filmed inside an enormous nineteenth-century mansion in the Welsh countryside. The old house with its faded chandeliers, spiraling staircases, and stunning stained-glass windows had been abandoned by its owners, the beds still draped in insect-infested linens and pillows.

"Old buildings are horribly expensive to maintain," I said. "I understand that, but it's a shame to lose them. They're part of our history."

"The top layer of history," Tom said. "With a few notable exceptions, the houses of ordinary people don't usually qualify for public funds."

"And their clothing wasn't usually saved for posterity—not like that red silk ball gown." I thought about the Nancy Thorne dress. Why had an ordinary workingwoman's dress, stained with blood and surely insignificant in the eyes of the world, been so carefully preserved? Whose blood was it? No one, not even Nancy Thorne herself, it seemed, knew what had really happened that night in September 1885. Had she truly no memory of the event, or had she taken her secrets to the grave? As much as I wanted to know the answer, solving that mystery wasn't in our remit. All we were expected to do was prove beyond a reasonable doubt that the dress was hers and then determine if the bloodstains contained enough genetic material to test. That part of our assignment was Tom's responsibility—finding a private lab that would agree to test the blood. Assuming the museum would allow a portion of the fabric to be removed.

Our car climbed through the high moorland, where a few stunted, wind-blasted trees punctuated the landscape. Soon Tom downshifted as the road descended again toward a crazy quilt of small, irregular fields separated by rough stone walls. Occasionally, in the folds of the land, we saw ominous pools of dark, peaty water.

We almost missed the road to Merivale House, as the sign was nearly overgrown with tall grass. The narrow roadway, hugged on both sides by high hedges and barely wide enough for a single vehicle, bent sharply to the left before opening up into a large gravel courtyard.

Before us rose the blunt stone face of a high wall, which merged into what looked like a barn with a pitched roof and narrow glazed windows. Parking under a leafless oak, we grabbed our jackets and walked through a stone archway into an inner courtyard.

There the stern facade of Merivale House met us. This was no posh country house in the home counties but a working farm constructed of stone painstakingly cleared from the land. We rang the bell and waited. And waited. We were beginning to think Lady Helen wasn't home when we heard the scuttling of a key in a lock. The door opened.

"Yes?" A tall, elderly woman eyed us suspiciously. "What do you want?"

"We're here for the tour," I said. "The brochure said you're open on Fridays between one and three."

"I know what day it is," she snapped. "I haven't gone doolally yet. You'd better come in. I can't afford to heat the entire outdoors." She beckoned us into a dank entryway lit by a pair of wall sconces. "Will you keep your jackets?"

We nodded. It wasn't much warmer inside than out.

Lady Helen Merivale must have been in her mid to late seventies. Her spine was straight and her gray eyes clear, but her hands, gnarled and roped with veins, betrayed her age. She wore a baggy tweed skirt and a pale-blue blouse buttoned to her neck, around which hung a single strand of pearls. Over the blouse, she'd layered a battered wax Barbour, and over that what appeared to be a man's heavy wool jacket with the sleeves rolled up.

Tom pulled out his wallet. "Forty pounds—is that right?"

"For the tour. Refreshments are extra, and the chapel is closed today." Her cut-glass accent was matched by an air of snobbery completely at odds with her grimy fingernails and thrift-store ensemble. She took the bills and shoved them into the pocket of her wool jacket, glaring at us as if daring us to reclaim our money. "Shall we begin?"

Moving farther into the gloom, she began without preamble. "Welcome to Merivale House. I am Lady Helen Merivale, widow of Sir Martin Merivale, the sixteenth owner. In March of 1539, Merivale House was granted by Henry the Eighth to Sir Charles Plympton." She began to reel off what was obviously a memorized presentation. "In 1653, when the Plympton family failed to produce an heir, the property was sold to the Merivales. We've lived here now for three hundred and seventy years."

It had been a few more than 370 years, but she apparently hadn't gotten around to updating her spiel.

We followed her into a long narrow room with walls of dressed stone and an intricately beamed ceiling badly in need of restoration. The room smelled musty—not surprising, as the stone walls were stained by the rising damp.

"This is the great hall," she said, "the oldest part of the house, built by the Benedictines in 1412."

The room was empty except for a long table of rough wood and a carved-wood sideboard of dark oak that looked Jacobean. If it was, it belonged in a museum, even in its present condition. At some time in the past, the beamed ceiling had leaked, allowing rain to pool on the carved oaken top and spill down the front, causing the old wood to swell and the old wax finish to whiten. This valuable antique needed saving. So did its owner.

The great hall was as cold as a refrigerator. I turned up my jacket collar and slipped my numb fingers into my pockets.

Next, along a dark corridor, Lady Merivale showed us the drawing room with its ruined fireplace, pitted plaster walls, and the remnants of what appeared to be Chinese silk wall coverings. The portrait of a handsome woman with dark curls hung over the mantelpiece.

"It must be a full-time job restoring a place like this," Tom said.

I wondered if Lady Helen would take offense, but she didn't. "The main thing is to keep the water out and make sure the electrics don't catch fire," she said, and then seeing the looks on our faces, she added, "Peeling wallpaper *isn't* important."

"No, of course not," Tom said. "But controlling the dampness might help."

"Houses are *supposed* to be damp." Lady Helen looked at us as if we'd just crawled out of some primordial slime. "People today overheat their houses. Weakens the structure. Fabrics crumble, wood deteriorates. My husband never lit fires in rooms that weren't occupied."

"Who's the lady in the portrait?" I asked, deciding we needed a change of subject. Despite the portrait's present condition, I could see the woman had been quite lovely.

"That's Lucy, wife of old Lord Merivale. She died in childbirth in the summer of 1885. Four months later her husband married again. His second wife, Esmeralda, was my husband's great-great-grandmother."

I looked at Tom. This was getting us nowhere. We needed to get her off-script.

When she took a breath, Tom asked, "Did you say there were refreshments?"

Lady Helen considered our request. "End of the tour. Tea and biscuits. Ten pounds each."

The price was outrageous, but I supposed we could consider it charity. "That sounds lovely. Just what we need on a cold January day." I could only hope there was a room in the old house where heating wasn't considered a danger to health.

The rest of the tour took less than twenty minutes. Each room was like the last—literally falling into ruin. Everywhere were signs that furniture and framed pictures had been removed. Had they been sold for cash or snatched up by other family members?

We ended our tour not in the cavernous original kitchen, obviously no longer in use, but in a side room fitted with simple furniture, including a sofa that might have doubled as a bed, an oak desk, a microwave oven, an electric kettle, and a deal table with three mismatched chairs. A two-bar heater produced just enough warmth to make the room habitable. Lady Helen was camping out in her own home.

She switched on the kettle. From a high, painted shelf, she lifted a tin decorated with the image of young Queen Elizabeth. Inside were cookies—biscuits in the UK. I hadn't noticed the small fridge shoved beside the desk. She pulled out a glass pitcher half filled with milk. She didn't offer sugar, and I decided not to ask. When the kettle squealed, she poured steaming water through a sieve strainer into three teacups.

I hoped they were clean. If there was a sink somewhere for washing up, it wasn't in this room.

"Merivale House was used in the 1960s for the filming of a miniseries, *Lorna Doone*." Lady Helen handed Tom a china teacup decorated with what appeared to be the family crest. "My husband was alive then. I'm constantly hounded by major film producers, but they never offer enough to make it worth my while." She handed me a cup. "The inconvenience, you know."

I thought this highly unlikely but had no intention of saying so. Her attitude toward us had warmed a bit. Maybe it was the extra twenty pounds. Time to get to the point.

"I learned recently that your husband's great-great-grandfather allowed a Romani family to set up camp on his land in exchange for seasonal work. The family of Queenie Squires, the one they named the tea shop after."

"That is correct."

"Do you know where the pitch was located?" I cradled the warm cup in my hands and tried not to shiver.

"The Gypsy Field, of course." She leaned toward the window sash and pulled back the curtains. "Do you see that stand of trees in the distance?"

I nodded.

"The Gypsy pitch was just this side of it. My husband's father gave that portion of land to the National Trust in the 1950s. There's a public footpath along the River Dart."

"I understand you donated some of your family treasures to the museum in Coombe Mallet," I said. "I saw an extremely beautiful red silk dress which will soon be on display."

"That wasn't me," she said. "My husband's half sister in London donated the dress. She has no real interest in family history. Which is why my husband left Merivale House to me."

Out of love or spite? I wondered.

Tom was pretending an interest in the landscape. I was to take the lead.

"Did the red silk ball gown belong to your great-great-grandmother?"

"Not mine or my husband's," she corrected me. "The dress belonged to Lord Merivale's first wife, Lucy—the one in the portrait. My husband's great-great-grandmother was his second wife, Esmeralda. They married in 1885, when he was forty-four and she was seventeen, just four months after the death of her predecessor. Her husband lavished her with the finest of everything. He even commissioned a local woman to make lace for her wedding gown. Did you know Devon was a center for the lacemaking trade back then?"

I felt a bubble of excitement in my chest. "Do you remember the name of the lacemaker?"

She looked at me as if I was the one who'd gone doolally. "Of course not. Who remembers such things?" She made a small dismissive gesture with her spare hand. "I do remember she was the sister of the seamstress who made the red silk dress. She made all the dresses for the Merivale women—the first and the second wife. They said she was a treasure—trained by a Frenchwoman with arthritic fingers. She couldn't sew any longer but had made gowns for the French nobility."

Finally we were getting some answers. "I believe you're talking about the Thorne sisters from Widdecombe Throop." I sipped my tea, which wasn't bad.

"I'm talking about the French court, dear," she said in the tone one might use with a particularly dim child.

"I mean the lacemaker, Nancy Thorne. The seamstress was her sister, Sally Tucker. Do you know what happened to Esmeralda's wedding dress?"

"Given away, I suppose. Or cut up for christening clothes."

"And the lace?"

"Oh, well." She waved her hand in dismissal. "In the end, they had to import lace from France. A shame."

"Why? What happened?" I tried to tamp down my excitement.

"A scandal. Contract had to be canceled."

"What sort of scandal?"

"My dear." She fixed me with a rather stern look. "This was more than a hundred and thirty years ago. Anyway, I don't know. Some impropriety."

I lifted my cup to examine the crest, a shield of black supported by a pair of winged griffins and emblazoned with three green, sprigged acorns. A helmet at the top was crowned with what appeared to be some sort of plant or flower. Along the bottom, a banner bore a motto: *Nostris Viribus Semper Novis*. "Is this your family crest?" I asked. "Can you tell me what it means?"

Lady Helen's lips parted in a smile, revealing long yellow teeth. "The motto says 'Our strength renews with each generation.'" She waved a hand. "Something like that, anyway. The shield of black means constancy, and the griffins represent courage and vigilance. The acorns refer to independence and self-rule. The fact that they are green means this will always be so."

Looking around the room, I couldn't help feeling pity for this proud woman. Strong she may have been, but the power of her adopted family had seriously waned.

"The trefoil symbol at the top represents past, present, and future," Lady Helen said. "Of course, it's also a nod to Dartmoor, where the yellow trefoil grows everywhere."

I pictured the acorn and the bird's-foot trefoil motifs plaited into the lace collar of Nancy Thorne's dress. The slight pressure of Tom's arm against mine told me he'd recognized the symbols as well.

"Lady Helen," I said, "Tom and I have been hired to investigate the provenance of a dress donated to the Museum of Devon Life. No, not the red silk. This is a calico dress, one that would have been worn by a village woman."

"What does that have to do with me?"

"I'm asking because a collar of exquisite lace, incorporating acorns and the bird's-foot trefoil, your family symbols, was sewn onto this calico dress. We believe the dress belonged to Nancy Thorne, the lacemaker, or possibly her sister, Sally, the seamstress. It was found in a trunk with items suggesting a Romani connection."

"The lacemaker was a Gypsy?" Lady Helen looked skeptical. "That can't be right."

"No, but there was a link. That's what we're trying to determine. Do any family papers from that time still exist?"

"All that was discarded when my husband died. None of anyone's business."

"You said your father-in-law gave the land to the National Trust in the fifties. Was the Squires family still camping there then?"

"Heavens, no. They'd stopped coming long before that. Toward the end of the nineteenth century, I believe."

"Do you know why?"

"Not sure I ever did." She gave me a curious look. "I don't wish to seem rude, but what does this have to do with a calico dress?"

"That's what we'd like to find out." I handed her my card. "If you remember anything, will you contact me?"

She didn't answer. Which told me everything I needed to know.

Chapter Twenty-Two

"Vague memories of a once-glorious past aren't really proof, are they?" We were back in the Range Rover, retracing our route through the high moorland with its austere beauty. "We need something in writing. Like an expense ledger listing the name of the Merivale family's dressmaker and lacemaker."

"If something like that still exists." Tom downshifted as the road rose sharply. "You heard her—all the records were thrown out."

"Or slowly decomposed."

As we traveled higher, the old oaks gave way to broad, rocky moorland. Since arriving more than a week earlier, I'd fallen in love with Dartmoor—with its myths and legends, its ancient ruins and mysterious stone circles. Living in such a remote place wouldn't be to everyone's taste. I could understand how the Merivale women must have longed for the London season with its balls, dinner parties, and charity events. Did they spend the long winter months planning the fashionable new gowns they would wear? I pictured Lord Merivale's first wife trying on the red silk brocade, exulting in the knowledge that she would outshine all the wealthy London matrons.

"We do have Julia Kelly's expert opinion," I said. "She's certain the bloodstained dress and the red silk ball gown were made by the same hand, an exceptionally skilled seamstress living somewhere near Merivale House in the 1880s."

"Sally Tucker."

"And we know that Sally's sister, Nancy Thorne, was a lacemaker, probably hired to make lace for a Merivale wedding, a project canceled because of an impropriety."

"Coming home in the wee hours with your dress soaked in blood could be called an impropriety."

I laughed. "People *will* ask questions, won't they?"

"There would have been all sorts of questions. And rumors. People are curious by nature. When they don't know the facts, they speculate."

"I've been thinking about the timing, Tom." I cast my mind back to the portrait we'd seen in Merivale House. "Julia Kelly told me the red silk dress had been made for a woman who wasn't exactly slim. I remembered that when we saw the portrait of Lord Merivale's first wife, Lucy. She died giving birth in the summer of 1885. Julia said the style of the dress places it somewhere between 1885 and 1888. I'm wondering if Lucy Merivale was pregnant when she wore the dress for the spring season that year. She was probably tight-lacing her corset in order to hide the fact. A very bad idea, in my opinion. Maybe that's why she and the infant both died. She wouldn't necessarily have been full-term."

"An interesting theory."

"And Lord Merivale married his second wife, Esmeralda, just four months later. If Lucy died in, say, July of 1885, the second wedding would have been in November. Which means Nancy Thorne could have been working on the wedding lace in September."

"Yes, I see." Tom turned the wheel, navigating a sharp turn. "That's when the so-called impropriety occurred. Which agrees with the date of the incident described in the documentary— the seventh of September 1885, when Nancy Thorne returned home soaked in blood. And it explains why the Merivale family symbols, the acorn and the bird's-foot trefoil, appear on the lace collar. But what was the collar doing on a calico dress?"

"It's speculation, I know, but I think Nancy Thorne had begun to make the lace for Esmeralda's wedding dress when the horrific events of that night occurred. Even though no body was found, her reputation was damaged. And she'd already put hours and hours into the work."

"And when the contract was canceled?"

"The Merivales probably refused to pay her for her work, so she used the lace she'd already finished to adorn her own dress." I turned toward him in my seat. "That's significant, don't you think? Everyone in the village would have recognized the acorn and bird's-foot trefoil symbols worked into the lace. I think she was making a statement."

"A statement against false accusation."

"She was suspected of murder, Tom—without a body."

"What about all that blood? Whoever wore that dress was involved in something pretty grisly."

I sighed. "I know. Maybe someone threatened her and she injured him while defending herself. Maybe she fought off an attacker and didn't think she'd be believed. Maybe her attacker was Lord Merivale himself. I don't know, but I feel comfortable connecting the lace collar on Nancy Thorne's dress with the Merivale family. And the Merivale family had a Romani clan camping on their land. And the bloodstained dress was found with items that point to a Romani connection. Each of these facts is like a single lace motif. We just don't yet know how they fit together into an overall pattern."

"Or how the dress ended up in the hands of Gideon Littlejohn." Tom reached over and rubbed the back of my neck.

"I am curious about one thing," I said. "How much longer can Lady Helen continue living in that house? Should we do something? Tell someone?"

"Who—the NHS? Age Concern? What would you say? *There's an old lady living alone in a big house*?" Tom raised a skeptical eyebrow. "Lady Helen Merivale looked perfectly healthy to me, and there's nothing wrong with her brain. If she chooses to live in a crumbling stone house, it's her right. Besides, people can't be helped unless they admit they need it. Did she strike you as likely to ask for help?"

"No," I admitted. "Quite the opposite."

On the verges of the lonely road, three or four small, dark ponies, similar to the ones I'd seen in the old photograph, munched on mounds of gorse. In the distance, several sheep grazed, splotches of pink dye on their wooly backs identifying their owner.

"You know I love uncovering facts about history," I said. "It's like solving a puzzle."

"Connecting dots is your gift." He grinned at me. One of them."

"The problem, as you say, is how Gideon Littlejohn ended up with that calico dress. That's the missing link. He bought the trunk containing the dress and the other items from the family of an elderly man somewhere in or near Devon. If Ivor comes up with the old man's name, we might be able to establish a connection between him and the Thornes."

"Then our job is finished. Except for DNA testing. Tomorrow I'm going to phone a private laboratory that's been recommended. I'll need Hawksworthy's permission to allow a portion of the bloodstained fabric to be removed for testing—and they'll have to agree to pay the upcharge for private testing. At least we'll know if the blood is human. At best, they might be able to tell us the blood type and likely origins."

"What if we never do connect the dots between the Nancy Thorne and the elderly man with the trunk? Will it be enough to authenticate the dress for Dr. Hawksworthy?"

"From all we've heard, Hawksworthy is eager to go forward with the dress, evidence or not."

"Yet he's the one who hired Nash & Holmes to investigate. I wonder why, when there was at least a chance we'd discover the dress didn't belong to Nancy Thorne after all?"

"Ask him," Tom said.

"I will, but don't you also want to find out the truth about Nancy Thorne?"

"Oh, so now you *do* want to solve a cold case—one that's probably unsolvable." Tom slowed our speed as a blast of wind buffeted the car. The weather was changing again. "Rumors aside, Nancy Thorne was never arrested. There was no proof she'd done anything wrong. No body turned up. Maybe she really did have some form of amnesia."

"I know. Still . . ." I thought about the forged note calling Nancy Thorne a murderess.

"We weren't hired to solve a cold case, Kate—remember? All we're paid to do is establish the provenance of the dress as far as we're able and see if DNA testing is possible. Then we can go home and start our new life together."

"Oh, that does sound lovely." It did, although leaving Devon with so many unanswered questions wasn't going to be easy. I wanted all those details to form an overall picture. Like the lace—all the tiny motifs connected to form a coherent design. "There is one more angle."

"Oh?"

"A connection between the dress and Littlejohn's death."

"What makes you think there is one?"

"Intuition?" I mentally cringed, knowing how that would sound to a policeman.

"You mean your famous overactive imagination." Tom slowed and pulled the car off the side of the road. Even with the lowering clouds, the view across the moor was incredible. "That's Hound Tor." He pointed to a heavily weathered granite outcropping dusted with snow. "It's supposed to resemble a herd of hounds, peering over the rocks."

"I don't see it."

"I don't either. Uncle Nigel and I used to come here. The remains of a medieval village are just over that hill. Houses, barns, four Dartmoor long houses dating from the thirteenth century."

"You're not suggesting we see it today, I hope." Rain had begun to drizzle down. "We didn't bring the right gear."

"Someday, maybe. I'd like to return."

"Me too." I watched one of the Greyface Dartmoor sheep, toasty in his rain-resistant woolly fleece, grazing in the grass near a stone outcropping. This one had a blue stain on his back. "How do the sheep—and the ponies, for that matter—keep from wandering off and getting lost? I don't see any fences."

"That's an interesting question." Tom loved talking about Dartmoor. "Each herd or group of animals on the moor—sheep, cattle, horses—instinctively knows its own grazing land. Kind of an ancestral or genetic memory. That's the theory, anyway. That's why the farmers always let some of the old animals graze with the youngsters. They know the boundaries."

"Is that true?"

"I've seen it. Uncle Nigel knew a farmer in west Dartmoor who bought a breeding pony from another farmer on the east side of the park. He got the animal home and settled, but in the morning, the pony was gone. He found it back on its own grazing land."

"Back home where it belonged," I said, and then noticed Tom's soft intake of breath. "What is it? What's wrong?"

"*Home.*" He glanced over. "Tell me the truth, Kate. Do you feel at home in England? Really at home, I mean. Will you come to regret your decision to settle here?"

"It's a little late to be asking." I meant it as a joke, but I *had* experienced a moment of hesitation before our wedding—not at the thought of spending my life with Tom but because I knew that, as a policeman, he would be putting himself in harm's way. Before the wedding, I'd been watching my mother unpack her suitcase in the lovely room she'd been given in Finchley Hall. "One day he might not come home," I'd said. "I could lose him—to a drugs dealer or a drunk in a bar. I'm not sure I can live with that."

My mother, who'd had a lifetime of experience with grief, had stopped what she was doing to sit next to me on the bed. "You're not asking the right question, darling. Instead of asking if you can live with him as the wife of a police detective, you should be asking if you can live without him."

"Kate—" I saw concern in Tom's eyes. "I asked if you regret your decision to settle in England, and you made a joke."

"I'm sorry. I was wondering why you're asking that question now."

"Because you've given up a lot—your antiques business, your friends in the States, the ability to see your mother whenever you like. Your home."

"You mean my house." I reached over to kiss him. "Home is where the heart is—and that means wherever you are will always be my home."

My cell phone buzzed. Reluctantly, I pulled it out of my jacket pocket.

"Hey, Ivor. Have you found something?"

"I found the solicitor who handled the sale of the household Littlejohn purchased. His name isn't Rutledge. It's Anton Rutley. He lives in Tedburn St. Mary."

"You brilliant man. How did you find him?"

"Found a listing of auctions in Devon and went through them one by one until I found an auction that offered an entire household of Victorian fittings and fixtures. Single buyer. Six months ago. July."

"Fantastic. Where is Tedburn St. Mary?"

"East of Exeter."

"The final piece of the puzzle. All we have to do is contact—"

"Not so hasty, my girl."

"What do you mean?"

"I spoke with Rutley. He remembers the sale because the man who purchased it—lock, stock, and barrel—dressed in Victorian clothing."

"That *would* get your attention."

"He located the inventory and the bill of sale, signed by Gideon Littlejohn."

"Does the family still live in Tedburn St. Mary?"

"The man's possessions were sold off by a niece who lives in London. She put everything in Rutley's hands. Couldn't take the time herself."

"So what's the problem?"

"The inventory included several hundred items, some large, some small. But listen to this, Kate—there was no trunk; no Victorian dress, bloodstained or otherwise; no Gaudy Welsh teapot; no Gypsy-set ring; and definitely no gold coins."

"What do you mean?" I was struggling to make sense of his words.

"It means, my girl, that wherever Littlejohn got the trunk, it wasn't part of the household he purchased at auction."

"He's sure about it, this Rutley person?"

"Positive."

"But . . ." I couldn't complete the sentence. If the trunk, the dress, and the Romani items hadn't been purchased at auction, where had they come from? "Okay. Thanks, Ivor. It wasn't the news I was expecting, but it'll save us some useless effort."

Ivor and I spoke for a few more minutes before we disconnected.

"What was that all about?" Tom asked when we'd rung off. "What useless effort?"

I told him.

"Well, that's just brilliant, isn't it?" The rain was now drumming down. Tom turned up the wipers. "So where did Littlejohn get the dress? And more importantly, why did he lie about it?"

"I think it's time to call Beryl Grey. Maybe she can steer us in the right direction."

Chapter Twenty-Three

My first three phone calls to Gideon Littlejohn's housekeeper went unanswered. On my fourth attempt, I left a cheery message for Beryl Grey, telling her I would keep calling until I reached her. I wanted her to know I wasn't giving up.

It seemed to do the trick, because that evening, just as Tom and I were sitting down for dinner at the Crown, she returned my call.

"I didn't see your messages," she said, although I felt pretty sure she was lying. "I seldom use my mobile except to check on my husband. So many scams out there."

"Of course. I understand." I wanted to stay on her good side. "Are you free to meet tomorrow? Some questions have arisen. You might be able to answer them."

"I very much doubt that."

"You worked for Mr. Littlejohn for—how long was it?"

"Almost a year."

"Well, then, you may know more than you think. I'd be happy to come to your house, by the way. So you wouldn't have to leave your husband."

"*No.*" The sharpness in her voice took me by surprise. I was trying to do her a favor. "Not the house. My husband is . . ." She hesitated, as if searching for the right word. "Well, he's easily distressed, and he's a big man. Strong. I don't mean he would harm either of us," she added quickly, "no, not at all. But he becomes agitated when he doesn't understand what's going on. I will meet you if you insist, but in a public place. Somewhere like Queenies."

"Queenies would be perfect." It sounded like her husband was suffering from Alzheimer's. Leaving him all day to work at the Old Merchant's House must have been a worry. "Are you sure you feel comfortable leaving your husband alone?"

"He'll be fine. He always is in his own house. He knows I'll be back."

We made a date to meet at the tea shop at ten o'clock the following morning.

I returned to our table near the hearth. A log fire was crackling. "It's all set. I'm meeting Beryl Grey tomorrow morning at Queenie's."

"Excellent." Tom craned his neck to see the daily menu written on the chalkboard. "Tonight's special is hunter's chicken with chips and homemade coleslaw."

"I need something lighter—a salad, maybe. All this honeymoon food is going to my waist."

"Your waist is perfect, but I know what you mean. I think I've gained a stone. What will it be, then?"

We ordered—the chicken and chips for Tom, a bowl of butternut squash soup and a salad for me. The waiter brought a jug of cold water, and we ordered a bottle of Chardonnay to share.

A perfect evening. And yet Ivor's news about the auction in Tedburn St. Mary had me feeling gloomy. *Back to square one.* Aloud, I said, "We were counting on that solicitor—Rutley."

"I know." Tom took a long drink of the cold Dartmoor water.

"If the household Littlejohn purchased at auction *didn't* include the trunk with the dress and the collection of Romani items," I said, "it means he lied. People lie to conceal the truth. And that means, whatever the truth is, he didn't want us—or anyone—to know about it."

"Could the solicitor be mistaken? Maybe the family threw in the trunk as an afterthought."

"No such luck. Ivor said the niece who inherited the elderly man's estate is a fashion designer in London. She was in the middle of designing a new collection, so she let her uncle's attorney, Anton Rutley, handle everything. She never even went down for the sale. Hired a removals firm to clear out her uncle's flat. They made a detailed inventory, and the trunk was definitely *not* on the list."

"It's odd," Tom said, pouring us each a glass of wine.

As I took my first sip of Chardonnay, I thought about our meeting with Gideon Littlejohn at the Old Merchant's House. "Remember how insistent Littlejohn was that the trunk not leave his possession?"

"A bit overprotective?"

"Dr. Hawksworthy said the same thing. The trunk was important to him in some way. If he was protecting it, I want to know why. I want to examine that trunk for myself. The crime scene team can't be still processing the house."

"I'll check with Okoje tomorrow." Tom swirled the wine in his glass and took a sip. "Let's think logically. Whoever initially preserved the dress must have known the Thorne sisters. Could Gideon Littlejohn have been related to the Thornes?"

"His sister, Donna, didn't mention it. She insisted she knew nothing about a bloodstained dress."

"Ask her again. People have been known to lie."

"As we've just discovered. I want to know why Littlejohn lied to us. There must be a reason."

Our dinners arrived, and we spent the next thirty minutes enjoying the food and talking about the tasks we needed to complete when we got home. We'd be moving into a lovely Georgian house outside Long Barston. Leasing it, actually. The house was owned by Tom's uncle Nigel, and even though Nigel had made it sound like we were doing him a favor—keeping the house in good nick until he decided whether or not he would sell—we both knew he was delighted to help his favorite nephew. We'd done most of the essential work before the wedding, completing a few simple repairs and combining the furniture already in the house with a few pieces I'd had shipped from Jackson Falls, Ohio. Tom's furniture would remain in the farmhouse he and his first wife, Sarah, had renovated in the village of Saxby St. Clare. Tom's mother would probably live there the rest of her life, causing as much trouble as possible, I had no doubt. But there was much more work ahead for us in Long Barston. Making the house ours. I was looking forward to it.

After dinner, over coffee, Tom said, "We need to regroup. Let's look at your questions again."

I pulled out my notebook. The only question we'd answered definitively was the one about Freya Little. She was dead. If Max Newlin had done as he'd promised, we might still hear from Mercy Abbott, but everything else was proving stubbornly illusive. But had we asked the right questions?

"Tom." I turned to him. "I didn't write it down, but the first question I had was why didn't Nancy's sister go to church that night?"

"Maybe she wasn't religious."

"Ah," I raised a finger. "But we know now she was pregnant. The census records indicate her son was five years old on the fifth of April 1891. That means he was born sometime between July of 1885 and early April of 1886. So if his actual birth date was in late 1885 or early 1886, Sally would have been four or five months pregnant when the incident with her sister occurred. Maybe she wasn't feeling well. Or simply didn't want to be seen in public."

"It's a possibility. Next question."

"Was Nancy ever examined by a doctor? The blood could have been hers."

"You mean a miscarriage?" Tom asked.

"Yes, but it doesn't make sense. All the blood was on the front of the dress—the skirt and the bodice."

"Like the bloodstains on Beryl Grey's white apron when she found Littlejohn's body. She said she cradled his head on her lap while she checked for a pulse."

"If that's what Nancy Thorne did, what happened to the body?" That image flashed into my head again. A woman, sobbing. *So much blood.* I had absolutely nothing concrete to go on. No facts that would hold weight with Okoje—or Tom, for that matter. But I knew with something very close to certainty that something dreadful had happened on that night in September of 1885. "There was a body, Tom. I'm sure of it."

"Maybe the person she tried to help didn't die." Tom's forehead creased in thought. "Although there was a lot of blood. Someone injured that badly couldn't just vanish. At least not without help."

"Next question. Was the blood on the dress human?" Once again, I had no evidence, but even so, I felt certain the blood *would* prove to be human. That image—the woman on her knees, sobbing—wasn't a reaction to the death of an animal, even a much-loved household pet.

"With luck, the DNA test will tell us," Tom said. "Always assuming the museum is willing to surrender a small sample of fabric. I'll ask Hawksworthy tomorrow."

"And I'll ask him why he hired Nash & Holmes."

Tom folded his napkin and placed it on the table. "Any more questions?"

"Loads. Like the connection between the dress and the Romani items found with it in the trunk."

"At least we know there is one," Tom said. "The Merivale family is the link."

"We need to know where the trunk actually came from, Tom. That means we need to speak with someone who knew Gideon Littlejohn personally, someone he might have confided in."

"Too bad his ex-wife is dead."

"But there's still Mercy Abbott and the other member of that Victorian club—Daniel somebody? I pulled out my phone. "Which reminds me—I haven't heard back from Max Newlin at the Agatha Christie festival. I'll text him now and ask if he's heard from Mercy."

I did, and the answer came almost immediately.

Great minds. Just about to text you. Mercy Abbott lives on Dartmoor. She's one of the managers at Beechlands, a country house hotel near Chagford. Days off Wednesday and Thursday. She's willing to meet up. I'm sure she'll get in touch.

I texted back. *Great. I'll wait for her call.*

"I hate to admit it," Tom said as I slid my phone back in my handbag, "but this feels like one of those cases that die for lack of information. Nobody saw anything. Nobody heard anything. Nobody knows anything."

"We still have a few leads, Tom." I wanted to encourage him. "All we need is one little fact to point us in the right direction." I held up my thumb and forefinger an inch apart. "One tiny clue that will unlock the puzzle."

"My money's on Beryl Grey."

Chapter Twenty-Four

Saturday, January 11
Coombe Mallet

My appointment with Beryl Grey was set for ten o'clock. At breakfast, Yvie Innes warned me that the temperature was dropping, so I layered a heavy sweater under my jacket. Frost blanketed the pavement and parked cars. My breath turned into little puffs of frozen vapor.

I arrived at Queenie's first and asked for a table in the corner, one that would give us as much privacy as possible in the small, public tearoom.

Beryl was ten minutes late. I was about to phone and ask if she needed to reschedule when the bell over the door jangled and I saw her bustle inside. She pulled off a scarf and a heavy tweed coat. I was momentarily surprised to see she was wearing modern clothing—a pair of navy wool trousers, a floral blouse, and what looked like a hand-knitted cardigan in rose-colored wool. I waved to get her attention.

"Hello," she said, unsmiling. "I warn you in advance—I can't stop long. My husband will be needing his lunch." She took the chair opposite me, set her large handbag on the floor, and stared at me as if I were the Spanish Inquisition.

I gave her my warmest smile and, relying on my mother's theory that honey attracts more flies than vinegar, said, "I'm grateful you came. It must be difficult for you with so many responsibilities."

"Thank you." Her voice softened slightly. "I don't mean to be difficult. You and your husband were awfully kind when . . . well, you know."

"You were very brave. If you don't mind me asking, what will you do now that your employment at the Old Merchant's House has come to an end?"

Our conversation was interrupted by a waitress who wanted to take our order. We decided on a pot of Darjeeling and a plate of traditional savory scones with cream cheese and chutney. A second breakfast, I decided, wishing I hadn't eaten every bite of the Crown's delicious sausages.

I repeated my question. "What will you do now, jobwise?"

"Look for another position. I've already put my name in at the employment agency. They tell me finding another job will be easy, but I shouldn't expect one that pays as well."

"At least you won't have to walk to work or use an antique flatiron."

"If it made him happy to live like that, who was I to question? It wasn't really that difficult to comply. The bus stops practically in front of my house. I'd get out on the High Street and walk from there. The other passengers noticed my costume, but they never blinked an eye."

"As I said, I have a few questions."

She bristled. "The police have questioned me—quite thoroughly, I assure you. Even if your husband *is* a policeman, I don't think I should be discussing the murder with you."

"I'm not here to talk about the murder." I tried to look shocked. "Our interest is in the items Mr. Littlejohn donated to the museum—the Victorian dress in particular. You know about that, I assume?" When she nodded, I went on. "Tom and I represent a private investigations firm hired by the museum to trace the provenance, the history, of the dress." This was true, although I hoped she might go over her movements the morning Littlejohn was murdered again. The problem was how to broach the subject. "I can only imagine how difficult it must have been to be interrogated. All those questions: *When did you arrive? What did you do? Did you see anyone? Hear anything unusual?*" I laughed. "When I'm stressed, I don't remember things very well."

"Well, I remember everything." She lifted her chin. "I arrived at the house precisely at twelve noon. I knew Mr. Littlejohn's visitor had already been, because he'd left the tea things in the sink. I washed them up and made lunch. At twelve thirty, I carried the soup tureen through and called Mr. Littlejohn to the table as usual."

Right there was the problem. "Now that's interesting," I said, trying for a casual tone. "Because I thought you said Mr. Littlejohn was always in the dining room at twelve thirty, already seated in his chair and waiting for you to serve his meal." I gave her a rueful smile. "See, I told you I get things mixed up."

"Well, yes, I suppose I did say that. But on that day . . . what I meant was—" She broke off, flustered. "That's not important now, is it?"

"Of course not." I smiled again, thinking it might very well be important. I'd mention it to Tom. "So you brought in his lunch at twelve thirty as usual. You'd prepared the food in advance."

"That's right. As I said, the soup just needed to be reheated. I'd made the sandwiches and wrapped them in cling film the previous afternoon because I wasn't to arrive until noon. Mr. Littlejohn was always precise in his instructions."

The waitress delivered our tea in a steaming brown pot with lovely cups and plates in tobacco-brown transferware. "The chutney today is apple and ale, house made."

The scones were warm and looked delicious. I took one, sliced it in two, and spread half with a thick layer of cream cheese and the chutney, which turned out to be sweet. "Do you know anything at all about the Victorian dress?" I asked between bites. "Where your employer found it, for example?"

Beryl Grey's mouth pleated in thought. What I'd said about calling her employer to lunch had rattled her, and I could see she wanted to make up for it. "I can't say I do remember where he found the dress. Mr. Littlejohn rarely discussed his personal life with me. Our verbal exchanges were limited to domestic arrangements—what he wanted me to cook, when he was having visitors, what in the house needed special attention, that sort of thing."

"Did you ever see the dress? Or the note that was pinned to it?"

"I did not."

"Do you know when he purchased the household?"

"Yes. I know because everything had to be moved into the cellar, didn't it? He asked me to sweep out one of the larger rooms down there, as they hadn't been used in a long time. Quite a job it was too."

"When was that exactly?" I was hoping her information would tally with Ivor's.

"The sale was in July, but arranging for delivery took time because of the cast-iron stove—the weight of it. Everything was delivered in early August. If you need to know the precise date, I can check my calendar at home."

"That won't be necessary." I took a sip of my tea and smiled. In spite of Mr. Rutley's assertion that the trunk hadn't been included on the auction inventory, I wanted to check for myself. And I wanted to see if Beryl Grey would lie. "Were you present, by any chance, when the items were delivered?"

"Of course. Mr. Littlejohn asked me to supervise, to make sure the deliverymen didn't damage anything."

"When my husband and I were there that first day, he showed us an old trunk with a domed lid, about two feet by three feet. Do you know the one I mean?"

"Certainly. He moved it into the morning room before you and your husband arrived."

A flock of tiny birds took flight in my chest. "Inside was a very beautiful quilt."

"I never saw that."

"Do you remember if the trunk was delivered at the same time as the other items from the auction?"

"Oh, no. You've got that wrong. The trunk wasn't part of that lot."

"How do you know?"

"Because Mr. Littlejohn owned the trunk when I began working for him last February."

"Really? Last February?"

She looked at me sideways, "Did he tell you otherwise?"

I shook my head. "It's not important. We're just trying to pin things down." I pushed the plate of scones toward her. "Please, have another."

"I think I might, thank you."

I spread cheese and chutney on the other half of my scone. "So you noticed the trunk last February when you began working at the Old Merchant's House. Did Mr. Littlejohn ever say anything about its history?"

"No. I assumed it had sentimental value—a family heirloom, perhaps."

If it had, his sister, Donna Nixon, would have known about it. "Besides his sister, did Mr. Littlejohn have any other relatives? Does the name Thorne ring a bell, for example? Or Merivale?"

She shook her head. "He never mentioned either name to me."

"I noticed that the house has a security system. Did Mr. Littlejohn tell you why he installed it?"

"He never told me anything."

"Do you remember when it was installed?"

She shrugged. "Three months ago, maybe?"

I wanted to ask her about the break-in, but I'd promised Okoje to keep it quiet. Instead I asked, "Had something happened recently—something that caused him to want more security?"

She looked blank. "Not that I know of. I assumed it was because of all that expensive equipment." If she was lying, she'd made a good job of it.

"Did he ever mention a Romani camp north of the Dart?"

"A *Gypsy* camp? No, although he gave a talk on the subject to that club he belonged to. I know because he'd checked some books out of the public library."

"Did you know the police questioned Mr. Littlejohn's sister, Donna, and her husband, Clive Nixon?" I was veering away from the dress, but she didn't seem to notice.

She gave a small snort. "If the police believe that lot, they'll believe anything."

Perfect setup. "Oh, I agree. You must have been incensed when they told the police you'd been caught stealing a silver box." I held my breath, waiting for the explosion.

Beryl's head shot up. "*Liars*, both of them. Making trouble. I *told* the police I was taking the box home to polish." A piece of the chutney had stuck to her upper lip. She dabbed it with her napkin. "Mr. Littlejohn expected me to keep the silver nice and shiny. Do you know how time-consuming that is? I couldn't spend every waking hour at the Old Merchant's House, could I? I have my husband to think about."

"Of course you do. I can see how hard it must have been to juggle your responsibilities. Did you often take work home?"

"Only when necessary. And it was very unfair of him to accuse me . . . if he did, that is." She flushed, realizing she'd given more away than she'd intended. "I'm not a thief, and Mr. Littlejohn never said I was. He always bought more food than was needed for a single gentleman. He knew I took the leftovers home for my husband."

She'd given away even more now. "Did you know he was planning to replace you?" I gave her my innocent-as-a-spring-lamb look.

"Did they tell you that—the Nixons? It's a *wicked lie*." Her eyes shifted. "He wouldn't have done that. It's absurd."

I could see she was shocked, but I could also see she was lying.

She stood, gathering her coat and handbag. "I'll have to be going now."

"If you think of anything that might—"

"I won't." She turned and marched toward the door, leaving me with the bill.

* * *

I remained at Queenie's for another ten minutes, finishing my tea. I hate to waste food. So, apparently, had Beryl Grey when she worked for Littlejohn. Or had she, as Donna Nixon implied, ordered more food than necessary in order to take the excess home? Even if she had, it wasn't a motive for murder, although being accused of the theft of a valuable sterling-silver box might be. And she'd been sensitive about the discrepancy in her movements the morning Littlejohn was killed. I couldn't see how that was important, but still . . .

I took the last bite of my scone. Beryl Grey wouldn't agree to any more interviews—that was clear. But I had learned a few things. She'd known Littlejohn was planning to replace her—I was sure of it. And Littlejohn had owned the trunk long before he purchased the household. Why had he pretended otherwise?

I paid the bill and left, feeling the waistband on my jeans cutting into my flesh.

"My goodness. Kate Hamilton. Hello."

Clare Jamieson was coming out of the butcher's shop, a carryall on her arm. "Have you tried the sausages here? My husband says he can't live without them."

"They supply the Crown. And I agree—impossible to resist."

"It's difficult, isn't it, keeping one's figure under control?" She gave me a conspiratorial wink, making my waistband feel even tighter. "Speaking of the Crown, I'm glad we ran into each other. I want to apologize for Quinn's behavior the other night. She's been under a lot of stress, the poor girl."

"It can't be easy being the target of attacks. And then the murder. I imagine the whole village is feeling the stress."

"They are." She shifted her carryall to her other arm. "Would you join me for a cup of tea at Queenie's? We're just in time for elevenses."

"Tea?" I was stuffed, but I wasn't about to pass up an opportunity to learn something. "Yes—I'd love to."

We entered the tea shop. The waitress who'd served me just minutes before gave me a curious look but showed us to a table and handed us menus.

"Let's treat ourselves, shall we?" Clare Jamieson clapped her thin hands. "Bring us the full cream tea, Dottie," she told the waitress. "I'll have the bill."

I groaned inwardly.

As we waited for our food, Clare said, "Teddy told us about your dinner together. Did they tell you about Quinn's relationship with her father?"

Where was she going with this? "A bit. I'm sure it's been difficult for them both."

"We've known Quinn since she was a little girl, you see. She's always been independent, strong-willed, but what you must understand is her father, Karl, is an exceptionally controlling sort of parent. He'd call it 'taking care of her,' I suppose, and he does mean well, I'm sure of it. The problem is, they're too much alike. Both controlling in their own way, which means they bump heads. Even at a young age, Quinn resented her father's attempts to set the course of her life. She's resisted his every attempt to steer her. It hasn't been a healthy situation."

"Wasn't Quinn's mother able to intervene?"

"Susan, yes. She tried—but she'd married Karl Benables. Old Devon family with bags of money. She knew what she was getting into. He likes to have his own way and generally gets it."

"Except when his daughter fell in love with a man he considered unsuitable."

"That's it exactly. Karl was determined that Quinn come to her senses and end the relationship. The more he insisted, the more she dug in her heels."

I thought about a similar case in Suffolk, one that had ended in the death of a young girl. The sight of her long blond hair floating in Blackwater Lake would never leave me.

The waitress delivered our tea, this time in a lovely pink flowered pot with a tiered silver tray—more scones, this time with jam and clotted cream; small glazed fruit tarts; pink and white meringues; cream puffs; and tartlets of phyllo dough filled with a sweet nut mixture. *Oh, man.* I'd have to eat something. Maybe I'd skip dinner.

"Here you are, dear." Clare poured the tea. "You must try the scones. You'll never find any better, I assure you."

I took one, feeling slightly sick. "But now that Quinn and Teddy are married and have the twins, things must have changed a little."

"You'd think so, wouldn't you? Quinn's mother has tried very hard, but Karl doesn't want her spending time with her daughter and granddaughters. He sees it as disloyalty."

"Wow." I knew a thing or two about mothers and daughters, but this was way beyond my experience.

"She's forced to see them when he's out of town. Fortunately, he's out of town a lot. He has business interests on the continent—Germany,

Denmark, Italy. But it's not a good thing, is it, to lie to your husband? He will find out."

"What will he do?"

"I don't think he's a bad man at heart. He's not violent. Just stubborn. We've never been great friends. He's on the opposite side politically. But we care about the family. Quinn's mother is lovely, and of course, we adore Quinn and the twins. Richard and I are their godparents."

"How did you become friends with Teddy Pearce? Through Quinn?"

"Politics. My husband recognized his talents and mentored him. Of course, Teddy's made his own way since then. Richard is content with local politics. Teddy has ambitions."

"I'm surprised that Teddy's election to the House of Commons hasn't changed Quinn's father's mind about him. I mean, he's making a success of his life."

"Ah, but that doesn't make up for Teddy's background. Not with Karl Benables. That's one of the reasons Quinn resents him so much. His precious daughter marrying a lad from the Burnthouse Lane estate? Unthinkable."

"Burnthouse Lane?" The name was ringing a rather large bell.

"A council estate in Exeter."

"Gideon Littlejohn grew up on the same estate—does Teddy know that?"

"Oh, I shouldn't think so." Clare Jamieson frowned. "There must have been thousands of people on the estate. But it had a reputation, and Quinn's father swore she'd live to regret her decision. She's never forgiven him for that, and she's committed to proving him wrong. That's why she's so defensive. She wants Teddy to succeed and to be *seen* to succeed. I'm sure she loves Teddy—he's crazy about her—but I'm afraid her overriding purpose in life is proving her father wrong."

Was that true? If it was, Quinn had more problems than I realized.

Clare used a pair of silver tongs to slide a pink meringue onto my plate. "Eat up, dear."

I smiled and raised my fork.

Chapter Twenty-Five

Back at the Crown, I lay on the bed and promised myself I wouldn't eat for a week. I had a lot to digest—both literally and figurately.

First, there was Beryl Grey. Even if she'd been telling the truth about taking the silver box home to polish, Gideon Littlejohn had accused her of theft and threatened to let her go. She'd as good as admitted it. Had she lied about other things as well? The discrepancy in her timelines the morning of the murder was significant in my mind. Earlier, she'd said she was surprised because her employer was always seated at the dining table when she brought in his food at twelve thirty. Later, she said she'd carried in the food and then called him to the table as usual. Yes, it was a minor discrepancy, but both versions couldn't be true.

Her defensiveness when I pointed it out was telling as well. And it caused me to rethink her other statements—her insistence that she'd arrived at the Old Merchant's House at precisely twelve noon, for example. She'd made a point of mentioning it, twice, which I found suspicious. As unlikely as it was, she could have shot Littlejohn herself. Traces of gunpowder residue had been found on her clothing, although the police said the particles could have transferred from his body when she tried to help him. The biggest problem was the gun. She would have had to dispose of it somewhere on the property, and in spite of a thorough search, no gun had been found. But had they searched everywhere? Victorian houses typically had lots of places to hide things—cubbyholes behind the paneling, hidden passageways, even secret rooms. My own Victorian house in Jackson Falls, Ohio, for example, had a hidden space in one of the bedrooms, the access panel concealed by three layers of ugly wallpaper. Inside, my first husband and I had found a reed basket filled with tobacco tins from the early 1890s—someone's secret stash?—and a child's storybook published in 1904. Was there a hiding place somewhere in the Old Merchant's House, one the killer had used to conceal the murder weapon?

I was also feeling sad about Quinn Pearce. I'd adored my own father and couldn't understand why the birth of those beautiful twin girls hadn't gone a long way toward healing their relationship. Even if Quinn and her father were both stubbornly insisting on their own way, the birth of children makes a difference. Or it should. Poor Susan Benables, having to hide her relationship with her own granddaughters.

None of this, however, was helping Tom and me determine the provenance of the bloodstained dress. What we needed was that one little clue my mother always talked about, a tiny loose corner to pick.

Feeling suddenly sleepy, I got up and pulled the curtains shut.

With the darkness and all that food settling in, I was almost asleep when my cell phone pinged. A text. I reached over to check in case it was Tom.

The text was from Maggie Hughes at the library.

Kate, I found some information about the Romani clan on Dartmoor. A physician by the name of Nutcombe served several villages in the late 1800s, including Widdecombe Throop. He kept a kind of daybook or diary, recording his calls, payments received, and often his thoughts on his patients. He was called on to treat Queenie Squires before her death and recorded a fascinating if brief account of the Squires family. His writing is often difficult to decipher, but his daybook has been digitized. Let me know if you're interested. I can email you a PDF.

Oh, yes—I was interested all right.

The email appeared in my in-box in less than five minutes. Slipping on my shoes and grabbing my laptop, I headed downstairs for a nice cup of tea. There's always room for tea.

* * *

The residents' lounge was deserted, which suited me fine. Outside the windows, a few flakes of snow drifted lazily down. Inside, a small fire crackled. I sat, a warm cup of Earl Grey beside me, and pulled up Maggie's PDF on my mobile. She'd marked the page.

Widdecombe-in-the-Moor

Thursday 20th August 1885

A miserable day, wet & unseasonably cold. Around dinnertime one of the Gypsy lads, a boy of perhaps ten or eleven, arrived on horseback with a message from Leverin Squires. His mother, Queenie, had taken ill. Would I attend?

I rode out to the Gypsy camp in a driving rain. It has been so cold of late I was obliged to wear my winter suit & rubber coat. Even so, I arrived stiff, soaked through & nearly frozen. I found the venerable old lady weak & feverish. She has a septic throat with an abscess already much advanced. There is no question of transferring her to hospital. They won't allow it. Her breathing is labored & her words, when she tries to speak, generally incoherent. Had they called me sooner I might have saved her. As is, I doubt she will last a fortnight. Of course chastising her family for their delay will do no good. Queenie herself probably forbade them. I helped her sit up a little which may aid her breathing & I have prescribed beef tea with brandy & a poultice for all the good it will do. As I was leaving, Leverin pressed a silver coin into my hand. I was loath to accept. I cannot cure her. But as he insisted, I took the coin. I shall call again tomorrow.

Placing the slice of lemon on the saucer, I sipped my tea as I skimmed down the page, reading several more entries very much like the first. Queenie Squires was dying, an event that occurred five days later.

Tuesday, 25th August 1885

The weather continues unseasonably cold. I arrived at the Gypsy camp just before noon to find Mrs. Squires had died in her sleep. There is much weeping & wailing in the camp. In spite of the seriousness of her condition they had not expected her to succumb as she was hale & hearty almost to the end. Dear me! How very sad life is when the feeblenesses of our declining years are realized. I wonder how the family will cope without her. A funeral is to be held in three days' time to give relatives an opportunity to make the journey. It promises to be an event to remember.

The next mention of the Squires family was the day of the funeral, and for the first time it dawned on me that Queenie's death and funeral had taken place literally just days before Nancy Thorne's trauma—whatever it was. I read with increased interest.

Friday 28th August 1885

The day of the funeral dawned cold & rainy. I did not attend the service at Widdecombe church but paid my respects by observing the committal ceremony conducted by the Reverend Edward Quick. I was surprised at the number of mourners, many of whom (I was informed) had travelled from other parts of Devon to see the old lady off. The procession to the grave was accompanied by loud expressions of grief, reaching a crescendo when the coffin was lowered into the ground. Men tossed coins after it. This genuine and most tender feeling for their matriarch was touching, and I confess that the venerable old lady's presence, a fixture in the lives of so many, will be missed. Not a year of my lifetime has passed in which spring did not mean the arrival of the Squires family. Truly an era has passed.

Later that evening Queenie's vardo and earthly possessions were burnt on the moor in a great bonfire, a tradition amongst the Gypsies. The flames & subsequent column of rising smoke could be seen for miles.

I would have liked to visit Queenie's grave. Dr. Nutcombe implied she'd been buried in the church graveyard which, like everything else in Widdecombe Throop, was under thirty feet of water. Had the bodies been reinterred? So far, Maggie Hughes at the library had found no information on the subject.

I read on.

Monday, 31st August 1885

Another cold & rainy day. Reports of a disturbance after the funeral of Queenie Squires have reached the village. The Constable was summoned by Sir Henry Merivale who had ridden out onto the moor to watch the funeral pyre. It is said that a dispute over the old lady's possessions ended in gunfire. I think this highly unusual as Gypsies have great respect for the dead & generally no regard for such things as inheritance. Fortunately no one was harmed or I would have been called out. The two men involved were detained briefly but released with a caution after Leverin Squires promised to handle the matter privately. Reports say the presence of the police was a serious affront to the family, as Gypsies have their own methods of administering justice. I fear Sir Henry's actions will have consequences. What trouble people make for themselves when a little patience might spare it.

At this point in the narrative, Maggie had added a comment, telling me to skip ahead to Dr. Nutcombe's entry on the eighth of October.

Thursday, 8th October 1885

A furious rainstorm was raging this morning. I took the lantern after breakfast & went to check on the chickens. The poor things were huddled together miserably but fortunately the repairs I made to the coop last summer are holding. Winter is arriving early this year. Seasons change & so does life.

The Drift was held on 3rd October after which the Squires family packed up every stick & stone and departed the village, perhaps for good. Queenie's death has brought an unwelcome change. Reports say that several of the younger men have left the family, perhaps to find work in Plymouth or Southampton. Queenie's daughter Naomi & her husband are to rejoin the Heron clan. The venerable old lady had held her family together by the strength of her character. Her departure has loosed the bonds. Hearing this I felt a kind of despair, thinking of my own loss & wishing things could remain the same all our lives. But it seems unwise to hope for it & I resolve to be more cheerful.

I wondered briefly if Dr. Nutcombe had lost his wife—or a child—but his misfortunes weren't my primary interest. Backtracking to the seventh of September, the night Nancy Thorne returned home in her blood-soaked dress, I skimmed the entries for that day and the following week, but there was no mention of the Thornes or any possible death. If medical advice had been sought, the authorities had probably called on the local apothecary rather than Dr. Nutcombe. Or perhaps Nancy Thorne, like Queenie Squires, had forbidden it.

Switching off my phone, I sat back and took another sip of the Earl Grey, which was now cooling. While the account of Queenie Squires's death and funeral was fascinating, the only information pertinent to our investigation was the dates. Queenie had died on the twenty-fifth of August 1885. She'd been buried and her possessions burned three days later, on the twenty-eighth, after which there'd been some sort of altercation, ending in shots fired. Nancy Thorne had come into contact with blood—lots of it—ten days after that on the seventh of September. Were the dates significant? I honestly couldn't see how. Isla had said the Romanies didn't mix with *gorja*, their word for outsiders.

I pictured the dress laid out on the workroom table. Whose blood was it? That's when it struck me. I was really asking, *Who died?*

Chapter Twenty-Six

It was just after three thirty when two American couples entered the residents' lounge. They smiled at me, and I got the feeling they were about to strike up a conversation—a conversation that would inevitably begin by asking me where I was from. *Near Cleveland? Really? Do you happen to know the Martins? They live in Chagrin Falls.* I wasn't in the mood, so before they had a chance to ask, I got up, gave them a brief smile, and returned to our room on the first floor.

Tom would be back from the police enquiry office by five. I had a lot to tell him, and I hoped he would have news for me as well—like Okoje's permission to enter the Old Merchant's House. I needed to examine that trunk, and I wanted to search for records that might reveal where Littlejohn had gotten it. Why was it taking so long? It had been six days since the death of Gideon Littlejohn, and they still weren't allowing anyone inside the house—even the Nixons, according to Tom. Which reminded me of the question I'd wanted to ask Donna.

Pulling out my phone, I dialed the Nixons' number. Luckily, Donna was home.

"It's Kate Hamilton," I said when she answered. "This may seem like an odd question, but are you and your brother related, even distantly, to the Thorne family?"

"Never heard of 'em."

"How about the Merivales?"

She snorted. "That'll be the day." At least she knew who they were.

When I asked about a connection to the Romani Travellers on Dartmoor, she went momentarily silent.

"Now that's an odd question, Kate. What makes you ask?"

"No reason," I lied. "Just curious."

"Our father was a Little. It's a Scottish surname, but his people have lived in Exeter for generations—scoundrels, the lot of 'em. Our mother was a Chilcott from up around Tiverton way, but she was orphaned as a child and brought up by a foster family, the Greens."

I thanked her and checked my messages to see if I'd missed a call from Mercy Abbott. I hadn't. If she didn't call soon, I'd have to contact Max Newlin at the Agatha Christie festival again.

Tom returned to the Crown at five. I saw a gleam in his eye. "Something happened today, didn't it?"

He grinned. "I'll tell you everything, but let's have a glass of wine first. I need to unwind."

In the bar, we took the comfy chairs near the window and ordered. "How did your day go?" he asked. "Learn anything from Beryl Grey?"

"Nothing except she tells slightly different stories about the chain of events the day of the murder. And she made a big point once again of saying she arrived at the Old Merchant's House that day at precisely twelve noon."

"Did she now?" His smile broadened. "You don't believe her?"

"I wouldn't go that far. But neither would I take what she says at face value. She as good as admitted that Littlejohn accused her of theft and threatened to fire her. I think she was taking advantage of him financially."

"And stealing the odd silver box when she could?"

"I don't know. It's just weird. She didn't want me coming to the house because she says her husband can become violent. She made it sound like dementia. Yet when she worked for Littlejohn, she had no problem leaving him home all day on his own."

"The police were at the Greys' house this morning. Before you met her at Queenie's."

"No wonder she was on edge. Did they meet her husband?"

"They didn't exactly meet him. When they got to the house, Alan Grey was sitting in an old armchair, covered with a blanket. Varma described him as an elderly man with thick gray hair and a full beard. He was mumbling to himself, not making sense. Beryl Grey told the police her husband was unpredictable and warned them not to disturb him."

"That's why she insisted we meet at Queenie's."

"We should pay a visit to the Greys ourselves," Tom said. "Catching people off guard is a useful technique."

"Would Okoje approve?"

"Oh, yes. I think he would." I saw the gleam again. There was something he wasn't telling me.

Yvie Innes delivered our wine. She stood there for a moment, perhaps hoping we'd ask her to join us. When we didn't, she wished us a pleasant evening and left.

"How did you spend the day?" I asked.

"Mostly viewing Littlejohn's videos. There are well over two hundred, all on YouTube—all about living the Victorian lifestyle. PC Doaks, poor sod, has been tasked with viewing the lot." Tom crossed his long legs, resting one ankle on the opposite knee. "Littlejohn had a surprising number of followers."

"I'd like to see some of the videos."

"We can do that tonight." He gave me a cheeky grin. "Great bedtime viewing."

Outside the window, a flock of glossy purple starlings in their white-speckled winter plumage swooped onto the lawn. They pecked at the grass, hoping to rouse the insects wintering there. Tom leaned back in his chair. "What else happened today?"

"I phoned Donna Nixon. They aren't related to the Thornes or the Merivales and had no connection with the Romanies on Dartmoor. And I had tea with Clare Jamieson." I told him about our conversation. "She says Quinn is super protective of Teddy's reputation and will do anything to prove her father wrong about him."

"We witnessed that ourselves."

"The most interesting bit of information today was an account of Queenie Squires' death and funeral. Written by a doctor who tried to save her. Maggie Hughes from the library sent it over."

"What did you learn?"

"I learned that the family sort of fell apart after her death. There was a disagreement at the funeral—gunshots fired. And no"—I held up my hand—"before you ask, no one was injured. No bloodshed and no mention of Nancy Thorne. After Queenie died, the Squires family never returned to this part of Devon."

Tom slid a finger slowly around the rim of his wineglass.

I gave him an exaggerated eye roll. "Tom, I know something happened today. Just come out with it before I die of curiosity."

"All right." He grinned. "I was going to tell you. First, though, you can get into Littlejohn's house tomorrow. You're free to look around before they release it to the Nixons."

"Excellent. Tomorrow, then. And the second thing?"

"The museum has agreed to allow a small piece of the bloodstained fabric to be removed from the dress, and they've agreed to pay for a private lab that will, for a fee, move our test to the top of the queue. Let's just hope the sample hasn't degraded too much over the years. The DNA test is scheduled for Tuesday, the fourteenth. We should have the results in a week."

"Will we still be here? We do have to go home sometime, you know."

"If we leave before the results are in, we'll just add the DNA results to our final report."

"I hope they can tell if the blood is human."

"Maybe Nancy Thorne came upon an injured animal or something."

"And was so traumatized that she suffered amnesia? Come on, Tom."

He shrugged. "At any rate, we should know something definitive, even if it's just that the DNA is too degraded to be of use." He leaned back, humming under his breath.

Why was I getting the impression he was waiting to deliver a punch line? "What else happened? I know there's more."

"An interesting new piece of evidence. A lady who lives three doors down from the Old Merchant's House swears she saw Beryl Grey arrive the morning of the murder."

"And?"

"And it wasn't twelve noon."

* * *

An hour later, after Tom and I had changed clothes, we ordered our food at the Crown's crowded little bar. The bartender, who knew us by now, had our favorite drinks waiting for us. When the food was ready, Yvie Innes showed us to our table. Unbelievably, I was hungry.

"Is the neighbor a reliable witness, do you think?" I asked.

"Seemed pretty sharp to me." Tom spread his napkin on his lap. "She's somewhere in her mideighties and has an elderly dachshund with bladder problems. She was outside, waiting for him to do his business, when she saw Beryl Grey arrive on foot."

"Except it wasn't noon."

"No. It was a few minutes before nine AM and still pretty dark, but she had no trouble recognizing the housekeeper. She'd seen her before in her costume."

"Was Clive Nixon in his car?"

"She saw a dark sedan parked on the street. Didn't know anyone was inside."

"Are you saying the figure Clive saw at Littlejohn's door was Beryl Grey?"

"No. That had to be later, because Clive told Donna the sun was shining when he saw someone at Littlejohn's front door. And the neighbor says the housekeeper walked around the rear of the house as usual. She didn't go to the front door at all."

"Did the neighbor see anyone else?"

"Unfortunately not. Herman—that's the dachshund—finished what he'd come to do, and they went back inside."

"What did Beryl Grey say—assuming the police have had a chance to ask her?"

"They have. They phoned her. She says the neighbor woman is mistaken—'halfway round the bend' were her exact words. She swears once again that she arrived precisely at noon and the woman was either confused about the time or trying to make trouble. Apparently they'd had a few run-ins over Herman doing his business on Gideon Littlejohn's front walk."

"Tom . . . ," I said slowly. An idea had formed in my brain. "I know I've said this before, but what if Beryl Grey was the killer after all? She was there. She was covered in blood. And she had a motive—to prevent Littlejohn from telling the police about the silver box."

"Was he going to press charges?"

"She says the Nixons made that up, but then she would, wouldn't she? We only have her word for it that she found him already dead. And now we have an eyewitness who saw her arrive earlier than she said."

"But we heard her scream. If she shot him, why would she draw attention to herself?"

"It's a point."

"Another reason we should talk with her again, informally."

"She's not going to confess to us."

"No, but she might tell us something the police can use."

"What if she sees us as a threat?"

"That's why we're going together. You're not threatening. What we need is a reason to show up at her house. Something logical—a question you forgot to ask before, maybe. Mention the neighbor in passing. I'll stay in the background. You have a way of getting people to tell you things. It's those innocent blue eyes of yours."

"Don't let them fool you." I winked. "So we show up on her doorstep tomorrow?"

"No—I think we let her stew about things for a day or two."

"About the Old Merchant's House," I said, changing the subject. "Okoje said something earlier—when we went to the police enquiry office that first time. He asked if Littlejohn owned something of value. Is that what he's hoping I can tell him?"

"I think he's hoping you'll notice something they didn't—or didn't recognize as important. Anything, really. It's been almost a week since Littlejohn's death, and they still don't have any credible leads."

"They found nothing at all in the house? What about the stuff he bought at auction?"

"Varma said it's mostly junk, but you're free to take a look."

"I could be wrong, but I don't think Littlejohn was killed for his possessions. He wasn't a collector. The objects he purchased were for practical use, and so far I've seen nothing more than a hundred and fifty years old."

"Practically brand-new in the UK."

"I want to see that trunk. I want to find out where he got the dress."

Tom nodded slowly. "And why he lied about it."

Chapter Twenty-Seven

Tom and I lay snuggled on the queen-size bed. He aimed the remote at the flat-screen TV on the wall. "Which episode do you want to see first?"

We'd found Littlejohn's videos on YouTube. Tom was right. There were hundreds, the first dating from 2014 and the last titled "Victorian Cursive Styles," filmed just weeks ago, before the Christmas holidays.

"Look, Tom. He had four thousand two hundred and fourteen people following him at the end."

"Impressive," Tom said.

I snuggled against him. "Let's start with one of the earlier ones. That one, for example." Tom had paused at a podcast titled "The Middle-Class Victorian Household." "What's the date?" I squinted at the screen.

"March of 2014." Tom clicked on the podcast. We watched, fascinated with the images of a younger and trimmer Gideon Littlejohn. I'd considered him attractive when we met him at the museum gala. In 2014, somewhere in his thirties, he was, as my daughter, Christine, would say, *lush*—meaning fanciable. His dark hair was cut on the long side, brushed back from his forehead but curling around his ears. The mustache and muttonchop sideburns had been added later. He was in the front parlor.

Hello. My name is Gideon Littlejohn. Welcome to the Old Merchant's House. I live in a village called Coombe Mallet, within

Dartmoor National Park in Devon, England. The date is March twentieth of 2014, but as you can see, I dress and live as if it were the middle of the nineteenth century. I hope you will join me twice a month as we travel back in time. Each program will explore a particular aspect of Victorian life. My goal is to show you how and perhaps why I have chosen to escape from the twenty-first century and return to what I consider a more rational and orderly way of life. This first program is entitled 'The Middle-Class Victorian Household.' Come along and see where and how I live.

The camera panned out slightly. Someone was filming him.

First a little history. The Old Merchant's House was built in 1838 for Thomas Nicholls, a well-to-do draper—a seller of fine wool, linen, and silk—who conducted his business from his shop on the ground level, facing the street.

His description of the history of the house was a slightly fuller version of what he'd told us on our first visit. "There's one thing we never thought of," I said. "Maybe Littlejohn found the trunk somewhere in the house when he bought it."

"It's possible. Let's listen."

My intention is to restore the entire house, cellar to attics, to its original condition in 1855. This transformation will be gradual and, in some cases, sadly incomplete. The fireplaces in each room, for example, are meant to burn coal—a practice banned in the UK—so I'm forced to use solid-fuel pellets. When it makes sense financially, I hope to switch to bio-coal, a carbon-neutral replacement. But back to the house as it was then. Follow me into the heart of the home.

The scene shifted to the kitchen, which was in a state of flux. Cheap oak cabinetry, circa 1960s, competed with a rather beautiful antique copper sink. A small electric refrigerator hummed next to an open hearth with a revolving spit. Littlejohn had made major changes since he'd filmed the video in 2014. All that tacky cabinetry, for example, was now replaced by period shelving, wall hooks, and hanging dish racks. How far would he have gone to achieve historical accuracy? Would he really have replaced the electric fridge with a genuine icebox, for example? Would he have rid the house of hot and cold running water, requiring Beryl Grey to draw water from an outside well and heat it on the stove?

A household such as this one would have had perhaps four to six live-in servants with quarters in the attic. I'm working on that, but in the meantime, I shall make do with contract workers. At the moment, my kitchen is fitted with a vintage cooker from the 1930s, which I intend to replace with an authentic Victorian cooker as soon as I can find one I'm able to restore.

Back in the front parlor, Littlejohn moved to an antique platform rocker near a glowing cast-iron fireplace insert. He sat and removed the glass chimney from an oil lamp that sat on a small round table. Lighting it with a match, he replaced the chimney.

If you have questions, put them in the chat. I'll answer as many as I can. One question I'm frequently asked is why—why do I chose to live as a Victorian gentleman? My answer is, I enjoy this life. I have done for several years now. I've always been fascinated with history, the Victorian age in particular. There's a certain propriety, an orderliness, that appeals to me. Perhaps I was born in the wrong century. A man out of his own time. The way I live isn't a hobby or an experiment. It's a little like choosing to live in a culture not your own. I'm not pretending. I am attempting to live as authentically as possible.

He looked directly into the camera.

You may consider my way of life strange, but this is where I feel most at home. So how do things actually work? That's what I intend to explore in future videos. If you're interested, follow me on this channel. And do put your questions in the chat below. Until next time, this is Gideon Littlejohn wishing you a pleasant day.

As the credits rolled, I looked at Tom. "What do you think?"

"I think it's strange. Discarding all modern conveniences on purpose? It's not quaint or nostalgic. It's . . ."

"Pathological?" I suggested. "There was something about the modern world he was trying to escape."

"Stay awake for another?" Tom reached up and stroked my hair.

I yawned. "Sure."

Tom clicked through the offerings, which covered a wide variety of topics—cookery, filling a pipe, tying a cravat, the hierarchy of household staff.

"Wait—how about that one?" I said. "The clothing thing. 'Dressing the Proper Victorian Gentleman.' That one's from 2017. Actually, I'm curious about his clothing."

Tom clicked on the chosen video. Littlejohn had become more professional. The program began with piano music—something classical I didn't recognize—and a series of historical images. A title flashed on the screen: *Living in the Past: The Life of a Modern-Day Victorian Gentleman.* The title faded, and again we saw a close-up of Gideon Littlejohn. He hadn't aged much since 2014, but now he had his mustache and sideburns.

Welcome, friends. This is Gideon Littlejohn. For those new to the channel, I live in a Victorian town house in a village called Coombe Mallet, within Dartmoor National Park in Devon, England. The date today is the fourth of June 2017, but as you can see—

The camera panned out.

—I dress and live as if it were the middle of the nineteenth century.

This time Littlejohn was filming in a bedroom. In the background, we could see a bed covered in a crocheted coverlet and flanked by twin molded-glass oil lamps. Over the bed hung a colored print of *The Lady of Shalott*, the oil painting by John William Waterhouse depicting Elaine of Astolat, confined by a curse to her quarters in Camelot, escaping in a small boat to face her destiny—and her death. A presage of Littlejohn's own fate?

Today's program concerns clothing, what I wear day to day. In the Victorian era, men's clothing basically consisted of a coat, a waistcoat, and trousers, not always of matching material. A coat or cloak was added for outdoor wear in cold weather. As you can see—

The camera panned out further.

—today I'm wearing a frock coat of gray wool, cut with a long waist and a short, full skirt. Mine is single-breasted, but many surviving frock coats from the period are double-breasted. This coat was made sometime in the 1850s by a custom tailor in London. Fortunately, it was in excellent condition and needed only minor tailoring. Trousers are the rarest survivors from the period. For this reason, I have mine custom-made, using an original pattern. Not an inexpensive proposition, but fortunately for the Victorians, a large wardrobe of garments, such as people expect today, was not common, even amongst the well-to-do.

Now let us consider a Victorian man's shirt.

Littlejohn moved to a large wardrobe and opened it to reveal several long, white shirts.

Victorian shirts were made of several materials—cotton, linen, even fine wool, and—

"Stop the video." I sat up in bed and pointed at the TV. "No, not there—go back a few frames. Okay, right there."

We looked at a still shot of Gideon Littlejohn in midstride, walking toward the wardrobe. On the floor near what must have been a draped window sat the trunk, open, the yellow floral lining exposed.

"The video was aired first in 2017, right?" I asked.

"He said so—the fourth of June, wasn't it?"

"There's our proof. Gideon Littlejohn owned that trunk long before the auction."

Chapter Twenty-Eight

Sunday, January 12

The bells of St. Petroc's rang out an exuberant recessional. A damp, chilly wind was blowing. Tom and I stopped at the door of the church to shake hands with the vicar. His cheeks were pink with the cold, but his eyes were friendly and his handshake firm.

Tom put his arm around me as we walked back to the Crown. "Ready to explore the Old Merchant's House?"

"More than ready."

Back in our room, I changed into a pair of black jeans, a pullover, and a pair of white trainers. If I was going to poke around inside the Old Merchant's House, I needed to be comfortable. As I was brushing my hair into a ponytail, I heard Tom's mobile buzz.

Tom appeared in the doorway. "That was Okoje. He wants me to spend a couple of hours at the police enquiry office this afternoon. Will you be all right at the Old Merchant's House on your own?"

"Sure. What's up?"

"Constable Doaks flagged several of Littlejohn's videos. Okoje and his team are planning to view them to see if they provide a motive for his murder."

"That's unlikely—unless some environmentalist found out he was surreptitiously burning coal. Of course, as my mother says, *Sometimes the moon turns blue.*"

Tom laughed. "What does that mean?"

"It means that sometimes the unexpected happens. Unlikely doesn't mean impossible."

"No, it doesn't. That's why the police will continue to pore over every available resource until the cyberforensics team manages to crack his computer. Oh, and Okoje said the key is in a lockbox. The code is 4785. Stands for *God Save The King* on the alphanumeric keypad, in case you forget."

"Clever."

Tom left on foot. I grabbed my warm jacket and the keys to our Range Rover and headed for the Old Merchant's House.

I parked on the street, several houses down from Gideon Littlejohn's experiment in time travel. Turning the key in the lock, I felt a flutter of anticipation.

Standing in the entrance hall, I thought about our first visit and the initial shock of seeing Beryl Grey in her Victorian housekeeper's getup. She'd said it was like being in a play. Today the place looked like a darkened stage after a premature closing, except for the obvious signs of police activity—drawers left partially open, a coating of dark-gray fingerprint powder on every surface.

I flipped the toggle switch on the wall. Flame-shaped electric bulbs lit up the wall sconces. Would Littlejohn have eventually replaced them with gas? Was that even legal today?

I began in the morning room, the octagonal room at the back of the house where I'd first seen the trunk. There it was, still in the alcove, half hidden by the draperies. I opened the lid and found the quilt still tucked neatly inside. *Excellent.* The quilt, with its exquisite workmanship, pleasing design, and vibrant, well-placed colors, was a work of art. It deserved to be displayed in the museum. I hoped Donna Nixon would agree.

The trunk itself was a standard nineteenth-century trunk meant for railway or carriage journeys—not the kind a wealthy woman would have owned but a plain oaken trunk with a domed lid, iron strapping, and handles. I knew from experience that these trunks were relatively inexpensive and usually lined with paper or even newsprint. This one, however, was beautifully lined with a padded fabric in a rose-and-green vine print on a soft yellow ground.

I laid the quilt on the sofa and stared into the empty trunk. I'd hoped to find a nameplate or some other kind of identification, but there was nothing to tell me who had owned it, except for the lining, which was not only in wonderful condition for its age but had been meticulously fitted and sewn. By the same hand that had produced the calico dress, the quilt, and the red silk ballgown? It sure looked like it to me.

I pulled the lighted magnifier out of my handbag and examined the lining fabric more closely. The trunk hadn't come from the manufacturer this way. The padded lining had been added later. I ran my hand along the fabric on the sides and bottom of the trunk's interior. The smooth cotton had been filled with a fine material, probably cotton or wool batting. Along the edges, I could feel a framework of wooden slats and the tiny brads—small wire nails used to secure the fabric in place. The brads had been concealed with a fine, fabric-covered welting, attached with stitches so tiny they were virtually invisible. I wasn't an expert like Julia Kelly, but I felt pretty confident this was the work of Sally Tucker née Thorne. If I was right, the same hand had produced the trunk lining, the quilt, and the bloodstained dress. That meant I could make a convincing circumstantial case for the bloodstained dress having belonged to one of the Thorne sisters—most likely Nancy, if the newspaper account was accurate. Dr. Hawksworthy would be thrilled, but would it really be enough to warrant attribution? The question remained: How had the trunk come into Gideon Littlejohn's possession, and why had he wanted to conceal that information?

Exploring further, I found a fabric tab under the domed lid that, when pulled down, revealed a lined tray divided into several compartments. The perfect place to conceal cash, travel documents, and jewelry. I went over every inch with my lighted magnifier. Stuck in the corner of one of the compartments were several tiny jet beads. It looked like they'd come from the broken choker necklace I'd seen at the museum. A hazy memory floated away before I could grab it. Using my fingernails, I retrieved the jet beads and put them in one of the zipper compartments in my handbag in case Julia Kelly want to try restringing the choker.

Pulling out my cell phone, I called Tom.

"Everything all right?" He sounded worried.

"Everything's fine. I'm wondering if DCI Okoje would let me take the trunk back to the Crown. I'd like to have Julia Kelly at the museum take a look."

"He's right here. I'll ask." I heard muffled conversation before Tom came back on the line. "Technically, the trunk belongs to the Nixons, but Okoje says you can have it for another few days. Is it heavy? Do you need help?"

"I can manage. Tell him thank-you."

"Have you found a reason to contact Beryl Grey?"

"Not yet. I'll keep looking."

"See you at the Crown around five."

I checked my watch. "I'll be finished well before then. Why don't I walk down and meet you at the enquiry office at five?"

"Perfect. I'd like to try that Thai restaurant on the High Street tonight."

After disconnecting, I refolded the quilt, placed it carefully inside the trunk, and carried the whole thing to the Rover, sliding it onto the rear seat. Then I went back into the house and spent some time simply enjoying the lovely architectural details and tight floor plan. Every room in a Victorian house had its own specific purpose—no open-plan concepts in that era. I also checked the furniture, floorboards, and wall panels for the hidden spaces the Victorians loved so much. I remembered my father saying once that if you haven't found a secret compartment in a Victorian house, you haven't looked carefully enough. Sadly, I didn't find any. DS Varma had been right about the items in the cellar, though. Besides some very pretty Victorian bathroom fixtures, the lot Littlejohn had purchased at auction was mostly junk. He must have bought it specifically for the cooker, which would probably never be restored now.

Seeing the cooker reminded me of the high-ceilinged kitchen. If I was going to find a convincing reason to contact Beryl Grey, that's where I'd find it—in her domain. And, sure enough, there in the corner of a rough oak corner cabinet was a Waitrose loyalty card in the name of Beryl Grey and an envelope containing £47.50 in cash and marked *Reimbursement for Groceries*. She would want the card and the cash, which meant we had a perfect excuse to drop them off at her house.

There was only one room left—the study. It was more of an alcove, really, off the parlor. Dark oak bookshelves flanked an ornate, marbleized slate mantelpiece. The books were old, and a quick glance suggested they'd been bought by the yard to give the impression their owner was an educated man of leisure. Several pieces of furniture stood on the parquet floor, but I was most interested in a mahogany secretary with glazed panel doors and an embossed green leather writing surface. The secretary was probably where Littlejohn had kept personal correspondence and financial records. I was proven right when I found one of the large exterior drawers filled with receipts. Other exterior drawers held several old-fashioned accounting ledgers, a checkbook, a supply of elegant writing paper, bottles of ink, antique steel-nib pens, and a brass-and-wood rocking blotter. Nothing that related to the dress.

Well, shoot.

Then I pulled out one of the small interior drawers and stared in amazement.

* * *

The policy enquiry office in Coombe Mallet was hardly more than a public waiting room. One of the community support officers, a woman in dark trousers and a black shirt with blue epaulettes, showed me into the inner sanctum. That's where I found Tom, staring at a computer screen. "Ready to go," I asked, "or do you need more time?"

"Hello, darling. No—I'm ready." Tom grabbed his jacket. "I've been thinking about chicken satay all day."

"Don't forget the umbrella. It's drizzling again."

We headed for Taste of Siam, the local Thai restaurant located halfway between the police enquiry office and the Crown. Tom held the umbrella as we tried to coordinate our steps. Not easy with his long strides.

"Did you learn anything from the videos?" I asked.

"No, but ask me anything about Victorian life—anything at all."

I took his arm. "I have a confession. I'm looking forward to one of those exotic cocktails with the little umbrellas."

He laughed. "I wouldn't mind that either, now you mention it. What we both need is a day off."

"I don't think we're going to get one—not just yet. Look what I found in Littlejohn's desk."

I pulled a sheet of paper out of my handbag, holding it up so it wouldn't get rained on. It wasn't Littlejohn's elegant writing paper with the engraved monogram but a half sheet of computer paper on which a series of words had been penned in a slanting, cursive copperplate.

Nancy Thorne is a murderess.
The blood of Nancy Thorne's victim.
Dress belonging to the murderess Nancy Thorne.
Dress belonging to Nancy Thorne, a murderess.

The last phrase, exactly as Dr. Hawksworthy described it on the note pinned to the dress, had been written five times. "It's his handwriting," I said. "I compared it to his financial ledgers."

"Why would he write all that?" Tom asked.

"He was practicing," I said. "Trying to get it right—the wording, the ink, the cursive. I know he'd been experimenting with copperplate. I saw similar examples in his check ledger."

"You mean Gideon Littlejohn wrote the note pinned to the dress himself?" Tom shook his head.

"Hawksworthy said it was a fake—a pretty good one. The faded ink and the paper looked authentic at first glance."

"How did Hawksworthy know the note was a fake?"

"Littlejohn tried too hard. Made it look too perfect."

"Was he hoping to generate interest in his videos? Nothing like a historical mystery. In 2016 he monetized them with advertisements. A video about a bloodstained dress and a murderous Victorian lacemaker strikes me as perfect clickbait."

"Did he make a podcast about the dress?"

"We didn't find one."

"If he wanted publicity, he could have insisted the dress be on display at the gala—with a big sign saying he'd donated it."

Tom nodded slowly. "If not for publicity, why forge the note?"

We'd arrived at the restaurant and ducked inside. Tom shook off our umbrella and added it to the jumble at the door. The light scent of jasmine and sandalwood hit our noses, and the soft sound of water cascading down a slate wall instantly banished the wind and the cold rain outside. We were somewhere warm and relaxing. Once seated, we ordered chicken satay and spring rolls as starters.

"Again, why would Littlejohn forge the note? What did he have to gain?" Tom asked.

"I've been thinking about that. If he wasn't trying to impress his followers, maybe he wanted to impress one person—Hugo Hawksworthy."

A pretty young Asian woman delivered our starters—house specialties that were probably always ready to go.

"What do you mean?"" Tom dipped a spring roll into the hot mustard sauce.

"What I mean is this," I said, trying to think logically as my mother had taught me. "We saw the dress and the bloodstains, right? And we read the script of a radio documentary produced years later. But what made everyone think the two were related? The note. Without the note, there was nothing to connect them. The dress could have belonged to anyone. A midwife, for example."

"I see what you mean." Tom's eyes were watering. "*Wow*—that sauce is hot." He took a long drink of water.

Our waitress, wearing a traditionally patterned silk sarong and matching shawl, delivered our cocktails with, yes, small paper umbrellas.

"We now believe the bloodstained dress belonged to one of the Thorne sisters," I said, "because Julia Kelly noticed similarities in the construction of that dress and the red silk ballgown donated by a member of the Merivale family. Lady Helen Merivale told us about the seamstress from Widdecombe Throop and her sister, a lacemaker who was hired to produce lace for a wedding dress but was subsequently fired for some kind of impropriety." I took one of the satay skewers and forked the chicken onto my plate.

"And it was you who noticed the acorn and bird's-foot trefoil motifs in the lace collar attached to the bloodstained dress. But all that happened after we arrived."

"Exactly. Until we made the connection between the Merivales and the Thorne sisters, we knew nothing for sure. And yet Littlejohn knew—don't ask me how—and decided to write the note." I dipped a piece of chicken in the peanut sauce.

"To persuade Hawksworthy to fund an investigation to prove it?"

"That's the only thing that makes sense," I said between bites. "Somehow Littlejohn *knew* the dress was Nancy Thorne's but needed us to prove it. I think he counted on the fact that after the medieval commentary had been proven to be a forgery, Hawksworthy would do his due diligence. He couldn't afford to take another chance."

"But why was it so important to Littlejohn that the dress be authenticated? What did he have to gain?"

"That's the part we don't know yet. We know he lied about the trunk. We saw it for ourselves in that podcast from 2017."

Tom took one of the satay skewers and used it to punctuate his thoughts. "Littlejohn donated the dress, lied about where he got it, and forged the note so Hawksworthy would fund an investigation."

"And now he's dead."

"Kate." Tom put down the skewer. "We have no reason to believe his death had anything to do with the dress."

"I know that," I admitted. "It could be a coincidence. Still . . ."

"Sometimes the moon turns blue." Tom smiled and scanned his menu. "Hawksworthy knew the note was a fake. I wonder if he suspected Littlejohn."

"He didn't tell me the note was a fake until I asked him to produce it. I'm going to ask Julia Kelly to examine the lining of the trunk. While I'm at the museum, I'll tell Hawksworthy that Littlejohn wrote the note. See how he reacts."

"Come on, let's order. I'd like to spend time with you tonight—alone." Tom gave me the half smile that never fails to melt my heart. "Maybe build a fire?"

"Or we could have another romantic evening watching video podcasts about living like a Victorian."

Tom groaned. "Spare me."

For the main course, we shared the house specialty, moo yang—grilled pork and vegetables with a spicy tamarind sauce—which was a good thing because there was plenty for two. The waitress had just dropped off the sweets menu when Tom's phone pinged.

"It's Okoje. Be right back." Leaving the table, Tom moved into the lobby.

In minutes, he returned and threw four twenty-pound notes on the table. "Grab your jacket, Kate. There's been an accident. Teddy Pearce is in hospital. Lucky to be alive."

Chapter Twenty-Nine

The hospital in Plymouth was forty-five minutes south of Coombe Mallet. It was close to nine thirty when we arrived. Tom showed his warrant card to the ward nurse, and we were ushered immediately to the hospital's accident and emergency unit.

We found Quinn Pearce in the waiting room. Seeing us, she burst into tears.

I pulled her into my arms. "What's happened? Is Teddy all right?"

"They think so." She dabbed at her eyes with a damp tissue. "Oh, Kate. It's just so awful. And it's all my fault." She looked at me. "How did you find out?"

"DCI Okoje called us. He told us where you were. He wasn't sure how serious Teddy's injuries might be."

"He was conscious when they found him. They called me, and I drove down as quickly as I could."

"Is Uma watching the girls?"

"My mum's been staying with us too."

"Have the doctors told you anything?"

"Teddy's in theater now. His wrist was broken—maybe his collarbone. They're checking for"—her voice snagged—"internal injuries."

A kind-looking nurse appeared. "Mrs. Pearce, the doctor will be in to give you some information very soon. But you can see your husband now. He's asking for you." She looked at Tom and me. "Go in with her if you'd like. Friends are the best medicine."

As we entered, the nurse took me aside. "Mrs. Pearce has been extremely emotional. The doctor told her straightaway her husband's injuries didn't look serious. I don't think she believed them. Keep your eye on her, will you?"

Teddy's cubicle was small. He looked alert, but his left cheek was raw and bruised. He had a bandage on his forehead, and his left arm was in a sling. Quinn ran to him, sobbing. "I'm sorry, darling. I'm so sorry."

"Hey—come on, now." He attempted a smile. "You're all right." He noticed us. "Tom, Kate—you drove all the way down from Coombe Mallet?"

"Okoje called. What happened?"

"Run off the road, wasn't I?" He tried to raise himself up, but he grimaced and sank back. "I'd driven down to the coast to open a new shopping center. Quinn thought it would be good publicity. I was on my way home when some eegit came up behind me—fast. Thought he was trying to pass, so I moved over. He made contact. I spun out. Car rolled a few times. Missed a couple of trees."

Quinn covered her face. "You might have been killed."

"But I wasn't, luv. I'm all right. Or I will be."

"Were you able to give the police any details about the car or the driver?" Tom asked.

"Single driver. Male, I think. It was dark, but I'm pretty sure the car was an older-model Toyota. Black or navy. Didn't have time to clock the number plate."

"And the driver didn't stop to see if you were all right?" Tom asked.

"What d'you think, mate?" He tried to laugh, then winced. "*Ah* . . . bruised ribs. Dislocated shoulder. They've got me wrapped up like a bleedin' mummy."

"You believe this was an attempt to kill you."

"I know it was, mate."

A young doctor entered the cubicle. "Having a party, I see. Am I invited?" He grinned, showing very white teeth. "Well, you've used up one of your nine lives, Mr. Pearce, but you're going to be just fine."

"When am I getting my ticket out of here?" Pearce asked.

"We'd prefer to keep you overnight."

"Only I'm meant to be in the House tomorrow afternoon. Any reason I can't leave in the morning?"

"That arm will be in a sling for a few weeks," the doctor said. "You can take paracetamol but nothing more if you plan to drive."

Pearce saluted with his good arm. "Taken as read. Thanks for your help."

He was doing a good job of minimizing what might have been a fatal accident. Maybe for Quinn's sake. "You need time alone," I said, giving Quinn a final hug. "And we've got a long drive back. We'll be in touch."

Tom was quiet on the way home.

"You're worried about him, aren't you?" I said.

"Of course. He's lucky to be alive."

"Will the police give him protection in London?"

"Okoje notified the Met."

"Something's worrying you. What is it?"

The headlights of an oncoming car lit up Tom's face. He wasn't smiling. "Did you notice something odd about Quinn's reaction to the accident?"

"She was distraught—naturally. The nurse told me to keep an eye on her. She must have thought we were family."

"No, it's not that. It's the guilt. Why would Quinn feel guilty about the attack on her husband? She wasn't responsible."

"I wondered the same thing. Although she was the one who urged him to accept the invitation to Plymouth."

"Hmm." Tom was unconvinced.

"We don't really even know it was intentional, Tom. Maybe the person was a bad driver, or drunk, and when they realized they'd caused the car in front of them to go off the road, they panicked and fled."

Our conversation was interrupted when my cell phone buzzed—a number I didn't recognize. "Hello?"

"Is this Kate Hamilton? My name is Mercy Abbott. I hope I'm not calling too late."

"Not at all. Thank you for calling. Max Newlin said you'd be willing to talk with me about Gideon Littlejohn. You were friends, members of the same club, right?"

The line went silent for a moment. "I was shattered when I heard about his death. I've known Gideon for a long time. He was still married when we met. What do you want to know?"

"Just some background information. I'm sure Max told you my husband and I have been hired by the local history museum in Coombe Mallet. We're tracing the ownership of a Victorian dress donated recently by Mr. Littlejohn. We're hoping you might be able to help."

"I'm willing to answer questions, only we have a wedding at the hotel this weekend and then we take our annual inventory. All hands on deck. What about Wednesday next week? It's my day off. Could you come to the hotel? I don't have a car at the moment. Beechlands is less than an hour's drive from Coombe Mallet. I'll treat you to lunch."

* * *

It was nearly eleven thirty PM. when we reached the roundabout on the southeast side of Newton Abbot. Tom took the first exit.

"Quinn Pearce is hard to make out," he said. "You said it. She looks fragile, but there's a core of steel in there somewhere."

"I agree. She told me she has no interest in politics, yet she's the one who persuaded Teddy to take the photo op in Plymouth because she thought it would be good publicity."

"The attacks on Teddy have created publicity, and they've also created sympathy. Everyone loves an underdog."

"If Quinn's father *is* behind the attacks, what is there in it for him? From what I can tell, the attacks have made Teddy even more popular with the people than he was before."

"It's a good question. The police have been in contact with Karl Benables. He's in Germany, all right. Hamburg. Has been since the second of January."

"Strange time to do business."

"He says he's negotiating some big business deal. Complicated. Couldn't wait. He's flying home Thursday."

"Where do the Benables live?" I asked. "I don't think Quinn ever said."

"Their main residence is in Exeter. Then there's the hunting lodge on Dartmoor—we saw the photo. Plus a flat in London—Holland Park—and an apartment in Paris."

"The man must live out of a suitcase."

We drove in silence for a few minutes. "Have the cyberforensics guys made any progress unlocking Littlejohn's computer files?"

"The software manufacturer isn't cooperating. In criminal cases, the company is required by law to surrender the cryptographic key, but they're pushing back, citing competing privacy laws and the likelihood of revealing personal information that has nothing to do with the crime under investigation. A judge will most likely grant access, but it may take a while. Depends on how hard they want to fight it."

Tom turned left onto the Ashburton Road. We'd be at the Crown by midnight. I was more than ready to forget everything and fall into bed, but Tom wasn't quite finished. "Earlier you suggested a connection between the bloodstained dress and Littlejohn's murder. I'd like to know why."

"No reason." I yawned. "Synchronicity, the chain of events, unexplained coincidence."

"Only if you're right, the killer may be connected with the museum."

"Or someone who knows something about the dress that we don't." I yawned again.

"Which reminds me, did you find a reason for us to drop by Beryl Grey's house tomorrow?"

"Two reasons. Both good ones."

Chapter Thirty

Monday, January 13

The end-of-terrace house where Beryl Grey lived with her disabled husband was near the center of Coombe Mallet. The small front garden had been cemented over. Three recycling bins and a couple of orange traffic cones had been shoved against the brick wall separating the house from its nearest neighbor. Beside the door hung a pot filled with dead flowers.

I was feeling jumpy—and glad Tom was with me. Our meeting at Queenie's hadn't ended well. I'd mentioned the theft of the silver box and Gideon Littlejohn's intention to terminate her employment, which she'd vehemently denied. She'd also denied knowing anything about his death, but the police now had a credible witness who'd seen her arrive at the Old Merchant's House much earlier than she'd said. I had no idea how we'd slip that into the conversation.

We stood in front of the Greys' rough-cast terraced house and put on our warmest smiles. Tom squeezed my hand and rang the bell. No one came. He pushed the bell again. When there was still no answer, he knocked. "Mrs. Grey—it's the Mallorys. Kate found something that belongs to you. A Waitrose card and an envelope containing nearly fifty pounds. Are you home?"

That got results. Beryl Grey opened the door a few inches. She was dressed in a bright floral caftan and held a glass vase filled with fake hibiscus. Her hair, which had been tamed into a tight bun every time

I'd seen her, now hung loose around her shoulders. She looked younger and—well, sort of tropical.

"I wondered where that check had got to." She opened the door wider and reached out her hand. "I'll take them now. Thank you for coming."

"Could we come inside?" I gave her my best butter-wouldn't-melt smile. "Just for a few minutes? I have a few more questions about that chest, the one we saw in the morning room at the Old Merchant's House. I'm wondering if—"

My sentence was cut short when a huge Gandalf-like man with a shock of gray hair and a full grizzled beard appeared behind her in the hallway. The sleeves of his jersey were rolled up, revealing muscular forearms. He hefted a wooden step stool over one shoulder and held a toolbox in his other hand. "Where'd you say you want that—" Seeing us, he froze.

"Alan Grey, I presume?" Tom held up his warrant card.

"*Bugger!*" The man dropped the toolbox and step stool and raced down the hall toward the rear of the house. Tom took after him, brushing past Beryl Grey and vaulting over the ladder.

Beryl threw the glass vase at me. It missed, shattering to bits on the concrete stoop.

* * *

Fifteen minutes later we all sat in the Greys sad little parlor. Alan Grey, Beryl's supposedly disabled husband, had made an impressive getaway, but he was in his late sixties and had run out of gas pretty quickly. About fifty yards up the road, he'd simply stopped running, put his hands behind his back, and said, "Fair cop." Tom had cuffed him. Who knew British detectives carry disposable nylon handcuffs? The police were on their way to charge the Greys with benefits fraud. And possibly murder.

They hadn't realized that yet.

"We haven't spent the benefits money," Alan Grey whined. "Not a penny. What will they do to us?"

Alan, they admitted, in spite of the fact that he was in perfect health for his age, had been receiving disability benefits from the government for at least a year and a half.

"I don't know what the authorities will do," Tom said. "But I do know things will go better for you if you cooperate."

"Haven't you ever had a dream?" Beryl Grey bleated. "It's all gray skies and government regulations here. We never wanted to hurt anyone. Just enjoy a little sunshine and joy before it's too late."

"How did the fraud begin?" Tom asked.

"Got laid off, didn't I?" Alan Grey sat rubbing his wrists. Tom had removed the cuffs after Alan swore he wouldn't bolt again. I believed him. He was still short of breath.

"There's me, trottin' down to the job center every week, being told I should take some menial dead-end job because I was too old for anything else. Thought I'd go off me nut." He finger-combed his grizzled hair. "Then I had what the docs called a ministroke. I recovered quickly enough, but that's when we started thinking."

"We realized he could make more in benefits by being disabled," Beryl said. "The whole thing's a game anyway."

"You didn't work at all?" I asked.

"Course I did. I'm no layabout." Alan scowled. "Drive down to Torquay in tourist season, don't I? Busking along the seafront."

"Magic tricks, mind reading. Makes good money," Beryl said. "In winter, he does odd jobs for cash. Just not around here."

"I assume you were examined by doctors," I said. "How did you fool them?"

"Easy." Alan mimed the face the police must have seen—eyes out of focus, mumbling, a bit scary. "They can't look inside yer head, can they?"

"A nurse stopped by every few weeks," Beryl added. "Not always the same one. He'd be in bed or sitting in that chair. All I had to do was tell them he could become volatile, and they'd be out of here quick as anything."

"In the meantime, Beryl got a job with that Littlejohn fellow. Pulling in good money."

"Which we saved—every bit of it," Beryl said. "And Mr. Littlejohn didn't mind me taking home the leftovers for Alan's tea. I'm telling the truth about that."

"The thing is," said Alan. "We'd found a nice little bungalow in Belize. Mango tree in the yard. Ten-minute walk to the beach. Small, but it's all we need. Beryl put a down payment on it with her savings."

Beryl Grey blinked away tears. "We'll never see it now—or the money."

"You really thought you could get away with it?" I was amazed at the boldness of their plan.

"Why not?" Alan shrugged. "Almost did until *Mr. History* accused my wife of stealing that silver box."

"And now he's dead," Tom said.

"Nothing to do with us," Beryl screeched. "Might have been anybody. He liked knowing secrets and using them when it suited him."

"What are you talking about?" I asked, remembering that Clive Nixon had said the same thing.

"Household staff are invisible. You hear things, don't you?"

"Like what?"

"Like those businessmen who've been cutting corners. I heard him talking to someone on the local council about that. Naming names. Said he had proof."

"That's not a secret."

Beryl Grey looked up. "He threatened someone on the telephone. I don't know who it was, and I don't know the details. I just know Mr. Littlejohn had looked into this person's background and threatened to go public with something if the guy didn't agree to . . . whatever it was he wanted. Quite a shouting match, it was. Later, Mr. Littlejohn called me into his study and said, 'One of the things I insist upon is loyalty and discretion, Mrs. Grey. Do you understand?' and I said, 'I understand perfectly, sir. I didn't hear a thing.' Of course he's dead now, so it doesn't matter, does it?"

"He knew a secret about you, didn't he, Beryl?" Tom said. "You'd been stealing from him."

"I told you—that's a lie," she shouted. "I didn't steal that silver box."

"Okay, that's enough." Tom checked his watch. "The police will be arriving soon. They'll take your statements."

"You mean stitch us up for his murder," Alan growled.

"I mean take your statements," Tom said. "But you will have to answer questions. Not just about the silver box. Your wife will have to explain why a neighbor saw her arrive at the house the day Littlejohn was murdered—much earlier than she said in her first statement."

"I didn't shoot him," Beryl squeaked. She looked at me. "You were there. You saw. I was shocked."

"We did," I said, wanting to calm her down but also remembering her former career on the stage. "But you lied in your first statement. Why?"

The Greys looked at each other, then at us. They were going to brazen this out.

"Beryl," I said, "the police are going to look into everything now—Alan's health, your finances, the witness statements they've already taken. And there's probably CCTV footage out there. You can't go anywhere these days without leaving a trace."

"She's right," Tom said. "The police will learn the truth one way or the other. And their main concern right now isn't benefits fraud. It's murder."

Beryl clutched her throat. "But I didn't do it."

"No way out of this, luv." Alan shrugged. "Might as well come clean."

Beryl started to weep. "They're gonna say I killed him. I know they will."

"Not if we tell the truth." Alan gave her a hard stare. "*All* of it."

I sat forward in my chair. This was going to be good.

"Hold on," Tom said. "I'm not in charge of this investigation. You have rights. You need legal advice. The police will arrange that."

"What if we'd rather talk to you?" Alan snapped, proving the power of reverse psychology. "We have the right to remain silent, and we have the right to talk."

"You need a solicitor. If you don't have one, the police will provide one for you."

"We waive that right, don't we, Beryl?" Alan looked at his wife. "Let's get this out of the way now—before the police go all narky on us." He stood and put his hands on his hips. "We want to give a statement—right, Beryl?"

She didn't look too sure. "I suppose we'd rather tell you than the police."

Tom *was* police, but saying so wasn't going to help.

"Look," Tom said. "This isn't the way things are done. You could say I pressured you to make a statement without legal representation. I'm not willing to do that. This is my job."

"Record it, then," Alan said, "on your mobile. We'll make it clear we're doing this over your objections."

I could see Tom's brain working. The police would soon arrive and take a proper statement, but the Greys wanted to talk. They might not feel that way later. He took out his mobile phone and handed it to me. "If you insist, we're going to do this properly."

"Why not?"

I pulled up his recording app and pushed start. "Okay—it's on."

Tom began. "This is DI Tom Mallory of the Suffolk Constabulary. It is eleven forty on Monday, January thirteenth. This voluntary recording is being made at the Grey residence on Chapel Lane, Coombe Mallet. Present in the room are Mrs. Kate Hamilton, Mr. Alan Grey, and Mrs. Beryl Grey." He read them their rights. Then he said, "I have advised them to wait for the arrival of the police from Newton Abbot. I have also advised them to wait until they have legal representation. Is that correct, Mrs. Grey? Mr. Grey?"

"That is correct, sir," said Alan Grey in a loud voice. "We wish to make a statement now and waive the right to remain silent and to counsel."

"Do you agree, Mrs. Grey? Do you also waive your right to remain silent and to counsel?"

She nodded.

"Aloud for the record, please." Tom gave me an exasperated look. "This is bizarre."

"I waive the right to remain silent and to counsel." Beryl Grey pressed her thin lips together.

"You said in your earlier statement that you first arrived at the Old Merchant's House on Saturday, January fifth, at exactly twelve noon. Was that the truth?"

"No."

"Louder, please."

"No, it wasn't the truth."

"When did you arrive?"

"A few minutes before nine. I knew Mr. Littlejohn had an appointment that morning. I wanted to speak with him before his guest arrived."

"What did you want to speak with him about?"

"About the silver box. He'd accused me of stealing it."

"Was he right about that?"

"No. I admit I was tempted, but you can't arrest someone for something they might have done, can you?"

"So you went there to convince him not to tell the police about the silver box? Was there any other reason you wanted to speak with him privately?"

"The whole truth, luv," Alan Grey said.

Beryl shot her husband a look. "All right." Her shoulders slumped. "Mr. Littlejohn had found out about Alan, about the busking."

"You mean he found out you'd been claiming benefits fraudulently?"

"Yes."

"How did he find out?"

"I don't know, do I? Something to do with those computers of his."

"He didn't offer any proof?"

"He said he'd checked our banking records. Things didn't add up."

"All those cash deposits," Alan explained. "And the down payment on the house in Belize. He knew."

"Let's talk about the morning of his death. You arrived at the Old Merchant's House a few minutes before nine because you wanted to speak with Mr. Littlejohn about the benefits fraud. What exactly were you hoping to achieve?"

"He'd told me he was hiring a replacement as soon as the agency found a suitable candidate. I wanted him to keep me on—just for another few months. I was going to tell him about our dreams. Plead with him not to go to the police. We weren't hurting anybody. I hadn't stolen anything. Not really."

"You wanted to convince him not to press charges."

"I thought if I told him about my husband's stroke and all those trips down to the job center, he might sympathize."

"And did you speak to Mr. Littlejohn?"

"Never got a chance, did I? I heard voices in his study. Realized someone was with him."

"Who was it?"

"A man."

"Did you recognize the voice?"

"No. I'd never heard it before. And I'm good with voices. Might forget a name but never a voice."

"Did you see the man?"

"No. The door to the study was shut."

"Was there a vehicle parked in front of the house when you arrived?"

"I didn't notice."

"But you heard something, didn't you?"

"I may have." Beryl studied her hands. "A phrase or two."

"Tell us what you heard, Mrs. Grey."

"They were arguing. The man said, 'This will ruin me,' and Mr. Littlejohn said, 'You should have thought of that. What's done is done.'"

"What did he mean?"

"I don't know, do I?"

"Was this the same person you'd heard your employer threaten on the telephone earlier?"

"How would I know?"

"What did you do then?"

"Got out of there as fast as I could."

Tom shook his head. "You do realize, don't you, Mrs. Grey, that you've withheld important information from the police?"

"How could it be important when I don't know who was there?" She squared her shoulders.

"A few more questions," Tom said. "Where did you go when you left?"

"Home."

Alan Grey held up a finger. "I can vouch for that."

"And when did you return to the Old Merchant's House?"

"Eleven thirty." She blinked. "I *know* I told the police twelve noon, but I figured his interview would be over and I might have a chance to speak with him before you arrived."

"And what happened?"

"That's when—" Her voice cracked. "When I found his body."

"You went upstairs?"

"He wasn't in his study or the morning room, so I went upstairs and called his name. The rest of what I said that morning is true. About seeing the door of his computer room standing open."

"You found Mr. Littlejohn's body at eleven thirty, not twelve thirty as you've testified?"

"Yes."

"Why didn't you call for help?"

"Because he was dead, wasn't he? I felt for a pulse. When I saw all that blood—it was all over me—I knew the police would think it was me as killed him. How was I to know he hadn't already told the police about Alan? I panicked."

"Are you saying Mr. Littlejohn had *two* visitors that morning?"

"He could have had ten visitors, for all I know. Maybe he had more than one appointment."

"You said earlier you saw the tea things in the sink at eleven thirty. Could they have been there when you arrived the first time at nine AM?"

Beryl Grey stared into space for a moment. "No. I remember. When I got to the house at nine, the tea things were still on the counter and the plate of biscuits covered with cling film."

Was that significant? Probably, but I didn't know how.

"What did you do after you found the body?" Tom asked. "I'm talking about the time between eleven thirty and twelve forty when we arrived."

"I was in shock. That's the truth. I decided to follow my routine. First thing, I went down to the kitchen and scrubbed my hands. Then I realized if they found traces of blood in the pipe, it would make me look guilty, so I poured bleach down the drain. Then I began preparing his lunch as always. I took the sandwiches out of the fridge and put the soup on the hob to heat, just like I told the police."

I pictured her going about her duties, her apron soaked with his blood. She must have been in shock.

"Why would you go through the motions when Mr. Littlejohn was already dead?" Tom asked.

"Because I wanted it to look as if I didn't know yet, of course." She looked at him as if he were slow-witted.

"But you were upstairs when we arrived. You screamed."

"Saw you coming, didn't I?" One corner of her mouth turned up. "I heard a vehicle pull up and ran to the front window. *Perfect*, I thought. *Witnesses.* I can think on my feet when I have to. I unlocked the front door because I knew you'd try the handle. Then I ran up the stairs and stood by the door to the computer room. When I heard you knock, I screamed."

"But you had fresh blood on your hands and apron," I said.

Beryl Grey's cheeks turned pink. "Had to make it look as if I'd just found him, didn't I?"

"You mean you went back into the computer room and . . ." I couldn't finish the sentence.

She nodded.

Tom sighed. "Is there anything you would like to add, Mrs. Grey?"

"Yes." She pulled herself up to her full height. "I didn't kill him. Someone shot him—someone who was there that morning. But it wasn't me. I don't even own a gun. I swear it."

I watched Tom tap out a text. "I'm sending this recording to Detective Inspector Okoje."

The faint sound of a siren outside told us the police were close.

Alan Grey reached for his wife's hand.

* * *

That evening, while we were getting ready for bed, Okoje phoned Tom. They spoke for less than five minutes.

"What happened to the Greys?" I asked when Tom rang off.

"They've been charged with benefits fraud, making false statements, perverting the course of justice, and wasting police time."

"Not murder?"

"No evidence—at least not yet. A solicitor has been appointed. They'll probably be released until their trial date."

"What do you think will happen to them in the end?"

Tom shrugged. "Assuming they're telling the truth about Littlejohn, if they pay back the money and if they're very lucky indeed, they might get a suspended sentence."

"What I want to know is, who got tea?"

Chapter Thirty-One

Tuesday, January 14

Maggie Hughes plunked a banker's box on the table in the library's glassed-walled conference room, raising a cloud of dust. She sneezed and fanned the air. "Dust and must—no wonder so many librarians develop allergies. I haven't had time to go through this lot yet. We've been working on our Valentine's Day exhibits. You know the kind of thing—romance novels, books with red covers, paper hearts."

Maggie had emailed me early that morning, following up on my request for more information about the Squires family. I peered into the open box, seeing an assortment of old printed materials—notebooks, folders, brochures, flyers, magazines, and papers clipped together. "What is this?"

"Local history. Forty years ago our head librarian—deceased now, of course—decided to enhance the library's local history section. She asked the community to donate books or papers of historical value." She gave me an ironic smile. "*Value* is a relative term, isn't it? Everyone in Coombe Mallet took the opportunity to clean out their attics. The library staff didn't have the resources to sort through everything then, so they did the best they could and stored the rest. You're lucky these didn't get sent to the county record office. This box is one of about a dozen. I'm afraid I can't let you take the box away, but if you have the time, you're more than welcome to look through it here."

"Thank you. Does this box cover a particular time frame?" I was thinking about those twelve boxes and mentally calculating the hours it would take to sort through several centuries' worth of detritus.

"Fortunately, yes." Maggie pointed out a label on the side of the box that read *1850 to 1900*. "That was one of the smartest things she did—setting out bins for materials, marked by date. Not everybody cooperated. Some just dumped stuff in the nearest bin and took off, but it saved us time sorting through. There were a few amazing finds—a broadsheet published on the death of Queen Anne in 1714, for example. That's on display in our history section. We also found an early edition of Samuel Johnson's *Dictionary of the English Language* and a third edition of Horace Walpole's *Castle of Otranto*. Beyond that, it was all local family history. Like this." She lifted out a red scrapbook and laid it on the table. "If you find anything you think may be of value, just leave it on the table. I'll take a look. If you have questions, give me a shout. I'll be in the children's section, just past the help desk."

I thanked her and got to work. I'd done this, or something similar, hundreds of times in my career, sorting through mountains of junk in the hopes of finding a single treasure. I started with the scrapbook, which was charming—filled, as I thought it would be, with Christmas cards and Valentines, calling cards, awards of merit from a child's teacher, poems, and Bible verses. On a good day, the scrapbook might fetch a hundred pounds at auction, but I saw nothing relating to the Squires family—or the Merivales.

After an hour or so, I'd found no treasures, but there were a few items I thought Maggie might like to check out. One was an inventory of Dartmoor ponies owned by one of the landowners. Obviously an animal lover, he'd given each pony a name and carefully documented their physical condition and any medical treatment they'd received. There was also a ledger for a ladies' haberdashery in the village of Buckfastleigh from the 1880s and a huge leather Bible with a family tree listing seven generations of a family named Chulmleigh. If there were any Chulmleighs still living, they might want their Bible back.

Near the bottom of the box I found a thick bundle of newsprint, rolled up and tied with twine. The bundle turned out to be several dozen editions of a newspaper called *The Village Tatler*, published in Widdecombe Throop between 1884 and 1886. Now this really was a treasure—at least to me. I was holding a contemporary account of a lost village.

Before diving in, I needed basic information.

I found Maggie in the children's reading room, sitting at a child-sized table with her legs stretched out in front of her. She was cutting out red paper hearts. "We're expecting a group of toddlers this afternoon. They're going to make valentines for their parents. How's it going? Can I help?"

"I found something you might want to see. Local newspapers from Widdecombe Throop, the submerged village. Do you know anything about *The Village Tatler*?"

"A newspaper? Really?" She put down the scissors and the heart she'd been working on. "I didn't know there *was* a newspaper in Widdecombe Throop. Well done, Kate. Let's have a look."

"Why would someone start up a newspaper in such a small village?" I asked on the way back to the conference room. "They couldn't have had a large circulation."

"Small local papers never expected a large circulation. All news was local news then. People didn't travel far from home, so events in other counties were of little consequence. They were interested in what was happening in their own particular area because that news impacted their lives."

I'd spread the papers on the table. Each consisted of two pages printed on both sides with seven columns of tightly packed text plus adverts.

Maggie thumbed gingerly through the sheets, touching only the edges. "My goodness. These should have been treated with more care. Looks to me like they were published weekly, but quite a few are missing. Probably used as kindling. What a shame."

I pulled a pair of white cotton gloves from my handbag. "Is it all right if I examine them?"

"Of course. Newspapers are a vital source of information." She straightened her back. "There's so much we'll never know about the past because the documentation wasn't preserved. History isn't just major events like wars and shocking crimes and changes in government. And it isn't driven only by wealthy, powerful, and famous people. History is the sum total of individual lives, the lives of ordinary people who lived in remote villages like Widdecombe Throop—what they believed, how they interpreted their lives, what actions they took to meet the challenges they faced, and how they changed their world, one day at a time. That's why historic newspapers are so incredibly valuable. They provide a snapshot of the lives of real people in a particular place on a particular day or week." Her cheeks were flushed. She laughed. "I'm sorry. I'm on my soapbox now. I guess you can tell where my interests lie."

"Mine too," I said. "That's the way I feel about antiques and antiquities. Not all of them are valuable in themselves, but they all have stories to tell."

"If only they could speak to us," Maggie said.

I thought about the dress and the Gypsy-set ring. They'd spoken to me, all right. The problem was interpreting the cryptic messages they'd conveyed.

Maggie touched my arm. "I should get back. Hearts don't wait forever." She laughed. "Let me know if you find something of interest."

Maggie left, and I began with the issue of the *Tatler* published on the twelfth of September 1885—five days after the incident involving Nancy Thorne. Page one was given to advertisements—for shoes and boots, fine leather gloves, wines and spirits, Yorkshire coal, and the services of Blake & Sons—coffins, undertaking, and general funeral requisites. I turned the page, and there it was on page two, the article about Nancy Thorne, in black and white—word for word. So the account had been published first in the local newspaper. Three weeks later the story was picked up by the *South Devon Post.* Finally in 1942, the same account appeared in the script of the radio documentary Hawksworthy had provided to Nash & Holmes.

I wondered how Nancy Thorne had felt about that first newspaper article and the suspicions that would cling to her for the rest of her short life. Why hadn't she ever revealed what happened that night? I could think of two possibilities: Either she really was guilty of murder and determined not to incriminate herself, or she truly didn't know what happened that night.

No, I thought with sudden clarity; there was a third possibility. She could have been protecting someone.

If only there was more to go on with. Letters, for example. Or a diary to give us insight into her character.

Someone, somewhere, knew what had transpired on the seventh of September 1885. The fact that I might never learn the truth was frustrating. My interest in the blood-soaked dress had expanded from a simple case of tracing provenance to a fascination with Nancy herself. I wanted to know what happened.

Returning to the *Tatler*, I scanned the subsequent issues—September nineteenth, September twenty-sixth, October third, October tenth. Fascinating as this snapshot of nineteenth-century village life was, I found nothing more about Nancy Thorne. Whatever the local gossip might have been, it hadn't made it into the newspapers.

I sat for a moment, wondering whether I should put the *Tatler* aside and finish off the box. A thought occurred to me: what about Queenie's funeral and the incident reported by Dr. Nutcombe? The funeral had been held on the twenty-eighth of August. Unfortunately, the issue of the *Tatler* published on the following day, the twenty-ninth, was missing. I moved to the next issue, published on September fifth.

And sure enough—there was a small article on the second page with a headline reading "Violence on the Gypsy Camp Raises Alarm." This had to be the incident Dr. Nutcombe mentioned in his daybook. I struggled to read the fine print:

> *A serious incident took place last Friday week following the funeral of Mrs. Queenie Squires, a Gypsy, a colorful character well known in this part of Devon. According to eyewitnesses, a dispute arose between Tawno Squires, 43, and Luke Heron, 31, both grandsons of the deceased. Gunfire was reported, although no one was injured. Sir Henry Merivale, fearing the altercation*

on his land might escalate, sent for the local police, but Constable Percy Chapel found no one willing to speak about the incident. Leverin Squires, son of the deceased woman and father of one of the young men, refused to give police any information but assured Constable Chapel that the matter had been settled and the family would be moving on in a matter of weeks.

It wasn't much, but as this had happened so close to the incident of the bloodstained dress, I couldn't help wondering again if they were connected. Almost a month later, on October eighth, Dr. Nutcombe had written in his daybook that several of the men in the Squires family had left to pursue work elsewhere. Were they the men mentioned in the article—Tawno Squires and Luke Heron? What had they argued about? Had the family expelled them? Possibly, although I had no idea how the Romanichals handled disputes. It did strike me that family ties wouldn't have been easily or thoughtlessly broken. If these young men had struck off on their own, something very serious must have occurred.

I found Maggie again. "Were Romani families counted in the census records in, say, 1891?"

"Yes, of course. The census records are a major source of information for Romani genealogists, as are parish records of baptisms, marriages, and funerals—even before 1841, when the information recorded was pretty basic. Why do you ask?"

I told her about the article I'd found concerning the incident following Queenie's funeral. "Remember the photograph you showed me, the one of Queenie Squires and her family? I'd like to search for Tawno Squires and Luke Heron in the 1891 and 1901 census records." I remembered Dr. Bob Smith saying there had been no Luke Heron in the 1891 census, and I believed him, but it wouldn't hurt to recheck. Besides, I knew from experience that census takers in the past sometimes got names wrong—or their handwriting was later misread and therefore misrecorded.

"I'll do that." She made a note. "Thanks for giving me an interesting task. Cutting out paper hearts isn't my favorite job at the library." Her eyes sparkled. "Give you a call if I find something?"

"Please. You might not find them in Dartmoor, or even Devon."

"No problem. With their names, ages, and the names of their parents, I can search for them in the every-name index. If they're there, I'll find them."

"Maggie, that's terrific. Would it be possible to get a copy of the photograph—the one taken in front of Queenie's vardo?"

"Of course. It's in my office. Follow me."

The photo was on her desk. Printed in white ink along the bottom was the date—August 1884. She laid the photo facedown on her printer. Turning it over, she printed the back side as well, so I would also have the names written there.

In minutes, I held the image in my hand and had located the faces of the two grandsons mentioned in the Tatler article.

Tawno Squires, strong, confident, proud of his young family.

Luke Heron, the beautiful young man with the mesmerizing eyes.

There was Queenie. I looked more closely. "Wait a minute." I fumbled in my handbag for my lighted magnifier. Holding it up to the photo, I focused on the old woman in all her finery, sitting in the midst of her family.

Suddenly I knew what my brain had been trying to tell me for days.

In the photograph, Queenie Squires wore an intricately woven jet-bead necklace, identical to the broken necklace at the museum, the one Gideon Littlejohn had said he'd found with the dress—and the jet beads I'd found in the compartmented drawer inside the trunk.

How had a necklace belonging to a Romani matriarch come into the possession of Gideon Littlejohn?

* * *

After an early lunch at the Crown, I drove to the Museum of Devon Life. I had the trunk with me, and I wanted Julia Kelly to examine it, especially the yellow print lining. I was confident that the workmanship would match that of the bloodstained dress and the red silk ball gown, but she was the expert.

Tom had texted to say Beryl Grey had been released from custody, at least for the time being. They were keeping Alan Grey, awaiting the arrival of a fraud investigation officer from His Majesty's Revenue and Customs. Alan was in trouble. They both were. But not as much trouble as they would be if the police thought they were responsible for Gideon Littlejohn's death.

I met Dr. Hawksworthy on the way in. "Let me take that," he said gallantly, lifting the trunk out of my arms. "So this is it, eh? The trunk where Gideon Littlejohn found the dress and the other items."

"That's what he told me. I've asked Julia to examine the interior."

"Will the museum get the trunk after all, do you think? It would certainly enhance the exhibit."

"It belongs to Gideon's sister now. She might sell it to you." I doubted anything but cold, hard cash would persuade Donna Nixon.

When we reached Julia Kelly's workroom, I held the door open for Hugo.

"Set it on the work top." Julia clasped her hands. "Oh, this will be fun."

"I'll leave you to it, then." Hugo headed for the door.

"Will you be in your office later?" I asked. "I'd like to stop by before I leave."

"Of course. Anytime."

Julia had already opened the trunk and was examining the padded lining. "The workmanship is exquisite." She straightened her back and gave an appreciative sigh. "Everything this woman did was performed with great skill and care."

"You believe the lining of the trunk was installed by Sally Thorne, then?"

"I'm sure of it. Look at the way she's handled the self-cording. Invisible stitches. And look at the seams, where the fabric meets the inside of the dome." She ran her finger along the padded edge of the fabric. "You can feel the wooden slats inside, but you'd never know they're there, even after all these years. The tiny stitches are absolute perfection. All you see is a bead of silk thread every half inch or so. Everything is precise and decorative."

"What about the fabric?"

"Well, that's amazing too, isn't it? Exceptionally fine cotton, tightly woven, probably French. The floral patterns are precise. See?" She pointed at one of the flower motifs. "The design was created with three colors, each rolled separately but with great care to match up exactly. This fabric would have been quite expensive. I imagine it was purchased for a client's commission, and Sally used what was left over to line the trunk."

"Is there anything else we can learn?"

"The lining has been repaired. See there?" She showed me a slight irregularity along the self-cording on the right-hand side of the domed lid.

"I see what you mean." Still, if Julia hadn't pointed it out, I might not have noticed.

"I'd like to keep the trunk for a few days," she said. "And with your permission, I'll release one of the panels—probably at the point of repair—in order to examine the construction beneath. I want to know what she used for padding—probably several layers. And how she managed to keep the fabric so uniformly stretched over the slats. I'll sew everything back with a slightly different thread. For historical purposes, we always show the work we've done as conservators."

"Yes, of course. I can stop back whenever you like."

"Thank you for the opportunity." She offered me her hand. "I can't wait to get stuck in."

Chapter Thirty-Two

Back on the ground floor, I saw Isla Ferris behind the ticket counter, arranging piles of museum brochures and maps.

"I'd like to see Dr. Hawksworthy," I said. "Is he free?"

"I'll just ask, shall I?" I got the message: *I'm the gatekeeper.* She disappeared into his office, returning moments later. "He'll see you. Don't stay long, mind you. He has a meeting with a donor in less than an hour." She eyed my jacket. "Let me take that. I'll hang it in the cloakroom."

Hawksworthy was at his computer. He looked up. "Come in. Have a seat. Coffee? Tea?"

I declined his offer, and we moved to the white leather chairs.

"You have questions?" he said, his face open and pleasant.

"Yes, but I have something to tell you first—about that note accusing Nancy Thorne of murder. You said it was a fake. You were right. Gideon Littlejohn wrote it himself."

"My goodness." He leaned forward. "How did you find that out?"

"He'd been practicing his copperplate—and the text of the note."

"I see." He ran his hand over his smooth jawline. "Extraordinary."

"My question is why? Why would he do it? Was he trying to entice you into accepting the dress for the local crimes exhibit?"

"*Entice* me?" Hawksworthy barked a laugh. "I was over the moon. We'd just announced the construction of the new wing and the local-crimes exhibit. I needed a centerpiece—something that would capture people's imagination. A bloodstained dress was just the ticket."

"But without the note, how would you have connected the dress with a crime?"

Hawksworthy frowned. "I suppose I wouldn't have."

"Did Littlejohn tell you where he found the dress?"

"You know that already. In the trunk he bought at auction."

"He didn't buy it at auction. The trunk wasn't part of the lot he purchased."

Hawksworthy's eyebrows shot up. "So where did he get it?"

"That's what we're trying to find out." I watched his face, seeing confusion. "Back to the note. What exactly did Littlejohn tell you about it?"

"Just that he'd found it pinned to the dress. He said he'd heard about our new exhibit and thought we might be interested in owning the dress. He had no use for it. Of course, we were delighted. When I asked if he would donate the trunk as well, he said that wasn't possible."

"Did he say why not?"

"No."

"Didn't that raise red flags?"

"Why should it? It was certainly his right. But I did hope he might change his mind."

"Why did you contact Nash & Holmes? Were you suspicious of the dress?"

"No, I wasn't. We'd found the radio documentary, the one I provided to Nash & Holmes. Everything seemed straightforward." He rubbed his ear. "Well, except for the obvious question: why would such a dress have been preserved—and by whom? But truthfully, we engaged private investigators—you and your husband, as it turned out—because Littlejohn insisted. He told me he had one requirement. He wanted to be sure the dress really had belonged to Nancy Thorne, and he wanted us to learn all we could about the circumstances surrounding the incident in September of 1885. Was Nancy Thorne a murderess as the note claimed? If so, whom did she murder and why? Of course I was happy to oblige. If the dress was going to be the centerpiece of our new exhibit, we wanted to know as much about it as possible anyway. From the museum's perspective, all we really needed to do was trace the ownership of the dress to Nancy Thorne. Littlejohn wanted more, and I thought, fine. If we can solve an old mystery, so much the better. I warned him we might not be able to answer his questions. He agreed as long as we did our due diligence."

"Why Nash & Holmes? Was it because of my husband's uncle?"

"Ah, yes—Nigel Hartley. He's one of our most generous supporters. His donation early on allowed us to begin construction on the new wing. But no—I didn't know Nigel had a nephew until recently. The truth is, Nash & Holmes has a reputation, Ms. Hamilton. They've done work in the past for other museums. You must know that."

I didn't, but I wasn't going to tell him. "So Gideon Littlejohn's goal was to find out if the dress really had belonged to Nancy Thorne and then if she had indeed committed murder."

"Exactly. He really wanted to solve the mystery. I did too, but he was insistent. He wanted the dress to be seen by the public, and he wanted the public to know exactly what Nancy had done. Almost as if he wanted justice to prevail after nearly a hundred and forty years."

Justice for whom? "What made him think we could find out what the police in 1885 never did?"

"I can't imagine, but if we wanted the dress, we had to comply. That's why we hired Nash & Holmes. No one here has the time to do that kind of research."

"What did you think when Gideon Littlejohn was murdered?"

"What did I *think*?" Hawksworthy glared at me as if I'd suggested he might enjoy a afternoon's excursion to an abattoir. "I thought it was appalling. Shocking. Disgusting."

"What I meant was, is it possible Littlejohn's murder had something to do with the investigation into the origins of the dress?"

"*Absolutely not.* What an idea. Now, if you'll excuse me. I have an important phone call." He strode to his office door and held it open. "I hope I've answered your questions, Ms. Hamilton. I'm afraid there's nothing more I can tell you."

Time to make an exit.

* * *

I didn't get far. Beryl Grey stood near the ticket counter, looking uncertain. She was dressed in conservative beige slacks and a thick navy coat. I was still having a hard time moving her mentally out of the nineteenth century. When she saw me, she rushed forward. "I saw your car outside. You have to help me." She grabbed my sleeve. "They're going to charge us with murder, and we didn't do it."

Two older couples who'd been examining the museum map looked up in surprise.

Isla Ferris fluttered her hand. "*Shhh.* Keep your voices down, *please.*"

"The police kept Alan in custody," Beryl said, ignoring Isla. "They're still questioning him about the fraud."

"But they released you. As far as I know, they haven't charged either of you with murder."

"They're going to. I know they are."

"You *don't* know that. Besides, what can Tom and I do? We have to tell the truth."

"But that's what *we're* doing." Her voice was almost a screech. "They don't believe us. You've got to help."

Isla came around the counter. "I'm afraid you're going to have to leave."

"Why tell me?" I asked Beryl. "I'm not the police."

"No, but your husband is. They'll listen to him."

"We've told the police everything we know."

"That's quite enough." Isla began steering Beryl toward the exit.

I followed.

"They appointed a solicitor for us. She's young, but she seems competent." Beryl shook off Isla's hand angrily. "I'm going. No need to get huffy."

Isla handed me my jacket. "Leave now, please."

"Well, then, take your solicitor's advice," I told Beryl. "Tell her everything—don't hold back. If you aren't guilty—of murder, I mean—she'll be able to help." I slipped on my jacket as we moved toward the exit.

"Go, go." Isla shooed us.

"Do you really think so?" Beryl looked like a lost child.

"Look—Beryl." I stopped at the door to zip up my jacket. "I shouldn't get involved, but they've released you for now. That means they don't have evidence you shot Mr. Littlejohn. And you just told me they're questioning your husband about the benefits fraud. They do have evidence against him on that count."

"I know." She shook her head. "Stupid to think we could pull it off."

"They may question you again about the murder. When they do, stick to the truth. They'll try to rattle you, see if your testimony changes. Just answer honestly and fully."

Beryl wiped her eyes on her sleeve. "Thank you. I—"

My hand was on the glass exit door when Dr. Hawksworthy came striding out of his office. "Isla, where's that folder I asked for? I need to review it before my meeting."

"It's right here."

I felt Beryl's fingers clutch my arm.

Outside, the first drops of rain speckled the concrete. "What's wrong?"

"*Who is that man?*" she hissed, glancing over her shoulder as if someone might have followed us out.

"Hugo Hawksworthy, the museum director. Why?"

"He's the person I heard that morning. With Mr. Littlejohn. They were together in the study when I arrived at nine o'clock."

"Are you sure?"

"I told you—I never forget a voice."

"Come with me." I pulled out my cell phone.

Chapter Thirty-Three

Ten minutes later, Okoje's Ford hybrid slid silently into the museum's parking lot. The doors opened. Okoje, Varma, and Tom stepped out.

Beryl Grey and I had been huddled inside my car for warmth. Seeing them, we got out and stood in the drizzling rain.

"Is Hawksworthy still here?" Okoje asked.

"We haven't seen him come out," I said, "and I'm pretty sure that black BMW over there belongs to him."

"Take Mrs. Grey home, please," Okoje told DS Varma. To Beryl Grey he said, "We'll need you to make a statement. Stop by the police station first thing in the morning."

"Are you going to let Alan go? He isn't going to do a runner, if that's what you're afraid of."

The fact that he'd already "done a runner" seemed to have escaped her. But all in all, I agreed. Once Alan knew he was caught, he'd folded like a paper fan.

"We'll let you know," Okoje said. "Mrs. Hamilton, come with us. We're going to have a chat with the museum director."

The glass doors of the museum swung open. Isla Ferris glared at us. "Yes? What is it?"

"We'd like to speak with Dr. Hawksworthy," Okoje said.

"I'm afraid that's not possible." She came around the counter and stood blocking the way to the offices. "He's on an important Zoom call with one of our donors. It might take some time."

"I'm afraid you're going to have to interrupt him."

"But . . ." She made a sound somewhere between a *tsk* and a *tut*.

"Just get him, please." Okoje folded his arms across his broad chest.

She bustled off, muttering under her breath. We heard a soft knock on the office door. Two minutes later, Hawksworthy emerged. "Couldn't this have waited?" he asked, sounding both irritated and wary. "I may have just lost a six-figure donation."

"You can call him back." Okoje managed a tight smile. "We have a few questions, if you don't mind. It won't take long."

Hawksworthy arranged his face in a more welcoming expression and made a maître d's flourish with his arm. "Step into my office. Unless you intend to do this in public."

"I'll wait here with Ms. Ferris," I said.

"No," Hawksworthy said, "Tom and Kate, join us, both of you. I have nothing to hide."

Isla stepped forward. "I'd like to be there as well."

"Afraid not," Okoje said.

Hawksworthy put his hand on her shoulder. "It's fine, Isla. We need someone out here." He must have noticed her dismay. "It'll be all right, really. I'll answer their questions, and they'll leave."

We entered Hawksworthy's office. He closed the door. "Have a seat. I'd offer coffee or tea, but as you say, you won't be here long. "

"This isn't a formal interview." Okoje's huge frame overwhelmed the white leather chair.

"Which means I can decline to answer?"

"Certainly," Okoje said smoothly. "If you'd rather come into the station for a formal interview, that can be arranged."

Some of the bravado on Hawksworthy's face melted. "What's this about?"

"Tell us about your relationship with Mr. Littlejohn."

"My *relationship*?" Hawksworthy shot me an accusing look. "He was one of our supporters. He had an—er, interest in the Victorian era. When he heard about our new exhibit featuring famous crimes in Devon's history, he donated a Victorian dress and a collection of objects found with it."

"Were there any stipulations?"

"Yes. Mrs. Hamilton and I just had this conversation. It's no secret. Littlejohn wanted us to undertake an investigation into the origins of the dress. We agreed to hire a private investigations firm, Nash & Holmes. They sent the Mallorys."

I gave Tom a side glance. I could tell he'd have liked to ask a few questions of his own, but this was Okoje's interview. He wouldn't interrupt.

"Why was Mr. Littlejohn interested in the origins of the dress?" Okoje asked. "What did he hope to learn from an investigation?"

"I told all this to Mrs. Hamilton. He wanted to establish the authenticity of the dress. So did we. But he also wanted to know if Nancy Thorne had indeed murdered someone in 1885. Frankly, I didn't believe an answer could be found. Not after all this time. Not unless further evidence was uncovered. That's why we hired Nash & Holmes—to satisfy his . . . stipulations, as you put it."

"Did you have a personal relationship as well—a friendship? You were about the same age. Did you socialize?"

"Never."

"All right. Thank you. Let's move to the morning of Sunday, January fifth, the day Mr. Littlejohn was murdered. A witness claims you were at the Old Merchant's House around nine AM, arguing with Mr. Littlejohn in his study. Why were you there?"

"But I wasn't there." Hawksworthy looked at Tom, then me.

"Are you sure of that, Dr. Hawksworthy?"

"Of course I'm sure."

"Where *were* you at nine a.m. on the morning of January fifth?"

"Well, let's see." Hawksworthy's brow creased. "That was a Sunday, so I would have been home. Yes—I was at home. I remember now."

"Is there anyone who can corroborate your story?"

"It isn't a story, Inspector. It's the truth."

"Can anyone corroborate that? Did anyone see you, for example?"

Hawksworthy's mouth hardened. "Are you accusing me of murder?"

"We're not accusing you of anything. We have a witness who says you were at Littlejohn's house at approximately nine AM on the morning of his death. You say you were at home. We're asking you to prove it. I repeat, sir, can anyone verify your statement?"

"There's someone I don't wish to involve."

"This person is already involved, I'm afraid. This is a murder enquiry, Dr. Hawksworthy. If someone can vouch for you, I suggest you give us their name."

Hawksworthy crossed his arms. "No comment."

"Then I have no option but to—"

"All right, fine." Hawksworthy licked his lips. "Isla. My assistant, Isla Ferris."

"How long were you together?"

"All morning."

"We're going to need exact times, Dr. Hawksworthy."

"We had dinner together on Saturday. She stayed the night."

"At your house?"

"Yes."

"What time did she leave?"

"I don't know exactly." Hawksworthy gazed at the ceiling as if he might find an answer there. "Must have been around eight thirty or eight forty-five. So I couldn't have been at—"

Okoje interrupted him. "Where did you and Ms. Ferris go from there?"

"I believe she, er, stopped at her flat to change clothes. I went for a run and then took a shower.

"Did anyone see you running?"

"I shouldn't think so. I don't remember seeing anyone."

"How do you account for the fact that you were positively identified by a reliable witness at the Old Merchant's House just after nine AM?"

"I can't account for it. Obviously, your witness is lying."

"Why would this witness lie?"

"I don't know, do I? To protect themselves, presumably." He folded his arms across his chest. "Are you going to charge me with something, Inspector? If not, I think we're done here."

"Do you have any questions, DI Mallory?"

"Just one," Tom said. "How far is it from your house to the Old Merchant's House?"

"Not far." Hawksworthy's eyes narrowed slightly. "Maybe ten minutes on foot."

"And how far from there to the museum?"

"About the same distance."

Okoje glanced at Tom. If Isla had left Hawksworthy at eight forty-five, he would have had just enough time to make it to the Old Merchant's House by nine, when Beryl Grey claimed to have heard him in the study.

"Thank you, Dr. Hawksworthy," Okoje said. "We may wish to speak with you again. Now if you'll just give me a few more minutes of your time, I'd like to get some details."

Tom and I stood. He took my arm and propelled me gently out of the office. "Okoje's going to spin this out as long as he can," he whispered. "Quick—we have five minutes if we're lucky."

"Five minutes to do what?" I whispered back.

"To find out where Isla Ferris was the morning of Littlejohn's death. Before Hawksworthy has a chance to warn her."

* * *

Back in the lobby, Isla eyed us with undisguised animosity. "How *dare* the police question Hugo? He's a respected academic, not a common criminal."

"You might be able to help him, Ms. Ferris," Tom said. "Would you mind answering a few questions?"

"Fine. I'll need someone to take over here." She picked up the telephone on the counter and punched in a few numbers. "Pat, I need you at the ticket counter—now."

A fair-haired young woman appeared, wearing one of the pretty, flowered gift shop tunics. "Is everything all right?"

"It will be." Isla led us into her small office. She stood behind her desk, cradling her mobile. "What do you want to know?"

"It involves the morning of January fifth," Tom said. "The morning Gideon Littlejohn was murdered. Do you remember where you were?"

"I was here. Pledges from the gala were still coming in, and I was adding them to the spreadsheet. You saw me, remember? I opened the break room for you."

"What time did you arrive at the museum?"

She blinked several times and licked her bottom lip. "Well, it must have been around nine, I suppose. You could ask Pat. I was here when she arrived at nine thirty."

"And where were you before that?"

"You mean before I came to work?"

"Yes. Where were you before you came to work?"

Her eyes narrowed. "But I don't understand why—"

Her mobile buzzed. She glanced at the screen.

"Let it go," Tom said. "Where were you before you came to work the morning of January fifth?"

Isla straightened her shoulders. "I was with Hugo."

"Are you certain?" Tom asked.

"DI Mallory." She gave him a knowing look. "I think I would remember something like that."

"How long were you with him?"

"All morning. I wasn't checking my watch."

"You left the museum around ten. Kate saw you with your coat on. Where did you go?"

"I met Hugo. We were together."

"Where were you?"

"What do you mean?" Her eyes slid from Tom to me and back again.

"Where were you?" Tom repeated. "At his place or yours?"

I watched a series of emotions pass over her face—uncertainty, wariness, and finally defiance. "Your questions are impertinent and highly personal. I don't have to answer them." She crossed her arms and glared at us. "When this is over, I intend to file a complaint."

* * *

"Of course it was Hawksworthy on the phone," I said, sipping my glass of Cabernet. "As soon as Isla saw his name pop up on her mobile screen, she understood what she had to do."

"Give him an alibi," Tom agreed. "Impressive, actually. She can think on her feet."

"And she knows when to stop talking."

Tom stretched his long legs toward the stone hearth in the residents' lounge. We'd left the museum at five thirty, dropped DCI Okoje at the police enquiry office, and headed for the Crown, where a warming fire was waiting for us. Yvie Innes had taken our dinner order and promised to fetch us when it was ready.

"I suppose it could be true," I said. "She might have been with Hawksworthy that morning. If they'd been keeping their relationship secret, she would have needed his permission to acknowledge it."

"And the phone call was that permission?" Tom crossed his feet and leaned back against the sofa cushion. "You think they were together, then, when Littlejohn was murdered?"

"I don't know." It was raining in earnest now. We could hear it drumming against the windows. "Their relationship might have been mostly in Isla's head. At any rate, I think she'd do just about anything for him. Including lying to the police."

"So it all comes down to Beryl Grey," Tom said. "Was it really Dr. Hawksworthy she heard the morning of Littlejohn's death, or was it someone who sounded like him?"

"Or is she making the whole thing up because she's the one who shot Littlejohn after all?"

Tom stared at me. "Is that what you think?"

"Not really." A log collapsed in the fireplace, sending a shower of sparks swirling up the chimney. "I can see Beryl Grey trying to persuade Littlejohn to keep her on, but I honestly can't believe she'd kill him. His death meant the end of her job, and she wanted to keep it until they'd saved up enough money to make the move to Belize."

"But she admitted he'd found out about the benefits fraud. What if he threatened to tell the authorities?"

"We need to get the timeline straight."

"Good thought," Tom said, his forehead creasing in a frown. "A neighbor saw Beryl Grey arrive at the Old Merchant's House just before nine AM. She's admitted it. And she says someone was there, with Gideon Littlejohn in his study. They were arguing."

"Clive Nixon must have slept through all that, because the first thing he remembers was seeing someone on Littlejohn's doorstep around ten. It couldn't have been Hawksworthy, because he'd arrived before nine—assuming Beryl Grey is telling the truth. How long that second person stayed, we don't know, because Clive drove off."

"Littlejohn had more than one visitor that morning." Tom recrossed his feet on the hearth. "Wonder which one got tea and biscuits?"

"Beryl Grey says the tea things hadn't been touched when she was there at nine. When she returned to the house at eleven thirty, the dishes were in the sink. That implies Littlejohn served tea to the person he was expecting—the second person."

"The one Clive Nixon saw arrive at ten."

"Maybe." I sipped my wine. "Anyway, we arrived at twelve forty and heard Beryl Grey screaming."

"That part was staged. She admitted it."

"So the critical time is between ten when Littlejohn admitted the person Clive Nixon saw on the doorstep and eleven thirty when Mrs. Grey found him dead."

"Always assuming Beryl Grey is telling the truth. She's a good liar." Tom downed the remains of his wine and set the glass on the side table. "We should hear something soon from the team working on Littlejohn's computer files. If he had evidence against the Greys, that's where we'll find it."

"Are the police still planning to release Alan Grey pending trial?"

"I'll find out tomorrow."

"*Oh.*" I sat up straight. "Tomorrow's Wednesday. I nearly forgot. I'm supposed to meet Mercy Abbott at that hotel near Chagford. The Beechlands. Five stars. Do you want to come along? She'll give us lunch."

"Do you mind if I don't? I think you'll do better on your own. And Okoje wants us to go over the witness statements from the night of the gala yet again. He believes the shooter really was aiming for Littlejohn. When he failed, he went to plan B."

"You mean showing up at his house and shooting him."

"Exactly. Okoje also believes there's something in those witness statements we've overlooked. Somebody saw something, even if they didn't understand what it meant at the time."

"I still can't imagine anyone taking a risk like that—firing a gun in the presence of so many potential witnesses."

"Except no one *did* see the shooter. All eyes were on the clock demonstration."

"And then there was general panic."

"When people hear a gunshot, the first thing they do is run for cover, not look for the shooter."

"Even so, Tom, the point is how could the shooter be sure he wouldn't be seen by someone? More importantly, how could he—or she—be sure they wouldn't hit the wrong person?"

"I think the shooter knew exactly what he was doing."

"Or she," I reminded him.

"He or she missed, but not by much."

"And knew in advance about the clock demonstration."

"Or took advantage of an opportunity. Quick thinking."

He'd said something very similar about Isla Ferris. *She can think on her feet.*

Chapter Thirty-Four

Wednesday, January 15

Tom left for the police enquiry office immediately after breakfast. I sat, drinking the inn's excellent coffee and checking my emails. I smiled, reading my mother's encouraging report about her new husband, James Lund, who'd injured his leg so badly he hadn't been able to attend our wedding. He was recuperating faster than expected.

> *James has started talking about a trip to England. Perhaps this spring, if that would suit you and Tom. I can't wait to see your house. Do enjoy your time together, my darling girl. An update on the mysterious dress would be welcome. We both send our love.*

I emailed back, telling her what we'd learned so far. *It all comes down to the tea,* I said. *Who got tea? Sounds like something from the Father Brown mysteries.* I pictured her face when she read that. If I knew my mother, she'd be mentally working on the puzzle for days.

In another series of emails, Debs, Ginny, and Lisa, my friends from Ohio who'd flown over for our wedding, had sent several dozen photographs from the minibus tour of England they'd taken after the festivities. I smiled, seeing the iconic tourist shots—Ginny on Westminster Bridge, pretending to touch the pinnacle of Big Ben in the distance; the whole group, standing arm in arm, in the garden outside Anne

Hathaway's cottage; Lisa and Debs pretending they were being chased by a peacock at Warwick Castle. They'd had an amazing trip.

The last email was from my best friend and matron of honor, Charlotte. She'd sent a short video of the four of them at Stansted Airport, waiting for their flight home. "We love you, Kate!" they said, waving and blowing kisses. I felt a lump in my throat. I'd told Tom I wouldn't miss my three-story Victorian house in Jackson Falls. That had been the truth, but I was going to miss the people I loved—my mother, my children, and my friends who'd supported me in the horrific, grief-filled months after my first husband's death. They'd promised to visit me in England every year, but I knew that wouldn't happen. They had families of their own. Charlotte's twin sons, much to the surprise of their nonathletic parents, had been recruited by an elite middle-grade football league. Lisa's father had been struggling with dementia, and her mother needed help. Ginny's son had gotten married the previous summer. A baby was on the way. I had a new husband, a new job with Ivor, and a new house.

We'd taken different paths in life. When I'd chosen to live in Britain, I'd had to let go of my life in Jackson Falls. I was happy with my new life, happy with Tom. I wouldn't change a thing, but that didn't mean the choice had been without cost.

The thought came out of nowhere—had Nancy Thorne faced a life-altering choice? What price had she paid?

Yvie Innes appeared. "More coffee?"

"I think I've had enough, thanks. By the way, I'm off to interview the young woman you told me about, Mercy Abbott."

"Say hello from me."

I left the Crown at ten, giving myself plenty of time to navigate the narrow Dartmoor roads. After more than a year, driving on the left side of the road had become almost second nature. I was even becoming adept at navigating England's often-complex roundabouts. But I wasn't brave enough to hurtle along one-track roads or take blind summits with abandon like the locals.

Crossing the River Dart at Hexworthy, I took the B3212 north to Chagford, a market town near the River Teign. Signs for Beechlands

Country House Hotel led me along the banks of the river, a lovely, wild place. I felt a sense of anticipation. Mercy Abbott was the last lead we had in our investigation into the origins of the bloodstained dress—apart from the mysterious Daniel somebody. Mercy might know how to contact him. And she'd known Gideon Littlejohn since before his divorce.

The sprawling Tudor-style country house was set on acres of woodland skirting the bubbling upper reaches of the river. While drinking my coffee that morning, I'd done a little online research. Beechlands had been built in the mid-seventeenth century by London entrepreneur Ephraim Beech as a summer retreat for his family. After the Second World War, the estate had been sold and converted into a luxury hotel. In the 1990s, it was sold again to an international company, who closed it for two years to effect a complete restoration.

I entered the oak-paneled reception area to find a woman waiting for me.

"Kate?" With her smooth, unlined skin, Mercy Abbott could have been anywhere from twenty-five to forty. She was Asian, probably Chinese, as Yvie Innes had suggested, with a pretty, heart-shaped face and glossy dark hair pulled into a ponytail. She wore slim jeans and a quilted vest over a white turtleneck sweater.

"Mercy, thank you for inviting me to lunch." We shook hands. "What a gorgeous hotel."

"Isn't it just," she agreed. "I came from an excellent hotel in Torquay, four stars, but Beechlands is in another category entirely. I'm the catering manager—weddings, private parties, business meetings. I live in a small cottage on the grounds."

"Lucky you."

"The only downside is being a bit farther from my family."

"You're a Devon girl, then?"

"All my life—well, all of it I can remember, anyway. I was adopted when I was two. My parents lived in Hong Kong then, but we moved back to England soon afterwards, to Brixham on the coast." When she smiled, a dimple appeared in one cheek. "This is our down time at the hotel. We reopen in March, so we're having our lunch in front of the fire in the library. Do you mind?"

"It sounds lovely."

"We don't have an actual menu. Just a daily lunch and dinner for staff. This is when the chefs try out new recipes." She offered an apologetic tilt of the head. "Today it's fairly plain—fillet of sole. Comes with a green salad."

"Sounds perfect." I followed her down a carpeted hallway to another oak-paneled room. A massive Portland stone hearth was flanked by twin sofas covered in coral-red and cream fabric. Shelved books, most bound in leather, lined two walls.

Mercy and I sat across from each other on the sofas. "Did you live in Coombe Mallet for a time?" I began. "I know you were part of Gideon Littlejohn's club—the Society of Victorians. By the way, Yvie Innes from the Crown says hello."

"Oh, *Yvie.*" Mercy smiled. "I always liked her. Very down-to-earth. But, no, I never lived in Coombe Mallet. I drove in for the meetings and stayed the night."

"You said you'd known Gideon for quite a while. How did you meet?"

"In London, at a symposium put on by the Victorian Society. That was in 2012 or 2013, I think."

"Did you know him well?"

"Not then, not until after his divorce." Mercy blushed slightly. "We were very close for a time."

"Close?" I gave her an encouraging smile.

"Close romantically. He asked me to marry him."

"You said no."

"I'm interested in the Victorian era. Gideon was obsessed." She smiled wistfully. "Did you ever see those historical re-creations on the BBC? There were four or five series, but the one I remember best was called *The 1900 House*. A modern family—husband, wife, two kids—agreed to spend three months living in a restored Victorian townhouse. They wore period clothing and weren't allowed anything that wouldn't have been available to them in 1900. It was a fascinating experiment, and I think it inspired Gideon to restore an old house and live in it like a Victorian gentleman. I probably would have agreed to a three-month experiment, but Gideon wanted it to be a permanent thing. He was so taken with the idea. As much as I cared for him, I couldn't do it." She looked at me curiously. "You're thinking about his wife, Freya, aren't you?"

I nodded. "I just heard about her death."

"I worked with Freya for a time on the Agatha Christie festival. The road accident was a real tragedy."

"Was there any suggestion of foul play?" Max Newlin hadn't said so, but I wanted to explore every possibility.

"None at all." Mercy's eyes flicked away, and I got the impression there was something she was reluctant to tell me.

"A single-car crash, I understand." I waited.

"Drink driving." She looked up. "I don't think Freya'd ever really gotten over the divorce—even though it had been her idea. That's why I mentioned her. It was Gideon's obsession with the past that caused the breakup. He wanted to buy a house and dive into the lifestyle. She couldn't do it. Neither could I."

I nodded. "We saw his house in Coombe Mallet."

"Then you'll know what I mean. He admitted he couldn't do it all at once, but that was his goal—to live the life of a Victorian gentleman as authentically as possible. He said once he'd been born in the wrong century." She laughed. "I think he probably was. The problem was finding a wife who'd go along with the idea. I thought for a time he was in love with me, but I finally realized he was in love with the *idea* of a Victorian wife and everything that went along with it. You know—the house as a sanctuary of order and contentment. Wife at home, making sure everything was perfect. The Victorians were big on that—separating one's work life from family life."

"But Gideon worked from home. He had a very sophisticated computer room." I deleted the part about finding his body there.

"He worked for himself, so he didn't have an office to go to. He had to have an income. Re-creating history is expensive."

"Did he see the irony in that?"

"I don't think he did. He was good at compartmentalizing. His computer lab was completely separate in his mind." She leaned forward, her face earnest. "Did you ever watch *Star Trek*, the one with Jean-Luc Picard? They had this holodeck thing on board the starship, a separate space. Inside that space, it could be any time or place at all. I always thought of Gideon's computer lab like that—a slip in time."

"Do you remember someone named Daniel—another member of the society?"

"Of course. Daniel Woodhouse. He used to do some filming for Gideon's videos."

"Do you know where Daniel is now?"

"Not exactly. He moved to Shetland in . . . well, I think it must have been 2019. He was offered a job at the hospital in Lerwick. Daniel is a surgical nurse and a hiker, so it was a good fit. And the pay was well more than he was earning here. We haven't kept in touch."

"Do you know about a Victorian dress Gideon donated to the local history museum in Coombe Mallet?"

"Of course. I read about it in the newspaper. Gideon's name was never mentioned, but I knew who the donor was because I'd seen the dress."

"You'd seen the dress?"

"Gideon showed it to me one evening. It was in an old trunk, folded up and wrapped in tissue. He actually wanted me to try it on."

"Did you?"

She shook her head. "All that blood? I thought it was disgusting, but Gideon was fascinated."

"Why was that, do you think?"

"Because of Billy Cole—an old man who'd befriended Gideon when he was a boy."

My pulse kicked up a notch. "Gideon told us about the old man. His sister, Donna, said he died in a fire. What did Billy Cole have to do with the dress?"

An arm appeared at my shoulder, making me jump.

"Sorry, madam." A man in a crisp white chef's tunic slid two plates onto the low table between the sofas and handed each of us silverware wrapped in white napkins. "Fillet of sole, lightly grilled, pureed squash with pumpkin seeds, and a rocket salad with Parmesan."

"It looks amazing," I said, feeling a little foolish. I'd been so immersed in Mercy's story I could have been in a time slip myself.

"This is our sous chef, Alex," Mercy said. "Alex, this is Kate Hamilton. She's a private investigator."

"Charmed." Alex gave a little bow. "I'll leave you to it." He headed for the door.

"You were telling me about Billy Cole," I said, moving the conversation back on target. "And the bloodstained dress."

Mercy took a bite of her sole and put down her fork. "That was the thing, wasn't it? The dress. And Gideon's fascination with it. He'd had a lot to drink the night he asked me to try the dress on. Which was unusual for him." She chewed thoughtfully.

"But that night was different?" I took a bite of the flaky white fish, hardly tasting it as I focused on her story.

"It *was* different. I think showing me the dress was a huge step for him. It meant a lot to him—because of Billy Cole. Gideon was a very private person. Hard to get to know. Secretive."

Just about everyone who'd known Littlejohn had said something similar. "What do you mean by secretive?"

"Well—that computer lab of his, for one thing. In all the time we were together, I was never allowed inside that room. I saw it once from the hallway. That was it. His specialty was preventing hackers from getting into his clients' software. I think he was almost paranoid about hackers getting into his system."

I could believe that. The break-in three months before his death must have rattled him—so much so that he'd installed a security system. "Tell me about that night. The dress."

"The trunk was Billy's. Gideon said it had belonged to Billy's grandfather. Billy had been named after him—William."

"You mean the dress belonged to Billy's grandmother? Do you know the surname?"

"I don't. Gideon mentioned a name, though—Nancy Thorne."

Nancy Thorne. I was almost hyperventilating. This was the first direct link we'd found between the dress and Nancy Thorne. And if this William was William Tucker, Sally's son, he would have been

Nancy's nephew. "I know there was a fire. Why didn't the trunk get burned up?"

"Because by that time, Gideon had the trunk. Billy had given him lots of things. He was old and in pain. He'd been living alone for years. His greatest fear, Gideon told me, was being forced into a care home. Having all his possessions tossed out as rubbish. I think he saw Gideon as a sort of grandson. Someone who would treasure his memories. And Gideon did treasure them."

"Where did the blood come from?" I forced myself to breath slowly. "Did Billy tell Gideon where the blood came from?"

"That's the funny thing, Kate. I asked him about it, but he changed the subject and somehow it never came up again. Maybe because that night Gideon was focused on Billy Cole's death." She hesitated. "And his part in it."

"His part in it?" I felt like someone had poured cold water down my back. "Are you saying Gideon Littlejohn was involved in Billy Cole's death?"

"Not exactly, no. You have to understand. Gideon had a rough childhood. He grew up on a council estate with people who didn't think much of intelligent boys who liked books."

"He was bullied?"

"Of course. And he had no support. His parents split up when he was six. His sister was much older. She left home when Gideon was ten. Billy's house was a sort of sanctuary for him, an escape from the difficult realities of life."

"Gideon told us they met in the park. The old man was feeding the ducks."

"They became friends. Billy had been born with a twisted spine. The kids on the estate called him a freak, a troll, a monster."

"What happened the night Billy Cole died?"

"You mean the night Billy Cole was murdered. Gideon had been to see him. It was dark and he was on his way home when he saw this gang of boys, some on foot, others on bikes. Gideon knew them. Everyone on the estate did. They were troublemakers—terrorized the residents, vandalized houses, set fire to rubbish bins, stole from local businesses.

Billy Cole was their favorite target. They would shove dog-mess through his letter box, Kate. They called him names, painted obscene messages on his front windows, tipped over his rubbish bin. Once they cornered Gideon, threatened to teach him a lesson—whatever that was supposed to mean. He avoided them if he could, so when he saw them that night, he hid. And he watched as they descended on Billy Cole's house. Some were chanting slurs, calling the old man a perv, a monster. But then they started a fire in Billy's rubbish bin. One of them grabbed a newspaper, lit it, and shoved it through the letter box. Gideon was nearly paralyzed with fear. If the gang knew he was there, they'd have beaten him up—no question. He ran home. Shortly after that, a neighbor saw smoke coming from Billy Cole's house. The neighbor called the fire service. They were there in minutes, but it was too late. Billy Cole was dead. And Gideon never told anyone. He was afraid of the gang. The problem was he felt guilty about not saving Billy, but what could he do, Kate? He was thirteen, I think, and small for his age. Just him against all those older boys. Even so, Gideon blamed himself."

"For what?" I asked.

"For not stopping them, I suppose. For running away. Maybe for not telling the police. He didn't like to talk about it. The fact that he told me anything at all was a miracle."

"Did he know who shoved the burning newspaper through the letter box?"

"He said he did."

I let out the breath I didn't know I'd been holding. "What was the boy's name?"

"He wouldn't tell me. Just that he'd made a vow that one day this boy—well, this man, now—would pay for what he'd done. He'd come up in the world, Gideon said. Made something of himself. No one knew that he'd killed a helpless old man. But one day Gideon would tell the world what this man had done, and the truth would ruin him."

This will ruin me. The words Beryl Grey heard Hugo Hawksworthy say the morning of Gideon's death. "Why hadn't Gideon already exposed the man?" I asked Mercy. "What was he waiting for?"

"I don't know. Actually, we were both pretty pissed that night. Honestly, I think Gideon had almost forgotten I was there. He was spilling out his story, almost to himself." She stopped. "Actually, I do remember him saying, 'There's something I have to do first. Promised Billy, didn't I?'"

"What had he promised Billy?"

"I wish I knew, Kate. As I said, we were both pretty pissed."

Possibilities swirled in my brain. Was there something Gideon Littlejohn had known about Hugo Hawksworthy that would ruin him if it became public? Was it the fire? Maybe, but then I remembered Teddy Pearce with his self-admitted record of youthful crimes. He'd actually lived on the Burnthouse Lane estate around that time. "Mercy, this is important. Did Gideon ever mention the names Hugo Hawksworthy or Teddy Pearce?"

"I don't remember hearing him mention either name. Actually, I don't know anyone named Hawksworthy. I do know who Pearce is, of course. If Gideon had known him, I think he might have said."

"And you never asked him about the man—well, the boy—who'd caused Billy's death? It's not a criticism, Mercy. I'm curious."

"I should have asked, but the next day Gideon was acting really strange, distant. Like he regretted telling me all that. I'm sure he did regret it. So I dropped it. We never spoke about it again."

"Gideon's housekeeper told us he had a visitor sometime in the week before he died—a woman, someone she thought he knew well. Was it you?"

"Me? No." She looked shocked. "Why would I want to see Gideon after all these years? My relationship with him is in the past—well, that's ironic, isn't it?"

"Mercy, is there anything else you can tell me? Anything at all? It could be important."

She thought for a moment before answering. Then she said, "There is one thing. I can't explain it, but I got the strongest feeling that the promise he'd made Billy had something to do with the dress."

Chapter Thirty-Five

I arrived at the Coombe Mallet police enquiry office in less than an hour. Parking the Rover on the street, I dashed inside, dodging the icy rain and feeling rather breathless. What Mercy Abbott had just told me could change everything.

The community support officer I'd seen earlier, the kindly woman in dark trousers and a black shirt, showed me into the room where Tom and DCI Okoje stood opposite each other at the laminate-topped table. The floor plans of the Museum of Devon Life were spread out before them.

Seeing me, they stood.

"Kate, darling." Tom gave me a side hug.

"To what do we owe this unexpected pleasure?" Okoje asked.

"I'm not sure what I have to say will be a pleasure, but I think you'll find it eye-opening."

"Take a seat." Okoje shoved a stack of papers to one side, making room at the table.

I sat. "Still working on the floor plans, I see."

"One of these names"—Okoje stabbed at the first-floor diagram—"is the person who shot Gideon Littlejohn the night of the gala."

"And maybe finished the job two days later," Tom said.

"Cup o' tea?" the CSO asked.

"I'd love one, thanks. It's freezing outside."

She smiled. "Milk? Sugar?"

"Splash of milk. Two sugars." I peeled off my jacket, draped it over the back of the chair, and sat next to Tom.

"What did you learn from Mercy Abbott?" Tom asked. "I told DCI Okoje where you went today."

I proceeded to tell them everything, exactly as Mercy had told me. "First of all, she saw the dress. And Gideon Littlejohn said it was connected to a woman named Nancy Thorne. So there's our first definite link, Tom. But more to the point, she also said Gideon Littlejohn knew the identity of a boy who pushed a burning newspaper through Billy Cole's letter box the night he died. This boy caused the old man's death. Littlejohn told Mercy this person had come up in the world and would be ruined when Littlejohn made the information public. That's important, because according to Beryl Grey, the man with Littlejohn around nine the morning of his death said, 'This will ruin me.'"

"Hugo Hawksworthy, if she's right," Okoje said.

Tom quirked an eyebrow. "And Hawksworthy was on the first floor when the shot was fired."

The community support officer placed a steaming cup of tea in front of me. "Thank you so much." I cupped my hands around it to warm my fingers.

"Hawksworthy claimed he and Littlejohn didn't know each other well," Tom said. "Do we know where Hawksworthy grew up?"

"First question we'll ask." Okoje stood, pulling one of the large sheets of paper toward us. "I'd like you to look at the floor plan of the museum again, Ms. Hamilton."

I took a sip of the hot tea, feeling the liquid warm me on the inside.

Okoje tapped the scale drawing of the first floor. "We know the shot was fired from this point, the first-floor balcony, while the mechanical clock demonstration was going on. Everyone was focused on the clock, but this is a small community. Most people remember who was standing near them, to the left and right. Before the demonstration began, you were here." He indicated one of the small paper squares with my name on it. "You were standing at the railing, looking down at the ground floor. When the demonstration began, you moved closer so you could see it." He peeled off the square with my name on it and stuck it down on the edge of a group of other squares. "Is that about right?"

I looked at the names. "I think so. I remember the Jamiesons, Richard and Clare, because I was thinking how lucky they were to be so tall. They could see over the crowd. I told you there were two men sort of in front of them. One was tall, the other short. And there was a woman with bright-red hair on their right. She was holding a small boy."

"Sharon Fogg and her boy Jacob. How about Quinn Pearce?"

The square labeled *Quinn P* had been placed to the left of the Jamiesons. "That's right. She was on their left, closer to me. Let me think for a minute." I closed my eyes and pulled up that final image—the little boy on his mother's shoulders, one chubby hand grasping her bright-copper hair; the Jamiesons, leaning forward, their shoulders meeting; the outline of Quinn's spine and her long swanlike neck; that flash of gold on the edge of the crowd—Isla's cocktail dress; the tall, red-faced man who'd backed off, allowing the shorter man a better view.

"I can picture the scene, but something isn't right. I just can't think what it is."

"It'll come to you," Tom said.

"You left the demonstration before it was over," Okoje said. "Why was that?"

"Truthfully, it kind of creeped me out—the figure of Death." I certainly wasn't going to use the word *premonition*. "I decided I'd seen enough. I wanted to find Tom, so I headed for the stairs."

"How long did it take you to descend the stairs and locate Tom?"

"I'm not sure, but, well, probably less than fifteen seconds. I remember the clock was still chiming. Actually, the final chime came just after the shot was fired."

"You're sure you didn't notice someone you hadn't seen before or someone who'd changed their location?"

I shook my head. But I had noticed something. If only I could remember what it was.

The conversation was interrupted when DS Varma burst into the room. "They've cracked the encryption on Littlejohn's computer.

There's a file you're going to want to see, boss. Should be coming through momentarily."

* * *

The four of us gathered around Varma's computer, riveted as links to files flashed on the screen. There were more than a hundred files, and they were numbered. No clue as to their contents.

Varma scrolled through the links. "Most of these are related to Littlejohn's work in cybersecurity—contracts, assessments of risks, reports and results." He placed the cursor over one of the larger files. "This is the one you need to see." Varma clicked on it. "It's raw data, but I think you'll catch the drift."

The file turned out to be a master document, a listing of links to other documents. They all concerned one person.

Tom looked up. "Well, well. Gideon Littlejohn was investigating Teddy Pearce."

Varma clicked through file after file. There were school records and the results of Teddy's O-levels, details of his brief stint in the military, a short document listing visits to the NHS, preemployment background checks, tenant screenings, financial disclosure documents from his political activities, bank statements, credit card statements, details about the mortgage on a house, the results of a surveillance operation. The amount of information Littlejohn had collected on Teddy Pearce was astonishing.

"Why would Littlejohn do that kind of an in-depth investigation?" Tom asked. "Was it his idea, or did someone pay him?"

"He was paid, all right. You ready for this? By Karl Benables."

"When was this?" Okoje asked.

"Spring of 2007."

"Around the time he and Quinn were engaged," Tom said. "Makes sense. Quinn's father was trying to find dirt on Pearce. Hoped to convince his daughter not to marry him."

"Ironic, isn't it?" Okoje said. "In 2007, Karl Benables hired Gideon Littlejohn to investigate Teddy Pearce. Fifteen years later, the council hired Littlejohn to investigate Benables."

"But here's the interesting thing," Varma said. "Look at the dates of the last files. Littlejohn continued to investigate Pearce even after Benables stopped paying him. He's included documents from Pearce's parliamentary campaign, recent bank records—from this year. And there are two files you're definitely going to want to see." Varma moved the computer mouse. "The first is an image, a photograph. A football team."

A photograph filled the screen—eighteen or twenty boys in two rows, all in their upper teens. The first row knelt, one knee up. The back row stood, their arms around each other's shoulders. They were flanked by two adult males, probably coaches. The boys were a diverse lot—white, black, Asian—dressed in navy shorts and navy shirts with the gray-and-yellow logo banner of their sponsor. Two boys had been singled out with red marker stars above their heads. Both were white, medium height with dark hair. One knelt at the end of the front row. The other stood in the back. He had a flat, lopsided nose and a distinct underbite. "That's Teddy Pearce," I said. "Who's the other boy?"

"See if you can trace him," Okoje told Varma.

"Won't be easy after all these years, boss—and maybe unnecessary." Varma clicked on another file, and the logo of the Devon Youth Justice Service, Exeter, flashed onto the screen. "What you're looking at is a detailed listing of offenses committed by one Theodore Pearce from the ages of twelve to seventeen."

"Is that legal?" I asked. "Aren't the records sealed or something?"

"Supposed to be." Okoje straightened his back. "Littlejohn knew how to stop hackers. Looks like he used his skills to hack into the juvenile court records."

Varma scrolled down the list of offenses. "Pearce was quite the lad in his day. Multiple truancies, stealing bicycles, shoplifting, purse snatching, intimidation, common assault, possession of a controlled drug, possession of a controlled drug with intent to supply, criminal damage."

"He made no secret of that," I said. "He admitted everything openly the night of the gala."

Tom had taken over the keyboard. "Maybe not everything. Look at this—a file dated June of 1992. 'Theodore Pearce. Charge: Criminal damage and endangering life during the riots in the Burnthouse Lane Estate. Gross negligence manslaughter arising from an unlawful and dangerous act in the death of William Cole, an eighty-two-year-old disabled man.'"

I felt my chest tighten. "Billy Cole, the owner of the dress. Pearce was charged. Was he convicted?"

Tom scrolled again. "Insufficient evidence. Never even went to trial."

"Mercy Abbott said Littlejohn was determined to ruin the person responsible for Billy's death. I asked her if Littlejohn knew Teddy Pearce. She said she didn't think so, but they both grew up on the Burnthouse Lane estate in Exeter. It can't be a coincidence."

"No." Okoje's expression was grim. "If Pearce was the visitor Littlejohn was expecting the morning he was killed, and if Littlejohn confronted Pearce about the death of Billy Cole . . ." He left the sentence hanging. "Varma, you're with me. We can be in London by"—he glanced at his watch—"seven PM if we hurry. Bring him in under caution."

"What if he's not there?" Varma asked. "He might have meetings—you know, government stuff. A dinner."

"He has to sleep. He's meant to be on the floor of the House of Commons in the morning. If he's not home, we'll wait—all night if we have to." Okoje grabbed his jacket. He put his huge hand on Tom's shoulder. "It'll take us three hours to get to London. I'll send you a text when we're in position. You and Kate head over to the Pearces' house. Stay with Quinn. Don't let her leave, and don't let her call her husband."

"What do we tell her?" Tom asked.

"Nothing if you can help it. Say we're following a lead and I sent you to provide security. That's it. We'll send someone to bring her in once we have Pearce in custody."

I felt unsettled. "Shouldn't we tell Quinn about her husband's arrest?"

"That'll be up to Mr. Pearce. Privacy laws. He'll be given the right to consult a solicitor and the right to have someone informed of his arrest. His choice. What I'm wondering is how much Mrs. Pearce already knows."

I was wondering the same thing.

Chapter Thirty-Six

Waiting three hours for Okoje and Varma to get to London was brutal. Tom and I returned to the Crown for an early dinner. Neither of us felt much like eating—or talking. We liked the Pearces. Teddy's transparency about his troubled past had been both admirable and disarming. He'd shown Quinn's father considerably more grace than he deserved. And we could sympathize with Quinn's intense loyalty to her husband, a loyalty that had led to a complete break with her father.

After dinner, because we couldn't just sit there and wait, we decided to walk around the village from the Crown to St. Petroc's, then past the shops and the guildhall on the winding High Street to the river. I couldn't get the sweet faces of the twins, Ivy and Lily, out of my mind. If their father was charged in Littlejohn's death, how would they ever cope? What if their mother had been an accessory? Who would take care of them?

My phone pinged—a text from Maggie Hughes. *Can you call me?*

Tom and I moved into a sheltered area leading to the local co-op store. I dialed Maggie's number. "You're not still at the library, are you?"

"Just about to leave. This project has been the most fun I've had in years. I love information."

"We're two of a kind, then," I said, thinking I should get to know the librarians at the Long Barston library. They might have another Maggie Hughes.

"I found what you wanted, Kate."

"Let me put you on speaker so Tom can hear."

"First, the bodies in the graveyard in Widdecombe Throop were exhumed before the village was flooded. They were reburied at the tiny parish church of Chalcombe, on the other side of the reservoir."

"That's wonderful, Maggie. Maybe Tom and I can visit before we leave Devon."

"That's not all. I also found Henry Tucker's military records. Sally's husband was a corporal in the Devonshire Regiment. They sailed for India in late February 1884. He died there—of malaria in August of 1885. Buried in a British cemetery."

"Maggie, you're a wonder. Thanks so much. Now go home and relax." When we disconnected, I turned to Tom. "That's so sad. Henry Tucker never got to see his son."

"Are you sure?" Tom took my arm. "Something's not right there. You said the son, William, was five on the 1891 census."

"Right."

"When was the census taken?"

"April fifth."

"So if William was five in April of 1891, when is the earliest he could have been conceived?"

I thought for a moment. "The earliest possible date? Well, if he was an older five—say, turning six soon after April fifth, he would have been born in April of 1885. And that means the earliest he could have been conceived would be"—I counted back nine months—"July of 1884."

"And yet Sally's husband had sailed for India in late February of 1884, five months earlier. Impossible unless Sally Tucker had a fourteen-month pregnancy."

"Or had a lover."

"Or wasn't William's mother at all."

I stared at Tom. "So who were William's parents?"

The mystery of William Tucker's parentage was forgotten when Tom got a text from Okoje: *In London. Go now.*

I felt sick.

Tom took my arm. "We're only a couple of blocks from the car. Let's get this over with."

Outside, snow was beginning to fall, the scattered flakes dusting the car park pavement. In the Rover, Tom turned on the heated seats, and we pulled out onto the street.

The windscreen was fogging. I reached over and turned on the defroster. "Why does Okoje want us to be with Quinn Pearce when they arrest her husband?"

"Because we don't really know what's going on yet, Kate. Okoje doesn't want the Pearces to communicate with each other, and he needs to know where she is. She may be complicit—or she may be in danger."

"This doesn't feel right. She's going to ask questions."

"She probably will. Police work isn't always straightforward, Kate, and it isn't easy. Innocent people are swept up in crime, and there's often nothing we can do about it except perform our jobs with as much integrity and compassion as we can. It's an imperfect system. All we can do is try to get it right."

Not all policemen had these standards. I knew that. If Tom did decide to leave the force, they would lose one of their best.

Lights were on at the Pearces' house. The only car was a large BMW sedan, one we hadn't seen before. Instead of pulling into the driveway, Tom parked in a lay-by near the gated entrance to a pasture. He took a flashlight out of the glove compartment. No moon to light our way.

As we walked toward the house, he squeezed my hand. "Remember—we're here to help."

Tom pulled the bell. In moments, we heard a female voice from inside. "Who is it?" It didn't sound like Quinn.

"Tom and Kate—the Mallorys. We'd like to speak with Quinn."

The door opened to reveal an older woman with Quinn's narrow frame, pale skin, and blond hair. "I'm Quinn's mother, Susan Benables. She isn't here." Her eyes were red-rimmed and puffy.

"Are the twins all right?" Tom asked.

"They're fine. The nanny's putting them to bed." Susan Benables was obviously making an effort to control herself, but her hands were trembling. "Who did you say you were?"

"We're friends of Teddy and Quinn. I'm a detective inspector, working temporarily with the Devon & Cornwall Police." He showed her his warrant card. "We know they've been the target of several attacks. Where is Quinn? Has something happened?"

Susan Benables pinned her upper lip with a knuckle. "I'm so frightened." Snow swirled down from the roof, enveloping us in a cold, wet shower. "What am I thinking? Please, come inside."

We followed Susan Benables into the expansive living room and took seats on the sectional sofa. Scattered on the floor were books, dolls, and dozens of flocked-plastic animal figures from a Sylvanian Families playset. My daughter, Christine, had adored the Sylvanians, woodland creatures dressed in Victorian clothing, for about three weeks when she was a preschooler, abandoning them for a chemistry set and a washable makeup kit.

A sweet little face appeared from around the corner. Then another. "It's Kate!" Ivy jumped up and down. Lily ran to me and hugged my legs. This time the twins wore heart-print pajama sets in a soft cotton knit.

"We're supposed to be in bed," Ivy said, "but we're not sleepy. It's not easy to go to sleep when you're not sleepy." Then, "If you've come to see Mummy, she's not here."

"Mummy was sad," Lily said solemnly. Suddenly her little face brightened. "Can you play with us? Do you like Sylvanians? We have the Tree House and the Fox Family and the Royal Princess set."

"I'd love to play Sylvanians sometime, but maybe not tonight."

"No, indeed," said a petite, dark-haired girl in a French accent. "I'm sorry, Madame Benables. They heard voices and thought it was their parents." She put a hand on each small blond head. "It's time you were in bed, *mes petits choux*. Say good-night to your friends."

"Goodnight. *Bonne nuit*." They scampered off.

Susan Benables began to weep. "My daughter's been beside herself for days—ever since Teddy's car crash. Crying, blaming herself."

"Why did she blame herself?" I asked.

"I don't know. She just couldn't settle, and she was having a hard time coping with the twins. I said I'd come, of course. I shouldn't be telling you this, but I don't know what to do." Now that she had someone to confide in, Susan Benables couldn't stop talking. "Yesterday, the doctor gave her some tranquilizers. I don't think she's taken any. Teddy had to leave for Parliament on Monday. He shouldn't have gone, not in his condition—his ribs bandaged and his arm in a sling—but he said he had to be there. He called this morning. He and Quinn argued, which isn't like them. She called him back, and they argued again. Then she packed a bag, told me to stay with Ivy and Lily, and drove off."

"When was this?" Tom asked.

"Just before the twins had their tea, so around five. It isn't like her to leave the girls while Teddy's in London."

"What did they argue about?"

"I don't know. Quinn took her mobile outside and stood there in the cold, shivering and crying. I tried to get her to come back in, but she wouldn't. She's that stubborn. Always has been."

"Do you know where she went? London?"

Susan Benables swiped her eyes with the heels of her hands. "That's the one thing I do know. She said she was going to our hunting lodge and I wasn't to worry. How was I not to worry? Her, driving alone on those terrible roads in this weather? I told her it was wrong, that she should wait until morning, but would she listen?" Her eyes filled with tears again. "I made her promise to phone me when she got there."

"Has she phoned you?" Tom asked.

"Not yet. That's why I'm so worried."

"Why the hunting lodge?"

"She's always loved it. It's been her special place, her bolt-hole where she can escape from the world. Quinn's terribly upset. They both are. I can't imagine what went wrong. They never argue—not like some."

"Are you able to stay with the twins until we get this sorted?" Tom asked.

"Yes, of course. My husband's due back tomorrow, and I—" She broke off, shaking her head. "It's complicated, but I'll stay as long as I'm needed." She looked up, her lips trembling. "Please find my daughter. Make sure she's safe."

"We'll do our best," Tom said. "How do we get to the hunting lodge?"

Susan Benables stared at us as if not comprehending. Then, wiping her eyes again, she drew in a breath. "Oh, yes, of course. The lodge is north of the Dart. Follow the B3357 past Two Bridges. Keep going—about six miles, I think. Take the first road on the right. There's a sign advertising a farm bed-and-breakfast. Just beyond that, you'll see a small road on the left. There's no sign, but that's the turning. After about a mile, you'll see the house."

"Try not to worry," I said foolishly.

"Call me." She scribbled her number on the back of a napkin and handed it to me.

Once we were back in the Rover, Tom had me text DCI Okoje:

Quinn's gone. We think she's at the hunting lodge.

Okoje's reply came in seconds:

Pearce no show as well. Concierge says he left with duffle bag at four o'clock. Called for taxi to train station. Get to lodge asap. You're closest. Meet you there.

I looked at Tom. "Where was Pearce going? They can't be planning to leave the country without their children."

"They wouldn't do that. They love those girls." He reached over and put his hand on mine. "Kate, you don't have to do this. Let me drop you at the Crown."

"Not on your life, Tom. There's two of them. You might need me."

Tom put the car in gear. "All right, then. Let's go."

Chapter Thirty-Seven

Tom wasn't normally a fast driver, but he must have been doing seventy. No moon. No stars. Just the pale beam of our head lamps bouncing along the dark, narrow road ahead. I gripped the seat around every curve and couldn't stop myself from frequently jamming my foot on the phantom brake. The snow had given way to a light drizzle.

"Are they dangerous, or are they in danger?" I asked.

"I don't know what they are. All I know is we need to get to the lodge as quickly as we can. Once we find them—if we do—we can figure out what's going on."

We swerved around a sharp curve, almost sliding sideways in the gravel. Tom slowed the car, but we both knew time was passing.

The directions Susan Benables had given us, without thinking, had been from Exeter, which wasn't helpful. Instead, we crossed the Dart at Hexworthy, which meant we had to travel east on the B3357 for a mile or so to locate the sign for the farmhouse bed-and-breakfast. There it was—rooms with shared bath, camping pods, and tent camping.

We turned left and passed the farmhouse on the right. Everything was dark. No sign of life.

Tom slowed again, this time to a crawl, on the unpaved one-track road as we peered into the blackness, searching for any road leading to the left. We missed it and had to back up. The left-fork road descended sharply into one of the folds of land. We were about half a mile in when a large, gray stone house emerged out of the darkness below us. We saw a light.

"Someone's there," I said.

"If so, they've seen us coming," Tom said. "I hope they recognize the car. This isn't the kind of place where neighbors drop by to have a chat."

The gravel crunched as we approached the house. It was old, built of the ubiquitous gray limestone. Four white pebble-dash chimneys rose above a steep slate roof. A number of outbuildings, some thatched, surrounded the main structure. We pulled into a kind of courtyard and parked next to Quinn's ice-blue Audi.

A shadow passed across one of the windows. Someone was inside.

We'd just gotten out of the car when the door flew open and Quinn stepped out into the cold air. She wore leggings and a huge cardigan sweater that made her look tiny, like a child. Under her right arm, she held a shotgun, the barrel pointed directly at us. Seeing who we were, she lowered the gun. "I'm sorry. I didn't know who you were. What are you doing here? How did you find me?"

"Your mother told us," I said. "She's frantic with worry."

Quinn placed the shotgun on a bench near the door. "Teddy's out there somewhere. I was going to look for him. He doesn't know the terrain." She'd been crying. I could see the resemblance to her mother, but I could see something else as well. Her eyes looked glazed, and her words were slightly slurred.

Tom grabbed the shotgun, broke it, and led her inside the house. "Where's Teddy's car?"

"In the barn. He didn't take the car. He's on foot."

"Which way did he go?"

"I don't know." She covered her face with her hands. "We had a terrible argument. He just walked out."

"When was this?"

"Fifteen minutes ago. Maybe a little longer."

"Why did he leave, Quinn?" I asked, shivering. The house was as cold as a mausoleum.

Quinn just shook her head. "He was upset. Said he had to think. But it's dark, and he doesn't know the area."

"Start from the beginning," Tom said. "Your mother said you and Teddy had two unpleasant phone conversations earlier today."

Quinn looked up. "It was my fault. I got upset. Told him I was going to spend a few days at the lodge. I had no idea he would follow me here. He's supposed to be in the House tomorrow."

"When did he get here?"

"I don't know. Half an hour ago?"

I checked my watch. It was almost nine. If Teddy had caught the train to Exeter immediately, he could have made it to the lodge by car at, say, eight or eighty thirty.

Tom tried again. "Why did Teddy walk out?"

"He said he needed time alone—to think about what to do next."

"To do next about what?" I asked.

She ignored me. "I told him not to go, but he wouldn't listen."

"Where's the kitchen?" I asked, hoping to find some heat. "I'll make us a cup of tea."

The kitchen had white walls with a low, beamed ceiling and treacle-colored wood floors. White-painted cabinets lined three walls. On the fourth was an Aga cooker, more cabinets, and a refrigerator, emitting a faint scent of kerosene. A long pine table stretched the length of the long room. I felt the Aga. The heat was still building. An electric kettle stood on the countertop next to a porcelain container marked *Tea*. I filled the kettle and flipped it on. Quinn slumped at the table, her forehead resting on the heels of her hands.

"Is the heating on?" I asked, standing with my back to the Aga.

"Yes, but it's oil-fired. Takes a few hours to warm up." She closed her eyes and took a breath. She looked exhausted—and not too steady on her feet.

Something was really wrong with Quinn. I looked around the kitchen, finding no evidence of alcohol consumption.

"All my fault," she said again. "Should have warned him about Evelscombe." Her words were really slurring now.

"Evelscombe?" Tom's eyes narrowed.

"The mire. Sheep get stuck there every year and die. Even ponies sometimes." She looked up, bleary-eyed. "You have to find him, Tom. If anything happens to Teddy, I'll kill myself."

I pictured the map of Dartmoor in Hugo Hawksworthy's office. Widdecombe Throop, the lost village, was located near Evelscombe, the deepest mire on Dartmoor—a giant peat bog where the waterlogged peat was as treacherous as quicksand. Animals and people who strayed into it became trapped and sank slowly to their deaths. And we'd had all that rain, making things worse. No wonder Quinn was worried.

"Do you have a map of the area?" Tom asked. "I need to see the footpaths."

"Take the Ordnance Survey map and a torch. In that drawer." Quinn flung an arm toward a cabinet near the sink. "If he took the road, you'd have seen him. Means he took the path onto the moor." She began to cry.

"Show me," Tom said, unfolding the well-worn map.

"There's the lodge," Quinn said, indicating an irregular shape shaded in pale pink. "That's where we are. And there's the footpath. See? It doesn't go anywhere. Just sort of peters out onto the open moor."

Tom took the torch Quinn gave him and zipped up his jacket. "Kate, you and Quinn stay here. If I'm not back in thirty minutes, text Okoje. He should be here"—he checked his watch—"by eleven thirty."

"No texting." Quinn frowned. "No mobile phone coverage. Haven't turned on the Wi-Fi. Don't know how to do it."

That explained why Quinn hadn't called her mother. Unless someone figured it out, we wouldn't be calling for help anytime soon either.

"Okoje will be here in about two hours," Tom repeated. "If I haven't found Teddy by then, we'll notify Search and Rescue."

How he would do that, I hadn't a clue. I wanted to go with him, but someone had to stay with Quinn. Something was wrong with her. I reached up and kissed him. "Be careful."

Tom picked up the map. Quinn grabbed his hand. "See there—the blue symbols like tufts of grass? That's Evelscombe. Dangerous. Don't leave the footpath."

* * *

I saw Tom out the door. When I returned to the kitchen, Quinn was slumped over the table.

"Quinn, something's wrong with you. What is it?"

She looked up. "Teddy's in danger." Her pupils were huge.

"No—you've taken something. What was it?"

"Prescription." She lowered her head again and started to moan. "My head's splitting."

"What sort of prescription?" When she didn't answer, I shook her gently. "Quinn, what prescription did you take?"

"Tranquilizers. Doctor gave 'em to me."

"How many did you take?"

"Don't remember." Her head was resting on the table now.

"Where's the bottle?"

"Bath." She flung an arm behind her, toward a dark hallway. "'S all right. Doctor said."

I ran along the hall, locating the huge, old-fashioned bathroom on the right. A plastic container of medicine stood on the porcelain sink. The label read *Lorazepam. Thirty tablets. Take two as needed.*

I poured them into my hand, wondering if Quinn would need an ambulance, and if she did, how in the world I was going to call one.

Counting by twos, I replaced the pills in the bottle. And took a breath. Twenty-eight left, which meant she'd taken the prescribed dosage.

"You need sleep," I told her, wondering when she'd swallowed the tablets and how long it would take for the effects to wear off. "Let's get you to the bedroom."

She shook off my hand. "No. Have to wait . . ."

"All right. You can sit in that big chair by the Aga."

I helped Quinn to the battered old chair and took off her shoes. She drew her feet up under her and closed her eyes. In another room along the hallway, I found a feather duvet and tucked it around her. That would keep her warm.

I'd forgotten all about the tea, but the kettle was hot, so I made myself a cup. No milk, but I added two spoonfuls of sugar from a glass jar on the counter.

Now what? I peered out of the curtainless window into the blackness. Rain spattered lightly against the panes. From the distance came an ominous rumble of thunder.

Had Gideon Littlejohn planned to ruin Teddy Pearce's political career—and perhaps his marriage—by revealing publicly that Teddy, as a teenager, had killed an elderly, disabled man? Had Teddy killed Littlejohn to made sure that wouldn't happen? Or . . . I stopped, the teacup halfway to my mouth, as several more possibilities jostled for position.

I had a sudden image of the crowd watching the mechanical clock demonstration.

Why can't I remember what's wrong?

I heard footsteps on the gravel, and the kitchen door burst open. It was Tom. Rain streamed from his hair.

I jumped to my feet. "Did you find Teddy?"

"I found him all right. He needs help."

"Come inside."

"No time. I need you both. Teddy's trapped in the mire. We need rope and—"

"Quinn's out of commission." I nodded my head toward the big chair. "She's taken tranquilizers."

Tom gave me an agonized look. "It's just us, then. We need rope and something slick—a plastic tarp or something." His voice was urgent. "You'll need wellies—and hats for both of us, if you can find them."

"Okay—I'll search the house. You try the sheds."

"We have to hurry, Kate. He's already in over his knees, and I'm afraid he's becoming hypothermic."

Chapter Thirty-Eight

"Will this do?" I held out a full-length rain slicker I'd found hanging with a collection of jackets and boots in the mudroom off the kitchen.

"It'll have to. I found some rope but nothing else useful. I see you found Wellington boots."

"They even fit me." I handed him a black knit watch cap and pulled on another knitted of thick gray wool.

Tom turned on the torch. I followed him out of the courtyard and onto a beaten track that led, as far as I could see, into nothingness. The rain, whipped by the wind, stung my face.

"The rain's coming faster now," I said, shading my eyes. "I can't see where I'm going."

He looked over his shoulder and gave me a brief smile. "All you need to see is the next step, darling—and my back. Pearce isn't far—no more than half a mile."

We trudged along the narrow, waterlogged track. "How did Teddy end up in the mire?"

"He doesn't know. Says one moment he was on solid ground, and the next he was up to his knees in the thick, spongy peat. There he is." Tom pointed ahead to a dark shape—human but oddly truncated. "Watch your step, Kate. When you feel your feet start to sink, stop. We'll have to get close enough to help him, but we can't do that if we get stuck in as well."

"Is he conscious?"

"Just about," came a weak voice, one I recognized. "Don't come any closer. Told you, Tom. It's hopeless. All you're going to do is get yourself trapped. And now Kate. Not worth it."

"Sorry, mate." Tom's tone was light, almost companionable. "We're not going to leave you here." Tom took several steps toward the shadowy figure. Teddy Pearce, wearing yellow waterproofs and a blue cotton sling for his injured arm, had sunk up to his thighs in the mire. His normally ruddy complexion was ashen. "I brought a rope," Tom said. "I'm going to throw you the end. Tie it around your chest if you can—tight enough to stay under your arms. We'll pull you out."

Tom sounded confident, but I knew his plan was anything but foolproof. I remembered using a rope to rescue him and two others in the collapse of a house the previous May, but then I'd had the power of a van to help me. This time the only power we had was our own—and I've never been famous for my upper-body strength.

A mighty crack was followed by a flash of lightning and the rumble of thunder. The storm was moving closer. The wind was picking up.

I moved forward cautiously as the ground beneath my feet felt increasingly squishy. Brown water oozed over the toes of my wellies.

Teddy sighed. His head slumped forward.

"Teddy, stay with us," Tom pleaded. "Don't go to sleep. We need your help to get you back to the lodge as quickly as possible."

As Tom got the rope ready to throw, I started talking to keep Teddy alert. "Quinn's at the lodge, waiting for you. The police are on the way. If we can't get you out, they'll alert Search and Rescue." I meant those words to be encouragement, but they had the opposite effect.

"The police?" He let out a strangled sob. "Don't let them take Quinn." Teddy struggled to take a step, using his good arm to propel him forward, but he subsided in exhaustion. He'd sunk farther into the mire. "She didn't do anything. It was me, I swear. I did it. Everything."

"What are you talking about?" I asked.

"Everything—the attacks on the family, rocks through the window, the car crash—that was me. I wanted sympathy. I killed Littlejohn. He was going to ruin me."

"We'll talk about that later, Teddy." Tom held a curl of the thick rope in his right hand. "The first thing to do is get you out of here. Then you can talk all you want."

"No, please." Teddy moaned. He was exhausted. "Better for everyone if it ends here. Tell them it was an accident. You couldn't save me."

"Quinn needs you," Tom said. "Think of Ivy and Lily. Your daughters need you."

Teddy let out a brittle sound that might have been a laugh. "I'll be charged with murder, sent to prison for life. Better they remember me this way."

"Sorry, mate," Tom said. "Can't do that."

"Why not?" Teddy was weakening. If we didn't do something soon, he wouldn't have the strength to hold on to the rope.

He was struggling again. The mire was up to his lower hip.

"Stop moving," Tom said sharply. "You're making it worse."

"Littlejohn was a blackmailer. Said I'd killed an old man years ago, when I was a teenager."

"Billy Cole," I said. "He died in a fire. Someone put a lighted newspaper through his mail slot."

"He said I'd go to prison." Teddy wiped his eyes. "Said he'd make sure everyone knew what I'd done. My girls would grow up knowing their father was a murderer."

"Are you saying you shot Littlejohn?"

"Tha's right. Tell the police. It was me. I admit it."

"Won't stand up in court," Tom said. "Hearsay."

"Record it on your phone."

"Don't have it with me. Sorry, mate. You're going to have to confess in person."

"Better it ends here, Tom. For Ivy and Lily's sake. For Quinn's sake. They don't deserve this."

"No, they don't." I said, because suddenly I knew what my brain had been trying to tell me. *The final image at the gala. The shot from the first-floor balcony. Littlejohn's unexpected visitor.* "It wasn't you, Teddy, was it? You didn't kill Littlejohn."

"What're you talking about? I just admitted it."

"Are you saying you shot Littlejohn at the museum gala too?" By some miracle, my voice was calm.

"Yes—I admit it. When it didn't work, I—"

"But you didn't." I cut across him. "You couldn't have. You were on the ground floor. The shot came from the first-floor balcony. Where Quinn was."

"No! You've got it wrong. It wasn't Quinn. I swear it."

Tom stared at me. "Quinn?"

The wind howled. Thunder rumbled. The sky split in a white-hot flash.

"I told you something wasn't right about that night, Tom. The last picture in my mind. Everyone's eyes were riveted on the clock. Except Quinn. I could see the outline of her spine. Her neck was bent. She wasn't looking at the clock like everyone else. She was looking *down*. I think that's when she pulled the gun out of her handbag. She intended to kill Littlejohn, but the shot missed. She tried again Sunday morning. That time she succeeded."

Teddy was crying now. "No. I'm the one who killed him. I swear it."

"All right," Tom said. "So tell me—what was he wearing when you shot him?"

Teddy's head shot up. "What was he *wearing*? I don't know. One of those frock coats."

I looked at Tom. Littlejohn had been wearing modern clothes when he was shot. The police hadn't released that information. But the shooter would know.

"Where was Quinn the morning Littlejohn was killed?" Tom asked.

"I'm not saying another word." Pearce teetered backward, nearly losing his balance as his legs struggled in vain to offset his weight. If he fell, we'd never get him out.

"You're trying to save your wife," Tom said. "Trust me—this isn't going to help her."

Pearce was sobbing, shaking his head. "You're wrong. It was me."

I knelt on the cold, soggy ground. "Teddy, listen to me. Time is running out. The police are on their way. Either they'll get here in time to save you, or they won't. Either way, your confession isn't going to hold up. They'll find out where you were the morning Littlejohn was killed. They'll find out where Quinn was. They'll know Quinn was to blame for the shooting at the gala, and she'll be taken into custody. What will your daughters do then, Teddy, if their father is dead and their mother is charged with a serious crime? They need at least one of their parents to survive, and I think it has to be you, Teddy."

He moaned like a wounded animal.

I pressed on. "Quinn needs you too. How will she cope with all this alone?"

I saw his jaw tighten. He drew in a breath.

"I'm throwing the rope," Tom said. "Catch it. Good lad. Now pull it toward you and wrap it around your torso. Do you know how to make a hitch knot?"

"I think so—yes."

We watched as Teddy pulled the rope around his body. Ripping off the blue sling, he used both arms to make the knot.

Tom gave a yank on the rope. "You've got it. Well done." He passed the other end of the rope to me. "All right, Kate. Crouch down—low as you can. Use your legs as a wedge and pull." He squatted down himself, bracing his legs. "Teddy, let your body slide forward onto the surface of the mire—like you're swimming. Your legs will release better at an angle." He took a breath. "Here we go. *Pull.*"

I strained at the rope, my hands slipping, the rough fibers abrading my flesh.

"Keep at it, Kate. Teddy, hold the rope in front of you. Let it pull you forward."

Nothing was happening. My muscles tensed as they struggled to shift a load way too heavy for them.

Teddy groaned as the rope dug into his armpits. "It's no good."

Tom and I collapsed onto the ground. "This isn't going to work," he said. "We need the slicker."

Standing awkwardly, I grabbed the long moss-green rain slicker and handed it to him.

Tom spread it out, slick side up, beginning at the edge of the mire. It didn't quite reach Teddy, but it was close. "We need to secure this.

See that dead tree over there, Kate? See if you can find three or four sturdy splinters to use as pegs. Long ones if you can find them."

It wasn't hard. The trunk of the stunted oak was disintegrating, but I found three sharp splinters. In the meantime, Tom had found a rock, which he used to drive the wood splinters through the slicker and into the soil. But would they hold in the soggy ground?

Tom said, "I'm going to try to pull him out myself."

"What's going to prevent you from sinking into the mire?" I asked.

"Distribution of weight." He wrapped the end of the rope around his waist. "Hold the end of the rope, Kate. Kneel on the edge of the fabric. If the whole thing slips into the mire, I'm in trouble. Teddy's right. Joining him isn't going to help."

I watched as Tom stretched his tall frame out over the slicker. He reached forward. They locked arms, which had to have been painful for Teddy. "Hold on," Tom said. "Let your body slide forward."

I knelt on the slicker as Tom pulled. I could see him straining against Teddy's weight while trying to wiggle his body backward.

After several minutes, the rope went slack. "It's not going to work," Teddy said. "Nothing will. They say hypothermia isn't a bad way to go." He made a guttural sound. "The truth is, Tom, I'm a coward. I don't really want to die."

"You're not going to die if I have anything to say about it." Tom slithered back. Once on solid ground, he stood, pulling off his knitted cap which was now soaked through and running a hand through his hair. "There's got to be a way." He began striding back and forth. "I've been counting on brute strength, and we're not strong enough—not with the resistance of the mire added to his weight. I have to think."

Teddy's eyes were huge and black in the pale oval of his face. His teeth were chattering.

Tom was still pacing. "We have to use physics—give ourselves an edge." He stopped moving. "Okay, let's try this. I'm going to thread the rope around that rock and then tie the other end around the trunk of that dead tree—low to the ground."

"What are you planning?" Rain beat against our faces, and I pulled off my knitted cap too. It wasn't keeping me warm. Rain pooled on the surface of the peat mire.

"We can't do it with arm strength alone," Tom said. "We need our legs and our backs."

Tom looped the rope around a large rock, then tied it to the dead tree, creating a sort of L shape—a distance of about twenty-five feet.

The wind howled as he worked. It had to be my imagination, but I could almost hear the ringing of those ghostly bells from the drowned church.

Tom finished tying the last knot. "Teddy, just as before—don't try to help. Relax your legs. Let the rope pull you forward, onto the slicker. Kate, come here. Stand next to me."

We stood side by side, our backs to the rope, about halfway between the rock and the tree. "We're going to create a fulcrum or pivot point. As we shorten the length of the rope between Teddy and the tree, the mire will have to give him up."

"Is this going to work?" I whispered.

"No idea," he said in a low voice. "I was never much good at physics. But if it doesn't, I'm out of ideas."

"It'll have to work, then. What do we do?"

"Thread your arms over and under the rope across your back and lock your hands in front of you. Like this." He demonstrated. "Then we're going to lean into the rope and push with our legs. The idea is to step backward—even a step or two will help. Ready? Hard as you can, now."

I felt the rope tighten against my back. Were we gaining ground? I couldn't tell. An inch, maybe, but it could have been the rope stretching. It wasn't enough. I tried not to cry as the rope bit into my flesh through the jacket.

The wind was howling even louder. Another massive thunderbolt lit up the sky, releasing a deluge of rain. I could hardly see. Gritting my teeth, I braced my legs and pushed with my back.

Tom grunted with a massive effort. We gained a single step. Then another.

The tree cracked ominously. If the rotten wood gave way, we were finished. I felt my feet slipping and regained my traction.

"Keep pushing," Tom said. "Just one more step."

In the bog, Teddy began to move. I could see it. With a massive sucking sound, the mire released its prey, and he flopped onto the rain slicker, which had pulled loose of the pegs.

"It worked." Tom sounded surprised. "Come on—help me get him out."

Together we pulled on the rain slicker, sliding Teddy onto solid ground. Tom and I collapsed. All three of us lay panting and covered with thick liquid peat.

Tom got to his feet. "No time to waste, Kate. He's lost body heat. Help me get him up. We're going to have to support him all the way."

Slinging Teddy's good arm over Tom's shoulder, we began the long trek back to the lodge.

And Quinn.

Chapter Thirty-Nine

An hour later, back at the hunting lodge, Tom, Teddy, and I sat in the large, square living room in front of a blazing fire. "At least we have plenty of logs and fire starters," Tom said, brushing ashes from his hands. He'd constructed a teepee of logs. Thankfully, the chimney was drawing well.

Tom and I had exchanged our wet, filthy clothes for whatever we could find. We'd helped Teddy out of his clothes, too, and into a thick velour robe that must have belonged to Quinn's father. Since the water in the boilers was still barely lukewarm, we'd wrapped him in another duvet and pulled his chair close to the fire. He'd been trapped in the Evelscombe mire for at least an hour and a half. In an attempt to raise his core temperature, I'd made more tea, adding lots of sugar. He really needed medical care, but with no way to reach out for help, this was the best we could do. I just hoped it would be enough.

Quinn was still sound asleep in the comfortable chair by the Aga.

"Why haven't the police arrived yet?" I asked Tom. "It's been well over three hours since you heard from Okoje."

"I don't know. I'm going to try to get the Wi-Fi working. Teddy, where's the router?" In our concern for Teddy, we'd forgotten all about the Wi-Fi.

Teddy held his mug of tea with both hands. He'd stopped shaking but his skin had turned red, and I knew he could experience heart arrythmia, even cardiac arrest. "In the main bedroom. Second level."

Tom returned quickly. "Success. Now if we'd only brought our power cords. My mobile's almost dead. How much charge is left on yours, Kate?"

I turned it on. "Eighteen percent."

"You're going to have to text Okoje—here's the number." He handed me his phone. "Tell him where we are. Tell him we need an ambulance."

"I'll need the password."

"It's Hector, the gelding's name," Teddy said. "All lowercase."

I logged on to the lodge's Wi-Fi and texted Okoje, then Susan Benables, telling her Quinn and Teddy were all right.

As I was texting, Tom said, "Littlejohn accused you of killing an old man—Billy Cole. Was he right?"

Teddy looked into the fire. He didn't answer.

"When was this?" Tom asked.

"He sent me an email a few days before Christmas. Said 'You killed Billy Cole. Soon everyone will know.' I tried to reason with him the night of the gala."

"I witnessed your argument," I said. "Just before the shooting."

"What did he say?" Tom asked.

"He said he'd seen me that night in 1992. He said I was the one who'd shoved the burning newspaper through the old man's mail slot. He said I was a murderer and needed to be punished. He'd make sure of it."

"Was he right? Did you do it?"

Teddy was silent for a long time. At last he spoke. "No. I swear it, Tom. I was there that night. I admit that. But it wasn't me. I couldn't convince him."

"You're saying you were there, but you didn't push the newspaper through Billy Cole's mail slot?"

"I was part of the gang, all right. Thought we were the dog's bollocks, we did. I've admitted it. But I wasn't responsible for the old man's death. I could prove it. Witnesses came forward. People who had no reason to lie. They saw me spray-painting a house blocks away when the fire was started. That's why I was never convicted." Teddy took a long drink of his tea—a good sign. "That night was a pivot point for me. I was shocked when I learned the next day about the old man's death. I was lucky. The police got me into a diversion program. Changed the course of my life. That's why I care about juvenile crime in the UK, in Devon. These kids need the same chance I got."

"What made Littlejohn think you were guilty?"

"We'd just come from a game. High on alcohol and ready to smash everything in our way. He said he recognized me, recognized my football jersey." Teddy's brows pulled inward. "But most of us were wearing our jerseys. I think he must have been testing the waters—seeing how I would react."

Was he telling the truth or setting up a defense? "Where does Quinn come into it?" I asked.

"Quinn? She doesn't." He sat up, his voice stronger. "Quinn had nothing to do with any of this. I was the one. Had to protect my family, didn't I?"

He'd just denied having a part in Billy Cole's death. I was confused. I thought he was too—confused and a little panicky.

"Did Quinn know about Littlejohn's accusations?"

"I knew." Quinn stood in the archway, still wrapped in the duvet. Her hair was disheveled and her eye makeup a mess, but she was awake. She ran to her husband and bent down to hug him. Then she looked at us. "He's innocent. Not just the murder of Billy Cole. He's innocent of everything. Thank you for finding him." She kissed the top of his head. "You're alive. That's all that matters. No more secrets. It's time to tell the truth."

Teddy's hand shot out, and he grabbed her arm. "Don't say another word."

Freeing her arm, she sat at his feet and turned to face us. "I was the one who staged the attacks—all of them. If you look into it, you'll find they never happened when the girls were home. No one was ever hurt. I made sure of that. Until the car crash." Quinn put a hand over her mouth. Her eyes filled. "I'm so sorry, darling."

"Don't do this." Teddy shook his head. "You don't have to do this."

"I do." Quinn wiped away her tears. "When Teddy was hurt in the car crash, I knew it had to stop."

"You staged the car crash?" I could hardly believe what I was hearing.

"I'd hired a guy to follow him from the supermarket opening. Teddy didn't know. The guy was supposed to get close, sort of threaten him, that's all. But he made contact. It was an accident, but Teddy's car spun out of control." She reached up and took his hand. "In the hospital, when I thought you'd been seriously injured, I realized what I'd done."

"Your mother said you'd been terribly upset since the crash."

"What about the shooting the night of the gala?" Tom asked. "That was you as well, wasn't it?"

Quinn's shoulders slumped. "Stupid of me. I'm a good shot—I really am. Just out of practice."

Teddy sat forward, his forehead on the heels of his hands. "Luv, don't do this."

"You tried to kill Gideon Littlejohn?"

"I didn't want to kill him, just frighten him. But it didn't work, because everyone assumed Teddy was the target. So, I thought, *fine.* More sympathy." She looked at me. "That's what Teddy and I argued about on the phone. I confessed. He was so angry. I thought he'd never speak to me again."

"I'm sorry, luv." Teddy kissed her hand.

"Why did you want to frighten Gideon Littlejohn?" Tom asked.

"Because he was going to tell everyone Teddy murdered a helpless old man. I couldn't let that happen. Teddy was innocent, and he was going to lose his reputation, probably his seat in Parliament, all because of a lie. And the scandal would prove my father right." She gulped down a sob. "My bloody, stupid pride."

"Littlejohn didn't get the message, though," Tom said. "He thought Teddy was the target like everyone else."

"His housekeeper said a woman visited him sometime after Christmas. Was that you?"

"Yes. He assumed Teddy hadn't told me. When I said I knew about his threats, he made me leave. I never had a chance to explain that Teddy was innocent. That's why I went to his house Sunday morning.

To plead with him again. To tell him he'd got it wrong. About the old man, I mean."

"You went to his house?" Tom leaned forward in his chair.

"No, luv. Please." Tears streamed down Teddy's face. "Don't do this."

"Was he expecting you?" I asked.

"No, and he wasn't happy to see me."

"When did you get there?" Tom asked.

"Around ten. I told Teddy I was going to the gym."

Tom and I exchanged glances. Quinn was the person Clive Nixon had seen that morning. She'd been there during that missing period of time when Littlejohn was murdered. I felt a sick coldness in my gut. "Quinn," I said, "Did Littlejohn offer you tea?"

"Tea?" She looked at me in disbelief. "Of course he didn't. I wasn't there long enough anyway."

"What did you do?" Tom asked.

"I begged him to have mercy." Quinn's hands lay still in her lap, but I could see the tension in her shoulders and spine. "I told him Teddy was innocent. That he'd turned his life around. We have the girls now. He's doing good things for Southeast Devon. Littlejohn wouldn't listen. He said nothing Teddy ever did would make up for murder. He saw himself as some kind of an avenger. Setting things right."

"Did you believe him?" I asked.

"Of course not. But he said he had irrefutable evidence. He'd made a video." She buried her face in her hands.

"So you had to stop him." Tom's face was completely blank.

"What?" Quinn looked up sharply. "What do you mean?"

"You shot him."

"No. Of course I didn't."

"You didn't?" Teddy blinked, his face slack. "I thought . . . when you told me you went there to stop him . . . I was afraid. I'm so sorry, luv."

"Don't be." Quinn grasped his hand. "For a while, I thought it was you."

"You're saying Littlejohn was alive when you left his house?" Tom asked.

"Very much alive. I was only there ten minutes. He said I had to leave. We had nothing more to talk about, and he was expecting someone at ten forty-five."

"His appointment," I said. *His murderer—the person who got tea and biscuits.*

"Quinn, think hard now." Tom went very still. "Did you see anyone when you left? Anyone at all—near the house or on the street? A car? Someone on foot?"

Quinn's brows drew together. "No, and I'm not sure I'd have noticed. I was terribly upset. I sat in my car and cried for a while. Then I drove away."

My mobile pinged. "It's Okoje—at last." I read it aloud.

Been trying to reach you all night. Tree across road near Holne Bridge. Cleared now. Be at the lodge in 30 min. Ambulance on the way.

Chapter Forty

Thursday, January 16

We'd gotten back to the Crown at two in the morning and stumbled into bed without bothering to brush our teeth or even turn off the lights. Teddy and Quinn Pearce had been taken to the hospital at Plymouth, the closest facility offering emergency services. On the drive home, Okoje had texted, saying they'd both been cautioned and, as soon as they were able, would give their official statements.

It was now ten in the morning. Having eaten our room-service breakfast, we lay in bed, fingers interlaced. At least we'd both showered. Dried peat isn't easy to get out of hair. Who knew? I was still in my cashmere robe.

"Will they be charged?" I asked Tom.

"I don't see how Quinn can avoid charges," Tom said. "She fired an unregistered gun in a public place. And wasted police time by staging the attacks."

"She thought she was helping Teddy by making him the hero standing up to corruption, and she ended up nearly getting him killed." I raked my free hand through my still-damp hair.

"He's not likely to press charges, is he?" It was a statement, not a question. "If she has a good lawyer and is very, very lucky, she might get a noncustodial sentence."

"Do they believe her about leaving Littlejohn alive that morning?"

"I don't know. Too bad she didn't see anyone hanging around when she left."

"Yes, it is." Images clicked through my brain—the photograph of the football team; the tea things in the sink at the Old Merchant's House; Littlejohn telling Quinn she had to leave because he was expecting someone.

"I know that look," Tom said. "You're making connections."

"The photograph of the football team. Pearce singled out two boys, marking them with red stars. One of them was Teddy Pearce. Who was the second boy?"

"Okoje's got someone tracking him down. It looked like an official team photograph. Someone else will have kept a copy. What are you thinking?"

"I'm thinking that two boys who vaguely resemble each other and who are both wearing identical football jerseys could easily be mistaken for each other in the dark. Gideon Littlejohn might not have known which of the two it was who put the burning newspaper through Billy Cole's letter slot."

"You mean by accusing Teddy Pearce, he was making a guess, seeing how Teddy would react."

"It's possible." My mobile buzzed. I'd left it on the table the night before. I moaned, getting out of bed. Every muscle in my body was objecting. I clicked on the phone. "Morning, Julia. What's up?"

"It's the trunk, Kate. I told you I was going to release part of the lining to examine the construction. I did that early this morning and—well, I got quite a surprise. I found two flash drives."

"*Flash drives?* What's on them?"

"Don't know. Thought you'd want to see them first."

"We'll be there. Give us half an hour."

When we arrived at the Museum of Devon Life, Isla was at the ticket counter. Seeing us, she turned on her heel and disappeared into the supply room. Hawksworthy was there too—somewhere. We'd seen his black BMW in the car park.

Julia was waiting for us. She held out two USB flash drives, cradled in a tissue. "They were hidden inside the lining, taped to one of the wood slats. I haven't touched them. I knew they might be important to the investigation."

"Well done." Tom retrieved a pair of latex gloves and an evidence bag from inside his jacket. He dropped the flash drives into the bag. "Show me where you found them."

The trunk sat on the worktable, the lid open. Part of the yellow-print lining had been peeled back and held in place with long pins.

"I told Kate I was going to open the lining here—where someone made repairs at one time. At least I thought they were repairs. Now I think someone opened the lining to hide the flash drives and then closed it up again with stitches meant to replicate the original. They didn't succeed. It was obvious." Carefully, she moved more layers of material out of the way—first a liner of unbleached cotton and then some fine cotton batting, exposing a thick layer of unspun wool. On one of the mounting slats was a piece of very modern electrical tape. "That's where I found them."

"Why there, of all places?" Tom said.

"Because he was paranoid about security," I said. "Especially after the break-in three months ago. He hid the flash drives in the one place he knew no one would ever look."

No wonder Littlejohn had refused to part with the trunk.

* * *

Varma slid one of the flash drives into the USB port of his computer in the police enquiry office.

Piano music began to play as a series of historical images rolled across the screen. The familiar title appeared: *Living in the Past: The Life of a Modern-Day Victorian Gentleman*.

"It's one of his videos," Tom said.

Gideon Littlejohn's face filled the screen. He wasn't smiling.

Hello again, friends. Gideon Littlejohn here. For those new to the channel, I live in a Victorian house in a village called Coombe Mallet, within Dartmoor National Park in Devon, England.

He stepped back from the camera to allow a shot of his costume.

I live and dress as a middle-class Victorian gentleman."

"Tom," I whispered, "did you notice? The camera is stationary. No one's filming."

Today's program will be different in style and subject matter to my usual videos. Instead of showing you how I live and what it takes to achieve fidelity to the past, I want to speak to you today about a different kind of fidelity. The kind we owe to each other as human beings. The kind that means telling the truth and holding ourselves and others to a higher standard.

He stopped, and when he spoke again, his voice was bitter.

Many years ago, I failed to protect someone. A man who'd been kind to me. A man who changed my life.

His eyes glistened.

I failed because I was afraid. I was a coward. And in all those years, I never spoke up because I was ashamed. Today I am speaking up, and in doing so, I intend to right an old wrong.

On a warm June night in 1992, a gang of teens on the Burnthouse Lane estate in Exeter went on a rampage, turning over rubbish bins, smashing car windows, and spray-painting houses with disgusting slogans. Some of them turned on an elderly, crippled man named Billy Cole. He was my friend. I owed him my loyalty. But instead of standing up to the gang or calling the police, I hid. And I watched as one of those teens, an older boy, someone I knew from the estate, pushed a burning newspaper through Billy Cole's mail slot. Billy died in the resulting fire.

Littlejohn moved out of the screenshot and returned, holding a file, from which he took a photograph. He held the photo close to the camera. It was the football team, the photograph we'd seen in the computer file on Teddy Pearce.

The boy in the front row is someone you know. Teddy Pearce, our new MP for Southeast Devon. Thirty-three years ago he murdered Billy Cole in cold blood, and I'm going to make sure he pays for his crime. I bear some of the guilt, I know that. But an old man died that night, and Teddy Pearce was never held accountable. I have the proof.

Littlejohn moved forward so his face, wet with tears, filled the screen.

Billy Cole will be avenged.

The screen faded to black.

"But Littlejohn was wrong about Teddy," I said. "Or at least uncertain."

"Maybe that's why he never aired the video," Okoje said. "Varma, let's have the second flash drive."

It was another video. We watched as the now-familiar music, images, and title filled the screen.

Hello again, friends. Gideon Littlejohn here. For those new to the channel, I live in a Victorian house in a village called Coombe Mallet, within Dartmoor National Park in Devon, England.

He stepped back from the camera.

I live and dress as a middle-class Victorian gentleman.

"It's the same damn video," Varma said, stopping the video.

"No, it isn't," I said. "Look at his clothes,"

Okoje tapped the monitor. "Start it again."

Today's program will be different in style and subject matter to my usual videos. Instead of showing you how I live and what it takes to achieve fidelity to the past, I'm going to speak to you today about a different kind of fidelity. The kind we owe to each other as human beings. The kind that means telling the truth and holding ourselves and others to a higher standard.

"The script is identical," Tom said. "Maybe he thought he needed a second take. Or maybe he included more information."

Littlejohn's voice was solemn as he continued.

Many years ago, I failed to protect someone. A man who'd been kind to me. A man who changed my life. I failed because I was afraid. And in all those years, I never spoke up because I was ashamed. Today I will speak up, and in doing so, I intend to right an old wrong.

We listened again to Littlejohn's emotional description of the rampage and the death of Billy Cole. He held up the photograph of the football team, positioning it this time so we were looking not at the front row but at the second. I held my breath.

The boy in the back row, second from the left, is someone you know—a respected academic, Dr. Hugo Hawksworthy, director of the Museum of Devon Life in Coombe Mallet. He is not what he seems to be, and I can prove it.

Littlejohn held up a folder.

His academic credits are fraudulent. He claims to have graduated with highest honors from the University of Glasgow. The transcripts show he barely passed his courses. He claims to have earned a doctorate in the States. The university he calls his alma mater says he never attended classes there. He claims to have interned at the Smithsonian Museum. They say he worked one summer as a security guard.

But these aren't the most important lies he's told. Thirty-three years ago, Hugo Hawksworthy murdered an old man, Billy Cole, in cold blood. Billy was my friend. I watched it with my own eyes, and I was afraid. Today I'm going to make sure Hugo Hawksworthy finally pays for his crime. I bear some of the guilt, I admit that freely. But an old man died that night, a man who deserved to be protected and esteemed, and Hugo Hawksworthy was never held accountable. His whole life is a collection of lies.

Littlejohn moved forward so his face filled the screen.

Billy Cole will be avenged.

Once again, the screen faded to black.

Okoje put the heel of his hand on his forehead. "Varma. Get Constable Doaks. Bring Hawksworthy in under caution."

"Tom," I said, "what happened to that blue file?"

Chapter Forty-One

It was midafternoon by the time Hugo Hawksworthy arrived at the police enquiry office, tight-lipped and indignant. He'd surrendered quietly enough, Tom and I learned, over the vociferous protests of Isla Ferris, who'd practically thrown herself between Hawksworthy and Constable Doaks.

Tom and I were seated in Okoje's office, facing a monitor on his desk. We held steaming mugs of tea. The old, waist-high radiator clunked out a comforting warmth.

"You can watch the interview from here," Okoje had told us earlier. "You've spent time with Hawksworthy, Mrs. Hamilton, and you know the museum personnel. If there's anything we should follow up, make a note."

"Ask him if he got tea," I said.

"Tea?" Okoje's mouth turned down. "If you say so."

"Is this usual procedure?" I whispered to Tom when he'd left. "Allowing private investigators to witness police interviews?"

"He says we deserve it, after all we've been through."

"I agree with that. Still—"

"The real answer is no—it's not usual procedure. If you ask me, Okoje's taking a chance. He's unconventional. If I've learned one thing about Elijah Okoje, it's he's willing to bend the rules to get results. So far he's got away with it. If he keeps getting away with it, he'll end up chief constable. If he doesn't, he might find himself back in uniform."

"You like him, don't you?"

"Very much. He's as smart as they come—and honest as an old penny, as Uncle Nigel used to say."

The monitor on Okoje's desk flickered. The camera in the interview room had been mounted near the ceiling, so we looked down on the small metal table. Dr. Hawksworthy sat on one side with his solicitor, a rather slick-looking man in a conservative navy suit and striped tie. Hawksworthy looked defiant. His solicitor looked worried.

Okoje entered the interview room, almost filling it with his height and breadth. He was followed by Varma and Constable O'Brien. The interview began with preliminaries. Constable O'Brien would be taking notes. Did Hawksworthy need anything? A cup of tea, perhaps? A glass of water?

Okoje let Varma take the lead. "We've brought you in today under caution because we've discovered new evidence in the shooting death of Gideon Littlejohn. We'd like to go over the account you gave earlier of your movements the morning of January fifth. You do not have to say anything, but it may harm your defense if you do not mention when questioned something which you later rely on in court. Anything you do say may be given in evidence. Do you understand your rights, Dr. Hawksworthy? It is *Doctor*, isn't it?"

"That's correct, but I don't insist on it. Yes, I understand my rights."

"Are you comfortable? Are you sure you wouldn't like something to drink?"

"I'm fine. Let's just get this over with."

"Very well," Varma said cheerfully. "If you need a break at any time, let us know. Now, you've stated previously you were with Ms. Ferris, your administrative assistant, the morning of January fifth. Is that correct?'

"Ms. Ferris is the assistant director of the museum. I said I was with her, and I believe Ms. Ferris confirmed it."

"You know a witness claims to have seen you at the Old Merchant's House that morning a little before nine AM. Can you explain that?"

"As I told you before"—Hawksworthy pretended a false patience—"your witness is either mistaken or lying. I wasn't there. I was with Ms. Ferris until about eight thirty; then I went for a run."

Varma nodded. "Thank you. Where were you born, Dr. Hawksworthy? Where did you spend your youth?"

Was it my imagination, but did a muscle near Hawksworthy's eye twitch?

"Exeter."

"Can you be more specific? What area of the city—a particular estate?"

Hawksworthy attempted a bluff tone. "It's no secret. I grew up on the Burnthouse Lane estate."

"A rough place to grow up in the 1980s and '90s. Would you agree?"

"Which is why I left as soon as possible."

"To begin your stellar academic career. Well done. You've certainly come up in the world. Did you know Teddy Pearce growing up?"

Hawksworthy relaxed. "I knew who he was. We were on the same football team briefly, but we weren't friends."

"Does he know you grew up on the same estate?"

"Actually, I'm not sure he does. We've never spoken of it." He blinked rapidly.

He was lying. I was sure of it. Whatever their involvement, both Hawksworthy and Pearce had put the horrific events of that night in 1992 behind them. Or tried to.

If Varma noticed the tell, he gave no indication of it. "Pearce is another lad from the estate who's come up in the world, wouldn't you say?"

"We're all very proud of him."

Tom leaned over. "Textbook police interrogation technique. I'm impressed."

I was too. Varma was relaxed, intimate, supportive, often nodding his head at Hawksworthy's responses. Putting him at ease. Okoje sat very still, a silent but ominous presence. Was Varma the so-called good cop and Okoje the bad cop?

"Did you also know a younger boy named Gordon Little?" Varma asked.

"Gordon Little . . . ?" Dr. Hawksworthy looked at his solicitor. "I . . . may have done. You know kids—stick to their own."

"Gordon Little changed his name to Gideon Littlejohn."

"I learned that quite recently. I would never have recognized him—or he me."

"Interesting that all three of you ended up in Coombe Mallet."

"A coincidence."

"Yes, and all three of you became involved in the new museum exhibit—Famous Crimes in Devon's History. Another coincidence."

"That's when I learned about Littlejohn's past—that we'd actually grown up on the same estate."

"I mentioned earlier that new evidence has come to light. We have a video we'd like you to view. Then I'll ask you to comment."

"Very well." Hawksworthy rubbed his eyebrow. He had no idea what was coming.

Varma pushed several keys on a monitor. The program began.

"Many years ago," Gideon Littlejohn said into the camera, "I failed to protect someone. A man who'd been kind to me. A man who changed my life. I failed because I was afraid. And in all those years, I never spoke up because I was ashamed. Today I will speak up, and in doing so, I intend to right an old wrong."

Hawksworthy shifted in his seat as Littlejohn spelled out the events of June 1992—the gang of teens terrorizing the estate, the targeting of Billy Cole, and finally the fire that killed him. When the image of the football team appeared, Hawksworthy's face went pale. "What is this?"

Littlejohn's voice continued.

The boy in the front row, on the left, is someone you know—a respected academic, Dr. Hugo Hawksworthy, director of the Museum of Devon Life in Coombe Mallet. He is not what he seems to be, and I can prove it.

Hawksworthy went completely still as he watched Littlejohn wave a blue folder.

He claims to have graduated with highest honors from the University of Glasgow. The transcripts show he barely passed his courses.

He claims to have earned a doctorate in the States. The university he calls his alma mater says he never attended classes there. He claims to have interned at the Smithsonian Museum. They say he worked one summer as a security guard.

"Stop the video." Hawksworthy stood. "This is slander. I don't have to listen to this. Stop the video."

No one moved.

Thirty-three years ago, Hugo Hawksworthy murdered Billy Cole in cold blood. I saw it with my own eyes, and I'm going to make sure Hugo Hawksworthy finally pays for his crime . . .

Littlejohn's face filled the screen. He was speaking, or so it seemed, directly to Hugo Hawksworthy.

His whole life is a collection of lies. Billy Cole will be avenged.

Okoje reached over and stopped the video.

"What is your response, Dr. Hawksworthy?" Varma asked.

"My response?" Hawksworthy's face had turned an ugly shade of red. "It's rubbish. It's—"

"We need a break," the solicitor said. "Now."

"Certainly," Okoje said. "Interview terminated at seventeen oh four."

Varma, O'Brien, and Okoje picked up their papers and left the interview room.

The screen we were watching went black.

* * *

In ten minutes, everyone reassembled, and Okoje resumed the interview. Once again, Tom and I watched on the small screen in his office.

"My client would like to make a statement," the solicitor said.

"Excellent," Varma said. "We're all ears."

Hawksworthy rubbed his chin. He seemed to have shrunk. "I admit to being part of the gang on the Burnthouse Lane estate in June of 1992, and I admit I was the one who caused the fire which took the life of Billy Cole." He took in a breath and let it out. "It was incredibly irresponsible of me, and I'm deeply ashamed. All I can say in my own defense is that his death was wholly unintentional. I wanted to cause damage, not death. I take full responsibility for my actions that night and will plead guilty in court—if it comes to that."

"*If* it comes to that?" I asked Tom. "This has to be manslaughter at the very least."

"Gross negligence manslaughter, I imagine." He smiled sardonically. "You know what's happening, don't you?"

"Tell me."

"His solicitor has advised him to plead guilty to the lesser charges. He knows they'll match his DNA to the samples found in Littlejohn's house. Keep listening."

"Three months ago someone broke into Littlejohn's house. Tried to access his computers. Was that you?"

Hawksworthy studied his hands. "Yes—I admit that as well. Foolish, of course, but I was desperate to find and destroy the evidence Littlejohn claimed to have."

"So Littlejohn told you about the video three months ago."

"Last September. I denied everything, of course."

"And he never did air the video. Why not?"

"I don't know. To make me sweat?" Hawksworthy gave a bitter laugh. "He succeeded. I lived in terror. Couldn't sleep, couldn't eat. But after a while—by early December—I'd convinced myself he was bluffing. He didn't have any real evidence, that it was all speculation, that he'd believed me when I denied killing the old man. Then, when Littlejohn told me about the bloodstained dress and proposed donating it to the museum, I was sure he was going to drop the whole thing."

"Is that the whole of your statement?" Okoje asked.

"Not quite, no." Hawksworthy glanced at his solicitor, then back at Okoje. "I also admit to forging my academic record—at least part of it. I did not earn a doctoral degree in heritage studies at Georgetown University, and I did not intern at the Smithsonian. None of that is true. What is true is my undergraduate degree in museum studies *and*"—he held up a finger to emphasize his words—"my proven expertise. I earned the respect of the team at the Mary Rose. You can ask them. And I have done my very best for the people of Devon. No one has raised more money than I have, and no one could have expanded the museum as quickly. That, I hope, will be taken into consideration."

Taken into consideration? Was the man completely deluded? "Did no one check his credentials?" I asked Tom.

"You'd be surprised how often something like this happens," he said. "Politicians, academics, scientists. I remember hearing about a cancer researcher in the States who claimed to have been a Rhodes Scholar to attain hundreds of thousands of dollars in grant money from the American Cancer Society. No one checked until the results of his clinical trials were published for peer review." Tom shrugged. "If people see something in print, they tend to believe it."

In the interview room, Hawksworthy shifted in his chair. DS Varma was closing in, and he knew it.

"You've made a good start, Dr. . . . er, Mr. Hawksworthy," Varma said, emphasizing the *Mister*. "We still have the events of the morning of January fifth. The shooting death of Gideon Littlejohn. You were there, at the Old Merchant's House, were you not?"

Hawksworthy glanced again at his solicitor, who nodded. "Yes, I was there."

Tom leaned in toward the monitor.

"When was this?" Varma asked.

"We had an appointment at eight forty-five that morning. Littlejohn got me there under the pretense of talking about a bequest for the museum. I was thrilled, and I was hoping to persuade him to allow us to display the trunk in which the bloodstained dress was found." He gave a bitter laugh. "Instead, he told me he hadn't forgotten about the death of the old man, Billy Cole. He said he'd actually seen me shove the burning newspaper through the letter slot.

"Once again I denied it. I said he was mistaken. He must have seen someone who looked like me. I told him there was no way he could prove anything after all these years anyway."

"You lied."

"Yes, I admit that. But then he showed me some files. He said it didn't matter that he couldn't prove it because he knew something that would ruin me anyway. Proof that I'd falsified my résumé. He said he was going to make everything public. I tried talking him out of it. I said telling everyone about my academic record would ruin the museum, hurt the citizens of Coombe Mallet, affect everyone in Dartmoor. Then he said there might be a way out."

"What was that?"

"The dress. If I could prove the dress belonged to Nancy Thorne, and if I could find evidence that she'd murdered a man named Luke Heron, one of the Romani Travellers on Dartmoor—"

I grabbed Tom's arm. "Luke Heron was the young man in that old photo, the one with the mesmerizing eyes."

"—and if I would make that information the centerpiece of the new crimes exhibit, he would consider keeping what he'd learned private."

"But you'd already hired the private investigators. Wasn't that enough?"

"I, ah"—Hawksworthy rubbed his mouth—"I'm not sure Littlejohn had full confidence in them."

I looked at Tom. He raised an eyebrow.

"What did you say in response, Mr. Hawksworthy?"

"What do you think I said? I agreed."

"What if you couldn't fulfill your promise?"

"I would have, trust me—one way or another. Even if I had to forge the evidence. What difference would it make after all those years?"

Okoje broke in. "Did Littlejohn offer you tea?"

"What?" Hawksworthy looked confused.

"Did he offer you tea?"

"No, he didn't offer me tea."

I looked at Tom. "Someone got tea. There must have been a third visitor that morning."

"When did you leave the Old Merchant's House?" Varma asked.

"Around nine fifteen."

"When did you decide to kill him?"

Hawksworthy sat up. "But I didn't. I swear it. I didn't kill him."

"What did you do?"

"I went home. Isla got there a half hour or so after I did. She was so happy. The night before I'd agreed to marry her. Not that I was all that keen, but she just kept pushing and pushing. I decided to make her happy."

"She didn't mention it in her statement. Why would that be?"

Good point. I looked at Tom. "Isla did seem unusually animated that morning, but I'd have thought she'd be shouting it from the rooftops."

"I made her promise to keep it quiet until I got the ring." Hawksworthy lifted one shoulder. "The truth is, I was keeping my options open. As soon as the words came out of my mouth, I regretted them."

"Did you tell Isla what happened with Littlejohn?"

"Yes, of course. She already knew I'd faked my credentials. She's loyal—I'll give her that. She'd do anything for me."

"What did she say?"

Hawksworthy looked down at his hands. I could almost see the gears turning in his brain. When he spoke, the words came slowly and deliberately. "She said, 'Everything will be fine, Hugo. Leave it to me.'"

I felt a sudden coldness. "Tom—it had to be *Isla* who killed Littlejohn. Remember? She left the museum that morning just before ten. She'd been in such a good mood. Hugo had just agreed to marry her. She must have returned to his house to find out how the meeting with Littlejohn went. When she heard he had the proof of Hawksworthy's deception, that he could ruin everything, she decided to take matters into her own hands."

Okoje strode into his office. "This is one for the books. Three suspects brought in under caution in two days for the same crime. If Hawksworthy is telling the truth, Isla Ferris is our killer. I sent Doaks and O'Brien to bring her in."

Chapter Forty-Two

Tom and I were leaving the police enquiry office when Isla Ferris arrived in handcuffs. Seeing me, she let out a sound I could only describe as a howl. "You miserable cow." She'd resisted arrest, we learned later. She was still resisting, attempting to wrench her hands free, kicking out at anyone who got close, and heaping abuse on everyone. She accused Tom and me of lying, Constables Doaks and O'Brien of police brutality, DS Varma of planting evidence, and DCI Okoje, unbelievably, of racism.

Tom and I stayed just long enough to hear Okoje formally charge Isla Ferris with the murder of Gideon Littlejohn.

Knackered, as Tom had put it, we returned to the Crown, ordered a light supper in our room, and built a fire in the fireplace. We were sitting with our feet on the brass fender when Okoje phoned.

Tom listened for several minutes, saying, "I see," a number of times. When they'd rung off, he said, "Isla's admitted everything. She went to the Old Merchant's House at ten forty-five that morning, pretending she wanted to discuss the exhibition of the dress. And yes, before you ask, she got tea. That's when he told her about Hawksworthy. He probably thought he was doing her a favor. They went to the computer room. He was going to show her the file of evidence. She shot him, took the file, and went immediately to her own flat to shower and change clothes."

"What happened to the file?"

"She destroyed it, of course. No idea Littlejohn had produced a video. They're taking her to the jail in Newton Abbot. The police are matching her fingerprints with those found in the computer room."

At around nine Tom got a texted update from DCI Okoje.

Teddy Pearce was recovering in the hospital in Plymouth. Quinn had been allowed to remain with him, pending a court hearing on the charge of public endangerment and carrying a firearm in a public place. She was facing a mandatory five-year sentence, but Okoje thought a skillful barrister might persuade the judge to make the sentence non-custodial because of the age of her children. Her father, Karl Benables, had returned from Germany and was now very much involved. Which was probably a good thing. He had clout.

Hawksworthy had been taken to a low-security facility near Newton Abbot pending his arraignment on charges of fraud, abuse of public trust, and the forging of documents. He kept insisting his stellar career should count for something, Okoje said. But whatever happened, his career was over.

"How do you feel now the case is solved?" I asked Tom.

"Like I've been hit by a lorry," he said.

"I know what you mean." We were still exhausted from the ordeal at Evelscombe mire. Every muscle in my body was complaining, and I had an angry red welt across my back.

"Tomorrow's our last day in Devon," Tom said. "Can't say I'm sorry to leave."

"No, neither am I. But I do regret not solving the mystery of Nancy Thorne. Did she really murder Luke Heron? If she did, why?"

"We'll probably never know. I think we can safely say the dress belonged to her, and the DNA results should tell us something about the blood. If the blood belonged to Luke Heron, it will show a significant link to South Asia. I emailed my preliminary report to Nash & Holmes while you were in the shower. I'll send along the DNA report once we get it."

"I wonder what the museum will do without its director," I said.

"They have an excellent board, from all accounts. They'll probably hire someone as quickly as they can. And go ahead with the new crimes exhibit."

"I hope so. There will be a lot of interest—especially when a contemporary crime is involved. Hawksworthy's arrest will lend an extra frisson, don't you think?" I shifted so I could put my feet on Tom's lap. "Speaking of crime, what's the penalty for forging your academic credentials?"

"That's a new one for me—not that I'm wasting any sympathy there. I'm more concerned about Quinn Pearce. We're really hard on gun crime in the UK these days. What she did was incredibly irresponsible."

I was thinking about Ivy and Lily when we heard someone tapping on our door. I got up to answer. It was Yvie Innes, and she was holding the trunk. "Julia Kelly from the museum dropped this off. She said you should take a good look at the tab in the lid." She turned to leave. "And, oh—she said to tell you she didn't touch anything."

I thanked Yvie, took the trunk, and placed it on the floor near the hearth. Opening the lid, I propped it on one of the decorative pillows from the bed. Tom and I sat side by side on the floor. I pulled on the fabric tab, revealing the compartmented tray. It was empty.

"Why does Julia want you to examine that again?" Tom asked.

"I don't know." I ran my fingers over each small compartment, feeling for any tiny beads or jewelry findings I might have missed. I found nothing, but even if I had, why would it be so important?

"I wish Julia had come up herself."

"She probably thought it was too late. She mentioned a tab."

I sat back and thought for a moment. Instead of the tray, maybe Julia meant the recessed area in which the tray was concealed. I ran my hand gently over the fabric along the underside of the domed lid.

Something crackled.

"There's something in there," I said.

Tom leaned forward to look. "Will you have to remove the lining?"

"I don't think Julia would have left that to me. There has to be something else. Hand me my lighted magnifier."

I trained the light on the recessed area, moving it slowly along the seams.

Then I saw it, a tiny tab of fabric, no more than an eighth of an inch long and lined up so precisely with the pattern it was virtually invisible. I straightened. "I know what Julia meant, Tom. There's a second tab. Can you see it?"

Using my fingernails, I pulled gently. Behind the tray compartment was a second space, smaller than the first but also meticulously lined with fabric. Concealed inside were letters, old ones, still in their envelopes and bound with blue ribbon. "Do you have a pair of gloves?" I asked Tom.

He reached for his jacket. "Last pair."

I pulled them on.

The letters—there were seven envelopes—had been sent by Sally Tucker, and they were all addressed to the same person, her son, William Tucker. "Look, Tom—the letters are still sealed, marked 'Uncollected. Return to Sender.'" I read the postmarks. "Sally mailed a letter to William every January from 1902 until 1907. He never received them." I laid the envelopes on the low table between our chairs in order of date. "Either she stopped writing after 1907, or the later letters didn't survive."

"Or Sally didn't survive."

"Good point." I picked up the earliest letter. "The return address is number four Brook Lane, Widdecombe Throop. That makes sense. The village wasn't flooded until 1906." I stopped, trying to figure out what the dates were telling us. "Sally must have started writing the letters soon after her sister, Nancy, died."

"When did we figure William was born?" Tom asked.

"Late 1885 or early 1886."

"That means he left home when he was . . . well, fifteen or sixteen."

"Four of the letters, the earliest ones, are directed to the post office in Plymouth. The last three were sent to a post office in Brighton. William never picked them up. Maybe he didn't have a fixed address—or Sally didn't know the address."

"Well—are you going to read them?"

I opened the first brittle envelope and pulled out a single sheet of paper, covered in a small, precise script.

12th January 1902

Widdecombe Throop

To William, my darling son, for that is what you will always be. I pray for you every night, asking God to protect and guide you. Can you not write to me? I shall not beg you to tell me where you are, just that you are alive and well. Today is your sixteenth birthday. I fear for you, my dearest boy, alone in the world, without friends. How are you living? How do you eat? But I must not torture myself with such questions.

I know how angry you were when your mother died.

I stopped reading. "His *mother*? Could she be talking about Nancy?" Several pieces of the puzzle fell neatly into place. "Mercy Abbott told me the trunk that contained Nancy Thorne's dress had belonged to Billy Cole's grandfather, a man named William. Tom—Billy Cole was William Tucker's grandson. How else would he have gotten the trunk?"

"And that means he was Nancy Thorne's great-grandson," Tom said. "Read on."

We should not have told you so abruptly, William, not without preparing you first. But Nancy was dying, and she would not go to that blessed realm without telling you of your true parentage. My only consolation is she died with a clear conscience. She didn't deserve your suspicion, nor your wrath. I don't blame you—how could I? But when you fled the house that night, without giving her an opportunity to explain, she gave up. Later that same night she breathed her last. I blame myself, but we did what we thought best at the time.

Dearest William, as much as I wish to relieve your mind, I cannot tell you anything of your father's death. I placed my hand on the Bible, you see, and took a solemn oath before God that I would tell no one what happened that terrible night. Woe to me if I do not fulfill that sacred vow. I can tell you this much: your mother lived her life carrying the burden of a shame she did not deserve. I can say no more. Please believe me, my darling son, you are all I think of. If I am doomed to live out my life alone, I shall bear it as best I can. Perhaps it is what I deserve.

May God soften your heart. Please write and relieve my pain.

Your mother, Sally Tucker

"If William was Nancy's child," Tom said, "could the blood on the dress have anything to do with his birth?"

"Not unless she lay on her stomach to deliver him. Trust me—that doesn't work. Besides, it was September when she returned home covered in blood. William wasn't born until January. Nancy, on her deathbed, must have told William who his father was."

"Whatever she told him made him angry—angry enough to leave home. Read another letter."

We read all the returned letters. All but the last were essentially the same. Every year on January twelfth, William's birthday, Sally implored her adopted son to come home or at least to write. As the years went by, the letters seemed less like communication and more like meditation. As if Sally were writing to herself.

The final returned letter, dated January twelfth of 1907, was different.

To William, my son,

This is the last letter I shall write. The doctor tells me I must die soon. It's cancer.

I'm not afraid. When I leave this poor earthly body, I know I shall be reunited with my parents, my beloved husband, and my dear sister. Your mother, dearest William, was a saint. Her love for you was so strong. Yet for your sake, she could not acknowledge you. I know I shall not see you again, so I picture your face as it must be now—the face of a strong young man of twenty-one. I pray you will never experience war or famine or grief, but that

God's face will shine upon you in blessing all the days of your life. At fifteen you did not realize the pain you caused by leaving. Perhaps you do not realize it still. I forgive you.

You know I must honor my vow. But death releases us from all vows, does it not? So I shall write an account of that night while I am able, knowing you will not read it until after I am gone. I am ready to die. God is my judge. To Him I shall answer and I believe I shall find grace. I die hoping that you will learn of my death and return to claim what is rightly yours. I wish it were more. If you return to bury me, I pray you will find this account and forgive us.

May the knowledge of what is good and kind and merciful sustain you always.

Your loving mother

Sally Tucker

I folded the letter and slipped it back in the envelope. My throat ached.

"Did William Tucker ever return to claim the trunk?" Tom asked. Even his voice held emotion.

I cleared my throat. "He must have. But it seems he didn't find the account Sally wrote." I held up the final letter. "This must be it. It's marked 'For William.' The envelope is still sealed. William never read it."

As the fire crackled, I read aloud.

To William. This is a true account of the events that took place on the seventh of September 1885, as they were told to me by your mother, Nancy Thorne.

The story began a year earlier.

Luke Heron was an exceptionally handsome young Romanichal man of thirty-two, a widower whose wife had died giving birth to a stillborn son. Like all men in the Squires family, he worked with the livestock on the moors, but he also worked with wood, producing fine objects of all sorts—bowls, carved boxes, platters, clothes pin and pegs, sturdy knife handles. His wares were prized by everyone, from farm wives to the landed gentry.

Before Christmas of 1884, Nancy was making lace by the fire. A mouse ran across her foot and she leapt up, dropping her bolster pillow, with the lace and all her precious bobbins, into the flames. Nothing could be saved. Somehow we found the money, and she commissioned Luke Heron to make new bobbins from dark, fine-grained cherrywood. Stated simply, my darling, they fell in love. But you must know such a marriage would never have been accepted by the citizens of Widdecombe Throop nor by Luke's family. For that reason, your parents kept their love a secret.

In June of 1885, your mother found herself with child—with you, dearest William. Do not blame her. Your father was an honorable man, and they were in love. When Nancy told him of her condition, he was determined they should marry. But not in England. They would sail to America and start a new life. Luke had relatives in Chicago who would help them. To that end, they saved every penny they could.

On the night of the seventh of September 1885, when Nancy was five months into her pregnancy, they planned their escape. I remained at home that night, as I could not conceal my sorrow. Nancy attended the evening service as usual. There Luke met her with a horse and cart, from where they intended to leave England forever. Sadly, this was not to be.

In late August, Luke's beloved grandmother, Queenie, had died. At her funeral, Luke's cousin, Tawno Squires, accused him of stealing some of his grandmother's possessions. This was not true. Luke had confided in his grandmother, and before she died, she gave her favorite grandson her wedding ring and other gifts, meant to help him and your mother on their way. When Tawno saw Luke leave the camp that night with the horse and cart, he followed him to the church and, with your mother, out onto the moor. They were travelling to Plymouth, where your father had bought passage on a ship. They never made it. At Evelscombe, Tawno accosted them and demanded that Luke return to camp and confess. When Luke refused, Tawno produced a knife and threatened to kill them both. The men fought. Both were severely injured. Both died on the moor—first Tawno, then, hours later, Luke.

Nancy did not kill your father, William. I swear it before God. She tried to save him. She loved him and he died in her arms. Before your father died, knowing your mother would be suspected of murder, he made her promise on all that is sacred that when he was dead, she would roll both bodies into the mire. It was all he could do for the woman he loved and for his child. She did what she promised.

The bodies were never found. She made me swear on my very soul I would never reveal the truth. She could not have known what that vow would cost us both. The dress she'd worn that night was horribly stained with blood. Yet she would not part with it. I washed it, but the stains remained, as did her grief and the stain of suspicion. She wore the dress every day of her life, a dress that held her beloved's lifeblood.

On a cold day in January, she gave birth at home. And I took you as my son.

This is a true account. May the Lord have mercy on my soul and theirs. And may He show you kindness and grace.

Your mother, Sally Tucker.

Tom and I sat back and let out a simultaneous sigh.

"They never knew the truth," I said. "Not Gideon, not Billy Cole, and not Billy's grandfather, William Tucker, the son born to Nancy Thorne and Luke Heron. They all believed Nancy murdered Luke Heron, and the truth was there all the time, within their reach."

"They died believing the lies." I thought about Hugo Hawksworthy, who, I was convinced, had ended up believing his own lies.

Chapter Forty-Three

Friday, January 17
Dartmoor National Park

Our final day in Devon was cold but sunny, with high clouds sailing over the moor. Yvie Innes at the Crown packed a picnic basket for us, and we took off in the Rover for the village of Chalcombe, forty minutes north of Coombe Mallet. We wanted to see the graves from Widdecombe Throop.

"Too bad we won't have time to stop at Fouroaks," Tom said. "I'm sorry, darling. I really wanted you to see it."

"There's always summer. And Uncle Nigel will be there then. I like him, Tom, and I think I'll like Devon even better when the weather's just a little warmer."

He laughed. "And without a murder."

"Yes. Definitely no more murders."

Maggie Hughes had phoned at seven, waking us up. She'd stayed up until three in the morning, scanning through the census records. "No wonder we couldn't find William Tucker," she'd said. "He'd changed his name to William Heron, and he moved to Plymouth. People could do that then. No official documents needed. Your theory was correct, Kate. Billy Cole was Luke Heron's great-grandson. I'll text you my results."

We drove over the high, barren moorland. A flock of sheep grazed contentedly, enjoying the sun on their woolly backs.

I was looking at my phone, reading Maggie's text, when Tom said, "William ran away from home, believing his mother had murdered his father. William must have lived the rest of his life believing that both he and his father had been betrayed by the Thorne sisters. That's incredibly sad, isn't it?"

"According to Maggie, William Heron eventually married and had a daughter. She married a man named Cole. William must have given the trunk to her, and she passed it on to her son, Billy."

"Who gave it to Gordon Little aka Gideon Littlejohn."

"Who vowed to find the truth about his murdered ancestor."

"Out of loyalty or guilt?" Tom asked.

"We'll never know. But that's why Gideon Littlejohn was so determined to learn what actually happened the night of September seventh. He wanted to prove Nancy Thorne was a murderess—for Billy's sake. That's why he forged that note." I leaned over and kissed Tom's shoulder. "And now Gideon is dead. Another tragedy."

"Nancy and Luke never got their future, and for William's sake, she could never acknowledge him as her son."

Chalcombe was a tiny village tucked into a fold of land on the north side of the reservoir. We found the small parish church, St. Brenden's, with its neat graveyard bordered by pollarded yews. The verger must have seen us parking. He came out to meet us.

"Can I help you folks?"

"We're hoping to see the graves relocated from Widdecombe Throop," Tom said.

"Are you now? Most people have forgotten all about that. Come with me." He led us to a well-tended corner of the graveyard. "I try to keep the stones clean, and we put flowers down on special holidays. Plastic ones in winter, but it's the thought, isn't it? Are you looking for anyone in particular?"

"Two graves—Queenie Squires and Nancy Thorne."

"Are you related, by any chance?"

"No," I said. "Just interested."

The two graves weren't far from each other. Both markers were simple limestone slabs, adorned with garish, flocked red poinsettias.

Queenie's marker bore a cross and read, *Queenie Squires. Born 1800. Died Aug 25, 1885. "Her children shall rise up and call her blessed." Prov 31:28.*

Nancy Thorne's stone said simply, *Nancy Thorne, a Lacemaker. Born 1855. Died 1901. Rest in Peace.*

"Is it all right if we stay for a while?" Tom asked. "We brought lunch."

"Of course. Take all the time you need." The verger left us, and we found a stone bench in the sun. I opened the basket, handed Tom a wrapped sandwich, and poured two plastic mugs of coffee from a flask.

"What's happening with Isla Ferris?"

"Since she pled guilty, she'll be sentenced by the Crown Court in Exeter."

"Where'd she get the gun?"

"Oh, she arrived at Littlejohn's house prepared. Stopped at the museum on the way and picked up a World War II pistol they had on display in the Devon at War exhibit. She knew how to load and fire it." Tom found napkins in the picnic basket and gave me one. He spread his on his lap and unwrapped his sandwich. "Okoje wants me to stay in Devon until the sentencing. I told him no. If they need a statement, I can do it from Suffolk."

"That brings up the big question, doesn't it?" I took a bite of my sandwich, sliced chicken with chutney.

"The big question?"

"Will you take the DCI position at the Suffolk Constabulary or the job with Nash & Holmes?"

"It's our decision, Kate—not just mine. What do you want?"

"Two simple things. I want you to be happy, and I want you to be safe."

"*Working on nice, safe historical puzzles*—I remember you saying something like that."

"Don't tease me, Tom. How was I to know Littlejohn would be murdered? I'm asking you a serious question."

"I know you are."

"And I know where your mind and heart have been these past two weeks. The investigation into the dress was interesting, but it was the police investigation that put a spark in your eyes."

He took a moment before answering. "I heard a parable once. Or maybe it was an allegory. I never get them straight. Anyway, it was a story about sheep and sheepdogs. The author—I think he was an American—said most people are like sheep. Not in a pejorative sense, not saying they're dumb animals. But for the most part, they live peaceably in the flock. They don't want to hurt each other, and they don't, except by accident or under extreme provocation. But there are wolves out there too. They prey upon the sheep without mercy. If the wolves have a chance to harm the sheep, they'll take it, and they look for the youngest, the weakest, the most vulnerable. That's why the sheep need sheepdogs. Sheepdogs are annoying to the sheep when everything's going well, but when the wolf comes, the sheep are glad, because sheepdogs live to protect the flock. Their instinct is to protect. When the sheep are in in danger, they come running." He looked almost embarrassed. "Trust me—I'm not saying I'm some sort of hero. And the analogy is deeply flawed, of course, and incredibly simplistic. Human beings aren't born into one of three categories. We have moral choices. We can change. We've seen that this week. Still"—he put his arm around me—"at heart I'm a sheepdog."

"Well, that's it, then, Detective Chief Inspector Mallory. You're a sheepdog, and I'm an antiques dealer. Private investigations aren't our thing."

"Not so hasty, my darling. I told you I emailed my preliminary report to Grahame Nash. This morning, while you were talking to Maggie Hughes, he replied. Even if I don't take the job with Nash & Holmes, they want you. He's offering you a consulting job on investigations involving antiques and antiquities. What do you say?"

Acknowledgments

The English county of Devon and especially Dartmoor National Park, where most of the book is set, is a magical place of myths, legends, ancient history, and stark beauty. Those familiar with the area will know I've taken shocking liberties with the geography. I hope I've also been able to convey some of its allure.

I'm deeply indebted to the people who shared their knowledge so generously: Phil Cornish of the National Association of Retired Police Officers, South Devon; Matt Newbury, Creative Director of the International Agatha Christie Festival, Torquay; Professor Mike Peixoto, who shared his extensive knowledge of medieval forgeries; Margaret Lewis B.E.M., Curator of the Allhallows Museum of Lace; and the Reverend Ash Leighton Plom, Assistant Curate of St. Michael & All Angels Church, Exeter. All errors are mine alone.

I am especially grateful for the help of Ms. Joyce McClennan, who kindly and patiently read my manuscript with an eye for the proper use of British syntax and expressions.

A very special debt of thanks is due to Dr. Thomas Acton, OBE, professor emeritus of Romani studies at the University of Greenwich; patron of the Roma Support Group in London; member of the committees of the Gypsy Council, the Advisory council for the Education of Romanies and Travellers, and the Churches Network for Gypsies, Travellers and Roma. He is also a board member of the Gypsy Lore Society and secretary of his local Gypsy Support Group. Dr. Acton read and commented on the entire manuscript. Without his encouragement, gentle corrections, and generous sharing of information, I could not have written this book.

Special thanks also go to my fabulous beta readers, Grace Topping and Lynn Denley-Bussard, who read this book in several iterations and offered their wise counsel, corrections, suggestions, and encouragement from beginning to end. I love you both.

As always, I'm thankful for the support of my agent, Paula Munier, and the team at Crooked Lane Books, especially my editor, Faith Black Ross. You are a joy to work with.

Last but not least, I must thank my family. My son David answered all my questions about technology and computers. My son John suggested an ingenious solution to a thorny logistical problem. My husband, Bob, encouraged me every step of the way, drove me all over the West Country, and followed me through endless churches, National Trust properties, and country villages without complaint. I love you.

Soli Deo gloria